DEVILRY

KING UNIVERSITY

MARLEY VALENTINE

D1522119

MARLEY VALENTINE

Cover design by PopKitty Designs
Edited by Shauna Stevenson at Ink Machine Editing
Edited by ellie McLove at My Brother's Editor
Proofreading by Hawkeyes Proofing

This book contains mature content.

DEDICATION

To Tanya.

You asked for more M/M Student Teacher Romances.

I hope I delivered.

Never ever apologise for who you love.

MARLEY VALENTINE

Cover design by PopKitty Designs
Edited by Shauna Stevenson at Ink Machine Editing
Edited by ellie McLove at My Brother's Editor
Proofreading by Hawkeyes Proofing

This book contains mature content.

PROLOGUE

ELIJAH

THREE YEARS EARLIER

"Do you really think we should be doing this?" I ask, adrenaline and fear my motivation for the question.

"What?" He brushes my wayward hair out of my eyes. "Hiding behind the church, while everybody is inside listening to the sermon?"

"Well, yes, that, but I mean this." I gesture between us.

Grabbing my hand, he brings it to his chest, my palm now privy to the frantic beat of his heart. Wanting him to know I feel it, too, I mirror his actions, until we're both standing there, staring at one another, vulnerable, exposed, and in absolute awe.

Is this finally happening?

"I've never done this before," I confess.

"I know." His eyes flicker between my eyes and my lips. "Are you sure about this?"

My stomach flips in anticipation. Am I sure? Absolutely not. Am I going to pass up kissing him? Again, absolutely not. Since the moment Alex crashed into my very small and sheltered world, it's been endless days and nights of uncertainty paired with an unhealthy amount of addiction.

I can't get enough of him, especially the way he makes me feel. The relief that these long sixteen years of my life haven't been wasted, the exhilaration that I've finally found the person I was searching for.

Surprisingly, it wasn't him I was looking for.

It was me.

The son of a pastor, my life is only supposed to run on the straight and narrow. Know your purpose, hear your calling. They're the words my father drums into me, every day. But no matter how hard I try to listen, to hear God's voice, I'm only ever left feeling out of place. Out of sync.

Until right now, I didn't even feel right in my own skin. Like God had sewn me up all wrong and the seams didn't meet up. I know I'm different. I also know exactly what it is that sets me apart, but that doesn't mean I've always been ready to accept it.

Nothing about me is straight and narrow.

Not my needs.

Not my wants.

Not my hopes.

Not my dreams.

And definitely not my sexuality.

With his unruly hair, piercing blue eyes, and unapologetic nature, Alex has been a breath of fresh air in my very stale and stuffy life.

Gradually, he's been teaching me how to be myself. Before him, I had feared the truth. Living every day with so much uncertainty, it's become painful to even look at myself in the mirror. Every waking moment I'm pretending to love myself on the outside, while I quietly, but painfully berate myself on the inside.

I don't want to live like this anymore, and he knows it. He's seen me for what I am and who I want to be.

Slowly but cautiously, he's bringing me out of my shell. Moment after moment he validates my existence, proving to me I can rid myself of the doubt and rejoice in my differences.

"Answer me, Eli, because we've been dancing around this for too long." He steps closer. "And I want to be your first so fucking bad."

"I've kissed someone before," I protest.

"Have you kissed a guy?"

Even though we've already had this conversation, my traitorous cheeks still flush at his forwardness. "No."

Alex's eyes melt from ice to liquid, from demanding to desire. Teenage hormones are no fucking joke, and the involuntary erection to the one hand job from my winter dance date, who was a girl, has nothing on this. My dick is so hard, one simple touch from him is all it would take to embarrassingly blow my load inside my pants.

Hands firmly grip either side of my face and I suck in a huge amount of air into my lungs. My chest hurts as the seconds pass us by, but I'm sure if I exhale, my fear will come rushing out, ruining the moment. Breaking our connection and taking away my first chance to experience what it's like to feel whole. Full. Complete.

"Breathe, Elijah."

His intention is to calm my nerves, but my body doesn't cooperate. My obvious panic forces him to take control. Softly but swiftly, he presses his mouth to mine.

Time stops.

My heart does too.

His lips are somewhat rough and slightly cracked from the way he habitually bites them, but the action still tender.

He moves his mouth against mine, taking the lead. Pushing me up against the brick wall, my back scrapes across the jagged exterior as his chest lightly caresses mine.

We're so close, but still not close enough. Finding the courage to take what I want, my hands travel up his arms, over his sleeves, and land on either side of his neck. Squeezing just a little, I bring him closer and deepen the kiss.

His tongue swipes the seam of my lips and I open up, letting him in. I can't help but compare this to the pitiful kisses I've stumbled through in the past. The continued experiments that always ended in disaster, ended in tears and frustration that I would never be normal. That I would never feel normal things.

But now... who wants normal? What is normal? Who wants to feel anything but this?

Eagerly, I graze my tongue against his and begin to match his languid strokes. A moan reverberates in the back of his throat, silencing the last of my anxiety and birthing a new kind of desperation.

His hips rock into mine, the clothes between us doing nothing to hinder the rush as our dicks rub against one another.

"Alex," I hiss.

"I know, but I can't stop," he breathes out. "What if this is our only time?" Hands trail down my chest. My stomach; fingers stopping at the button on my jeans. "Can I?"

With his forehead resting against mine, he holds my stare, his eyes patiently waiting for me. Even though I know just how complicated things are about to get, I don't have the strength to argue with him. I don't think I even want to. Even if it kills me, I want *everything* he has to give.

Crashing my lips to his, I answer his question. Slipping

into my jeans and under my boxers, he wraps his fingers around my solid length. Gripping me tight, we both still.

Time stops.

My heart does too.

"I'm going to come," I warn.

"Good."

Our kiss becomes a feasting frenzy as he moves his hand up and down, jerking me off with all the skill of a boy who is comfortable in his own skin.

With shaking hands, I unbutton his pants and shift my movements till he's throbbing under my touch.

"This is going to get messy," he chuckles against my mouth.

Our fists move faster, our tongues battle for dominance. Together we're chasing the high, going against everything we've ever been told. Every teaching. Every expectation. We're just two boys literally hiding behind the church. Hiding from the world of judgement and harsh realities.

While everyone in the congregation is down on bended knee, offering thanks, saying their prayers, and begging for absolution, Alex and I are giving in to our deepest desires.

Heat rises from the soles of my feet, tingling up my legs and tightening around the base of my spine. My body jolts with the anticipation of my release. Breaking our kiss, I look down, enthralled by our public indecency, as simultaneous orgasms ripple through us.

With heavy and labored breaths we stare at the outcome of our attraction. The stickiness of our pleasure. The confirmation of *my* truth.

"Are you okay?" he whispers.

His words break through my sated mood. I look up at him with a weak but satisfied smile. "Never better."

I inhale the scent of him and the perfection of this moment, as he drops a quick kiss on my mouth.

"Elijah?"

An unexpected but familiar voice penetrates the moment. Paralyzed by fear, I stare into Alex's now apologetic eyes. I take in every feature, committing everything we just shared to memory, because I know without a doubt, this is the first, and last, time I will ever touch him. Taste him. *Be with him.*

"Is that you?"

Time stops.

My heart does too.

"Yeah, Dad. It's me."

1

COLE

PRESENT DAY

"Fuck," I shout, as I stub my toe on the corner of my coffee table. Again.

My new apartment appears to be a little on the small side, or maybe it's the ridiculous amount of paraphernalia I've lugged across the country with me that errs on the side of excessive. Either way, I'm overwhelmed by the never-ending number of boxes that sit in every corner of every room.

Lumping myself on the couch, I grab the remote control and lay down. While thanks to my hoarding tendencies the rest of this place is in shambles, my priorities in regards to entertainment are intact. Clearly evidenced by the sixty-inch flat screen that I had mounted onto the wall before I even spent my first night here.

When moving into a new place, there are some things that are negotiable; access to every sports channel known to man is not one of them.

As soon as I switch the television on, my cell rings. I

groan into an empty room, frustrated by the disruption. Looking down at my phone, I see my sister's name on the screen.

I hit mute on the remote control before answering. "Hey. Long time, no talk."

"How's the new place?" she asks, launching straight into the conversation.

"Small."

"You ungrateful shit," she teases. "Only you would be unhappy with free housing."

When you're offered a job at King University, they make it impossible for you to decline. With one whole building dedicated to--it's so cheap it's almost free--staff accommodation, it's one of King's lucrative incentives to acquire all the educational talent from around the world, and keep them.

"I am not," I protest. "I'm grateful. I thanked them, but I don't want to be living this close to campus. Nobody wants to see their students inside *and* outside the classroom."

"When you put it like that," she muses. "So, what's your plan?"

"I'm going to line up a few houses in Georgetown to inspect over the coming weeks, and hopefully I like one enough to place an offer."

"Got my fingers and toes crossed for you."

"Thank you." There's an extended length of silence between us and it dawns on me, my sister didn't just call to see how I was settling in. "What is it, Megs?"

"Nothing," she says, a little too squeakily.

Rolling my eyes, I pick up the remote and turn the volume up just a smidgen, and settle in to watch a rerun of a Blackhawks game. "I'll just wait here till you're ready."

Meghann and I are as close as siblings can get. Only fourteen months apart, we used to often get mistaken for twins. My parents got the raw end of the deal with two kids still in diapers, but my childhood was all the better for it.

"Why do you do that?" she huffs. "I didn't call to lay my shit on you."

"Didn't you?" I joke, pairing it with a soft chuckle. She doesn't laugh back. "Okay, so maybe it wasn't your intention to sound all mopey, but there's clearly something bothering you and you'll end up telling me, so while you're on the phone, why not kill two birds with one stone?"

"I just miss you."

Guilt eats away at me as I imagine her pouting on the other end of the phone. This is the first time we've ever been more than a twenty-minute drive away from one another and I didn't anticipate a struggle. "I'm sorry."

"No, don't do that. This is the job of a lifetime, there is nothing to apologize for."

Even though she's kicking ass in her own career, at one of the top law firms in Chicago and is happy living with my best friend, I throw the suggestion out anyway. "You're always welcome to pack up and move here."

"When you find a place, I'd love to stay for a few weeks."

Red flag number one.

"And what about work?" I probe.

"They owe me a whole lot of vacation time."

Red flag number two.

"And Trey? He won't mind sleeping without you for that long?"

"Of course not. He's not going to stop me from seeing you."

While this is very true, my sister has been head over heels for Trey Simpson since the second he walked through our front door and I introduced him as my best friend. They've been inseparable ever since.

Red flag number three.

"Spill it. Now," I demand.

"I think we're breaking up." My chest tightens as her voice cracks. "Nothing seems to be the same anymore."

"Change isn't always bad," I console. "Have you spoken to him?"

"I've tried."

"He hasn't said anything to me," I say, hoping to offer her some comfort.

"Like he's going to tell you he plans on breaking my heart," she scoffs. "Just move into your own place will you? I need time with my brother."

Even though she isn't intentionally trying to guilt me, her distress eats at me more than a little. Despite the fact that I'm now living hundreds of miles away from them, my family was and always will be everything to me. And though I consider Trey family, Meghann is blood. I could call and talk to him, but my sister would kill me.

When they first got together, we set ground rules. What goes on in their relationship is their business. It's never been a problem. Until now. I never would have imagined that Trey might hurt Megs. He's a great guy, an amazing friend, but you better believe those guidelines I mentioned will mean nothing if he breaks her heart.

"Promise you'll keep me updated."

Her loud sigh travels through the phone. "I couldn't keep something from you if I tried."

"Good." Trapping my phone between my ear and my shoulder, I twist my watch the right way up and check the time. "Fuck."

"What?" Meghann asks with worry.

"I didn't realize that was the time. I had plans to kick back and watch TV before you called, but now I have to rush and get ready. I have a black-tie event for the university tonight and I don't even know what I'm going to wear."

"I put all your formal wear in those long clothes bags, " she informs me.

"Huh?"

"For fucks sake, Cole, how can you be so fucking smart, yet so unorganized?"

"Get off my dick, Megs," I rib as I stride through my bedroom and into the walk-in wardrobe. "Okay, I see what you're talking about. So there's a pressed suit in one of these?"

"Yes. All your more expensive stuff should be in there. I made sure of that."

"Thank you," I say, unzipping each of the bags. "I've really got to get going. I need to get ready."

"Have fun," she sings. "And call me if you can't find anything else."

"You know I'm allergic to fun." Meghann snorts, the sister gene guaranteeing a laugh to all my bad jokes. "Megs."

"Yeah."

"I'm here if you need me."

"I know. Now," her voice picks up, hiding her anguish. "Go get ready. Have fun tonight, and don't scare off potential new friends."

Chuckling at how well she knows me, I don't bother defending myself. "Love you, Megs."

"Love you, Cole."

Ending the call, I toss the cell phone onto my bed and begin to sift through the piles of clothing in front of me. I would never admit it to anyone, but I might have a slight apparel obsession. I mean, nobody needs as much clothing as I have, but I just can't seem to part with any of it.

Finding what I want, I lay it gently across the made up

mattress and go on a hunt for the rest of the shit I'll need. Once my shoes, belt, and socks have been found and neatly placed at the foot of the bed, I head to the bathroom.

After tidying up my short and usually well-manicured beard, I jump in the shower. It takes all of three minutes for me to clean myself up, because if you aren't having shower sex, there's really no reason to be in there for any longer.

Forty-five minutes later I'm standing in front of the maître d, waiting to be ushered to what I assume is a nearby function room.

"Sir, could I please have your name?" she asks.

"Cole," I supply. "Cole Huxley."

"Thank you, Mr. Huxley." She slides the black ballpoint pen through my name and lowers the clipboard. "If you could follow the waiter." She gestures to a young man dressed in a white button-down shirt and black slacks standing beside her. "Peter will take you through to the rest of the party."

Straightening my tie, I run my hands down my suit jacket and undo the buttons. Looking down, I ensure my dress shirt is tucked in correctly and swiftly slip my hands into my pockets. I follow Peter and get a wonderful view of his firm ass. There's nothing like a man dressed in well-fitted pants, but seeing as he's probably just turned eighteen, and that isn't my style, I don't let my gaze linger too long.

From what I've been told, King University has hired new teaching staff for almost every single department. As one of the most prestigious schools in the country, this is a huge opportunity for anyone who is trying to climb up the career food chain.

Offering only a handful of scholarships to freshmen students every year, the school population mainly consists of snotty, bratty, rich kids, whose parents are either the older versions of their children, or they jumped through hoops to have them attend here.

Pushing the heavy door with his shoulder, Peter steps inside and holds it open for me. "Everyone's toward the back of the room."

In a few long strides, I'm closer to the crowd. I met a few important people at the interview, and hope they're here to see that I showed up. Scanning each set of eyes for someone familiar, I come up blank and decide that parking myself at the bar is always a safe bet.

"Can I have a gin and tonic, please?" I ask. "Preferably Hendrick's."

"Not a problem."

Turning away from the bartender, I look back out to the crowd one more time, appreciating the opulent decor. Silver satin is draped in a perfect design across the length of the high ceilings, looking like waves on a beach overhead. Topped off with large, eye-catching chandeliers and matching table centerpieces, you would almost think it's a wedding.

"You look lost." A soft, female voice sounds from beside me. I turn to find a beautiful, tall, brunette leaning against the marble bar top.

Returning, the bartender lays out two napkins and places both our drinks in front of us.

"Thanks." I tip my head up to him in gratitude before he retreats to serve other guests. I look back at the gorgeous woman, who seems as equally unimpressed about being here as I am. "No, I'm in the right place."

"Are you new?"

"What gave it away?" I take a much-needed sip of my drink.

"I don't know, maybe because we're the only two people staying at the bar." She holds up her glass. "Or it's because you look as awkward as I feel?"

"I'm Cole." I offer her my hand.

She takes it. "I'm Harper."

Before we can continue the conversation, another body slides up beside Harper. A little wobbly on his feet, the man grips onto the bar to balance himself.

"A whiskey neat, please," he slurs.

The bartender pulls at his ear, clearly working out how to cut off the gentleman without making a scene. My gaze flicks from Harper to the stranger and back again. She gives me a quick nod, so I push myself off the bar and squeeze between them.

"Hey, man." I clap him on the shoulder. "How about some water instead?"

He shrugs, forcing my hand to fall off. "Do I know you?"

"Not yet, but the night is still young."

"Take this," Harper interjects.

Too shocked to argue, he takes the water and drinks it. All at once.

"Can we get another, please," I call out.

Another bottle of water is placed in front us, and surprisingly our new *friend* takes it without protest. Sobering up with each sip, he finally gets out of his own head and takes inventory of his surroundings, especially Harper and me.

"The whiskey would've tasted a million times better than this," he quips.

"I think the words you're looking for are thank you." Harper's take no shit attitude reminds me of Meghann, and I can't help but smile at the interaction.

"In case you didn't notice, I was on a mission to get absolutely wasted."

"Oh, we noticed." Harper links her arm through his and begins to drag him to a nearby cocktail table.

Waving down the bartender, I ask for another bottle of water before picking up my own drink and following them to where they're now seated. Noticing a chill in the air between them, I raise an eyebrow at Harper. "Everything okay?"

"Someone was just continuing his ungrateful tirade," she informs.

"My name's Miles," he interrupts.

"I'm Cole."

He glances at a pissed off Harper. "Are you still not going to tell me your name?"

"It's Harper," I blurt out.

"What the fuck?" she chides.

"What?" I shrug, an unapologetic smile on my face. "We're new, let's not make enemies before we've even started."

I take a seat beside a perturbed Harper and face a much more focused Miles. "Are you new too?" I ask him.

He shakes his head. "No, I've worked here for five years."

"What do you teach?"

"Criminology."

"What kind of classes does that include?" I ask, continuing to be polite.

"Introduction to Law Enforcement, Forensic Psychology, Interview and Interrogation, and Juvenile Delinquency," he rattles off.

"So, why aren't you mingling with everybody else?" I tip my head back to the crowd behind us.

"King is a great school to work at, but the staff are snotty as fuck."

Harper laughs, the tension between them dissipating at the sound. "When the third guy in a row refused to look anywhere else but my tits," she chimes in, "I gave up trying to play nice." She finishes off her wine and places the empty glass down with force. "I'm here for nothing more than that beautiful paycheck. And the notoriety."

"They're a nice set of tits," Miles says with a smirk.

She backhands his shoulder. "Fuck off."

"I'm kidding. Kind of." He takes a long pull of water, finishing off the bottle before continuing. "I've sworn off women. For a while, anyway. You and your tits are safe."

"Thank you?" Her shoulders rise in confusion. "Either way, I don't shit where I eat, so the point is moot."

"So elegantly said," Miles teases.

"I only use my good words when I'm getting paid for it," Harper sasses back. "So, what about you, Cole? What will you be teaching?"

Their attention shifts to me, and thankfully distracts them from their bickering. "I'm floating between the Arts and History faculties, but Studies of Religion is my specialty."

"So you're religious," Miles says as more of a clarification, and less of a question.

"Definitely not," I respond with a shake of my head. "I majored in teaching, minored in history, and here I am."

"And you?" He turns to ask Harper.

"I'm the new head of the Languages Department."

Impressed, Miles whistles. "So, what are you doing slumming it over here?"

Avoiding our gaze, she fiddles with the stem of the wine glass. She cocks her head from one side to the other. "He looked so lost, and you could barely stand up. You guys needed me."

I watch Miles' eyes soften as Harper unsuccessfully tries to sound nonchalant. Without the alcohol overindulgence he seems like a nice enough guy.

"So, what, we're your friends now?" He gives me a slight smirk as he begins to wind her up again.

"You're on probation. If I catch you staring at my tits, we're done."

"Tell her how nice they are though, Cole."

I roll my eyes at him. "Sorry, man, I wouldn't know good tits even if they hit me in the face."

He looks at me thoughtfully and I hold his stare, wanting to see his reaction. "It's all about the dick for me."

He doesn't flinch, and I'm impressed. His acceptance, or anybody else's, isn't an issue for me. I don't care how the rest of the world perceives me, because they aren't living my life. I am, and I've always done it on my terms.

He looks back at Harper. "Sorry, sweetheart. Out of the three of us, my dick beats your tits as most popular. You like dick. He likes dick. I'm the winner."

Harper makes a gagging noise with her mouth and I bark out a laugh. "Sorry, man, I don't think you're either one of our type."

He raises up his hands in defeat. "I'm kidding." He looks pointedly at both of us. "I promise I'm not as creepy as I've made myself sound tonight. Let's just say it's been a rough week." Harper coughs and he smiles. "I'm going to get myself a soda. Let me grab you both a round to apologize and we can start fresh."

Feeling more comfortable, I'm content to not end the night anytime soon. "Hendrick's and tonic, please."

A sigh of defeat sounds beside me, and I bite back my smile. "Fine. I'll take a pinot grigio."

"He's not that bad," I say as he retreats toward the bar. "I think his bark is bigger than his bite."

"I like the way you handled that." Catching me completely off guard with her comment, it takes me a few seconds to process what she's talking about. "I know you shouldn't even have to worry about telling other people, but you found the perfect segue and ran with it."

"I've had a lot of practice."

"Is it hard? Being gay and having to worry about what people think?"

"It's about as awkward for me as it is when guys stare at your tits before your face," I explain. "Most men think it immediately means I want to fuck them, so they feel the need to gently let me down. That's why I like old mate over here." I tip my chin up at a returning Miles. "Not everybody can hide their reaction that well. Unless they really don't care, and fortunately for me, it seems like he doesn't."

"And what if I cared?" she challenges.

"You came and kept a complete stranger company after noticing me alone from across the room." I gently nudge her shoulder. "You're too nice to care."

"I'm back," Miles sings, effectively ending our conversation. "Stop talking about me now." He hands each of us our drinks and takes his seat on the stool.

"You're assuming we have nothing better to talk about," Harper retorts.

"So where are you two from?" I jump in, interrupting them.

"Oh my god," Harper groans. "Dean Billings is coming this way."

"Hello, Miss Martínez. Huxley. Decker."

"Sir," we all say in unison, like God fearing teenagers, instead of the adults we are.

"It's wonderful to see you all mingling with one another, especially you, Miles."

Miles' jaw clenches, but the dean is too busy ogling Harper to notice.

"I just came to borrow Miss Martínez." He stretches his arm out, inviting Harper to take his hand. "The rest of your faculty has arrived and I would love to introduce them to the new Head of Languages."

Harper visibly stiffens and both Miles and I instinctively turn to face her. She plasters on a smile, ignoring our concern and takes his offered hand. Gracefully, she stands and lets him lead her to his side.

Without another word, he places his palm on the small of her back, his fingertips settling right above her ass.

"Is he always like that?" I ask, unease swimming through me.

"Courtesy of the dick in my pants, I've never experienced anything more than his condescending attitude, but there's always rumors that get shut down as quickly as they pop up."

"I don't feel comfortable leaving her," I say, as Miles blurts out, "We should just keep an eye on them."

In a few quick strides, we're at the other end of the room, drinks in hand and Harper and the dean in our line of sight.

Miles leans closer to me, making sure nobody else can hear him. "I don't think we had anything to worry about."

Harper is working the room like a natural, all the while Dean Billings tries to keep her at his side, like a trophy. Showing off her worth, she dodges his touches with a smile that has the rest of the faculty eating out of her hands.

Just as she's moving on to introduce herself to the next

person, she notices us. Raising her glass, she nods and smiles in appreciation.

Tonight might have shed light onto things about King University I wasn't prepared for, but whatever the change brings, I feel a swell of comfort building, knowing I've managed to find people I could eventually call my friends.

Miles and I lift our glasses in the air, returning Harper's gesture. "I think you're right."

2

ELIJAH

"Hello," I groan into the phone.

"Elijah." My mom's perky voice pierces my eardrums.

"Mom," I answer groggily. Pulling the phone off my ear, I bring the screen into view to check the time. "Why are you calling me at six a.m.?"

"It's your first day of college. Can't a mother wish her son good luck?"

I refrain from answering with the truth because for most kids, a parent calling their child to offer any positive encouragement is normal. For mine? Not so much. Any show of affection I get from my mother is to appease her own guilt. Whenever she tries, it's a measly attempt anyway.

"Of course," I supply, playing into the charade. "Thanks, Mom."

"Your father sends his love too."

I try to muffle my snort at her lie, baffled by why she thinks I would believe he would willingly send any positive thoughts my way. I couldn't tell you the last time my father said more than two words to me, and none of them had been, or would ever be, him expressing his love. "Thanks for calling, Mom, but I'm going to try and get an extra hour of sleep in, okay?"

"Of course, honey," she coos. "Be sure to call if you need anything."

Highly unlikely. "Promise."

"Love you."

"Love you too."

Sliding my thumb across the screen, I quickly check my alarm is still set to go off in an hour and a half, before placing it back on the nightstand. Dragging the blanket over my head, I push my mom's farce of a call to the back of my mind and pray that I can fall back asleep.

I arrived at college a little earlier than most students; a combination of wanting to leave home as soon as possible, and wanting to make myself comfortable and familiar in my new surroundings before classes started.

Coming to King University has been my dream for as long as I can remember. I worked my fucking ass off to get accepted here, and despite the nervousness, I'm excited. Not only is it far enough from Kent County, Texas that I'll only have to see my family twice a year, but it offers the most prestigious History degree in the country.

With each department only offering a ridiculously low number of scholarships per year, the competition was huge, but when there's nothing else worth your attention in your shitty shanty town, you lock yourself in a room and plan your exit strategy.

A door slamming immediately sets me on high alert, reducing any chance I have of falling back to sleep. Other than my roommate, there isn't really anybody else it could be. But seeing as his room has been set up since before I arrived, I can't help but be curious as to where he's been all week.

Clearly not caring about how much noise he's making, I take it as my cue to head into the common area and pretend his ruckus is what's woken me up. Now seems as good a time as any for introductions.

The shared space is bigger than I had anticipated before arriving. With not only functional kitchen facilities, but room enough for a couch, a decent sized rug, and a coffee table, it's pretty much a miniature two-bedroom apartment. I don't know how I got assigned to what feels like the penthouse of dorms, but I'm not complaining.

Dressed in my sweats and a black t-shirt, I stand in my doorway and come face-to-face with two people. One is, I'm assuming to be, my very unsteady, and possibly drunk, roommate. And the other is a petite-framed girl, trying to hold him up.

Standing inches away from the couch, he awkwardly tries to take his socks and shoes off while maintaining his hold on the girl.

"Just sit down," she huffs. "I'll get them for you." Whatever it is impeding his coordination wins out and he ends up stumbling onto the solid piece of furniture, taking her with him.

"Shit," I call out. "Are you two okay?"

Surprised by my presence, the girl quickly jumps off him, bumping into the nearby coffee table. Swiping her hair off her face, she looks up at me with wide eyes. "I'm so sorry. Did we wake you?"

"No," I answer honestly. "I just wanted to make sure nobody was hurt."

Completely oblivious to his surroundings, my roommate

tilts his head up and looks between me and his friend. "Who are you?"

"Eli," I say flatly.

"Nice to meet you, Eli," he garbles. "Can I sleep on your couch?"

I don't bother to argue or even question if he knows where he is. Instead, I watch his friend head for his room and grab the duvet spread across his bed. In the few seconds it takes for her to return he's already asleep. Gently, she places the blanket over his body before looking back up at me.

"I'm so sorry," she repeats. "I didn't want Aiden walking home alone."

"No worries." I wait for her to offer up any information on where he's been or why he's so drunk, but she doesn't. Nor does she offer me her name. Turning back to Aiden, she fusses over the blanket, and I take that as a sign to leave them alone. I tip my head back to my room and she nods. *Weird.*

Checking the time, I see I still have an hour before I need to start getting ready for school. Instead of hanging around feeling trapped by the four walls of my room, while whatever goes on outside continues, I change into my running shorts, find my sneakers, and decide to brave the outdoors.

Securing the Velcro on my armband, I slip my phone inside the protected pouch and put my wireless earphones into my ears. Walking out to the lounge room, I'm surprised to now see two sleeping bodies on the couch. Careful not to wake anyone up, I slip outside with ease and head through the emergency exit, instead of waiting for the elevator. Walking down six flights of stairs is the perfect warm-up.

The crisp, early morning breeze soothes my already

clammy skin as I exit the building. The student residences at King are a circular formation of apartment buildings with an oversized courtyard in the middle. Each entryway opens out on to the housing area's main attraction: a cute boutique-like café. King Koffee is situated like an oasis in the desert for all the tired, hungover, and overworked students that make up King's population.

With its usual overpowering smell of coffee beans wafting through the air, I'm surprised to see it in its sleepy stages of setting up. As I survey my surroundings, looking for the best running route, I realize six o'clock in the morning on campus might just be my favorite time of the day. With not a single body in sight, I inhale the fresh, cool air and indulge in the serenity of not just a brand-new day, but the promise of a new school year. The change in seasons. The potential of a new me.

Wanting to shake off the remnants of the phone call with my mother and the unconventional meeting with my roommate, I press shuffle on my playlist and start at a warm-up pace.

For as long as I can remember, running is something I've turned to when everything else doesn't make sense. I don't view it as a sport, or something I bother with competitively, but it's my one constant. The one thing I can depend on when I need to disengage from the world, detangle my own thoughts, or, more often than not, to simply just breathe.

Brisk walking turns into running, and soon I'm gaining more speed and momentum with every step. The scenery begins to blur, the solid color of bricks meshing into a never-ending expanse of green, while the sun peeks out from behind the clouds, brightening up the sky.

My feet find their rhythm and my chest expands and contracts with the bass of the music. Subconsciously, I close my eyes, basking in the now warm air that kisses my skin. Caught up in feeling, I hold my lids closed two seconds too long. Jolting out of my stupor, I fling my eyes open, acknowledging how consequential the simple slip can be. But it's too late.

Crouched down only inches in front of me, is a man fiddling with his shoe, or more likely, redoing his laces. I want to stop. My mind tells me to stop, but that one extended blink holds my movements hostage, stunting my coordination, and making it impossible for me to avoid the body before me.

"Sorry," I shout in warning. His head whips up, just as one of my legs leaps over him and the other knocks him in the shoulder. The bulk of his body means my lagging leg struggles to catch up with my other, and before I know it, we're both haphazardly tumbling toward the asphalt.

My hands meet the ground first, shielding my face from the gravel. Painfully, my legs follow, one knee throbbing and the other ankle feeling strangely out of place.

Shocked, I look down to take better inventory of my body, but my eyes are momentarily distracted by the man who's staring at me like he wants to kill me. *Shit.*

"I'm so sorry," I stammer. Hoping to get myself out of this situation as quickly as possible, I try to push myself up, but am welcomed with a rush of pain shooting through the leg I landed on. "Fuck. Ouch."

"What is it?" he asks, my moment of weakness changing his expression from pissed off to concerned. "What hurts?"

"Nothing." Avoiding his scrutiny, I keep my head down and attempt to sit up without putting any pressure on my sore foot. "I'm fine."

The sun that was strongly bearing down on us is now blocked as he maneuvers himself into a standing position in front of me. With seemingly no plans to leave, he hovers over me with his hand stretched out in front of my face. "Stop being so stubborn and take the help."

Embarrassed and defeated, I slip my palm into the one he holds out. The second our skin meets, his grip turns firm and unyielding.

"Put the pressure on your good leg," he demands knowingly. On instinct, I hold him tighter to give myself leverage, but he takes it as his cue to pull me up in one swift tug.

His hands find my waist and steady me before I collide into his chest and into him once more. Wanting the ground to swallow me whole, I bite the inside of my cheek and limp out of his touch.

With my head down, hair covering my face and eyes, I mutter for the hundredth time, "I'm sorry."

"You should really watch where you're going." The earlier inflections of worry and helpfulness in his voice have disappeared, changing to a gravelly reprimand that sends a shiver running up my spine.

Wanting to get this exchange over and done with, I run my fingers through my hair, flicking it off my face, and bring my gaze up to finally meet his.

I still.

Caught completely off guard, every single part of me freezes. I stop and stare. Stop moving. Stop blinking. Stop breathing.

In the haste of my limbs flailing all around him, and my failed attempt to get away, getting a good look at the man I careened into wasn't my number one priority.

And as steel colored eyes drag their appreciative gaze from my face down my body, I guess it wasn't his either. Slowly, different parts of me react to his perusal.

My mind. *Confused.*

My body. *Intrigued.*

My dick. *Very interested.*

With him being slightly taller than I am, I angle my head up and then let my gaze roam over him. He's got dark colored hair, closer to black than brown. Short around the sides and heavier at the top, it's the perfect length to run your fingers through. His face is adorned with a short, well-manicured beard that accentuates his full lips. It's obvious running, and probably other physical activities, is a priority. He takes care of his appearance, his broad and muscular shoulders can attest to that. Sinewy arms peek out from the sleeves of his t-shirt, as protruding veins run up and down the length of them.

Unable to look away, I shamelessly continue my perusal, admiring the way his shorts hang off his hips. Slowly, I work my way back up his body, taking it all in.

God, he's sexy. Herculean perfection.

"Move out of the way," a disgruntled runner shouts, disrupting our stare off. Frantically trying to get out of his way, I forget about my sore ankle and end up right where I shouldn't be. In his arms. Back together, toe-to-toe, even closer than before.

Trying to avoid what would be my third fall, my hands grip his shoulders for balance. I should let go. I need to let go, but the parts of my brain that control my movements refuse to cooperate. A light chuckle leaves his mouth, shifting the mood. "If you wanted to get close to me, all you had to do was ask."

Please don't say things like that.

"I'm sorry." Shaking my head, I ignore his harmless attempt at what I think is flirting and force myself to move away from him. "I've gotta go."

He smirks at my dismissal, but steps aside all the same.

"I guess you won't be buying me a drink to apologize for almost killing me earlier."

I'm so inept at conversation, flirting included; I want the ground to swallow me whole. He can't be interested in me, that's impossible. He's totally kidding.

"I'm kidding," he blurts out. As if he's read my mind, his face offers a sympathetic smile. One that tells me he wasn't really joking, but somehow he knew I wanted him to be. "Are you sure you don't need help getting home? You could lean on my shoulders that you seem to like so much."

My cheeks heat in embarrassment, at both his comment and the thought of being near him for the whole walk home.

Cautiously, I back away before I get myself into any more trouble. "Look, again, I'm really sorry for bumping into you."

As if he's committing every inch of me to memory, his eyes follow the same path as earlier. His gaze drifting between my shoulders, down my torso, and lingering at my shorts. He trails his way back up, licking his lips as he meets my stare. "Don't be."

Enjoying his appraisal a little more than I should, my dick thickens from a semi to a full blown hard on.

Get a grip, Elijah.

Knowing that if he takes one more look at my body he'll see my reaction to him, I point behind me quickly, desperate to escape. "I'll see you later."

Choosing not to wait around for a response, I limp away. Saving my foot from any more pain and saving myself from any more embarrassment.

It takes me double the time to get back to my dorm, making my early morning wake up pointless, and leaving me already running behind on my first day of classes.

Great fucking start.

After an uncomfortable shower, where I balanced on one leg, a breakfast of rice crackers and plastic cheese, and a two-hour nap, I try to take my mind off my disaster of a morning. Seeing as the couch is now unoccupied, and my roommate's bedroom door is closed, I get myself comfortable, keeping my foot elevated on the wooden table. With one of my t-shirts now saturated in cold water, I wrap it around my ankle as a substitute for a frozen bag of peas. It's not perfect, but it'll do. Hoping this alleviates the swelling of my tendon, I situate my Mac on my lap and get comfy. It's obvious I'm not going to make it to any of my lectures today, so I need to make sure I don't fall behind. Picking up a fresh packet of Werther's Originals, I unwrap the single butterscotch candy. They're my favorite, and have been since I was a kid.

Popping it into my mouth, I let the rich sweetness settle on my tongue as I log in to the student portal.

You're only allowed to miss two classes per subject. And even though the access to podcasts would have you feeling a sense of security when it comes to your education, it's a false one.

Here at King, you're banned from listening to podcasts if you exceed two unexplained absences. It's essentially a military camp for your brain, and even though pride rushes through me every time I think of being given the opportunity to earn my degree here, everything about this whole institution still intimidates the absolute shit out of me.

Assuming I've only missed an introductory lesson, I put my headphones on and search for my Studies in Religion elective. Foregoing a pen and paper, I close my eyes and let my head fall onto the back of the couch while I listen.

The authoritative voice streams through the speakers,

laying down the rules, listing the expectations, trying to put the fear of God into every student. And if I was in the classroom, being stared down by a face that matches that voice, there is no denying I would've felt it.

Religion: Texts, Life, and Traditions was one of the only classes I had where face-to-face contact with the Professor was limited to once a week. With what was said to be a gruelling online testing schedule, making up fifty percent of the grade, it was a sound decision to allow students to take full advantage of the upscale technology the university has to offer.

My attention begins to wane as I realize I need the unit outline to continue following along. Seeing as the only way to get my hands on it was to attend today's class, I decide to make it tomorrow's problem, and let my thoughts detour to my run in with the sexy stranger.

With the lecturer's deep voice playing as a soundtrack in my ears, my mind conjures up the mystery man and replays the way his gray eyes bored into me, slid down my body, while he unabashedly got his fill.

I'm a complicated mess when it comes to relationships and the laws of attraction, but as I swam in the depths of the embarrassment pool, it was a nice ego boost to be the subject of his desire, even if only momentarily.

A hand on my knee pulls me out of my thoughts and startles me, my body jolting in response. I snap my eyes open and glare at my now refreshed and sober roommate.

"Whoa." His hands fly up in surrender as I yank my headphones off. "I didn't mean to scare you, man. I was just trying to get your attention, and"— he points to my ears —"you couldn't hear me."

"Well, I can now," I say sarcastically.

"Look." He runs his hand over his short-clipped hair. "I

was hoping we could introduce ourselves, and I could apologize about earlier."

I give him a slight nod as he rambles, letting him talk it out.

"I don't make a habit of getting drunk, or coming home like that," he continues. "Just some last minute fun before school starts, you know?"

I didn't actually know what he meant, because I was purposely reserved. I kept to myself, stayed out of trouble, and constantly chose to blend into the background.

Drinking.

Getting drunk.

Being out of control.

Not. My. Thing.

"Are you going to say anything?" Exasperated, he drops to the couch beside me.

Not sure what to say, I ask him an easy question, even if I did hear his friend from earlier say it in passing. "What's your name?"

"My name?"

"I think people that live together should know each other's names."

"Yeah. Of course. Yeah." He buries his head in his hands, his shoulders sagging in unexpected relief. He turns his head to face me. "It's Aiden."

"I'm Eli," I offer. "I already told you that this morning, but I'm not sure if you remember."

He gives me a sheepish smile. "So, Eli." He glances down to my foot on the coffee table. "What happened to your foot?"

I simultaneously laugh and groan at the memory. "I'd rather not relive the embarrassing moment."

"Worse than me passed out on the couch?"

Focusing on the incident itself, and not the eye fucking I was reliving only minutes ago, I keep my answer to a minimum. "It was pretty bad."

"Are you going to be okay?"

"I think so. I might be hobbling my way around campus for the next few days, but I'll make do. Missing today was bad enough." Putting the laptop down on the table, I raise my leg and bend it toward me before placing it cautiously on the ground. "Did you make it to class today?"

"Don't start till tomorrow."

"And your girlfriend?"

"Who?" He looks perplexed.

"The girl from this morning?"

"Oh. That's Callie," he says despondently. "She's not my girlfriend."

"Noted."

Silent again, the usual getting to know you awkwardness ensues. While I appreciate Aiden's need to apologize, I'm not someone who expects it. I only set rules for myself, everybody else's business is theirs and I do my best to respect those boundaries.

If people want to spill their secrets, I'll listen. But I don't ever ask. All I do is observe, and it's obvious to see Aiden's apology is more his way of justifying this morning's actions to himself, not me.

Feeling like an imposition as he wages a war with himself, I shakily try and stand. Reaching for my laptop, I point to the open door behind me. "I'm going to head into my room and finish listening to this."

"Oh yeah, sorry, man. I didn't mean to disturb you." His face falls and I feel like I've kicked a puppy.

"It's not like that at all. I'm just pissed I missed my first day." It's a partial lie, but he buys it. "Maybe we can order pizza tonight?"

"Yes." He claps his hands together and jumps off the chair. "My treat. An apology."

"I do—"

He raises his hand, cutting me off. "Please. It will make me feel better."

Eager to stop the back and forth, I soften my voice and offer him what he's desperately seeking. "Aiden."

"Yeah?"

"I accept your apology."

3

COLE

S ince arriving, I've hit the ground running. Trying to find a new apartment, as well as getting into the swing of my new routine, the weekend can't come fast enough.

It's week two, and being the new teacher spread thin across the Arts and History faculties hasn't proved to be that bad. However, replacing someone that the older students had grown to know and love is a whole different ball game.

Professor Herald was a well-known Studies of Religion professor. He dabbled in other areas of interest, but his extensive contribution to academic literature on Christianity means having him as your professor was the equivalent to having Beethoven teaching students piano.

Saying I've got big shoes to fill is an understatement, but knowing he left on good terms upon his retirement makes everyone slightly more receptive to the replacement.

Shuffling paperwork around on my desk, I move the senior lesson plans out of the way and prepare for my next freshman class. The first lesson wasn't too bad. As usual, I had a few latecomers, and some no-shows. Even at a prestigious place like King, the beginning of the semester is always a case of weeding out those who enrolled in your class for the wrong reasons, or better yet, don't even think college is for them. Typically, I don't plan the heavy workload until week four. It seems to be a sweet spot, giving the apprehensive students enough time to decide if they're in or out.

The timer on my phone goes off, letting me know I've got five minutes till the students start piling in the room. Placing the remainder of the course outlines on the edge of my desk, I set the electronic student sign in machine next to it. Lucky for me the History department has been chosen to trial the new recording strategy––customized for each class I teach and portable to take to all the rooms I'm in.

That's right ladies and gentlemen, King University is planning on introducing little electronic devices that students swipe their ID cards on before collecting their unit outline. A similar scanner is also placed at the entryway of each lecture room, and students are required to tap into that as well. Both these machines collate the data and send a list of attendees straight through to my email on a daily basis.

It's the roll call of the future, and it's fucking fancy.

But when the cost of a degree is equivalent to that of a mortgage, and scholarships are limited, you can bet your ass parents want to know if their children are attending; and King only wants the dedicated. I'm sure if it wasn't frowned upon, each kid would be wearing an electronic ankle bracelet so their parents know of their every move.

One single beep notifies me that my first student has arrived. Finishing up, I scribble a few more points on my notepad and then stand. Walking around my desk, I shove my hands in my pockets and situate myself on the edge and wait.

With each noise, another person enters, talking to their

new friends and taking the seat that will eventually become their usual.

I love freshman classes, their enthusiasm for something new never gets old. Wide-eyed and curious, and a little bit frightened, I try not to scare them off right from the get go, no matter how much entertainment it might bring me.

Watching as the last student takes his seat, I pull the hand-sized, electronic remote that connects to the interactive board behind me, out of my pocket. I twist my torso, and point it at the screen.

The voices quiet down the second they see the screen come to life.

"Welcome, again, to Religion: Texts, Life, and Traditions. I'm glad to see most of you returned." A light hum of chatter flutters through the room at my comment. "For everyone who read the course outline, what are we doing today?"

While the majority of students nervously flick through their booklets, an eager kid at the front raises his hand.

Surprised, and pleased, I gesture to him. "Your name?"

Before he has the chance to answer, a sound indicating someone's arrival interrupts the class. Instinctively, every head turns to the back of the room, waiting.

Someone's late.

The door opens, and a young man uses his back to keep it open, while holding a backpack out to someone in front of him. Not at all concerned with being late, he smiles at whoever is out of sight. A hand takes the bag out of the young man's hold and a few more words are exchanged.

Knowing my voice echoes, I give an exaggerated cough, hoping to get their attention. Whoever plans on walking in is taking their sweet ass time, and I'm not impressed. Painfully slowly, the hidden student finally steps into view.

Fuck. Me.

My mouth dries up at the sight of him. Knowing that it's definitely the first time he's stepped foot in my classroom, I watch the attractive guy that fell in to me last week with unmistakable curiosity.

He looks up to meet the hundred or so pairs of eyes staring at him, his face turning an unmissable shade of red as he scans the room for a spare seat. My annoyance at his tardiness is shelved, and my greed to see him up close pushes its way to the forefront.

Selfishly wanting to know why he wasn't here, I knowingly use my power as his professor to find out what I need.

"Lost, late, or new?" I call out. His head whips up, and I watch as recognition takes over his features. Stunned, he stares at me, indecision written all over his face. Should he stay or should he go? "Well?" I press.

He clears his throat and speaks louder because of the distance between us. "New."

I try to appear as nonchalant as possible, to seem unaffected by the presence of a young man who's unexpectedly occupied my thoughts since he ran into me, and eye fucked me senseless.

"In that case, you might want to come down here and pick up what you missed."

With a small limp in his gait, he begins to descend the flight of stairs.

He's still hurt.

Even though I can see he's injured, I don't back down on my request. I want him in front of me, knowing who's in charge, and wanting to know if our run-in was the reason he didn't show up.

I pray that up close his face is somehow less tempting than I remember, and that my attraction to him is dampened by our circumstances.

As he takes his last step, I realize it's impossible.

Last week, shock and annoyance quickly turned into startling intrigue, and my lust filled reaction to him was instant and obvious. As the voice in my head kept reminding me of the perils of being too close to campus, my eyes continued to devour him and the words out of my mouth tried to lure him in.

Full of remorse and undeniably skittish, his behavior after our accident only highlighted the age gap between us. Even disheveled, I saw how innocent and honest he was, and under any other circumstances, I wouldn't have looked twice.

Young isn't my thing. Not usually, anyway. But as he stands before me, I realize denying my attraction to him is futile. Rivaling any Hollywood heartthrob, his hair is now brushed back into a perfect quiff, out of his eyes and show-casing every enticing angle of his face.

Fuck.

He's a freshman, and he's not just a student at King, he's *my* student. This is the part where I should be turned off.

But I'm not.

As he stands before me, holding my gaze, his face flushed and Adam's apple bobbing in his throat, I'm even harder for him now than I was last week.

Diligently, he waits for my next directive, and fuck if it doesn't make him that much more alluring. The second his forest green orbs lock with mine, he tips his head to the side and, like a choreographed move, his hair falls over his eyes, hiding his gaze.

Irrationally, I feel rejected, and I fucking hate it. Taking it as my cue to get back to what's important, I grab the stack of papers and thrust them in his direction.

"Name?" I say a little more curtly than I need to.

"Eli."

"Eli," I repeat, hoping he'll look back up at me. "Here's what you missed."

Mumbling an almost inaudible thank you, he unclenches his hands to snatch the outline from me. Twisting his upper body, he looks around, searching for somewhere to sit. Worried about his injury and selfishly wanting him to be close to me, I take the decision out of his hands. "Sit here at the front." He doesn't move at my suggestion. "It looks like it might take you longer than we've got to get back up those stairs."

His shoulders deflate at the reminder, and I momentarily hate myself for putting him on show in front of everyone. The whole class watches as he makes his way to the front row. When his body lands on the seat, I shift my glance and gesture to the student from earlier. "Ok, where were we?"

"You asked what today's lesson would be about," he pipes up.

"And do you have the answer?" The sarcasm drips off my voice, and just like that I slip back into professor mode, leaving the distracted and turned on man behind.

"Yes. Of course," the kid supplies. "Today we should be discussing global religions."

"Excellent." Focusing on all the attentive eyes aimed my way, I push Eli to the back of my mind and dive right into the lesson.

Listing each major religion, discussing their countries of origin, and their transcendence through time, has the students eating out of the palm of my hand and immersing themselves in all the information I'm giving them. "Ok, now, we're going to play a quick word association game before we tie this lesson up."

Impassive faces fill the auditorium. *Tough crowd.*

"Ok," I start. "I'm going to call out a series of words and you will say the first thing that comes to mind when you hear it." A student to my left narrows her eyebrows, so I clarify. "The words will be taken from things we've discussed today, and other words that may pop up this semester. Therefore, so will your answers."

Blank stares.

"I'm not expecting a definition, but just words that pop into your head. There's no wrong or right answer, and there will almost always be multiple interpretations. Got it?" I catch sight of a few students nodding. The purpose of the game is to pinpoint people who are listening and retaining information. It doesn't change anything when it comes to their final grade, but it's a nice little way to keep tabs on the success of my teaching methods. It also offers an abundance of affirmation to those students who do know what the fuck is going on and choose not to lurk in the shadows of the classroom.

"Ok." I rub my hands together. "First word is anthropology." Silence ensues. "Anyone?"

"Humans."

Stunned, my head turns to face Eli. Composed, and much more relaxed, he waits for the next word. "Sociology."

"Karl Marx," he rushes.

"Dogma."

"Catholic."

Knowing I need to address the rest of the class, I drag my attention away from him. "Theology, anyone?"

The class fails me, and Eli jumps in, pulling me right back to him. "Religion."

Smart and attentive, I'm caught up in a surprise round of intellectual foreplay with the only student I don't want to pay attention to, and I never want it to end. *Unfuckingbe-lievable.*

"Deity."

"God." The answer comes from the far back of the room, and just like that our connection is broken.

I school my face, trying to look indifferent, and focus on the student who answered. "It's nice for someone else to join us."

The timer on my desk goes off, putting an immediate end to the game, and, simultaneously, today's lecture.

"Well, that's it for today, folks. I'll see you all next week. Same time, same place."

The noise in the room heightens as books slam, desks retract, and students engage in nonsensical chatter. I should feel relieved the class is over, but as I sneak a look in Eli's direction, an insane urge to be in his presence railroads my rationale.

I call out to him as he packs his bag. "Eli."

He stiffens.

"Could you stay back, please?"

Sitting back down, he remains rigid, his body language closed off and weary. *Nice going, Cole.*

Against my better judgement, I take the seat beside him. "Your foot still hurting?"

Obviously not expecting my concern, he tilts his head to the side and faces me. "So, you remembered me."

A loud laugh escapes me. *Like anybody could forget a face like yours.* Redirecting my thoughts, and the conversation, I point to his leg. "Is that why you missed the first class?"

"It took me a while to walk back to my dorm, and in the end it was too much pain to even bother."

"Nice to know my class is a priority."

He shifts in his chair, nervously tapping his student card on his knee. "That's not what I meant."

I place my hand on his leg, stopping his fidgeting. "It's okay, I'm just teasing."

We both look down, but unlike the shy man from the other day, he doesn't move and he doesn't push me away.

Wanting to prolong the conversation, I take the rectangular piece of plastic out of his hand and bring it up to my face.

Elijah Williams.

"Your full name is Elijah?"

"Everyone calls me Eli," he corrects.

Loving the way the six letters come together and the way his name sounds coming out of my own mouth, I take a mental note to never call him Eli again.

I hand him back the card. "Are you going to be okay to catch up?"

He drags his bag up his body and tugs out a composition notebook. Wordlessly opening it up, he offers it to me. Taking it, I notice there's a heading that says 'Lesson One' and what looks to be like notes from everything he would've heard on the podcast. Falling back into my chair, I cross my legs, so that my ankle rests on my knee, and continue to flick through the pages. With a highlighted heading for every new topic, I appreciate Elijah's accurate dissection of the lesson. Turing more pages, I find lesson two, the one he was late to, and his legible scrawl filling up every line.

Questions. Explanations. Highlights. There's things in here that I haven't even covered yet, and things he would've missed without the outline, but just as I suspected, this proves his mind is a wealth of information, exploring and delving into everything this class has to offer.

Rendered speechless, I look up at him, and he's smirking

at me. His intellectual charm has returned, and it's in this moment I realize it's the exact same thing that changes him from cautious to confident. If it were possible, he's even sexier like this. "Looks like you've got it covered."

Fingers find the spine of his notebook and he drags it out of my grasp. "Failure isn't an option."

"If you continue like this, it won't even be on your radar," I commend.

"I'm here on a scholarship," he says, explaining his studious nature.

I nod in understanding. "What are you studying?"

"Double major. History and Education."

An unwarranted sense of pride rushes through me. "You want to teach?"

"Eventually."

"What made you choose this class?" I don't get a lot of students who are wholeheartedly into exploring religions. Usually it's just another class they take to fill up their arts requirements, or an elective they think they'll enjoy, but end up dropping. It's an intense and intricate exploration of a world that I have always loved to get lost in, and curiosity has me hoping Elijah is in this class for those reasons.

"A few reasons," he answers vaguely. Applying pressure to the arm of the chair, he pushes himself up. "But the teacher seems like a good enough reason to stay."

At his veiled compliment, I rake my eyes up his body. Standing in front of me, he hooks the bag strap over his shoulder, and the white shirt he's wearing rises. My eyes falter at the sight of his skin, his jeans low on his hips, and the thick waistband of his briefs peeking out.

Noticing the silver crucifix that hangs low from his neck, and the way both of his wrists are adorned with leather and silver bracelets, I'm reminded that Elijah really isn't my usual type. He's my student for fuck's sake, and students can never be my type. But that piece of information holds no weight on my conscience, because I can't stop staring at him.

He clears his throat, pulling me out of my ogling. "I'm going to start my long walk home now."

"Of course." I rise with the intention to move toward my desk, as far away from him as possible, but we both continue to stand there, prolonging the inevitable.

Everything about this is unprecedented for me. Personally, I'm carefree, spontaneous, and would gladly date a guy who looks like he belongs in a magazine centerfold. But professionally, I've made it my mission to follow the handbook. Success isn't an option, it's an expectation. One that I place on myself and take very seriously.

I've come too far to fall flat on my face, and being attracted to Elijah isn't something that should throw me off my game. But it has.

I don't want to walk away from him, and it looks like he doesn't want to walk away from me either.

But I have to.

We have to.

"I'll try and be on time next lesson."

"Sounds like a plan, Mr. Williams. Otherwise, you'll be sitting at the front of the class for the rest of the semester."

Stop trying to flirt with the kid, Cole.

"It could be worse," he says, surprising me.

Elijah lowers his face in embarrassment as he realizes he's spoken his thoughts out loud, and I bite my tongue to make sure we remain in neutral territory.

"I'll see you next week, Elijah."

"Eli," he reiterates.

I ignore his request and offer a smirk instead.

He shakes his head while tucking his bottom lip

between his teeth, and it takes every ounce of willpower I have to stop myself from running my fingers across the seam of his mouth.

"Prof—"

I put a hand up to stop him, not wanting the reminder of who I am to him.

Running a hand through his hair, he gives me an understanding nod and turns to leave. Each step seems harder to watch than the one before, and it pains me to watch him hobble his way up the stairs.

My concern morphs into an unrestrained ogle as I shamelessly watch him from behind. I've hit on plenty of straight guys, and last week, because he was so awkward, I would've bet my left nut that he was.

But today... Today he was interested. Still nervous. Still scared. Still embarrassed. But there's no denying he was interested.

He's everything I know I shouldn't look twice at, but I can't turn away. There's no in-between for me here; nobody cares if it's *just* a physical attraction, there aren't levels of punishment based on how far you go. I'm a professor. He's a student. It's wrong on *every* level.

As he reaches the top landing, I tell myself to take advantage of this moment and to take him all in, because the next time I see him I *need* him to not be a problem.

He turns my way one last time and gives me a two fingered salute. I raise my hand in a half-hearted wave and mentally lock that door the second it's shut.

Elijah Williams will not be my distraction

Elijah Williams will not be my temptation.

Elijah Williams will not be my mistake.

4

ELIJAH

H oly. Fucking. Shit.
Walking out of the lecture hall, I'm an over-
flowing bundle of nerves.

Was I actually flirting with him?

From the minute I rose to the challenge with his word
association game, I couldn't help but show off. He was
impressed by the knowledge that I had worked so damn
hard to attain, and hell if it didn't feel good to have someone
notice me for all the right reasons.

It doesn't hurt that there's an air of authority and sophis-
tication that enhances just how handsome and intelligent
he is. It makes paying attention to him a very dangerous and
addictive pastime.

He was good looking in running clothes, but in gray
tailored pants that match his silvery eyes, and a crisp, white
button-down shirt, he's an image that I am unlikely to forget.
And with a scheduled meeting once a week, also known as
my Religion: Texts, Life, and Traditions class, where he's
required to wear variations of that exact outfit, it will

undoubtedly be seared into my memory by the end of the
semester.

"Earth to Eli."

Aiden's voice reaches my ears and I'm surprised to see
him and Callie leaning on the brick wall in front of me.
Ever since he apologized, and Callie joined us for pizza
night, it's been the two of them dragging me along, while we
all find our way through freshman year, together. "What are
you guys doing here?"

"Well, we came to walk with you to grab some lunch,
but, dude," he looks down at his imaginary watch. "We've
been waiting for ages."

"Yeah. Um—"

Just as I'm about to apologize, the door I recently walked
out of swings open. Callie's and Aiden's eyes look past me,
and the look on their faces hints at all the reasons I
shouldn't turn around. But it doesn't matter, because like the
Red Sea, we part as he walks right between the three of us,
and I get another glimpse at the man whose attributes I'd
just been mentally cataloguing.

His cologne wafts right past me. All man, with a hint of
spice, citrus, and wood, it takes me right back to the stolen
moments we just shared. Right back to where I was just the
guy who ran into him, and he was the guy who caught me.
Right back to where I didn't feel the need to hide *anything*
about me.

My eyes follow him as he walks away, enjoying the way
the material stretches across his ass with every step. It's a
nice consolation for missing the opportunity to look at his
face one last time.

"Is that the reason you got held up?" Callie says.
"Because I would stay back with him. Any day."

A humorless laugh leaves my mouth. I run my fingers

through my hair, styling it any which way to distract me from the obvious fact that Professor Huxley is attractive to *everyone.*

"Yeah, he's okay," I mumble. "Are we going to lunch or what?" I ask a little too enthusiastically.

Aiden narrows his eyebrows at me suspiciously, and I wonder what it is that's got him curious.

Flanking either side of me, they protectively walk at a slower pace. It's a nice gesture but completely unnecessary. "I'm not an invalid, guys."

"You kind of are, though," he jokes. "And maybe, you're the only other friend we have."

A hand brushes over mine, and I falter when I realize it's Aiden's. I glance over at him and he's watching me intently, waiting for my reaction. I offer a tight-lipped smile, because I don't want him to think I'm shocked that another guy touched me. I don't want anyone to feel rejected because of their sexuality, but I do want him to know I'm not interested in him, or anyone else for that matter.

A relationship isn't on my to-do list. In fact, it's not even on my radar. I don't have the time or luxury to even think about getting involved in one. And it's always been this way.

"So, what's cafeteria food like?" Callie asks, unknowingly disrupting my thoughts. "I've been a little too busy to visit."

"And by busy she means having lots and lots of sex with her boyfriend."

"Ha," she laughs. "He's not my boyfriend. I barely even know him."

"Oh, sorry, my bad," Aiden scoffs. "You don't know him well enough to call him your boyfriend, but enough to let him stick his dick in you."

"Do you have to be so crass?" She feigns offense. "You're going to scare Eli away."

"Nope." I raise my hand up in protest. "Don't involve me. I'm happy being a spectator."

Aiden and Callie bicker constantly, and even though I was almost certain there was some underlying sexual tension between them, Aiden's actions earlier and news of Callie's extracurricular activities confuses me a little.

"Please," Aiden drolls. "If he was scared, he'd be gone by now."

"In case you didn't notice, I'm low on friend options," I joke. "You guys are all I've got."

They both pretend to look offended and simultaneously nudge me in the shoulders. "Whoa, guys. Invalid here."

"Oh now you're an invalid."

The three of us laugh, successfully ending their banter, and settling into comfortable chatter as we make our way to the cafeteria.

When we get there, Aiden holds the door open for us, and I keep my head down while walking in. Crowds make me a little self-conscious.

We find a table for the three of us, and then Callie and Aiden leave to get food, insisting that I sit and wait. Apparently a sore ankle means I can't carry anything on my own. I guess I'll just milk it then.

Minutes later, a plastic tray is being slid across the table, stopping in front of me. I take a quick peek at the very gross looking lunch. "Is this edible?"

"It is unless you want to fit a part-time job into your study schedule," Aiden informs me. "But the fries are there just in case the rest really tastes as bad as it looks."

"Speaking of jobs, actually, I think I need one," I admit. "Scholarships only get you so far. And even though I've been saving all summer, I don't have too much spare money to throw around."

"Can't you ask your parents?" Callie naively asks.

While spending time with my new friends, I've also found out that Callie and Aiden are rich. Trust fund rich. They grew up together in Connecticut and went to the most prestigious high school this country has to offer. This doesn't necessarily make them insensitive to other people's financial situations, but it does mean more often than not, they're clueless to the way the world works for the rest of us.

Honestly, it doesn't bother me that they have access to money, and their parents shower them in it. It's what parents *should* do, but if I was ever going to be jealous of these two, it wouldn't be about their money. It would be about their parents. Even if they believed money solved everything, and often used it as a bargaining chip, they still cared. In a fucked up way, they cared, and it was a lot more than mine did.

"My parents aren't well off," I say flippantly. "And I'd rather wait till hell freezes over before asking them for anything."

The dismissal in my voice is enough that they don't probe, and I'm grateful for it. I've already said a little too much, and if I can help it, family is never something I want to talk about. I figured out early on, if you don't talk about it, nobody can ask you about it.

"I would really love a job, though," I say, steering us back on topic. "Have you guys seen anything around?"

"What are you good at?" Callie pulls out a pen and paper. She does this a lot, I've noticed. According to her, everything deserves a list. "And what job experience do you have?"

"Um." I run my hand over my face. "I worked in a diner back in Kent, and I can make café style coffee."

"Oh wait," Callie claps in excitement. "Can you do those cute designs on them too?"

I hold up a finger for her to wait while I finish chewing my food. Taking a quick swig of water, I answer. "I have been known to make some fancy looking hearts in my time."

"Excellent." Without any more discussion, she continues to add to the list and I wonder what else she's writing since 'making coffee' and 'diner' don't take that long.

"What about working in the library?" Aiden suggests. "Or asking some of your professors if there's stuff you can assist with?"

Just like the word association game, the mention of a teacher triggers an all too appealing visual of Professor Huxley in my mind.

"But do those jobs pay? I thought they just helped you earn extra credits," Callie muses. "Unless it's that professor of yours we just saw. I would work for free, for him."

You and me both.

"I would like to earn extra credits." They turn to me confused. "Why not?"

"You want a job, you want to give up your time to the people who already take enough of ours, and you expect to have a social life?" They both stare at me with disapproving looks as Callie continues to dress me down. "Are you trying to run yourself into the ground?"

"I've never had a social life, so I'm not really giving anything up." I pick up a fry and pop it into my mouth. "I don't need one." They're both so horrified it's almost comical.

"What about us?" Callie pouts.

"Come on, guys, be serious for a second. I need to keep my scholarship and have a little bit of money to help me get by. Plus, no social life means I'll spend less money."

"You're one hell of a party animal," Aiden sneers.

Callie backhands his shoulder, and I try my best to not be bothered by his assumption that I'm the boring kid. I remind myself it's by choice, and it's a necessity.

"Honestly, Eli, it's a good idea." Callie is speaking to me, but looking at Aiden. "And it will mean that we'll remain your best friends, because you won't have time for others. I like it."

"I guess that's one way to look at it."

"You'll soon come to realize I'm the queen of the glass half-full movement."

She smiles at me, happy and infectious, and I return it. Unlike Aiden, she's never sullen or moody. She also isn't taking my life choices unexpectedly personally.

Losing my appetite, I fork my food around my plate, while Callie and Aiden fill in the silence with unnecessary babble. Reminiscing about their pasts and laughing at their own jokes, they are talking enough that I never have to.

Dragging my cell out of my pocket, I check the time to see how long I have before my next class.

"Guys, I'm going to head out," I announce, rising from my chair. "I'm going to stop in at the library and see if they have any jobs available there."

"Are you going to be okay?" Aiden asks, glancing at my leg.

"Yeah, man, it's getting better each day."

"Don't forget to take a hard look at the notice boards," Callie pipes in. "Sometimes businesses leave flyers there for students to see, but they get buried."

Placing my hand across my stomach, I bow slightly. "Thank you, my queen."

"That's what I like to hear."

I give her a wink and tip my chin up at Aiden. "I'll see you guys later."

AIDEN and I are holed up in a room in the library studying, and after my third week at college, I've decided I could easily give up.

Leaning back into the reading chair, I bring my coffee up to my nose and take in a lungful of the enticing smell. *Coffee is magical.*

"My brain is exhausted," I say on a sigh. "I know I'm a book nerd, but I'm on information overload."

"Now imagine what it's like for the rest of us," he jokes. "Maybe I should just give in and work for my dad. He might be so happy he'll allow me to skip the degree altogether."

From the little things he's mentioned about his family, they own a multi-million dollar computer software business, and like all kids who have options, Aiden doesn't want the one his parents have chosen for him.

"Oh, I forgot to give you this." Pulling a scrunched up piece of paper out of his bag, Aiden hands me a flyer. "I found this for you."

I take it and give it a once over. "Where did you get this?"

"They were just putting it up at King Koffee as I was buying our drinks."

My eyes take in all the details. Hours. Requirements. Starting date. I think this might actually work.

"I think I might apply for it."

"That's the idea, Einstein." He laughs then looks down at my ankle. "Do you think your foot is up for it?"

With only slight discomfort, I manage to roll my ankle

around, in all directions. It feels a million times better than it was.

"It's perfectly fine," I say, showing off my improvement. "It's been three weeks, and it was only a minor sprain, if that."

"Well, they don't want anyone to start for another week, so you should be fine, as long as you stay off the running course."

I groan dramatically. "I fucking miss running."

"Dude, why do you even do it? It's not like you play a sport." He drags his gaze up and down my body. "Or even need to stay in shape."

Ever since the unassuming hand graze, Aiden has made it his mission to throw simple advances my way. It's not making me feel uncomfortable, In fact, the small part of me that's deprived of attention relishes in it. I should be ashamed for not putting a stop to it, but as a small consolation to myself, I don't do anything to encourage it either.

Aiden isn't unattractive by any means; he wears preppy like it's an art form, and when he isn't apologizing for being a drunken mess, his confidence is in overdrive.

I'm waiting for the moment he blatantly asks if I'm gay, but the more time I spend with him, the more I think he's a guy that isn't concerned with labels, but he's someone who's emboldened by the chase just as much as the catch.

"Running gave me the space I needed when I was a kid," I divulge. "Some kids love football or baseball, I just love running."

"Maybe when you're all healed up, I'll join you."

"Ha," I scoff. "All your classes are scheduled after ten for a reason, and I haven't seen you ever get up earlier than twenty minutes before a class."

He shrugs. "You may have a point, but maybe I just need incentive."

And there he goes again.

"Right. Are we going to study or not, because I want to go to the café before I head home, and check the notice-board downstairs again too."

"You still after extra credits?"

"Hey, if I can cover an elective with some extra work, and get out of here a semester earlier, then why not?"

"When you put it like that," Aiden ponders. "I'll keep my eyes and ears open for you."

"Thanks, man. And if this job works out, I'll owe you big time."

Aiden's phone rings and he obnoxiously puts it on loud speaker. "Hey, baby," he greets.

A female voice purrs through the phone, surprising me.

I guess he's into girls too.

Aware that I'm not going to get any actual studying done with Aiden, the phone call urges me to get going. Rising, I catch his attention and point to the door behind me with one hand and carelessly pack my books up with the other.

Slinging my backpack over my shoulder and holding my folder to my chest, I offer Aiden one last wave before making my way out of the room.

As I've been doing almost every day for the last three weeks, I head to the noticeboard near the exit doors and scan through all the miscellaneous flyers that have been pinned there.

There are at least fifty pieces of paper crammed all over the felt board, and the unorganized placement of each notice has me giving up on the idea of finding something altogether.

I should just focus on getting the job at the café; it seems like the more doable route right now. And maybe Callie and Aiden are right, there's no absolute rule that says I have to exhaust myself from both ends and maintain my status as a loner.

Wanting to get to the coffee shop before someone else swoops in and takes my job, I spin on my heels and collide with a solid wall of muscle.

Immediately, my folder dislodges from my grip and lands open and face down on the floor.

"Shit," I utter under my breath as I bend down to pick up the casualty of my clumsiness.

"I'm really sorry." The voice is vaguely familiar, and as I raise my eyes to meet the person who's also crouched down trying to retrieve my belongings, I realize why. "Elijah."

My eyes zero in on his masculine lips, and a knowing smirk pulls at either side of his mouth. Unable to speak, I pull my folder out of his grasp and stand, trying for some distance between us.

In acknowledgement of the effect he has on me, I have purposefully stayed away from him since that day in class. I have forced myself to continue being boring, rigid Eli, even though I promised myself I wouldn't do that here. But I need to, because boring is safe, and around Professor Huxley, I need safe.

Entertained by my continuous display of awkwardness, he just stares at me while I swiftly fix the papers in my folder and clutch it back to my chest.

"I think my flyers got caught in the mix up," he informs me while eyeing my folder.

Fucking Hell.

Not trusting myself to speak or move with coordination, I hand him the bulky folder. He can find them himself.

With ease, he flicks through the mess and finds what

he's looking for. "I was just coming over to pin these to the notice board." He hands me a paper. "Maybe I won't need to put them all up, if you're interested?"

Taking it from him, I look down to see what he's talking about. It's a research project funded by the History department. If you're successful, it's a guaranteed spot on the team for the duration of your degree. It might not give me extra credits, but to have this listed down as one of my achievements is a once in a lifetime opportunity.

If there ever was a right place at the right time moment it would be this. "Wouldn't you need more than one student for this?"

"I would only need one freshman. We're taking on one student from each year," he explains. "I'd really like it to be you."

So forward.

Stepping closer, he crowds in on my personal space. "What do you say, Elijah?"

Regardless of how seductive my name sounds falling off his tongue, I correct his blatant dismissal of my request. "Please call me Eli."

"How about I make you a deal?" My heart hammers in my chest at his closeness. "Say yes, and I'll call you Eli."

I press my teeth into my bottom lip while I weigh my options. It might be a once in a lifetime opportunity, but it also means being swept up in Professor Huxley's intoxicating presence.

The attraction is there. I can feel it, and it's nothing like the innocent and harmless flirting from Aiden.

It's dangerous.

It's addictive.

It's wrong.

He hands me back my folder, as I mull over the decision.

When I take it off him, he purposefully grazes his fingertips over mine in the exchange, and his touch zips through me like an electric shock. Pulling my hand back, I catch the sliver of desire that he can never seem to hide when he's around me.

Certain that this is the best and worst decision of my life, I answer with the only real option he's given me.

"Yes."

5

COLE

L ike a warm whisper that kisses every inch of my skin, his answer is needy and wanting; sending my mind into a spiral of scenarios where I could feel him under me saying the same word.

Yes. Yes. Yes.

My cell chooses this moment to ring, and it gives Elijah the chance to—literally— run away from me. There's no goodbye, no I'll see you soon, just the back of a young man who's probably trying to figure out what the hell he just signed up for.

When the head of the History Department came to me with the idea, Elijah was the first person who came to mind. Take away whatever physical attraction I have to him, there's no denying he's a dedicated and deserving student.

I stopped myself from seeking him out after class to see if he was interested; told myself I needed to remain professional. Every student needed to be given a fair and honest opportunity to apply for the positions, and my biased dick didn't get a say.

Until I saw him again.

It wasn't an accident that he bumped into me, but rather stupidity on my part for standing so close to him. I had planned to tap him on the shoulder, and possibly enjoy the look on his face when he turned around and saw it was me. What I didn't expect was the way the air thickened around us once his eyes found mine and recognition set in.

The smallest part of me wants to believe the attraction I feel for him, and that he seems to have for me, isn't real. I want to be wrong about how flustered he becomes when he looks at me. I want to be wrong about the electric current that zips through me whenever I think of him. I want to convince myself that his interest in me is because of what I teach and not because of how I make him feel.

But I'm not wrong, and trying to persuade myself is hopeless. It's there, plain as day, written on both our faces.

"Hello. Hello? Is anyone there?"

Shit.

"Yes. Hello. Sorry, it's a bad connection," I lie. "Who's this?"

"Hello. It's Liam from Century 21. I've got some details on some of the properties you inquired about."

Still frazzled by Elijah's rushed exit, it takes me a while to respond. "Yes. Okay, what do you have?"

"There is an open house for two of them tomorrow night, if you're interested." Pinching the bridge of my nose, I do my best to concentrate. This call is important. "They're only a few minutes away from one another, so you could come and check them out and discuss prices."

"Yeah," I answer, finally focusing on the conversation. "That sounds great. What time?"

"Both houses are open from seven thirty to nine."

"That works fine with my schedule," I inform him. "If

you can email me the details and directions after we get off the phone, that'd be great."

"Not a problem. I'll do that right away."

"Thank you, I appreciate it. I'll see you tomorrow."

"See you then."

With a loud exhale, I slip the phone back into my pocket and step up to the notice board, continuing with what I originally came here to do. Rearranging some flyers, I carve out a little space, front and center, to put up my own.

In my own personal daydream, I stand in the middle of the library, staring ahead, looking pensive. But really, I'm only thinking about Elijah. I need to get back to my office. Better yet, I should go out.

I just need to fuck him out of my system.

Leaving the library, I pull out my cell and flick out a message to Harper and Miles. Ever since the school soiree, the three of us have kept in touch. Harper and I have fallen into an easy routine, seeing as she also lives in the same block as me, but Miles is harder to nail down. Recently divorced and a full-time parent, his schedule isn't always free.

Me: Anyone free for drinks tonight?

It's not until I reach my office that I get a response from either of them.

Miles: I'm low on babysitter options these days.

Harper: I'm free.

Me: No worries. Harper, I'll swing past at 7:00.

Harper: See you then.

Just as I lock my phone, it lights back up with my sister's face blown up on the screen. For a minute I consider letting it go to voicemail, but I know my sister. Leaving a message isn't her style, but continuing to call until I answer, is.

"Hey."

"Hey, stranger." Her voice immediately puts me at ease and we fall into an easy banter as I enter my office.

"Stranger," I scoff. "Is this because we don't live near one another anymore? Because I'm sure we've spoken every day since I left home."

"It's not the time for technicalities, Cole. You're not here and that's all that matters."

"Is everything okay?" I ask. I haven't forgotten how upset she was when I first moved out here, but since she hasn't mentioned anything lately about her and Trey, I've taken it as a good sign.

"Everything is fine. I only called to see if you'd be able to make it back for Mom's birthday."

Sitting down on the leather office chair, I swivel it around until I'm directly in front my yearly planner. I flick the pages over to November.

"I figured if we could plan something early enough, there would be a better chance of you being able to make it."

"It's so close to Thanksgiving," I say. "I don't know if I'll be able to swing both trips, or if I can even be there longer than a weekend." I scribble Mom's name on the calendar and add 'look for flights home/work out best option for visiting' on my to-do list. "I know it's a big birthday, so I'll do what I can because I don't want to miss it."

"I was going to throw her a surprise party, but—"

"She'll hate it," I finish for her.

"Right. That's why you're going to be the surprise."

"I am?"

"Yes. Whenever you speak to her, just keep telling her you can't come till Christmas, okay?"

"Got it." My hand hits my computer mouse and the large screen comes to life, my email inbox in front of me. "Actually, Megs, while I've got you, I'm going to send you an email."

"I guess I'm okay with you sending me gay porn."

"Things every brother loves to hear." I open the email Liam sent and forward it straight to Meghann. "I'm going to look at a few places tomorrow night and I want your opinion on them."

"I'm not living in them, though."

"You know I'm not going to make an offer without your opinion."

"Your dependency on me is comical, big brother. Somewhat cheesy, but extremely satisfying."

"Can you just stop with the gloating and check them out, please?"

A loud beep comes through the phone, followed by the sound of her personal assistant's voice advising her she has a phone conference in ten minutes. She sighs. "I've got to take this call if I ever want to get out of here at a decent hour. Not all of us are lucky enough to finish at three."

"It's five o'clock," I retort, unfazed by the dig. "Just let me know what you think before tomorrow night, okay?"

"Love you, Cole."

"Love you too."

Looking at the time, I tell myself another half an hour here would be time well spent, then I'll go home and get ready before meeting Harper.

An email alert pulls me out of my reading. Meghann has sent her reply with the heading 'For the right price this is the one.' I laugh at her choice, because just as I predicted, it was mine too. Fingers crossed it looks just as good in real life.

Unable to get back into the zone with my reading, I pack what I need into my leather laptop bag and head home.

After a quick shower, I opt for comfort, throwing on a pair of dark blue jeans with a white, short-sleeved button-down shirt and brown leather boots. Dressed casually and less restrictively, it's the perfect combination, because it's the exact way I want to feel tonight. Shoving my phone and wallet in my pockets, I'm ready to go.

Knocking on the hollow door, I wait for the familiar face to appear.

"I'm coming," Harper calls out. The door opens and she appears in black jeans and a loose, black blouse, with a towel twisted on top of her head holding her wet hair up. "You're early."

"Well, hello to you, too, Beauty." I look down at my watch and follow the seconds as they tick by until the digital numbers flip over to seven o'clock. "I'm right on time now. Are you ready?"

She huffs at me in irritation. "I just need to dry my hair. Come inside and wait for me?"

"I don't mind hanging here."

"Don't be the creeper at the door, Cole. Just come inside and sit on the couch."

With no room left for argument, I step into her apartment and awkwardly stand in the middle of the space, waiting for her to finish up.

Just like me, Harper was offered housing to get her to move here quicker. Where I am messy, laid back, and in no rush to settle in, a quick scan shows none of that is a problem for her. Clean and clutter free, the layout of her place is the only thing our apartments have in common.

Five minutes later, she steps out, her hair now somewhat dry and flowing in long, loose curls that frame her face. "So, what is it you want to do? Eat? Drink? Dance?"

"How about all three?" I answer honestly.

"It's like that is it?"

I raise an eyebrow at her. "Like what?"

"Nothing."

Not wanting to take the bait, I give her a noncommittal shrug. "You ready to go?"

"Yep." She throws a light jacket over her forearm and gestures to the door. Walking out first, I turn to face her in the corridor. "Do you have any ideas on where we could go?"

"What kind of guy asks someone out with no idea where to go?" She rolls her eyes at me. "Lucky for you, I never move somewhere without finding out everything I need to know about my surroundings." Locking her door, she shoves her keys into her black clutch and we head to the elevator. "If you trust me, I've got your dinner, drinking, and dancing sorted."

"I trust you."

STOMACHS FULL, Harper and I now sit opposite one another sipping on our drinks and discussing what life is like at King.

"You can't be serious?" she asks, mouth hanging open. "A history nerd like you hasn't been to The National Archives? You didn't want to relive *National Treasure* and reminisce about Nicolas Cage?"

"No." I chuckle, bringing the beer bottle to my mouth. "I don't think I ever want to reminisce about Nicolas Cage."

"What have you been doing since you got here?"

"I've just been busy." It shouldn't bother me that Harper is pointing out how boring my life has been since I arrived. If I'm not at school, I'm doing school things, and apart from her and Miles, I'm not really doing anything to make this place feel like my home.

For some reason it eats at me more than I expect. I was excited to come here, but most days I just feel off-balance.

"I thought you wanted this job."

"I did." Harper eyes me curiously, and I quickly correct myself. "I do, but I wasn't exactly running from anything when I left home. It's a lot harder to detach when you have no reason to."

"But that also means you didn't have much to keep you there, either."

I'd never really thought of it that way, but the more I mull it over, the more I realize maybe Harper is right. While I'm missing everyone at home, and the ease of my old life, there wasn't anything that stopped me from making this life-changing decision. I didn't have anyone to answer to, to beg me to stay, to make me want to stay.

"I was sure you had a guy back in Chicago."

"I had many guys in Chicago." I wink and she shakes her head at me. "You were right before. I didn't have anyone keeping me there."

"Really?"

"Why are you so surprised?"

"You just look so put together." My face must look confused because she tries to simplify what she's saying. "You know? Stable. Long-term."

"I'm flattered. I think. But I've never been in a long-term relationship."

"Scared of commitment?" she guesses.

"Hardly. I've just never been with anyone who's made me want to change the different-guy-every-other-day routine."

"That many, huh?"

"Maybe?" She stares at me pointedly and I begin to feel

defensive over my choices. "What can I say, I enjoy sex." I shrug shamelessly. "I've slept with one guy for a long period of time, if that counts."

"But you weren't together?"

I shake my head and take another swig of my drink. "We were exclusive in the bedroom. Outside of those four walls we lived very separate lives."

Harper stares at me while mindlessly running her finger across her lips. "So, it was like friends with benefits?"

I contemplate her question and try to answer it without sounding like a douche. "Without the friends part. We were physically compatible *only*, and it was enough for me to settle for only him in my bed when I wanted him."

"And how did it end? He wanted more?" she speculates.

"Not from me, he just wanted more in general. So, I let him go."

"How long did that go on for?"

"Six or seven months?"

Her eyes widen, horrified. "There is no way I could sleep with the same person for that long and have it remain platonic."

"Without sounding like a pretentious asshole, I have a checklist of things I want in a guy before I pursue more than sex."

"Oh, I know that list." She steeples her hands together and leans forward on her elbows. "It's the 'elusive' list."

"What?" I question, frowning.

"Has anyone even come close?"

"No."

"Exactly," she deadpans. "The perfect person is elusive because your standards are ridiculously high."

"Not at all," I scoff. "There is nothing wrong with

wanting to be with someone who can turn you on in more ways than one."

"Yeah, otherwise known as mouth, fingers, dick." She puts three fingers up in the air. "One, two, three."

I almost choke on my beer trying to stifle a laugh. "I meant conversation, Beauty."

"So, you don't want to date anyone dumb?"

"Now I sound like the perfect catch," I mutter before taking a long pull of my drink.

"I'm kidding." Harper's voice loses its humor and is replaced with a tone of understanding. "I get it. I think on some subconscious level everyone seeks a partner who is similar to them in more ways than not. Intelligence included."

Wanting to steer the conversation away from myself, I take the plunge and ask Harper something that's probably a bit too personal. "What about you? Nothing to keep you back in..." I rub my hand over my forehead trying to remember if she's ever said where she was from.

"California."

"That's right," I say, now remembering her mention it once before. "So, nobody there?"

I watch as she bites the inside of her cheek, stalling her answer.

"There was," she finally responds.

Choosing not to probe, I subtly put my hand up in the air to get the waiter's attention. When he notices, I motion for him to come our way, giving Harper space to get lost in her own memories.

"Can I help you, sir?" He stands there attentively waiting.

"Yes, do you have a dessert menu we could look at?"

"Of course." He looks down to the huge pocket that's embroidered with the restaurant's name, at the front of his apron, and pulls out two small menus. Handing one to each of us, he runs through the specials and tells us he'll be back in a few minutes to take our order.

I put my arm up to stop him. "You can take the order now, we know what we're going to get."

"We do?" Harper chimes in.

I wink at her and point to the tiramisu on the menu. "We'll have one each, thank you."

"No worries, sir." He picks up the menus and puts them back in his apron. "Any drinks?"

"Another round of the same, please." Nodding, he writes it down on his notepad and heads back to the kitchen.

"So, how's school going?" Harper asks, the inflection in her voice a little too high considering how pensive she looked only moments ago.

Internally I groan, knowing exactly where this conversation is going to lead my train of thoughts. "It's been really good."

Her face scrunches up. "Why does it seem like you're lying?"

"I'm not," I say defensively, "The students," *One student.* "Are really attentive."

"Really?"

"Okay, maybe not all of them," I admit. "There is this one kid, though." Wistfully, I think of Elijah and I hate myself. "He's going to do great things, I'm sure."

"Having one student really love the content makes all the difference." She closes her menu and looks up at me. "I know a lot of people don't think there's the same sense of achievement for a college professor as there is for a middle or high school teacher, but this is like the last stop in their journey, where you can still make a difference. They're open to change and opinions, and they're much more adventurous and willing to explore before they take the final leap into adulthood."

"You make it sound so romantic."

"Or maybe, I'm just trying to remind myself why I'm here," she confesses.

"That bad?"

"Let's just say I haven't found the student that makes it worth it, yet." Her shoulders slump in defeat. "It's been close to a month and all I've been blessed with is an abundance of arrogance and privilege."

"Fucking rich kids," I mutter.

"My parents would've kicked my ass if I acted so entitled."

"My mom used to wash my mouth out with soap."

Harper's eyes widen at me. "That would've been disgusting."

"I haven't even told you the worst part." Inspired by the shock all over Harper's face and wanting to lighten up her mood a little, I share one of my most embarrassing moments. "The last time she did it, I was seventeen."

Bringing her hands to her face, Harper muffles the loud laugh that leaves her mouth at my revelation.

"What the fuck did you do?"

Two plates, holding the largest portions of Tiramisu I've ever seen, are placed in front of us, momentarily interrupting my story.

"I can't eat all this," Harper argues, while contradicting her words by dipping her spoon in the dessert, then taking a bite.

"You can, and you will."

She moans as she drags the silverware out of her mouth. "Okay, maybe I can. Now, tell me, what did you do?"

"Well, you'd think I actually did something offensive

with said mouth," I start. "But no, my mom just loved to use it as a form of punishment. She never hit us, or lost her cool screaming. Instead, she came up with consequences that were completely irrelevant and equally humiliating." I quickly take another spoonful of the decadent coffee flavored dessert before continuing. "I wrapped up my best friend's car with plastic wrap after school one day."

Harper's spoon stops mid-air. "The whole car?"

"Multiple times," I clarify.

"Why?" she asks. "Actually, don't bother answering that." She waves her hand at me. "I know how stupid teenage boys are, and clearly your mom did too."

"I would like to add that in any other circumstances she wouldn't have cared, but Trey's stepmom went into labor and his car was the only way to the hospital."

She gasps before covering her mouth with her hand. "You fucked up big time."

I nod sheepishly. "She had the baby at home. The ambulance didn't even get there in time."

"Hence the soap," Harper confirms.

"My mom was sneaky, though. She waited till Trey's mom was back home with the baby, and then she took me over to apologize and washed it out in front of everyone."

Harper slams her hand on the table as she doubles over in laughter. "Your mom is my freaking hero."

We both continue sharing stories, the conversation between us effortless. With each laugh and trip down memory lane, I feel the tension within myself start to dissipate. Satisfied with how the night is progressing, we polish off our dessert and add a few more drinks to our tally before deciding it's the right time to move on to our next destination.

"You brought me to a gay bar?" Incredulously, I look

between the plethora of men walking into the club and the neon sign above the entry door that obnoxiously reads 'Hard Heads.'

"Did I miss the memo where you announced you no longer like dick?"

"No." I chuckle. "But the dick that likes *you* isn't in there."

"Not that it's any of your business," she sasses, " but I've sworn off men for a while. So, a night of dancing where nobody is going to hassle me, touch me, or try to get into my pants is exactly what I need."

Picking up on the same vulnerable vibe from earlier, I don't ask questions, and I don't try to change her mind. Instead, I place my hand on my hip and wait for her to link her arm through mine.

Grateful that I don't pursue the conversation further, she leans in to me as we walk over the threshold. It seems tonight we're both running or hiding from something.

At least we can do it together.

6

ELIJAH

Class is over, and just like the last few lessons, I'm sitting in the back, as far away from Professor Huxley as possible.

After seeing him in the library and agreeing to the research project, I should be banging down his door and demanding to hear more and wanting to start work on it as soon as possible. Any eager student would be.

But I can't.

I'm too scared to follow this opportunity, knowing very well that I should stay as far away from him as possible.

Surprisingly, he hasn't pushed me. Come for me. Asked for me. Begged me. And I hate *that* more than I hate how scared I am.

I think about him more than I've thought about anyone since Alex, and it's fucking with my head. When you leave the carefully constructed bubble you've lived in for so long, there's bound to be intrusions you didn't prepare for. But I never thought, for one second, my professor, with his gray eyes and sturdy build would be what held all the appeal.

Hurriedly, I pack my books into my bag, hoping to blend

into the sea of students exiting the room. Just as I'm about to leave my seat, a body slides into the chair beside me, cornering me in. "You always drag your ass in this class."

Aiden has made it his mission to make his presence known any chance he gets. It doesn't matter that we live together, or that he really is my only friend; he is determined to push me until I give him *any* reaction.

"What are you doing here?" I ask.

"Callie is waiting outside. It's time to eat."

"Half the class hasn't even walked out yet. Your patience sucks," I say, keeping it light.

My hair falls into my face, and Aiden gently pushes it back in place, brazenly staring at me; waiting for *something*.

Awareness of where we are and who might be looking surges through me. "Don't," I warn.

"Whatever."

"Mr. Williams." Professor Huxley's voice booms through the auditorium, surprising us both.

Aiden's face twists in frustration at the interruption. "We'll meet you at the cafeteria."

"Honestly?" I say in frustration. I stand and he follows the action. "I'm just going to meet you back at the dorm."

"Fine," he says petulantly. "I'll let Callie know we can go ahead without you."

Shaking my head, I know I'm going to have to get to the bottom of whatever it is he's waiting for from me, because I really like Aiden and Callie, and as much as I am used to being a loner, they're the first friends I've had in years. I don't want to lose them over a misunderstanding.

With the class finally empty, I courageously stare up at him without caution, missing something I shouldn't be, knowing my desperation for him is written all over my face. I want nothing more than to watch him walk up here to me, and yes, chase the thing he seems to want so badly. To chase *me.*

"Am I going to have to come up there to talk to you?"

Please.

But, despite my internal yearnings, I sling the strap of my bag over my shoulder and head down the stairs. With my sprain now a distant memory, I walk with much more confidence and ease, despite the drum beat pounding inside my chest.

With a predatory stare, he meets me at the last step, stopping me. "I've been waiting for you to see me about the research project."

"Yeah, about that," I say, trying to swallow down my nervousness. "I don't think it's a good idea."

He doesn't miss a beat. "You said yes, Elijah."

"It's Eli," I say through gritted teeth.

"One day, you're going to have to tell me why you hate your full name so much." He steps closer. "But until then, you need to come to the History faculty offices tomorrow afternoon to meet the other students for the research project."

I lower my eyes to avoid his scrutiny. "I don't think I can."

Fingers gently take hold of my chin and tip my head up. "Why did you agree if you didn't want to do it?"

"It's impossible to say no to you," I regretfully confess.

"Words every man wants to hear." With his hand still on me and his eyes locked on mine, he asks something unexpected. "Is that your boyfriend?"

"What?" He tilts his head to the door, and I realize he means Aiden. Taking hold of his wrist, I pull his hand away. "I don't do boyfriends."

"Girlfriends?"

Dismissing his inquisition, I set him straight. "I'm not here for a relationship. With anybody."

"Does your friend know that?"

"What?"

"That guy who seems to be attached to your hip."

It's on the tip of my tongue to ask him if he's jealous, but the question is inappropriate and in direct opposition to the distance I'm trying to put between us.

"He's just a friend," I tell him.

"Does he know that?"

I don't know.

Interpreting my silence as a brush off, he leads the conversation back to what's important. "This is King University, Elijah. It should be your only priority."

"It is," I reply firmly.

"And that's why it would be stupid for you to turn down the research project."

"It's not the research project I was turning down."

"It wasn't?" he challenges.

"I can't lose this scholarship."

The crack in my voice causes a flash of guilt to cross his face. He reaches for me, but quickly thinks better of it. "Elijah." He shakes his head. "I'm sorry if I ever made you feel like that was a possibility. I would never…"

Instead of finishing the sentence he runs a hand over his face in frustration.

"Professor Hux—" I start.

He drops his hands at the sound of my voice. "It's Cole. *You* can call me Cole."

His name sends shivers down my spine. Like he's giving me permission to cross the line. To want more. "I think it's better if I go."

"Wait." He gestures to the front row of seats. "Can we just sit down for a second? I think I need to explain myself."

A loud exhale leaves my mouth as I ignore the alarm bells blaring inside my head.

Side by side, we sit in the narrow chairs, bodies facing one another. Just as Aiden did, he sweeps the hair out of my face, but the annoyance I felt before is replaced with an unexpected moment of intimacy.

Please touch me.

His eyes bore into mine, making it impossible to look away. "Anyone ever tell you you're fucking beautiful?"

My tongue lodges itself to the roof of my mouth, unable to respond to his adoration. He's older, and experienced in all the ways I'll never be. And hearing words he's probably said to countless other men before me hits me harder than it should. The way he's staring at me, and his unfiltered confession, make me realize how starved I am for attention. Not just his. Anybody's. And I hate that.

"I know it's completely unprofessional to lay it out there like that," he continues. "But it's the elephant in the room, and I want you—scrap that. I *need* you to know, you're one of the smartest students I've come across in a long time. It would be a fucking waste for you to turn this opportunity down because of me."

Looking away from him, I keep my eyes trained on an inanimate object ahead. Under his gaze, nothing comes out right, and since he's being honest, I want to be too. "I didn't mean to imply that you would abuse your power like that. The issue is mine; I don't like feeling out of control."

"And I make you feel that way?"

A humorless laugh leaves my mouth. "Among other things."

"Is that right?" he drawls seductively.

Giving in to the urge to look back at him, I catch him watching me intently. "I'm not usually this forward."

"Forward?" he scoffs. "This is like pulling teeth."

A soft chuckle leaves my mouth, cutting through the tension that's been building since the moment we met. "I meant being attracted to you. I've always been able to hide how I feel about someone, but whenever I see you, I know it's written all over my face."

"When you say hide," he probes, "do you mean your attraction to men?" The tone of his voice is now low and soft, erring on the side of caution. "Between the looks and the guy, I just assumed..."

Jittery and nervous, I shoot out of my seat and begin pacing. "I don't flaunt my sexuality." I stop when I realize how it sounds. "I don't mean it in an 'I'm still in the closet' type of way, either. I'm definitely only attracted to men. And if someone feels the need to ask, I don't have any issues telling them."

"But..."

"But I prefer when nobody asks."

"Because you don't want anyone to know."

Less of a question and more of a statement, his observation makes me feel like shit, and automatically I go on the defensive.

"Because it isn't their business." Confusion is written all over his face, and I don't know if it's because of the forceful way my words come out, or if it's what I'm saying. I try to simplify it. "It's something I like to keep to myself."

"So, let me get this right. If you don't feel something for someone, you don't have to tell anyone you're gay, right? That's a fine line you're treading over there, Elijah."

The accusation and disappointment in his voice causes an unwelcome tightness in my chest. Even though he's got it all wrong, my insecurities are still triggered by his assumptions of me.

"I don't need your judgement, Cole," I spit out. "I get plenty of that from more people than you can imagine."

"Elijah." He reaches for me apologetically.

"Don't." I take a step back and shove my hands in my back pockets. "You said your piece. You promised professionalism, and against my better judgement, I'll do the research project. Are we done here?"

"I didn't mean to make it sound like I was judging your choices," he explains, ignoring my question. "I say this with complete objectivity, it never ends well."

Picking up my bag, I keep my eyes trained on his, so he knows none of this is up for discussion. "It's a good thing there's nothing to end then."

A KNOCK on the door pulls me out of my reading, and I consider pretending to be asleep and not responding. When it happens again, I call out, "Come in."

Callie's head appears and I'm surprised it isn't Aiden. "I didn't know you were here."

"I got here not long ago," she responds. "Hoping the three of us can do something tonight."

Considering I've rejected Aiden every time he's asked to do something not school related, I figure he's sent in Callie as his back up.

"What do you guys have in mind?"

Her eyes sparkle in excitement. "Is that a yes?"

"Maybe," I tease.

Walking in, she closes the door behind her and takes a seat on the edge of my bed. "What if we start slow? We'll get some alcohol and food, and spend the night here drinking."

"You guys don't have to stay in for me." I place the book on my nightstand and sit up. "I'm perfectly fine hanging out here."

"It's not a big deal," she reassures me. "Just something we all could do to get your head out of your books."

"I happen to like my books." It's supposed to lighten the mood, but comes out sounding too close to the truth. Callie looks at me like I just told her Santa Claus isn't real, and I know I can't keep declining their invites any longer. "So, how will you buy the alcohol?"

As soon as she registers my interest, a wide smile graces her lips, followed by excited clapping and a loud squeal.

"What do you like to drink?" She pulls her phone out of her pocket. "I'll tell Aiden, and he can bring it on his way home."

"I'm guessing you guys have a fake ID?"

"Doesn't everyone?" she responds flippantly. When I don't answer, her eyes widen. "Have you ever drunk alcohol?"

Trying not to sound like the naive and inexperienced guy that I am, I give a little shrug. "It just wasn't on my radar at home."

"This is going to be so much fun." She launches herself at me and I catch her with a loud oomph. "It's better that we're home and you don't get sloppy drunk in public."

I don't bother telling her that sloppy drunk isn't going to happen; here or in public. Instead, I plaster on a smile and tell her I trust her and Aiden to introduce me to whatever corruption they have planned.

After a much-needed shower, I step into our small living

room and see Aiden for the first time since he left me earlier today, annoyed with my response

Not wanting to continue with any awkwardness, I head to the drawer full of food menus, courtesy of Aiden, and place them on the table. "What do you want to eat? My treat."

"No, it's cool, we can go three ways," Callie interrupts.

"I want to. Think of it as a thank you for putting up with my antisocial ass."

The smallest smile appears on Aiden's lips. "Works for me."

An hour and a half later, Aiden is back with the food, the alcohol is lined up, and the three of us are sprawled on the couch and the floor passing around Chinese take-out containers.

"So, you never played seven minutes in heaven?" Callie starts. "What about spin the bottle?"

"Is it going to be like this all night?" I ask in between spoonfuls. "Twenty questions for the freak show?"

"Only if you're willing to answer them," Callie teases.

Aiden picks up three shot glasses from beside him, followed by the bottle of Sambuca. "Let's get this party started then."

Dread settles in the pit of my stomach at the thought of being uninhibited and unfiltered. Alcohol wasn't readily available growing up, and I made sure not to hang around with people who would draw any more negative attention to me. I wanted to leave that place behind me, sooner rather than later, and teenage temptations weren't going to stop me.

A little voice makes itself known inside my head, telling me to relax. I got what I wanted; getting into King, getting away from home. It's time to at least try to enjoy the freedom. Even though the chains of my past have been nothing but stifling and restrictive, I'm scared of who I'll be without them.

"For every shot, we each answer a question," Aiden tells us, a wicked gleam in his eyes.

"Can we at least finish our food first?" I protest. "I don't really want to drink on an empty stomach."

Callie leans over and ruffles my hair. "It's so cute how innocent you are."

It doesn't come off as patronizing, but it makes me feel small and inadequate all the same.

Aiden looks between Callie and I. "Why don't we watch something while we wait for Eli to feel comfortable?"

"Why do you guys insist on making this a big deal?" Frustrated, I place my food down on the coffee table and grab the liquor. Unscrewing the cap, I fill the small glass up to the rim before clumsily raising it to my mouth and forcing the black liquid down my throat.

My whole face scrunches up as a potent licorice taste hits my tongue and burns all the way down to my stomach.

Keeping my eyes closed until the woozy feeling passes, I feel rather than see a glass being pressed into my hands. Looking down, I sigh in relief at the water, chugging it down without a second thought to who gave it to me.

Feeling settled, and finally rid of the afterburn, I fall back into the couch and take inventory of both Callie's and Aiden's expressions. I'm surprised and slightly impressed that they both have ridiculous and infectious smiles plastered across their faces.

Secretly glad to have broken through the awkwardness, I hold on to my courage and place their empty shot glasses in front of them and fill them up to the brim.

"Your turn," I announce, feigning confidence.

They both toss them down without even thinking twice, and a wave of calm washes over me.

I can do this.

One shot turns into four as I continue shoveling food into my mouth, hoping not to succumb to the lightheadedness swirling around me. Chasing each shooter with water, I trick myself into thinking I may come out of this unscathed. Each question turns into a story about Callie and Aiden in high school, and I'm enjoying listening to their version of our formative years.

As we line up our sixth shot, Aiden shuffles a little closer, asking the one thing I was hoping to avoid. "When are you going to tell me which team you bat for?"

Counting down from ten, I try to muddle through the fog blanketing my thoughts. I remind myself nobody here cares.

Just be you.

Callie gets up off the floor and sets herself on the arm of the chair beside me. "Don't worry, Eli," she coos while stroking my hair. "Aiden isn't the best at being subtle, but in case you didn't know, he's interested in you."

The desire written all over Aiden's face as his whiskey colored eyes flick between the both of us floods me with equal amounts of eagerness and shame. He's more than interested, and not surprisingly, he's interested in more than just me.

"What do you say," Callie whispers into my ear. "You gonna put him out of his misery?"

"How about another shot?" Aiden suggests. "Something to tip us all over the edge."

I know where this is heading, and as I shakily take down another shot, I have to decide if I care.

I could kiss him.

I think I want to kiss him.

Just like every other mistake teenagers make, I could pretend it's the peer pressure and the drunkenness fueling my decisions and not the aching desperation to be touched.

Unexpectedly, Callie walks around me, placing herself between Aiden and me. It's a tight fit, but it works. Like a well-practiced dance, Aiden and Callie move toward one another. Their heads tilt in opposite directions as they softly press their lips together. Slow and seductive, their mouths begin to move against one another. Licking. Tasting. Sucking

Curiosity has me shifting on the chair, twisting enough to get a full view of them making out. My gaze moves from Callie and stays on Aiden. My dick twitches at the thought of feeling a man's mouth on me, to have his tongue plunge into my mouth, to have his large hands cup my face.

And not just any man. I get harder at the thought of Cole kissing me like that. Touching me. Wanting me.

I don't realize I've leaned closer till they pull apart and both face me. We're all closer than I intended, but I'm the only one that seems to be taken aback by it.

Aiden searches my face for indecision, but mustn't find anything worth stopping over, because without hesitation his lips are now on mine and he's kissing me.

Thoughts of Cole have my mouth moving on autopilot. Kissing Aiden back, letting him finally have the prize he's been wanting, and I hate myself for it. I should be stopping him. Stopping us. But instead, I shamelessly use him to fulfill a forbidden fantasy.

It's not until hands that aren't Aiden's start tracing circles on my back that I freeze. Sobering up immediately, I know I can't take this any further. Not with him, not with Callie, and most definitely not with them together.

I peel my mouth off of Aiden's and hastily move myself off the couch. "I shouldn't have done that," I blurt out.

Callie reaches for my hand and squeezes it in comfort. "Hey. It's no big deal if you like guys."

Because that isn't the issue, I ignore her and look at Aiden. He isn't the person I should've used to play out my own daydream. He was enjoying it. I felt it, and by the way he's staring at me, he wouldn't mind more.

He rises so we're toe-to-toe. "It's okay if this is the first time you've kissed a guy."

"This isn't about what team I bat for," I say, forcefully throwing his own words back at him. "This was just a really bad idea."

"You mean kissing *me* was a really bad idea?"

Callie cuts in and puts her hand on Aiden's chest. "Aiden, babe. It's nothing personal. I just don't think he's ready."

The way she feels compelled to soothe him adds another layer to this clusterfuck of theirs that I'm in no way equipped to deal with.

Without another word, I turn away from them and walk toward my room. I don't know what they are to each other, or what they expect of me, and as I slam the door and throw myself on the bed, I know I have no plans to find out.

7

COLE

I check my watch, noting that it's about five minutes until Elijah and the rest of the students meet me to discuss the faculty's expectations of each candidate and the final research project.

I'm equal parts giddy and nervous, and I shouldn't feel either of those things.

When he left the lecture theatre yesterday, there were so many unanswered questions, unspoken speculations, and unfortunate misunderstandings that should make me feel uneasy about him. Or at least discouraged at the idea of wanting to be around him.

Distance is imperative, keeping it is the smartest and most appropriate thing to do in this situation. I should adhere to his original wish and relieve him of his commitment to this research project.

But I can't.

I know the difference between right and wrong, but the minute he acknowledged the attraction between us out loud, it flicked a switch that I can't turn off.

Clearing the air was supposed to make it all better; give

us a fresh start and offer us a clean slate. But all it's done is make me want to push my luck. It's like every part of me refuses to give up the opportunity to be in close quarters with him, to watch him light up as he shares his knowledge with those around him; including me.

Even though it's torture not to touch him, or know that I'll never get to kiss him, I'll grin and bear it. For the sake of being able to stare at him for a few extra hours every week, I'll fucking *grin* and *bear* it.

Low murmurs gather outside my door signaling everyone's arrival. I wait for the first knock to sound before fixing my tie and rising from my chair.

I'm expecting four students, including Elijah, but when the door opens and only three sets of eyes are looking at me, my heart drops down to my stomach.

Putting on my teacher's mask, I usher the three bodies into my office and instruct them to sit around the table and pick up the manila folder labeled with their name.

Just as we're about to delve into specifics, a succession of knocks plunges the room into silence. They all look at me, waiting for me to acknowledge whoever it is on the other side of that door.

Scared and excited it could be Elijah, I clear my throat and call out, "Come in."

A nervous looking Elijah walks through the door, his usual backpack replaced with a crossbody satchel he's wearing as a shield.

Everyone around the table is all smiles and he couldn't look more uncomfortable if he tried.

"You're late," I say sternly.

Running his fingers through his hair, he looks more disoriented than I've ever seen him. His green eyes are glassy and guarded; dark, tired circles surrounding them.

He takes in the other students, directing his attention to them. "Sorry, guys. Won't happen again."

With the only spare seat beside me, he trudges my way without even a second glance. Trying to give him space, I get up as soon as he sits down and decide that anything I need to say can be done with a comfortable distance between us.

Something about his demeanor screams embarrassment and discomfort, and for the first time since we've been in a room together, I don't think it has anything to do with me.

"Elijah, that remaining folder is yours," I say, pointing to the middle of the table. "And I was about to have you all introduce yourselves. Jenna, can you start?"

From the corner of my eye, I see a slight slump in Elijah's shoulders, telling me I made the right decision in steering the attention away from him.

"Um, okay, what should I share?" she asks looking up at me.

"As much as we all are dying to know your favorite television show and favorite food, I think what you're studying, what year you are, and, of course, most importantly, why you wanted to do this research project, should be sufficient."

While the mood lightens at my dry humor, I take a step back and sit behind my desk, leaving them to get to know one another without me hovering. My ears work well enough to listen from a distance.

The four of them all realize their interest in religion, history, architecture, and sociology is why they were chosen for this project. Each of them has a different strength that I have been able to identify through classes, observations, and past transcripts. With funding from the American Historical Association and the notoriety of King being one of the best Arts and History schools in the United States, being selected is an opportunity of a lifetime.

For the duration of this school year, they will research the relationship between cultures and religions, and their transition through the centuries. They will have access to documents, artifacts, statistics, and everything else their hearts desire in order to produce the best possible result.

It's a broad topic, but as the years pass, change is inevitable and that's what the research project wants to capture. With a focus on the relationship between religion and politics, the school feels this is a perfect way for students to connect with the current social climate.

There is no guarantee their end results will get published, but since it's practically a national investment, it's almost improbable they won't.

Once all is said and done, the faculty and the students get to walk away with an extra achievement on their curriculum vitae that will open doors and opportunities otherwise unavailable to them.

Even though I stuck flyers up offering all students an equal opportunity, the amount of work and time a project like this requires turns almost every student off. It makes it easier to fill the spots with those who are the most dedicated. Jenna, Louis, and Shari are those students.

Elijah, is too. He's just too green to know it yet.

As all their gazes fall on him, I realize it must be his turn to introduce himself. I busy myself with shit around my desk while he talks, not wanting to make him any more uncomfortable than I usually do.

"I'm Eli," he starts. "It's my first year here. I'm originally from a small town in Texas. And I'm doing a double major in History and Education." His answers are quick and concise, lacking the invitation of questions and casual conversations all the other students provided.

"What made you want to do this research project?" Louis prompts.

"I can't say no to you."

The memory of his words forces me to look up at him, to catch a quick glimpse before I go back to pretending I'm busy with paperwork. I'm surprised to see him staring straight at me. The look of vulnerability from earlier is now replaced with a look of longing.

It's unexpected, yet welcome, no matter how impossible he and I seem. I want him to look at me like that always.

"Professor Huxley was really convincing," he says, still staring at me.

All eyes turn my way, and his cheeks redden as he realizes they've all caught on to what's in his line of sight.

Trying to appear unperturbed, I give them all a shrug. "Don't all look at me like that. I've been known to give a good pep talk or two in my time. Elijah earned this spot just like everyone else. Only difference is, he wanted to give it up and I had to remind him why that would be a *very* bad idea."

"He's so right," Shari confirms. "You would be out of your freaking mind to pass something like this up."

A light chuckle leaves his mouth. "Let's just go with temporary insanity."

Louis playfully slaps him on the shoulder. "Glad you're here, man. You saved me from being the only guy."

A shy smile stretches across Elijah's face, accentuating his reserved and innocent nature. Realizing he's not often like this, I don't want to rush his relaxed moment. An odd sense of protectiveness tugs at my insides, wanting nothing more than to be responsible for the contentment that's written all over his face.

"Are we going to discuss what's in these folders?" Jenna asks, interrupting my thoughts.

"Of course," I respond, shaken out of my stupor. "As you can see, they're all personalized."

Standing, I walk around my desk and sit back at the table with the students. "The first booklet is a contract of sorts. It states how many hours are required by each of you, and that those hours will be signed off on by me, every week. It also covers a confidentiality clause, stating whatever information you find, provide, etc, cannot be used anywhere else, including if you are removed from, or choose to leave, this research project."

"What are the grounds for getting kicked out?" Louis asks.

"If you all flip to the back page, you'll see it all listed there in black and white." Papers ruffle, so I continue talking. "The next booklet is a rough timeline to keep you all on track, and I will ask for periodic proof of work to ensure all your time is being used wisely. The rest is just a resource booklet." I place my own copy on the table and wait for them to do the same. "It all seems pretty straight forward, right, guys?"

Nods and murmurs circle the table, approval and understanding the main consensus. I run through a few more discussion points and then ask them to pull their planners out to organize a time and a place for our next few meetings.

They all begin stuffing shit in their bags and rising from the table. I follow them to the door and say goodbye to them one at a time.

"Elijah, could you stay back, please?"

He freezes at the threshold.

Reaching around him, I grab the door handle and pull it closed. Even though I shouldn't, I lock it. When the click of the door sounds, I move back and he lets his body sag onto the hard surface behind him. My eyes flick from the locked door back to his face before putting a somewhat safe distance between us— not a lot, but enough that we both get a good enough look at one another. It's then I can see, without the interference of everyone else, his troubled and tired look from earlier has returned.

"Are you okay?" I ask him. "You look..."

"I look?"

"Are you okay?" I repeat, a little more forcefully. "You were unusually late today."

"I can make up the time—"

"Elijah," I say with an exhale. "You don't need to make anything up. I'm asking because I'm worried about you."

He rubs the back of his neck, his apprehension calling to me. The longer he stays silent, the more time there is for worry to seep in, and I don't like it.

"You don't have to talk to me about it." I step toward him. "But if there's something bothering you, you should talk to someone."

He looks at me, the yearning from earlier calling to me even more than before.

"I kissed someone." His voice is just above a whisper. His eyes hold my gaze, green pools of unnecessary regret staring back at me. While I'm stunned by the words that've come out of his mouth, it's the way they make me feel inside that takes me by surprise.

To care or not to care.

"Elijah, you can kiss anyone you want."

My stomach rolls, my body protesting at my lie.

"Then why have I been up all night worrying about what you'll think of me instead of worrying about the potential mess I've put myself in?"

Confused, I only focus on the one part of the conversation that appeals to me. "Why would it matter what I think of you?"

"How the hell am I supposed to know?" he shouts, irritated. Every part of him screams desolation as he tries to figure out a riddle neither one of us has the answer for. "I don't know anything about anything anymore."

"And that kiss?" I pry, stepping close enough to touch him.

"It wasn't you," he blurts out.

I skim my thumb across his plump bottom lip. "And that's a problem?"

He lets out a shaky breath, his gaze moving up from my mouth and settling on my face. "Apparently it is."

"What are we going to do about it?" His eyes darken with desire at my question, but he doesn't answer. "Elijah," I prod, more forcefully. "What are we going to do about it?"

"Kiss me."

His request hardens my dick, as if he wrapped his hands around me and stroked it himself. "Do you know what you're asking of me?"

"Please."

I push myself up against him, our bodies flush, both our cocks hard. "Are you sure?"

"Cole." My name comes out like a strangled cry. He places his hand on my chest. "Kiss me. *Please.*"

The crack in his voice combined with the simplest of pleas, is what pushes me over the edge. The caution. The trepidation. The fear. It all should be there, but the second my mouth touches his, it doesn't matter. Everything but the two of us is nonexistent.

Soft and pliable, his lips effortlessly meld into mine. The

perfect contradiction to the way the hard planes of our bodies press into one another. My hands settle around either side of his neck, relishing the way his pulse flutters under my touch. A frantic rhythm that matches my heart beat.

I hold him to me. I hold him close. Hold him tight. Hold him still.

Scared that the magnitude of what we're doing is going to bury itself between us and force him away from me, I stay frozen. I don't want time to pass, or even our lips to move, because then I won't have to deal with the very high likelihood of Elijah coming to his senses and walking away from me.

A second hand joins the one on my chest, offering the slightest amount of pressure. Encouraging me. Calling to me.

He wants this.

Taking the small but significant contact as all the permission I need, I decide to start this moment over. Pulling back, I take one last look at him, ensuring the want is still written on his face.

It's there.

The tip of his tongue peeks out, wetting his bottom lip, inviting me in. Without hesitation, I greedily take his mouth, hard and hungry. The way I've wanted to since the day I laid eyes on him.

The loud groan at the back of Elijah's throat vibrates against my palms as our mouths collide. He takes hold of the collar of my button-down, forcefully returning the kiss. Showing me he wants this just as much as I do.

Itching for more of him, my tongue plunges into his mouth, seeking his out. Fervently, he opens up, greeting me with strokes of appreciation and enjoyment. With a delicious hint of butterscotch, he tastes as sweet and innocent as I expected.

The kiss deepens, the caress of our tongues spurring on both of our desires. We fall into an unexpected rhythm of strength and desperation, our bodies now so close, even air couldn't get in between. Wanting to feel more of him, but not wanting to scare him, I let my hands slowly fall from his neck, down his body, settling them softly on his ass.

I grind his erection against mine, over and over till we're practically dry humping on my office door. With every arousing stroke, a little voice in the back of my head tells me it's wrong. Even if every single touch feels right, this is so *very* wrong. I contemplate moving, but then he whimpers into my mouth, and I become a glutton for punishment. The noise has me ravaging his mouth with renewed vigor, wanting to hear it again, wanting proof that I'm the only person responsible for that sound.

He moves his hands from my chest, up past my shoulders, and sinks them into my hair. He grips at the strands, and somehow everything feels a little more frantic than before. Slightly shifting, I bend my knees and move my hands to the back of his thighs. With our lips still glued to one another, I manage to raise him off the floor and instinctively he wraps his legs around my waist, just like I wanted.

Our hips are now bucking, and I have to stop myself from slamming him into the door. I'm certain the overwhelming sensations, coupled with the rush from our predicament, will have me coming in my pants in no time.

I try to still his hips as I pull my lips away, our breaths loud and labored.

"Fuck, Eli," I groan. "I'm so hard for you right now."

"Elijah," he pants. "I like it when you call me Elijah."

"Do you now?" I grin.

"Don't look so smug." He presses his lips to mine and the initiation takes me by surprise.

He rubs his dick up and down my own, and I begrudgingly pull back.

"I'm going to come in my pants like a fucking teenager if you keep doing that," I warn.

"I don't care, I am a teenager," he quips. It's said so flippantly, but the harsh reality hits us both like a freight train.

"Elijah."

He unlocks his legs from around my waist and I let them drop. Expecting him to grab his bag and leave, I'm surprised when he rests his head on my shoulder.

Worried he's internally berating himself, I wrap my arms around him protectively and speak directly into his ear. "Elijah, we can pretend this never happened. I told you I would be professional and I went back on my word." I squeeze him tighter. "I'm the only one in the wrong here. I'm sorry."

He raises his head, and our similar height has him looking directly into my eyes. "I asked you to kiss me, remember?"

And I'll do it every time you ask.

"Yes, but I should've shown some restraint." I step back to prove my point. "I'm not the teenager, after all."

"I didn't mean to say it. It just came out, and now I've ruined the best kiss I've ever had." His emotion filled eyes widen as he slaps his mouth with his hand. "Pretend you didn't hear that."

Despite the dire circumstances, I smirk. "Not a chance."

"You're not helping."

"Neither are you. Every time you open your mouth my cock gets even harder."

"Don't say cock," he reprimands.

I'm about to say it again when his expression sobers. "What are we going to do, Cole?"

Certain he isn't one to give in to temptation and is the more responsible and restrained one out of the two of us, I tell him to choose. "Whatever you want to do, Elijah, I'll do it."

Sure he's about to set some new boundaries, or threaten to leave the research project, I brace for the worst, but he surprises me. Knocks the wind right out of me when he steps forward, takes hold of my face, forcing me to concentrate on only him.

"We can never do this again," he says with a heavy sigh, running his fingers through the scruff of my beard. "But I'm not leaving till you kiss me goodbye."

8

ELIJAH

The words are bittersweet, but the action itself even more so. He presses his lips to mine, so much softer than before. Slower. Less greedy. Trying to savor the moment.

The kiss with Aiden—while it's possibly made my life a little more complicated—has made me realize how much I've been sacrificing all these years. How much affection I was missing.

After holing myself up in my room last night, too embarrassed and confused by what I had done, all I could think of was the idea of kissing Cole. In my mind, I was replacing Aiden's mouth with his.

I'd laid in bed for hours, wanting just one taste, and now that I've had it, I don't know how this will ever be enough.

My body trembles at his tenderness, trying not to read in between the lines. I don't know all the signs. I don't know what's normal, or if this is any different to him than the million other times he's done it. But for the guy who's been alone and untouched for so long, this is euphoria.

Pity it all has to end.

His lips keep moving, his tongue keeps on tasting, and my heart keeps beating excitedly inside my chest. It's in this moment I hate myself for being so rigid with my rules. I hate that I've denied myself these small little moments because of my family and the shame and embarrassment they've made me feel.

Maybe if I didn't cocoon myself up all these years and was more of a risk taker, like Alex wanted, I wouldn't have let myself be tempted by the thought of kissing any guy, or dipping my toes into a forbidden romance with my professor. I wouldn't feel like the desperation is leaking from my pores, on show, and so obvious for everyone to see.

Hands find my waist and skate down to my ass, pulling me out of my own head and back into the moment. Dragging my own hands down his body, I mirror his actions, hoping to feel his arousal. Just as my hardness grazes against his own, Cole pulls his mouth away.

Before I have the chance to chastise myself, he gives my ass a little squeeze in reassurance. "You're going to have to tell me when you want me to stop, otherwise I'll be saying goodbye till the sun comes back up."

Stunned at his admission, I can feel the blush climb up my neck and settle on my cheeks. His brows furrow in confusion. "What is it?"

"It's stupid."

"I still want to hear it," he presses.

"You have the freedom to kiss anyone, and you're here, wanting to kiss me."

He shakes his head in disbelief, but there's a hint of playfulness twinkling in his eyes as he pushes into me. Our faces are only a breath away from one another when he says, "If I could, I'd do a lot more than just kiss you, Elijah."

My breath hitches at his implication, and my dick

hardens at the thought. I try to shy away and lower my face as the images his words conjure become too much for me to bear.

Fingers take hold of my chin as he tips my head back up to look at him. "I felt how much that turned you on, but I want to know why you find me wanting you so hard to believe."

Honest answers sit at the tip of my tongue, but I don't see the point in telling him *years of being told you were a pariah makes it hard to believe you're worth any more than the scum you're made out to be.*

As if he can sense me being swept up in my memories, he reaches for my hand with his free one. "Come with me."

He leads us away from the door and back further into his office. We walk around his desk. "Sit," he orders, guiding me to the wooden surface.

He takes his place on his leather chair and then rolls himself closer. Laid back, his legs are wide, one on either side of mine, caging me in, while his eyes trace over every inch of my body. He stops his perusal at my dick, and I feel every nerve ending in my body begin to delight underneath his stare.

"If we only get now, I want to know as much as I can about you." His voice is low and steady, his gray eyes piercing through me. "Tell me about the Elijah who exists outside the walls of King University."

I situate myself a little further back on the desk, feeling a little bit too exposed by his scrutiny. Not only is my physical yearning for him on display, but he's looking at me like he can see *all* my insecurities, and that's something I don't think I'll ever be ready for.

I shrug nonchalantly, hoping to cover up the raw truth. "There isn't an Elijah outside of here."

"No?" He tilts his head to the side. "What about the guy who kissed someone else and felt the need to tell me?" he coaxes.

A loud groan leaves my mouth as I bury my head in my hands, remembering last night, and regretting every bit of it. "I can't believe I did something so stupid," I confess.

"Kissing someone is stupid?"

His voice sounds wounded, and I'm worried he thinks I mean kissing him is stupid.

"Last night was stupid," I clarify.

"Why did you kiss him then?"

"Why do you want to know?" I ask, hating that this is even a conversation we're having.

"Just tell me," he insists.

Realizing he's not going to let me get away with not answering, I concede. "It was my roommate. The guy you asked me about."

"The guy who's always waiting for you after my class?" He sits up in his seat, his expression changing from interested to annoyed. "That's the guy you kissed?"

He's almost angry as I nod my head in confirmation.

Is he jealous?

"Of course that's the guy you kissed," he says, throwing his hands up in the air. "Not like I can blame him. Someone would have to be blind to not see how attractive you are."

Now I know he's definitely jealous, and I feel guilty for loving it.

"So, how did it happen?" he probes.

"You don't really look like you want details," I say half-jokingly, hoping to lighten the mood.

Placing his hands on the top of my thighs, he moves himself closer, looking at me with the utmost sincerity. "I do. I want to know all the details," he presses, tightening his grip, digging his fingers into my legs. "I want to know whose arms you'll be running into when you're no longer in mine."

My heart trips over itself when he refers to me being in his arms. There's nowhere else I'd rather be.

I cover his hands with mine, knowing nothing I say will adequately do this moment justice. We're stuck. For whatever reason, he wants me, and I want him. But even if every part of me wants to assure him that kissing Aiden would be a poor substitute to how his kisses have made me feel, it would be like rubbing salt into a fresh wound. And I've already done that to myself one too many times over losing Alex.

"Whatever you're imagining," I say, trying to comfort him. "It's nothing like that."

"How do you know what I'm thinking?"

"You're probably thinking I'm just going to make a habit out of this. Kiss everyone that shows any interest in me," I explain. "I'm not like that."

"I don't think that at all." He slides his hands from underneath mine and sits them on his lap, my body missing the contact immediately. "If anything, he is someone you should be with. The perfect, safe, and non-risky option."

Not wanting to hear it any longer, I hop up off the desk and stare down at him. "If this is what you want to spend our time talking about, I think I'm better off going home."

As soon as the ultimatum registers, his jaw clenches, and I wait to see if he'll revert to his usual offhanded arrogance. I can tell in any other circumstances, or if I were any other person, he would call my bluff and show me the door.

"What's it going to be, Cole?" I challenge.

He shocks me by tugging at my belt buckle and pulling me close to him. His large hands take hold of the back of my thighs and his beautiful face looks straight up at me. "I'm irrationally jealous of a fucking teenager," he spits out. "And I don't know what the fuck to do with that."

I run my fingers through his hair, glancing back at him with a relieved smile. "That's a lot of fucks."

"And none of the good kind."

On cue, I feel myself heat up, still not used to the way he casually mentions sex.

"You're fucking adorable, you know that?" An approving smile graces his face before he puts his hands on either side of my head, bringing my face down to his.

Slamming our mouths together, he straightens his body, rising to his feet and taking control. With our lips still locked, he pushes me till I hit the edge of the desk. He presses himself into me, his thick, hard cock rubbing against mine.

Cole's kisses move across my jaw, his stubble leaving marks down the length of my neck. Licking, biting, scraping, he buries his face in the hollow of my neck and sucks on my skin, causing an embarrassingly loud moan to leave my mouth.

"God, you make the best sounds," he murmurs against my ear. "I wonder what sound you'll make when I do this?"

His mouth returns to mine as he palms my erection, grazing my length up and down. With every stroke, I become impossibly harder, my resolve waning, and the need to feel more of him becomes all consuming.

"More," I breathe out. "I need more."

Without being told twice, he skilfully unbuttons my jeans and slides his hands down my front. I release a loud shudder as he grips my cock over my boxer briefs, teasing me.

Desperate for friction I push my crotch into his waiting palm, and he bites my bottom lip, like a reprimand. With mischief dancing in his gray eyes, and a devilish smirk spreading across his face, I know he's going to make me ask for it.

"Want something?" he teases.

With no preamble, or room to play hard to get, I pant, "Touch me."

"Where?"

"Cole," I groan out in frustration.

"Tell me, Elijah," he demands. "I want to hear it from that cute, shy mouth of yours."

Everything about this is out of my comfort zone, and he knows it. But for the first time since I've met him, these four walls are giving me freedom. Right now, they're no longer the reason we can't be together, but they're the one thing barricading us from the rest of the world and giving us this moment. As if he knows what I need, he pushes me, and I let him, because it allows me to revel in the very same things I have denied myself for so long.

"Grab my dick," I spit, thrusting my hips into his waiting hand. He sinks his hands past my waistband and wraps his fingers around my shaft.

My lungs refuse to work at the feel of his skin against my own, struggling to breathe, scared for more. The first time another guy touched me it was all brand new. There was trepidation. There were nerves. Every move was filled with fear and worry of the unknown.

We were just two young guys, trying to figure life out. There was excitement in our innocence, and purity in our race to the finish line.

This isn't like that.

Cole's got his hand around my cock, and I have to hold myself back from relentlessly fucking his fist. He rolls the pad of his thumb around the slit in my crown, spreading my pre-come all over the head. He raises his hand to his face and salaciously slips his thumb into his mouth before resuming his hold on my hardened length.

Fuck.

Desperate to touch Cole, I reach for his pants, but his forceful hands stop me.

I look down at his hard on and then back up at him quizzically.

"I need you to come first," he says explaining himself. "I can't risk it if you touch me."

"I'm sure we could work out a way to come together," I offer lightly.

Cole's hand begins to slowly move up and down my dick, but it isn't until he sinks to his knees that I'm caught completely off guard.

He glances up at me, his expression serious, but the lust in his eyes is unmistakable. "I want you to come in my mouth."

Clearing my throat, I look down at Cole, my mouth opening and closing as I try to focus on what I'm trying to say, instead of the fact his face is mere inches away from my cock.

He hooks his hands into my waistband, dragging my jeans and boxer briefs down my thighs. Stopping just above my knees, my ass and dick are now on full display. I want to feel self-conscious, because it seems like the only way I've ever felt, but I don't.

I feel the best kind of crazy. Horny and amped up, I'm fucking starving, for *all* of this.

I feel everything I've been told I shouldn't, and for the first time, in a really long time, I feel liberated. I feel free. I feel like me.

Smooth hands grip the base of my shaft just as his

tongue circles the head of my dick. I suddenly feel no reason to share that this is the first time anybody has ever sucked me off, knowing there's a very high chance he'll stop if he knows.

Cole maneuvers me into his mouth, his head bobbing up and down on my length. Finding his rhythm, he licks and sucks, pushing me deeper down his throat.

My hands settle on his head, while my hips pick up pace. Thrusting in and out, I'm fucking his face, chasing the high. When I hear him gag, a telltale whimper leaves my mouth, highlighting how little to no self-control I possess right now.

Mesmerized by the way he looks, I watch him devour me, loving the way his face is pressed up against the dark crevices of my groin, like he just can't get enough. With one hand working in sync with his mouth, the other reaches for his own erection, squeezing it over his pants.

As he tries to contain his arousal, mine skyrockets to unimaginable heights. My body is buzzing, electricity racing through me, and all I want is to see him as uncontrolled as I am.

"Take it out," I order, my voice husky and unrecognizable. "I want to see it."

Sliding off me with a pop, he looks up, the thrill of my command written all over his face. Frantically, he unbuckles his belt and his slacks, and lowers the zipper. He tugs his dick out of his underwear and lets his hard, thick cock rest against his lower torso.

He's big and beautiful. Virile and masculine, his pulsating veins wrap around his girth, steering my gaze to his strained and slick crown.

He takes hold of his erection and begins to methodically stroke himself. The sight would bring any man to his knees, and that's exactly where I want to be. Touching him. Tasting him.

"Cole," I breathe out. "I need..."

"What is it?" he asks, his hand moving faster. "Tell me."

"I need to come."

Seeking release, I lower my hand to touch myself, but Cole swats it away.

"I told you," he warns, flicking his hungry eyes up to mine. "In. My. Mouth."

Long fingers circle my shaft as he begins effortlessly matching his own ministrations. He has a dick in either of his hands, expertly jerking us both off.

Closing the small distance between us, he covers the head of my cock with his mouth. A loud hiss leaves my mouth as his tongue works my tip, feasting on my pre-come.

Needing release, I pull at his hair and brazenly buck into him, no longer able to hold back. Abandoning his own gratification, I feel his hands settle on my ass, squeezing and kneading my bare flesh.

My hips continue to piston into his mouth, but when he stretches my cheeks apart and lets a finger trace my rim, I halt and try to steady my breathing. Mistaking my reaction for discomfort, he starts to move his hands, but I quickly cover them with my own, keeping them in place. The anticipation of any part of him penetrating my hole has me dizzy with lust, thinking too far ahead, imagining all the possibilities.

"Keep going," I urge.

His poise disappears at my instruction, our movements now faster, unhinged, and frenzied. An eager digit returns to my hole, dipping the tip inside, and it's enough to push me over the edge, to send me free falling. My body begins to shudder as his finger and mouth move in tandem. In. Out. Up. Down.

Unintelligible moans echo off the old brick walls; fear, worry, and embarrassment, are all nonexistent as a familiar buzz rushes through me.

"Fuck. Fuck. Fuck," I chant, unable to keep silent. My balls tighten with every short and hard thrust, and I feel myself ready for release.

Holding Cole's head, I push myself further into his mouth one last time before every taut, rigid, inflexible string that holds me together begins to snap.

Rules.

Snap.

Doubt.

Snap.

Confusion.

Snap.

Control.

Snap.

Restraint

Snap.

"Cole," I groan as I give myself to him and empty my load into his mouth. My body weakens, sagging onto the desk as he enthusiastically licks and sucks every drop of my come.

Lazily, my eyes open and look down at the beautiful man who, even on his knees, has the most commanding presence of anyone I've ever met.

Eventually, Cole loosens his grip and begins to slide his mouth off me. He works his gaze up my body, his lips wet and sticky, his hooded eyes dancing with want and satisfaction.

My gaze drifts down to his stiff, angry, and abandoned

cock, and it takes less than a second for me to decide on how I want this to end. I push myself off the edge of the desk and swiftly pull my pants up, tucking myself in as quickly as I can.

Sinking to my knees, I mirror his posture and look at him expectantly.

Understanding, he shakes his head. "I'm so fucking hard even I can't touch myself right now."

"I want to know what you taste like," I state simply.

"I won't last if you put your mouth on me."

"You don't need to last," I reassure him. "Just fill me up. Please."

"Fuck," he groans. He cups the nape of my neck and smashes his mouth to mine. Tasting myself on him stokes the small fire within, building it up ever so slowly. I suck on his tongue, enjoying how new, different, and sexy this feels.

He pulls back and peers at me. "How do you do that?"

I look at him, clueless.

"That," he emphasizes. "You look so fucking innocent, but then you say the most erotic things and I want to do them all. Fulfill all your fantasies. I want to shove my dick so far down your fucking throat I can hear you choke on it."

My cock stirs underneath my pants, my recent orgasm evidently forgotten. Thickening. Lengthening. Reacting to the aggression in his desire.

His observation is right, and while a part of me is just as surprised by my boldness, I don't need to dissect it. In some way I knew it would always be like this. This is what my father meant when he said the devil is disguised as your deepest desire, and the second I let myself cross that line, there's no turning back.

I should've known it would be like making up for lost time.

Greedy.

Thirsty.

Wanton.

I want everything he's threatened me with. His dick. His come. I want to choke on his hard length and then let him taste himself on me.

I want, and I want, and I want.

But the question is, how much will I let myself take?

9

COLE

He looks at me with his big, emerald green eyes, the yearning that always lingers in them still potent as ever, but it's the flecks of desire that dance around in his irises that beg me to fulfill every single one of his needs.

Even my own touch is too much as I take hold of my shaft and squeeze it. I try to tell myself to calm down, will my cock to retreat even a little, so I can finally get his mouth on me and fucking enjoy it.

"Please, Cole," he whispers against my mouth.

With my pants undone, my shirt slightly untucked, and my exposed dick standing at attention, I'm sure the sight of me is as crazed and off-center as I feel. But denying him isn't an option.

I press my lips against his before standing up, never taking my eyes off him. I take in the vision before me, Elijah down on his knees, watching me with a hungry gleam in his eyes, and licking his lips in anticipation.

Stroking myself, I slide my pre-come up and down my cock, teasing Elijah. I feel more than wanted. I feel worshipped, and I fucking love it.

Hanging on by a single thread, I reach out to him, ready and aching. "Let me fill you up."

Elijah's hand replaces mine, holding firmly onto my shaft. He glides his hand along my erection with innocent fascination before lowering his head and lazily licking the tip.

He tongues the head of my cock, lapping up all the proof of my arousal. He moves like we have all the time in the world, and even though we don't, there's something about his cautious movements that have me not wanting to rush him.

Hands slide to my balls as his tongue glides up the underside of my shaft. Once he reaches the crown, he gazes up at me expectantly.

"Suck me."

Taking my words for the permission he must've been seeking, he covers my length with his mouth, surprising me by how much of me he can take.

When I feel the back of his throat, I grip his head with my hands and groan. "So good. So. Fucking. Good."

He moves faster at my praise, taking me deeper, sending me further down this rabbit hole of lust we've dug ourselves into. Fucking his mouth at a perfect pace, every part of me is consumed by the view in front of me. I watch myself slide in and out of his lips, enjoying the way he gasps for air when I nestle myself deep into his mouth, loving how he's at my mercy.

"Fuck," I pant in between thrusts. "You ready for me?"

Green eyes flick to mine, sex and soul staring back at me. He's hungry for it. Hungry for me.

I tug onto his hair and piston fiercely into his mouth, letting him bring me to the brink. Every part of me heats up as a rush of electricity pulses through me, loosening every one of my coiled muscles.

Pushing one more time, I feel every nerve ending in my body erupt in fireworks. Elijah's hands dig into my ass, stilling the tremors, pressing me to him. I flood his mouth with my release, his throat humming around my sensitive flesh as he greedily swallows my come.

Both of us sated, he relaxes his hold on me while the adrenaline wears off us both. Loosening my grip on his hair, I slowly run my fingers through his thick, soft strands, enjoying the come down.

Slow and steady breaths fill the room as Elijah rises to my height. Our eyes zero in on one another, neither of us wanting to break the silence.

Unable to look away from him, I robotically tuck myself back into my boxers. Shoving my shirt into my pants, I pull up the zip and situate my belt buckle. The second my hands are no longer busy, Elijah throws himself at me, grabbing my face and plunging his tongue in my mouth.

I wrap my arms around his body, pulling his lean frame toward me and let him devour me. Licking and sucking, he drags the taste of himself off my tongue while offering my own scent up in return. Wet and tangy, slick, and salty. We're floating on an erotic cloud, enjoying the forbidden fruit in all the ways we possibly can.

Just as Murphy's Law would allow, a shrill ring bounces off the walls. He freezes, but I ignore the intrusion by squeezing him tighter to me. This is not how I want our time to end.

The interruption ends, but quicker than I'm able to sigh in relief, it starts back up again.

"I think you should get that," he says against my mouth, a smile curving his lips.

"If I ignore it, they'll go away."

It starts up for the fourth time, and I know avoidance is no longer an option.

"Let me just see who it is."

Begrudgingly, I step away from him. Holding only his hand, I use my other to grab my phone off my desk.

"It's my sister," I tell him, my annoyance shifting into worry. Before I can call her, my phone starts again. Swiping my thumb over the screen, I bring it to my ear, but keep my focus on Elijah. Uncertainty creeps back into his eyes, and I know he's convincing himself to leave. I don't want him to go. Covering the speaker end of my cell, I whisper to him, "Just give me five minutes, okay?"

"Cole." My sister's panicked voice tears me in two.

"Megs, what is it?"

For some reason she doesn't answer straight away, the sound of muffled voices reaching my ears instead.

"Megs," I repeat.

Debating whether or not to hang up and call her back, I watch Elijah grab a pen and scribble on the yellow legal pad sitting in the middle of my desk. Ripping the bottom of the paper off, he looks back at me, and presses it into my chest.

I have to let go of his hand to catch it and he uses the opportunity to catch me unaware and kiss me goodbye. It's quick. Chaste. And not enough.

"Cole. Sorry. Are you there?"

"Yeah," I say, staring at Elijah. While my eyes plead with him not to go, he steps out of my reach and walks around my desk. "Megs, can you hold on a second?"

I slide the phone to the middle of my chest, ensuring my sister can't hear me. "Please wait."

Offering a sad smile, he glances down at the paper, his

green eyes urging me to read it. I flip it over in my hand, and read his bittersweet words.

"I don't want to have to make a big production out of our goodbye. It'll ruin it, and I don't want that. Thank you, Cole. For more than you'll ever know."

A tinge of sadness is woven through every curve of his legible scrawl, hitting me harder than any of this should.

Whatever this is hasn't even started, and I'm already gutted it has to end.

With one hand on the door knob and the other pressed against his mouth, he's ready to go. Wistfully he rubs his fingertips across his lips before raising his hand to wave goodbye.

I don't get the chance to say anything back, because my cell vibrates against my chest. Giving Elijah the getaway he so desperately seeks, he backs out without a second glance.

I curse into the empty room and bring the phone back to my ear, all my attention finally back where it belongs.

"Yeah," I grunt.

"Shit, I'm so sorry, Cole," she rushes out, the alarm in her voice from earlier pushing Elijah to the back of my mind. "The service here is a fucking nightmare."

"The service where? Aren't you at work?"

"No." Her voice cracks on the single word. "Mom's at the hospital."

"What the fuck?" I roar, frustration and guilt filling my veins. "What happened? Is she okay? Fuck, are you okay?"

"Yes. No. I don't know," she cries. "She was in a car accident. They said she's fine, but until I see her, I can't stop imagining the worst."

"How long till you know more?" I sink into my chair and

scrub my hand down my face. "Actually, you know what? Don't answer that. I'm booking the next flight over. I'll call you when I have details."

"Cole," she shouts, stopping me from hanging up. "Just hold on a sec, okay. Calm down."

"I'm not cal—"

"Cole," she says sternly. "You just started your new job. It's still early in the school year, I don't think it's a good idea for you to pack up and come back here so soon."

"I don't give a fuck," I respond too harshly. "She's my mom."

"She's going to be okay," she soothes. "They said she was fine. Just some breaks and bruises."

"I don't like being so far away," I confess.

"I know. It's the reason I didn't want to tell you. If I could've gotten away with keeping this from you, I would've. I knew you'd stress out."

"Can I speak to her?"

"Not yet," she squeaks.

"Meghann, are you fucking lying to me about something?"

Silence.

"Meghann."

"I'm not lying. I told you she had some breaks," she says defensively.

"But," I coax, my voice firm, but not angry, knowing that will only force her to shut down.

"Her hip bone is shattered; they're putting in steel plates." She sniffles, finally giving in to her worry. "It's going to be a lot of work."

Trying to steady my breath, I remind myself to not take my anger out on my sister. She's doing the best she can.

"Is Trey with you?" I ask, wanting to make sure she's got support too.

"He's on his way."

"Good." I rub my hand across the nape of my neck. "Let me work out my schedule and I'll see you as soon as I can."

"Cole—"

"Don't," I warn. "Don't tell me it's fine. I'm not going to be able to stay and settle her in, or take her to doctors' appointments, or the therapy she's probably going to need. So let me come and see her for myself. See that she really is okay."

A loud, resigned sigh makes it to my ears. "I want you here too much to argue," she admits. "Just let me know when you fly in, and either Trey or I can pick you up."

"Sounds good."

"Love you, Cole."

"Love you more."

Rolling my chair closer to my desk, I pull up a few web pages and start searching for flights. Too frantic to bother searching for the cheapest option, I end up clicking on a flight for tomorrow afternoon. It should give me enough time to tell the dean and organize a temporary replacement. Opening up my desk drawer, I pull out my wallet and flick through it for my credit card. Just as I type in the last of my information, a succession of knocks sounds at my door.

"Come in," I call out absentmindedly.

Shocked to see Elijah walking back in, I throw my wallet in the drawer and stand on instinct. As if that will somehow close the physical distance between us.

"Is everything okay?" I query.

His lips lift up in a shy, nervous smile. "So much for my quick escape. I left my bag here."

I look over to where I remember him putting it down, and sure enough it's still there.

"Oh. Yeah. Of course." There's no way to disguise the disappointment in my voice, so I scrub a hand over my face and try to smooth the expression that I know sits there.

I watch him awkwardly make his way through my office to retrieve his belongings. Tongue tied, I'm too over-whelmed with conflicting priorities to formulate anything coherent.

"Are you ok?" he interrupts, his brows pulled together in worry. "I'm sorry if the note..."

"Shit. No." I raise my hand up to stop him. "It wasn't that."

He lowers his gaze to the ground and backs up again, his expressive eyes unable to downplay the unwelcome change between us. "I'm just going to go."

"My mom was in a car accident," I blurt out.

"What?"

Steadying myself, I grip the edge of the desk and explain. "That was why my phone wouldn't stop ringing."

"Oh my God." Discarding his bag, he takes three long, purposeful strides toward me. "I'm so sorry, Cole. Is she okay?" Placing his hand on my shoulder, he effortlessly shelves his personal feelings. With nothing but genuine worry written all over his face, he turns me to face him. "Are *you* okay?"

It's a simple, expected, common question. But hearing it out of his mouth dangerously tightens my chest. His concern is welcomed. Appreciated. Wanted.

Common sense tells me that anybody with a heartbeat would ask if I was okay, but with Elijah, the gentle gesture has me mentally creating a list of all the good things about him. A list deeper and more complex than his ability to kiss and suck me off.

Trying to tamp down my attraction to him, I reluctantly shrug out of his touch and take a seat, pretending to focus on the screen. "She shattered her hip in the accident. She's in surgery now."

With all the comfort in the world, he takes a seat on my desk and points to the open web page on my computer screen. "I guess that means you're going to see her?"

"My sister said I didn't need to, but I would feel better if I did. To be able to see for myself."

"Of course. I can understand that."

"You'd go back and fly home for your mom, wouldn't you?"

The question must catch him off guard, because he just stares at me, his mouth opening and closing, his words a struggle. "Umm." He scratches at his temple nervously. "Honestly, I don't think anyone would even call me to tell me my mother was in a car accident."

"What?" I whip my head around to face him, but he's too busy pulling at invisible threads on his jeans. "What do you mean nobody would tell you?"

I know I have no right to ask the question, but this, coupled with his reluctance to voice his sexuality the other day, puts me on edge and makes me even more curious about him and his family.

"We're not as close as you guys seem to be," he supplies nonchalantly. "So, what are you going to do now?" The subject change is quick, his intention clear. "Do you want to be left alone?" His voice loses its confidence. "Is your flight soon?"

Flicking my wrist, I check the time, then look back up at

him. "How inappropriate would it be if I ask you to stay a little longer?"

He mulls over my question. "Not any more inappropriate than what we've already done."

"If you want to leave, you can." Wanting to give him an out, but wanting him to stay is the hardest balancing act. "I know you didn't want anything to ruin it." As casually as possible, I place my hand over his forearm. "I know it felt rushed, but thank you for the note. It was kind of cute."

A beautiful blush ascends up his neck and face. "This isn't ruining anything." He settles his palm on the top of my hand. "I don't want to leave if you're not okay."

"It's fine. I'm fine," I insist. "I'll be even better when I'm on that flight home."

"And where's home?"

If any other student asked, there would be no hesitation in saying where I moved here from. Everyone knows only a small percentage of students and teachers in an Ivy League University are not actually from here, but now it feels so much more than an innocent question. A risky step into unchartered territory.

Recognizing my hesitation, Elijah removes his hand off mine. "Sorry, was that overstepping?"

I blow out a loud breath, not really sure about anything between us. "It's fine. I'm from Chicago. Where in Texas are you from?" I ask casually.

"Don't you need to print out those tickets? Or pack your bags? You can ask me this stuff another time."

I raise a questioning eyebrow at him, becoming well versed in his unsuccessful deferral tactics, knowing very well *another time* isn't really an option for us.

If things were different, I would call him on it. Instead, I face my computer and press print on my tickets. The noise from the machine fills the silence, giving us less of a chance to talk, less time for misunderstandings, and hopefully fewer reasons for Elijah to feel compelled to get up and leave.

Since the moment I met him, the idea of him walking away from me suffocates me. After tonight, I downright hate it.

Needy and unsettled, I ignore my conscience and turn my body to his. I let my hand rest on his thigh. "Maybe we can bend the rules one more time." *Cole you're an idiot.* "Start fresh when I get back from seeing my family?"

"Cole."

The strain in his voice has me retreating. *Leave him the fuck alone, Cole. Is this even the right time to be discussing this?* "I'm sorry, I fucking know better. You should go."

Pushing off the chair, I try to walk away from Elijah, but he grabs on to my wrist, effectively stopping me.

"You know that was the first time I'd ever given someone a blowjob?"

Pulling out the big guns, he renders me speechless with his admission. I don't protest or pull away, but I let my gaze roam over him, trying to work out where to go from here.

"And receiving?" I push the words out slowly, knowing the answer, but wanting to hear it all the same.

He swallows hard, guilt and fear filling his eyes.

"Why didn't you tell me?"

"You wouldn't have touched me." His voice is pained, his words somewhat true. If he'd been upfront with me, I would've used all my strength to walk away from him. Unknowingly, I've crossed a line where a lust-filled exchange has now turned into a moment of importance. A moment of significance. And no matter how badly we both want to deny it—this changes *everything*.

"Elijah." I shake my head at him. "We shouldn't— No," I say more firmly. "*I* shouldn't have taken it that far."

He lets go of my wrist. "Don't do that."

"Do what?"

"Put all the blame on yourself." He straightens his stance, injecting confidence into his argument. "There may be some things I haven't done in my life, but that doesn't make me any less responsible for *my* actions."

"I had a feeling you were inexperienced," I say more to myself than him. A wave of shame passes over him, and I take hold of his face, imploring him to look at me. "Elijah," I breathe out. "Don't you dare feel embarrassed or ashamed for things you have or haven't done."

I mistook his innocence for naivety, not realizing just how guileless he was. He is practically untouched in every way that matters, and that stirs every single protective bone in my body.

"I'm sorry," I whisper.

"I told you—"

I cut him off with a soft kiss. "I'm not sorry it happened, Elijah. I'm sorry it can't keep happening." I press my lips to his again, trying to memorize the feel of them. "I think it's best if you go."

He closes his eyes, hiding his most expressive feature. "This is why the note was a good idea," he says against my lips. Separating our mouths, he takes steps backwards, away from me. "I hope your mom's okay."

Picking up his bag, he hangs it over his body and turns his back to me. I call out to him as he places his hand on the door handle.

"Elijah." He looks at me over his shoulder, resignation consuming him. "Don't give yourself to anyone too freely."

My implication is obvious and inappropriate. If he'd

never sucked dick before tonight, there's no way he's gone any further with somebody else.

"Like you?" he challenges.

It comes out too quickly, my selfish mouth—that can still taste and feel him—running away from me. "Like your friend."

Without missing a beat, he gives me a two-finger salute. "Have a safe trip, Professor Huxley."

10

ELIJAH

Parking myself in a corner booth at King Koffee, I sip on my fourth cup of joe for the day, while frantically trying to lose myself in my studies. It's been my routine for the last three days. Going to class, trying to avoid Aiden, and simultaneously filling up my brain with so much information I'm too exhausted to think about anything or *anyone* else when I go to sleep at night.

I wish I could say it was working, but my increased caffeine intake says otherwise. The addictive liquid is the only thing keeping me sane. Every night, I toss and turn until I give in to the needs of my traitorous dick and jerk myself off remembering every touch and taste of Cole Huxley.

The only successful part of my days has been making sure I stay out of Aiden's way. Seeing how we've barely run in to each other, it seems there's a good chance he too isn't ready to face what happened between us. Or as usual, I'm overthinking it, and he's just busy.

Either way, I'm drowning in emotions, consumed by the

multitude of feelings, and for the first time ever, burying myself in my workload and studying isn't cutting it.

The sound of a chair scraping against the concrete floor pulls me away from my shitty attempt at reading. Surprised to see Callie sitting in front of me, I grab a stray piece of paper and slip it between the pages before closing it. "Hey."

"Hey," she responds casually. "How are you?"

"Good." Shifting in my seat, I try to combat the awkwardness by rearranging my strewn-out belongings. Noticing my empty coffee mug, I pick it up and give it a little shake. "Want me to get us a coffee?"

"No, I'm okay." She points over her shoulder. "Aiden is getting us both one."

My body visibly deflates at the mention of his name and I immediately start counting to ten to calm my nerves.

Leaning over the table, Callie grabs my half-eaten packet of Werther's Originals and takes one butterscotch candy, popping it into her mouth. "I forgot how good these taste. It makes sense that you would be addicted to them."

Confused, I patiently wait for Callie to reveal the reason she came over to see me. She turns back, looking at Aiden and then back at me. "I wanted to tell you, you don't need to feel that way."

"What way?" I ask, eyeing her curiously.

"Nervous." She gives my hand a little squeeze. "It's written all over you."

"I can't help it," I admit.

"If you think he's mad at you, he's not."

I sigh in relief as she alleviates my main fear. "I feel like an apology is in order, anyway."

"Actually, that's what I wanted to do before Aiden got back."

"What?"

"Apologize." She bites the corner of her mouth, looking pensive. "I didn't mean to scare you, or make you feel uncomfortable. I would never—."

"Hey," I interrupt. "It wasn't that." Feeling self-conscious, I pull my hand away from her and fold my arms across my chest. "In case it wasn't obvious, I've never done anything like that before, and I chickened out."

"Been propositioned for a threesome or kissed a guy?"

"The first one," I answer, barely audible. "Maybe I over-reacted."

"It's not for everyone," she soothes. "And sometimes Aiden and I forget that."

"You two do that all the time?" The change in my voice accentuates my surprise.

"It sounds so much worse than it is, but yeah..." her voice trails off as she lowers her head, hiding her eyes. "Sometimes we sleep with the same person. At the same time."

"It's none of my business, Callie, and I would never judge you. Either of you," I add quickly

"You just looked so horrified," she hides her face in her hands.

"Hey. Hey." Moving forward, I mirror her actions from earlier, grabbing her hand between mine and hoping it gives her some comfort. "My reaction was because of what I was feeling and things I was processing. I can assure you, it wasn't because of you two."

"I thought that might be it. I even tried to tell Aiden that's what it was, but he's been pretty insistent you're repulsed by him."

"Repulsed by him?" I straighten in my chair, shocked. "God, I knew I'd upset him when I couldn't go through with it, but I definitely was not repulsed. He's attractive, but I'm not looking to complicate things right now," I clarify. "Without sounding like a complete loser, so much of this is new to me, and if he's in to me, it was never my intention to hurt his feelings."

"I get it," she assures me. "And he will too. Your issues are yours, and he's also got his own stuff to work through. You guys just need to get back to 'before' the kiss."

Accepting her advice, I clear my throat, wanting to ask her something a bit more personal. "Can I ask you something?" She gives me a quick nod. "Are you and Aiden... together?"

"Ha," she scoffs. "Aiden only wants what he can't have."

"But the sex?"

"It's just sex, Eli."

She drags her hand away from mine, resting it over the one sitting in her lap. We stare at each other in silence, her tired eyes giving away more than she plans on saying. I know there's more to that story, but just as Callie hasn't probed into my vague explanations, I know she deserves better than me trying to dig into hers.

"Hey," Aiden's voice interrupts our stare off and Callie takes it as her cue to go. Putting her fun face back in place, she rises out of her chair and half turns, so she can look at both of us. Kissing him on the cheek, she takes the hot drink, clearly labeled with her name, out of the cardboard coffee tray. "I'll see you guys later, okay? I have to get back to class." Putting her fingers over her lips, she blows me a kiss. "It was good talking to you, Eli."

Feeling more confused about Callie than I am about myself, I watch Aiden nervously sit down in what was her seat. He hands me a takeaway cup full of hot, fresh java. "Just how you like it."

"I'm sorry," I blurt out, taking the peace offering from his hands.

"For...?"

"Avoiding you."

"So, you were doing that," he sniped out accusingly. Avoiding my gaze, he focuses on taking the lid off his drink and pouring an unhealthy amount of sugar into his steaming cup.

"Like I told Callie," I continue, wanting to get it all out in one quick go. "I know I rushed to my room and made you guys deal with the aftermath, but the whole thing overwhelmed me." Scrubbing a hand over my face, I stay silent long enough for Aiden to wonder why I'm so quiet. When he notices my apprehension, he looks away from his coffee and back to me, his demeanor softer, more patient. "I didn't want to admit that my awkwardness may have cost me the only friends I have."

His remorseful eyes look so big in his sullen face, and just like with Callie, I've come to realize I'm not the only one hiding.

"It was really stupid of me to think kissing or anything more between us wouldn't pose a problem," he says. "Only Callie and I roll like that; we keep our fucking and friendship separate."

I inwardly cringe at how crass and offhanded his experiences with Callie are made out to be. The familiar look of sadness and longing on her face making his words even harder to hear.

"So, you're into guys and girls?" I ask, trying to decipher the details I've been privy to.

A cheeky smirk erupts onto his face. "I'm into anything that makes my dick hard."

"Good to know." I chuckle.

"So, we're okay?"

"Unless you try to kiss me again," I tease. "We should be fine."

"How about we make an agreement? Some sort of compromise." Taking a sip of my coffee, I look over the rim of the cup and eye him skeptically. "We can put the shitty misunderstanding behind us, but you need to agree to a new game plan."

A nervous noise slips out of my mouth. "Why am I already feeling uneasy about this?"

"Come out with us more. Callie and me. The three of us," he insists. "As friends."

Seeing as losing my only friends was one of my biggest fears, his request doesn't make me feel as anxious as I thought it would. I hold my hand out to him. "Deal."

He takes it, and holds on to it. "Being gay isn't a death sentence, Eli." A lump forms in my throat, his candor unexpected and unsettling. "Enjoy it. Enjoy being you. Better yet, just enjoy being here. Young and free."

I pull my hand away. "I think that's the most mature thing you've said to me since we've met."

He laughs. "I'm a selfish dickhead most of the time, Eli, but I would never intentionally hurt you or make you feel uncomfortable about your sexuality. That's not me."

"I appreciate that, man. A lot." And I do. When you're so starved for acceptance, you look for it everywhere. Searching for it in everyone's words, and all their actions. It becomes your only focus. "So, can I take the spotlight off myself now, and ask you about Callie?"

"Yeah. What about her?"

"Do you like her?"

"What?" He seems confused, almost like he's never given the possibility any thought. "Like more than friends?"

"Yeah"

"We're best friends," he deadpans. "I can't say I think of her as a sibling. Considering the sex we've had, that would be awkward."

He means it as a joke, but for some reason I can't seem to find it funny. "So how does it work? You sleep with whoever you want? Who invites whom?"

"You haven't changed your mind, have you?" he jests.

"Ha. You wish." I sit back in my seat, much more comfortable with the mood between us. "I'm curious. Young and free, the 'act your age Eli' wants to know."

"She does it for me," he confesses. "The threesomes, I mean. If there's a guy I want, but I'm not sure where he stands, I pull in the big guns. He'll either reject me and be ok with both of us fucking her, or he'll swing my way."

What a fucking mess.

"Don't let anybody ever tell you you're not full of surprises."

He shrugs. "It works."

"You're not the only one who doesn't judge," I admonish. "But it doesn't mean I can't be concerned."

"There's nothing for you to be concerned about. Callie knows how it is."

"Yeah," I say casually, even though I feel anything but. "I'm sure she does."

IT's LATE SATURDAY AFTERNOON, two days before my Religion lecture, when a mass written email pops up in my student inbox. It informs all enrolled students that their lectures with Professor Cole Huxley will be cancelled for the next two weeks, but all materials will be uploaded with a podcast taken from the archives to assist with the workload.

Two weeks?

I don't know how long I was expecting him to be away, but two weeks sends a jolt of panic racing through me. Is his mom okay?

There's a closing line at the bottom of the email reminding students if they need Professor Huxley for any reason, he has advised that students can email him directly and he would endeavor to get back to them as soon as possible. I let the mouse hover over his contact details.

Fuck it.

I click on the email address and a new screen pops up. Without overthinking it, I let my fingers fly over the keys of my keyboard. Simple and succinct.

Professor Huxley.

Ugh. Too formal. Delete.

Cole,

Got the official email about your leave of absence. Two weeks seems like a long time.

Is your mom okay? Are you okay?

Elijah

Closing my eyes, I hit send and slam my computer shut. Tossing it beside me, I get up from the couch, head to the kitchen, and rummage through the cupboards looking for something to make for dinner.

Grabbing a packet of raw penne, I make a mental note to resume the job hunting I briefly thought about before I got sidetracked with the research project and all the complicated strings that have attached themselves to it.

Aiden is always offering to throw his money around and have the dorm fully stocked, but it doesn't sit right with me.

I don't want to feel indebted to anyone, even if I know that isn't his intention.

Just as I'm almost done boiling the pasta and simmering the horrible—from a jar— sauce, my phone pings.

Aiden: Want to go to a gay bar?

Me: We're only 18.

Aiden: They have wristbands. Nobody will serve us alcohol with it on.

Me: I'm not sure.

Aiden: Remember our agreement?

Me: I don't think coercion was part of the deal.

Aiden: Kidding. I knew you weren't up for it, but what about a party?

Me: I guess I could come.

Aiden: I'll be home in an hour and we can head out together.

Me: Callie?

Aiden: She's meeting us there.

Plating my meal for one, I scoff down my food in record time, thinking of excuses to get out of tonight. Another message pops up on my screen before I even have a chance of formulating a good idea.

Aiden: Don't even think about bailing on me tonight.

Fucking know-it-all.

AIDEN and I arrive and the party is in full swing. Just like in the movies, the huge Greek letters sit proudly on the gable of the historic looking building. Students spill out of the door and music blares through the large windows. It looks exactly like I would expect it to.

"Don't you have to be part of a frat to come to these parties?" I ask Aiden.

"Most of the time. But like with anything, if you know a guy who knows a guy you can pretty much do anything you want."

I look over to him and offer a bemused smile. "Of course, you're the guy that knows a guy, right?"

He offers me an arrogant smirk, paired with a wink. We've settled back into a routine with one another, our friendship even better than it was before the kiss. I've yet to see Callie since the day at the café, but I've made the decision not to get lost down their thorny road. We're all friends, and if either of them need a pair of ears or a shoulder to cry on, I'm happy to be their guy. But for now, I've got enough of my own problems to try and work through.

Reaching the entryway, Aiden and I cross the threshold and shuffle to an empty corner, out of the walkway. Pulling his phone out of his pocket, he begins to furiously tap away at the screen. "If you see Callie, can you let me know? She's supposed to meet us here."

"She's here." I lean closer to him, inconspicuously trying to point her out. "She's in the kitchen. Can you see her?"

Laughing and drinking with another girl, Callie looks like she's in her element. Carefree and happy. Aiden starts toward her and I follow.

As we get closer, I feel tension beginning to radiate off Aiden; Callie's face when she notices us confirms this isn't a friendly visit.

"Hey," I greet, hoping to break the ice.

"Eli." Callie takes hold of my shoulder, but stares at Aiden. "This is my friend, Sophie. Can you hang here with her while I kill him?"

Sophie and I both stifle a laugh. "I think that can be arranged."

We both watch them walk off and huddle in a darkened corner before turning to face one another. "I'm Sophie," she supplies, sticking her hand out for me to shake. "Nice to meet you."

Effortlessly beautiful, Sophie would make anybody double take with her long, wavy brown hair and petite frame. Comfortable in her own skin, she's wearing short, low heeled boots, blue, ripped vintage denim jeans, and a white, off the shoulder top. She's the gorgeous girl next door.

"You come here often?" I joke, taking her hand.

"Is it that obvious?" she says looking around.

"What?"

"This is my second party. We're almost two months into school, and that's all I've managed to attend," she reveals.

I smile knowingly. "It's my first one." Shoving both my hands into my back pockets, I sway on my heels. "I don't think it's something I could, or want to, get used to."

"What?" She feigns shock. "You don't want the all-American college experience?"

I laugh, enjoying how her humor matches mine. "I came here for the education and education only. I'm on a scholarship."

"Thank fuck," she breathes out. "Someone who understands why parties just aren't on my radar."

There's no denying that every student that steps on this campus is smart, or has been accepted based on some intellectual merit, but not all students have the threat of being kicked out if they don't maintain their grades at a ridiculously high standard all year round.

"How did you meet those two?" She points at Aiden and Callie who are animatedly arguing with one another.

"Aiden and I are roommates. You?"

"Callie and I take a Juvenile Delinquency class together."

"That sounds interesting."

"You can say that again," she mumbles.

Something about her tone insinuates she's not talking about the class. I give her a small smile, not really sure how to continue. I'm bound to make it awkward.

"I've heard a lot about Aiden. Callie is always talking about him." We're both blatantly staring at them as she keeps talking. "He seems intense. Are they together?"

"No." I take too long to answer, my hesitation forcing Sophie to side-eye me.

"What is it?"

"Nothing," I lie, rubbing the back of my neck. "They've been friends since they were kids, and moved here together. I can see how it looks like they're together from the outside looking in, but they're just really close."

Watching, it's obvious from their faces just how serious their conversation has turned, their body language has become more rigid, more tense. Aiden's eyes catch mine, and I raise my eyebrows at him, hoping he realizes he's starting to gain more than just me and Sophie as an audience. Placing a hand on Callie's lower back he speaks directly in her ear.

Whatever he says forces a fake smile across her face while she quickly glances around the room. Locking eyes with Sophie and me, she straightens her back and confidently walks towards us.

"Because that wasn't weird," Sophie mutters to me.

Glad she voiced what I was thinking, I give her shoulder a nudge with my own. "I like you, Sophie. You should hang around us three more often. You could balance out whatever that," —I tip my head to where Aiden now stands alone. — "Is."

Looking past Callie, I catch Aiden watching her intently. When his gaze moves to me, he puts up a finger, signaling for me to wait. Back on his phone, it isn't until mine vibrates in my pocket that I realize he's the one who's sent me a message.

Aiden: I'm going to head to another party.

I glance up at him and then to Sophie and Callie.

Me: Are you okay? Do you want me to come?

Aiden: Stay here, watch over Callie for me. I just need to blow off some steam.

Knowing I'm going to regret putting myself in between them like this, I tip my chin up at him and let him know I've got it covered.

My phone vibrates just as he steps out of view. Not expecting anybody else besides Aiden to contact me, I'm surprised to see an email notification pop up on my screen.

He replied.

11

COLE

"I can't believe I had to find out through the staff intranet that you were on a leave of absence for two weeks," Harper whines.

"I was going to tell you. Both of you," I emphasize, glancing between her and Miles. "You just beat me to it."

"I would've driven you to the airport, or checked on your apartment while you were away," she continues.

"Cut the guy some slack, Beauty," Miles interrupts. "He was rushing home to his mom."

"Firstly," she raises her finger in the air. "Since when did you start calling me that? I thought only Cole called me that. And secondly, nobody asked you to be the voice of reason, Miles." She mock glares at him before looking back at me "So, how is your mom, anyway?"

Resting my elbows on the table, I lightly massage my temples. "She's good. It was a bit of work setting the house up for her recovery, but it's not permanent and my mom is a fighter, so I'm no longer as worried as I was when I first arrived back in Chicago."

The last two weeks were a tumultuous rollercoaster, and

not at all for the reasons I expected. After Elijah walked out of my office, I swore to myself that it was the end of it. I would organize my leave the next morning and I would spend much needed time focusing on my family, what they needed, and righting my skewed priorities.

What I didn't anticipate was an email from Elijah checking if I was okay. Just like the time we were in my office, his compassion and concern surprised me more than it should've. It's not like I've never been around people who cared about or for me, but it was knowing how much his care could cost him that made the meaning and sentiment behind the email mean so much more.

I tried avoiding it for hours, but as it sat in my inbox, it mentally weighed me down, throwing me off balance until I laid in bed that night and gave in to the absurd need to write back. It was the most straightforward response I could give, without venturing into any form of inappropriateness. I didn't want to give him closed-off answers, but I didn't want to ask him any open-ended questions, either. We were stuck, and all that was required was for me to say thank you for the email and I'd see him when I see him.

I did that. And just like he should've, he didn't respond.

Hour after hour. Day after day. Nothing. And it crushed me. As if he was the first guy I'd ever wanted in high school, desperately seeking his attention, wanting him to notice me. It was childish, and even though I could acknowledge how pathetic I was being, it did nothing to diminish how much his silence crushed me.

What is wrong with me?

"So, what have you guys been doing since the last time we all caught up?" I ask, trying to retrain my focus. "Surely your lives have been much more interesting than mine."

"Well, Miles is getting his dick wet," Harper blurts out.

I whip my head around to a shocked Miles. "You are? That's great, man."

"What?" he shakes his head, as if he's trying to make sense of what Harper is saying. "I'm not sleeping with anyone."

"Yes, you are," she insists.

"I think I would know."

"You do know, you're just lying about it."

"No, I'm not."

"Fine." She slaps both hands down on the table. "Explain why you've been less of an asshole lately then."

"I'm not an asshole," he counters.

"I'm going to ignore that statement, because everybody at this table knows you're a dickhead from time to time, and give you one more opportunity to confess the truth."

Amused by their banter, I'm torn at whether or not I want this to end or escalate.

"Maybe he doesn't want to talk about it," I offer to his defense.

Unexpectedly, Miles looks at me, his eyes filled with relief and gratitude. It's all the proof I need to confirm that he is, in fact, hiding something. Thinking of my own secret obsession with Elijah, I wonder what his reasons are for staying quiet.

"All he had to say was he didn't want to talk about it, instead of lying," she pouts.

"Anyone told you that you two fight like siblings?" I say, pointing between the two of them.

"I already have a sister," Miles huffs. "And she's plenty."

"And I already have four brothers."

"Four brothers?" Miles and I repeat incredulously. "Older or younger?" I add.

She juts out her chin. "What do you think?"

"Definitely older," Miles answers. "It would explain your take no shit attitude."

"I'll take that as a compliment," she says dryly.

"It is," he says, surprising me. Harper focuses on him, a mixture of confusion and curiosity on her face.

"Don't look at me like that." He shakes his index finger in front of her face. "You don't get to where you are without big fucking balls. I know it's not easy for women to assert their authority and be acknowledged appropriately. But your job here is proof you've earned it."

Harper swallows, the apples of her cheeks reddening. "Thank you."

He gives her a quick nod before taking a sip of his beer. "But on a serious note," he continues. "How the fuck did you bring anyone home to meet four brothers?"

"I think the fact I'm single answers that question."

The three of us laugh, picturing a young Harper getting into it with four older brothers.

"So, your mystery girl," Harper presses, trying to corner Miles again.

"Will remain a mystery."

He isn't as heated when he answers her, a little more resigned.

"So, there is someone?" I pry.

"Please don't ask me questions." A humorless laugh leaves his mouth. "I'm in way over my head with this."

His words make me think of how desperate I was to talk to anyone about Elijah while I was away. I could've told Meghann, but she would've been my voice of reason. The person to tell me I was wrong, or stupid, when all I really needed was someone who would shut up and listen. The puzzled expression on his face makes me empathize with how crazy Miles must be feeling trying to sort through his own stuff.

"What about you, Cole?" Harper asks, turning her focus on to me. "Did you hook up with anyone when you went back home?"

"Do we really need to be doing this? Miles and I aren't asking you about your sex life."

"Doth protest too much," Harper quotes, looking at Miles.

"He's guilty," Miles says, encouraging her. "I would know."

"I did not hook up with anyone. I don't like to fall back into bad habits."

"Oh right," Harper quips, like she's just remembered something. "He's the commitment phobe out of the three of us."

"I am not. I just haven't found the right one."

"Trust me, you do not want to end up with the wrong one," Miles says, speaking from experience. "If it doesn't hurt to walk away from them, then they're not the one."

"Was it easy to walk away?" I ask.

"I didn't have a choice. Leaving was her decision." His voice picks up. "That's neither here nor there. I'm just saying, the thought of leaving my ex-wife before we were married, would've killed me. But when she walked away last year, the feeling was nowhere near the same."

"And what, you believe because she wasn't *the one*, you were spared heartache?"

"I didn't say there was no heartache, but it would've been worse if we were meant to be forever."

"It's warped," Harper says, mulling it over. "But he kind of makes sense."

Harper raises her glass for us to cheers her. "Who would've known our Miles was a hopeless romantic?"

"Could it be the new mystery woman?" I joke, clinking our drinks together.

Miles glares at us both. "Shut up."

———

It's my first day back, and my first class is the one where I teach Elijah. My nerves are shot to shit. It's been radio silence from him. As it should be, but I need it to not be a fucking issue.

He sits all the way at the back, and my ego takes a hit that he doesn't even want to try and sneak up closer to me. How is it that he's turned into the adult and I'm the one wanting us both to be reckless and irresponsible?

The class ends, the students faring better than I expected considering my absence. I wait for Elijah to stop and stay behind, but much to my dismay he leaves the class without even a second glance.

Not even bothering to stay back and sift through my paperwork, I pack up my shit and head out of the lecture hall.

I swing the door open, and like a slap in the face, Elijah is just behind the door, his *friend* stuck to his side as usual. His surprised face morphs into guilt and anguish, and I don't even let myself feel bad for making him feel like he's been caught with his hand in the cookie jar.

"Elijah," I greet through gritted teeth. Something about my tone must incite his friend to interrupt and introduce himself.

"Hi, I'm Aiden."

I give him a nod, my body too tight and tense to provide any words.

"This is Professor Huxley," Elijah fills in for me.

"Yeah, I've seen you around. Eli loves your class."

The offhanded compliment unknowingly breaks the ice. My shoulders sag, every part of me acknowledging my irrationality.

"He's a great student." I clear my throat and glance at him one more time. "I'll see you next week."

"Aiden, do you think I could meet you and Callie later? I just want to ask Professor Huxley something about the research project."

"Yeah, man," he eyes me suspiciously. "I'll see you later."

When Aiden walks off, I look at Elijah expectantly. "Something you need to say?"

When he doesn't answer me, I start to walk away.

Catching up to me, he blows out a long breath. "Please, don't walk away from me."

"I figured maybe we can do this in private," I bite back.

Side by side, step by step, our long strides match until we reach my office.

The second the door closes, he pounces. "You can't look at me that way."

"What way?" I challenge, walking to my desk and placing my bag down.

"Like I'm doing something wrong."

"I don't know what you're talking about." Turning around, I rest my backside on the edge of the desk and cross my ankles. There's a significant distance between us, and it takes everything in me to stand my ground.

"Fine. I must've misread the situation." He pauses, as if he's waiting for me to say something. To argue or defend myself. When I do neither, he shakes his head in disappointment. "I'm going to go." He throws his hands up in the air in defeat and turns to leave.

"Elijah, wait." He stills, but doesn't look back at me. "Why didn't you respond to my email?"

"What?" he whirls back around, his eyes incredulous.

"You emailed me and then when I emailed you back you didn't reply."

God, I sound so pathetic.

"And say what?" he shouts. "Hey, I know your mom needs you, but I can't stop thinking about your dick in my mouth."

It takes less than a second for me to reach him, my hands gripping the sides of his head, my mouth slamming onto his. There's no finesse in this kiss. No delicacy or caution. With nothing but shared desperation, I feast on the taste I've shamelessly been missing.

"Fuck," I pant. "I can't—"

"Don't." He kisses me quiet, brushing his hard cock against mine. "Don't think."

"We can't," I argue. "I want all of you, and I can't have it." I dive in for one more taste, caressing his tongue with my own. "And I want you so fucking bad."

"What's another secret?"

The words come out like a whisper, and the look on his face is an admission that they accidentally fell out of his mouth. But the meaning hits me in the chest, like a hot branding iron, painfully burning me. He doesn't deserve to be a secret; he doesn't need to be at college hiding. He deserves to be out and proud, and not in the sense of just his sexuality, but just from whatever chains I know he has bound himself with.

"You deserve better than this, Elijah."

My hands slide down from his face and circle around his torso, and he instinctively wraps his arms around my neck.

"This isn't about what either of us deserve, Cole. This is just us being realistic."

"Nothing about this is realistic," I dispute.

"Us trying to stay away from each other is the only unrealistic thing going on here."

"When I saw you standing next to him," I close my eyes wishing the image of the two of them together away. "I felt sick."

"We're just friends," he says, trying to placate me.

"But you could be more. He's Aiden, right?"

Elijah nods.

"You could be his."

"Ha," he scoffs. "No, I couldn't."

"Yes," I counter. "If you let yourself, you could."

"I need to sit down," he says, looking around. Stepping to the working table sitting center in my office, he pulls out a chair and takes a seat. "I need to explain something to you."

Dragging another chair out, I sit down next to him. "What is it?"

He runs a hand over his jaw. "I have taught myself to be unaffected by every single guy I've come into contact with."

"Eli—"

He raises a hand. "Let me finish. If I didn't let myself touch, or look, I couldn't get into trouble. I didn't need to give my parents more reasons to be disgusted with me." Elijah closes his eyes before continuing, taking a large breath of air and holding it. When he finally exhales, more comes spilling out. "Since my parents found out I was gay, I have lived a very isolated life. Some of it was done on purpose, especially the part where I never allowed myself to acknowledge or even indulge in someone else." He pauses. "Until you."

"What does that mean?"

"I don't know, but from the first time I saw you, I was sucked in. At first, I thought it was just a physical attraction. You're sexy as fuck and *everyone* can see it."

A soft chuckle leaves my mouth, and his lips curve at the edges. "Don't act like you don't know." Twisting in his chair, he reaches for my hand and holds on to it. "But the more I saw you, the more I wanted you. And after..." He lets the sentence die, neither of us needing clarification. "I can't stop thinking about you. And when you saw me with Aiden," he shakes his head, ridding himself of a memory. "I can't have you look at me like that... Like you're disgusted with me."

"Fuck. No," I say, horrified. "I could never be disgusted with you." I squeeze his hand. "I'm fucking jealous, Elijah." Needing to feel more of him, I hook my arm around him and drag him onto my lap. He fits in my arms perfectly. "He gets an all access pass to my fucking main attraction."

"All access is a bit of an exaggeration, don't you think?"

"Shut up." I press my lips to his. "I'm not used to not getting what I want, and not having you is driving me insane."

"This is the part where we're both supposed to encourage one another to go and find this feeling with someone else."

I know he's right, but I'm too selfish, too horny for him, too fucking interested to be the voice of reason.

"Maybe we could see where it goes," he suggests hesitantly. "I know you've got your job to worry about."

"It's not any more of a worry than your scholarship."

Shy and needy, like a kitten, he curls himself around me and buries his head in the crook of my neck.

"I could pull out of the research project."

Annoyed that we're revisiting this, I pull away from him. "We discussed this already. That is yours. And for what? To see how good we can fuck?"

He flinches and I immediately regret my offhanded comment, knowing whatever it is between us has a little more depth than just sex. "I'm not worth a sacrifice that big, Elijah."

"Well, if it's just to see how good we fuck, maybe we should just get it over and done with," he states. "Fuck and run."

"And how's that worked out for us so far?" I cup the back of his neck and bring his face closer to me. "One kiss turned into a blowjob, and you think we're going to be able to fuck and run?" The tone of my voice deepens as my eyes lock onto his wet lips. "All it did is make me want you more."

"That's the anticipation of sex talking," he says. "Once you've had it, you would've had it all, and I'm sure you could walk away then."

"You have no fucking idea, do you?"

"What?" he questions innocently.

I slide my hand up his thigh. "Once wouldn't even come close to being enough."

He grabs my hand and brings it up to his hard dick. "We need a solution, Cole."

His breathing becomes shallow, and I know how easy it would be for me to slip my hand in his pants and bring him to the brink. Instead, I take the lead, make the decision, and give us a solution.

"I want you to know, I don't know what's going to happen from here. I don't have all the answers, but whether we only see each other in class or for the research project, nothing is going to stop me from wanting you." He perks up, and my instincts tell me he loves to hear how much I want him. "But what we did, it changed things. It was like a taste tester and now I want the whole fucking meal." I feel him get harder underneath my hand. "Let me take you out to dinner?"

He sobers quickly. "What?"

"My hand on your dick is okay, but when I mention dinner you freak out?"

"Outside this office?"

"One time isn't going to kill anyone." I rub firmly along his erection. "What's wrong with wanting to take a guy out for a meal before I try to slip it in?"

He laughs, his body relaxing in my hold, the mood shifting to exactly where we need it to be.

"Feed me, Cole."

A loud groan erupts from the back of my throat and he laughs, the innuendo not lost on either of us. I take his mouth, my tongue swooping in and tasting every corner available to me.

I flick open the button on his pants, but he stops me. "What?"

"I don't want you to start something we're going to have to stop."

"Fine."

"It's still early afternoon and I have a few things to finalize, especially if I'm going to be otherwise occupied later." He stands, unabashedly adjusting himself. Sticking his hand in his back pocket, he pulls out his cell and throws it at me. "Text yourself from my phone and then text me the details for our date later."

He throws a hand over his mouth, stunned at his slip up.

"I can take you out on a date," I concede, not too worried about the right terminology.

"Really?"

His eyes light up with excitement, and my chest expands with pride at making him feel the way he does.

Bending down, he grips both arms of the chair, hovering over me. "You're going to get a lot of firsts, Mr. Huxley."

"First place is all I ever strive for."

12

ELIJAH

As usual, when I'm away from Cole, common sense tries to worm its way into my psyche, but this time it isn't trying to talk me out of seeing him. Instead, it's a montage of memories, of how every time I take what I want, it's followed by a series of disasters. Reminders that whatever I want in this life is not mine for the taking. No matter how much I yearn to feel whole, there will always be empty parts that I'll never know how to fill.

Letting my head roll under the spray of the shower, I try to push the negativity aside and let myself get excited about seeing Cole. As much as I enjoy everything about him, I also love the freedom of being able to talk to a man, ogle a man, and be touched by a man.

It's the simple pleasures that so many other people take for granted. The things that used to keep me up, imagining all the different ways my life would pan out once I left home. Every night, I would close my bedroom door, climb under the covers, and let myself succumb to the barrage of my desires. With my hand around my dick, my imagination ran wild, conjuring up images of faceless guys getting me off every which way.

I feel myself getting hard as I get lost in the moment. The same movie reel playing in my mind, the strangers' faces now replaced with Cole's.

I make a fist around myself, stroking up and down, thinking of him.

His mouth. His hands. His cock.

My movements are frantic as the familiar tingling that runs up from the soles of my feet begins to settle over me. My balls become tight in anticipation, a warning that I'm close. It only takes a few more pumps before my body shudders and I come all over my hands.

As quickly as my release came, it's gone. The water washing it down, along with all the knots of tension and arousal that frequently battle it out.

After one more quick rinse, I switch the water off and step out into the small but efficient bathroom. Situated between the two rooms, the bathroom has access on either wall, opening up into each of our bedrooms. The water running through the pipes is loud enough to ensure neither of us walk in on one another.

Once I'm dry, I wrap a towel around my waist and rummage through my clothes, searching for something appropriate to wear. Settling on army green, cuffed chinos and a white t-shirt, I search around for my white, low top Chucks and step out into the common room.

"Where are you going?" Aiden asks almost immediately.

"Out," I stammer.

"Without me?"

"Hey. I know other people," I quip.

"Seriously, where are you going?"

"You know that research project I told you I was part of?

We're all meeting up to discuss what we've got so far and make sure we all stay on track."

His gaze roams over the length of me before he flicks his eyes back up to mine. "Something is different about you."

I wave him off and slip my wallet and phone into my pockets.

"You've never come home and showered before going to meet people from school," he presses. He flips his wrist and looks down at his watch. "It's dinnertime soon. The time people usually meet someone for a date."

"Please," I scoff. "Me, on a date? What have you been smoking today?"

"Firstly, don't act so surprised. I'm not the only guy who's going to want to tap that ass. Secondly, I'm on to you, Eli. You really are a terrible liar."

His comment catches me off guard, reminding me how everything about Cole has made me want to be carefree and obvious. A stark contrast to the guy I was growing up.

"Aiden, we don't have to do this, you know?"

"Do what?"

"Pretend that now we're no longer walking around on eggshells with one another, I'm actually okay about speaking about myself."

My rebuttal sounds harsher and more dismissive than I intended, but Aiden doesn't even balk, continuing with his inquisition.

"You mean speaking about sex."

"There's nothing to talk about. I'm going out to study," I lie.

"Fine, take all the fun out of it." I roll my eyes at him. "But just so you know, I just wanted to fuck you. Dating isn't my thing, so if you're worried about hurting my feelings or some shit like that, don't."

Grasping at the lifeline Aiden has unknowingly thrown at me, I run with his thought process to try and take the spotlight off myself. "Thanks. Not that I think we need to worry about me dating anyone, but I'm glad I'll be able to talk to my friend if I need to."

He smiles. Genuinely. And I feel like shit for lying to him. There's no way I would talk to anyone about this. Especially Aiden.

"I got to get going before I'm late," I announce.

I head to the door, swinging it open.

"Eli," Aiden calls out.

"Yeah."

"If you were meeting someone tonight? You look perfect."

I give him a small smile, grateful for the confidence boost. "Thank you."

COLE TEXTED me an address with the instructions to meet him at seven p.m. When I googled the location, it was a beautiful brownstone in the middle of Georgetown. I replied to his text asking if it was his place, but he evaded the question and told me to hurry up. He didn't want me to be late.

Standing in front of a set of steps that lead up to a large, black front door, I'm grateful for the lingering sunset, offering a warm, orange hue. Giving me enough light, I feel less creepy about standing alone outside of someone's house.

Should I go home?

Just as I'm about to pull up my Uber app and see how long it would take for one to drive me back to the dorms, a black sedan drives up to the curb.

Effortlessly, Cole steps out, his eyes honed in on mine with every move he makes. Expecting to see the same impeccably dressed man I saw earlier, I'm surprised to see Professor Huxley has retired for the evening. No longer wearing his mask of authority, he's dressed down, out of his suit, and looking sexier than I ever thought possible.

Even if he's older than me, he still looks younger than his profession makes him out to be. He's in black jeans and a casual, black, linen button-down. Rolled up at the sleeves, his thick forearms are on display, giving me a glimpse of how built and sturdy he is underneath his clothes.

Shoving my hands in my pockets, I rock on the heels of my feet, thoroughly enjoying the view. The freedom of being *able* to enjoy the view.

Finally reaching me, he stretches out his hand. "Hi, I'm Cole."

Finding it impossible to stop the smile from stretching across my face, I take his hand. "It's nice to meet you, Cole. I'm Elijah."

"Are you looking to rent this house too?"

I can play along with this.

"Actually, I'm checking it out for a friend," I respond, slipping into character. "Seeing if it's fit enough for him to live in."

"What do you think so far?"

"I'm not really one to judge a book by its cover." I drag my eyes up and down his body, "Even if it does look perfect on the outside. I'd like to get a good look inside before I made any final decisions."

"That's probably for the best." He pulls keys out of his pocket and rattles them in front of me. "Shall we go inside?"

I gesture my arm up the stairs, signaling for him to take

the lead. As he walks up to the door, my brain short circuits, watching the denim stretch across his firm ass.

Noticing I'm not behind him, he stops and turns. "What are you doing?"

"Taking in the view," I quip. "I want to make sure I don't miss a thing."

"Don't make me drag you inside," he threatens, a mischievous smile stretching across his face. Taking the stairs two at a time, I stop right behind him, my chest grazing his back.

He steps inside first and quickly punches some numbers into the keypad right next to the door jamb. I follow him further inside, taking in the inviting layout.

The front door opens up to a narrow foyer. A staircase leading upstairs stands directly in front of us, and an opening on our right takes you straight into an open plan kitchen and living room. The dark hardwood floors compliment the light tone of all the furniture.

"Do you live here?" I ask.

"I will be," he supplies. "I signed the lease the minute I got back from Chicago."

"Where do you live now?"

"King has housing for staff who transfer here from out of state. We can stay there for the length of our employment, but most people only use it temporarily, until they find what they're looking for. And," he adds, "it's on campus. After a whole day of classes, the last thing you want is to be bumping into all your students."

"So that explains why you were running near my dorm that day."

He gives me a knowing nod. "I was going to buy this place, but after what happened to my mom, I'm not certain I want to tie myself down like that."

"Oh. So you don't see yourself teaching here long-term?" I don't know why I feel deflated at the thought of anything changing from this very moment. It's not like King is home to me either.

"I don't have plans to leave, but if I needed to go back home for an emergency, or even permanently, I'd like it to be as hassle free as possible." I nod in understanding, much happier to listen to him tell me more about himself than contribute anything of my own. "So, I asked the owner if he was open to me leasing it instead of buying it, and luckily he wasn't in a hurry to sell."

"Seems like it's meant to be."

"He called me while I was away. I was itching to get back here to see it and begin moving in." He walks into the living room and looks at me over his shoulder. "What do you think?"

"It's beautiful." I step closer to him. "Is this stuff staying, or are you moving your own furniture here?"

"He offered to take it all, but I only have a television and a bed, and I was happy to not have to go furniture shopping."

"That seems easy enough. When do you officially move in?"

"Tonight." He holds up the keys. "I probably won't have all my stuff in here till next week, though. Want to look around?"

I answer him by placing my palm onto his.

The air thickens the second our skin touches, the two of us in his house becomes more intimate than I'm prepared for. We walk through in silence, my eyes locked on our hands instead of my surroundings.

After going through the living room and adjoining kitchen, we walk out of another entryway and head up the stairs. This time he guides me to go up first. "It's my turn to take in the view."

Feeling brazen, I work my way up the stairs, clenching my ass with every step. As soon as I reach the landing, I feel Cole grip my cheeks and press his lips to my neck.

"My room is the one on the left," he instructs. He hooks his fingers in my back pockets, following me into his private space.

It's a decent sized room, the light gray walls and white cornices opening it up even more. There's a door on the far right that I assume leads to his ensuite bathroom, and plantation shutters that let the perfect amount of outside in. Apart from a set of drawers, the center of the room is empty.

"When does your bed arrive?" I ask, a small part of me disappointed that the piece of furniture is missing.

"It's scheduled for Thursday. I finish classes early and can be home to let the movers into the apartment."

I turn around in his arms and waste no time kissing him. Unlike the other times we've been together, Cole's hands roam down my torso, finding the hem of my t-shirt. Fingers slip under the material and begin to skim my skin. His hands enjoy the dips and lines of my body and my lips eagerly try to commit his taste to memory.

"Is there a bed in the spare room?" I ask, pushing my hard shaft into his.

"There is, but I'm not taking you tonight. The only place I'm having you for the first time is my bed."

The confirmation that there will be a next time has me deepening the kiss, wrapping my fingers around the bulge in his pants and squeezing him tight.

A loud moan leaves my mouth as he sucks hard on my tongue.

Unexpectedly, he pulls his head back from mine. "Let's go eat."

"Food?" I question, my mind still lagging behind, stuck on the way I wanted to suck on his dick like he was just sucking my tongue.

"Yeah," he chuckles. "I'll want this," he grabs my junk, "for dessert, but how about we get dinner first?"

Talking my dick off the ledge, I steady my breathing and loosen my hold on him. "I guess I could eat."

"Good. We'll lock up here and then head to this place I know on the next block over. It's got the most mouth-watering steak I've ever tasted." He looks at me intently, while leading us back down the stairs. "You do eat meat, don't you?"

"I eat almost everything," I say with a smirk.

He tips his head to me and smiles. "Hurry up and get your ass down these stairs."

When we finally make it outside, the sun has officially set and a light breeze has picked up. "Are you cold?" he asks. "We can take my car."

"No, I'm good." I shove my hands in my pockets. "I think a walk will be nice."

The first few minutes are filled with a comfortable silence, the streets of Georgetown luring me in with every step. Kent is nothing like this; the town and the people so dated, small, and sheltered. "The size of these streets is beautiful," I comment, disrupting the quiet. "I told myself when we had Thanksgiving break I would use the opportunity to venture around Washington and spend some quality time seeing what else this place has to offer."

"I'm assuming that means it's your first time out to D.C.?"

"This is my first time anywhere," I confess. "Before coming here I'd never even stepped out of my hometown."

"You're only eighteen, though, right?"

"Is this your way of indirectly asking me about my age?"

"Actually..." He stalls, and I narrow my eyes at him. "Without sounding like a complete stalker, I already checked how old you were on the school records."

"You did?"

"Every now and then there's a kid that skips grades and goes to college early because they're some kind of genius." Confusion must be written all over my face because he goes on to explain his motives. "I wanted to make sure you were definitely over eighteen. Knowing made me feel less guilty for wanting you."

"Pity about not being a genius though," I offer light-heartedly.

"Don't sell yourself short, Elijah. You're a lot smarter than most of the students I've come across."

"Is that favoritism I hear?" I mock. "Are these the type of compliments I can look forward to because I gave you a blowjob?"

He stills, and I regret the joke immediately. "Elijah, I know you're not serious, but nothing about the success of your school work correlates to what we're doing here. Every grade and opportunity you get is because you've earned it."

His words are earnest and truthful, and such a meaningful compliment to how hard I've worked to get myself here. "You know, my dad told me to quit working so hard because nobody was ever going to acknowledge me as anything more than 'that gay kid.'" His steps falter, and I choose not to acknowledge it, not wanting to turn and look at him. Not wanting to see any pity in his eyes, I keep my gaze to the floor. "It means a lot to hear that I am more than that."

The silence returns, but this time, I can feel the tension radiating off him. He wants to say something, but for whatever reason, he holds back and I'm grateful. Rehashing the things I intrinsically know are wrong about my parents isn't something I want to do. Especially with Cole.

"I didn't really see much until I left for college, either," he divulges. "But since then I've traveled a fair bit around the country."

It's a simple fact about himself, but one I appreciate wholeheartedly. There's no judgement in the delivery, or reference to how much I still have to do and learn. It's like two people, strangers, slowly getting to know each other. Which is exactly what I want.

"Since I don't have the luxury of school records, am I allowed to ask how old you are?"

This seems to lighten the mood. "As long as you promise not to make any old man jokes."

"Please," I scoff. "You've got to know you're far from an old man."

"I'll be thirty-two December twenty-eighth."

"You're a Christmas baby," I muse.

"What? That's all you're going to say? Nothing about my age?"

"Surely you know age means absolutely nothing when you're as hot as you are."

"You think I'm that hot," he says with a knowing smirk.

"Don't act like you haven't been hit on every time you've left the house for most of your adult life."

A booming laugh leaves his mouth, filling the empty street. "I will have you know I've had to work for it a time or two."

I raise an eyebrow. "I find that really hard to believe."

"Whatever." He waves me off. "Back to the more important stuff. When's your birthday?"

"The end of this month. October thirtieth."

"Are you doing anything for it?"

"I don't think so. I haven't really celebrated my birthday since I was sixteen."

His shoulders graze against mine in understanding. "It's your first year at college. Your first year away from home. You should do something."

"Aiden has been bugging me to hit up a local gay bar. Maybe I'll make my birthday the night I take him up on the offer."

We reach a string of storefronts and stop outside one that says Carne. It's the perfect time to stop the conversation because I can see Cole's jaw working overtime at the mention of Aiden.

The hostess directs us to a booth in the back corner. With high partitions, it feels like we're boxed in and secluded from the rest of the restaurant. It's perfect for us.

"Welcome to Carne." The perky blonde hands us each a laminated square of decorated cardboard. "Here's our menu, and I'll be back in a moment to take your drink order and run through tonight's specials."

"Thank you," Cole answers.

Cole looks through the menu and then up at me. "Aren't you going to see what you want?"

"You promised me steak."

"I did," he says. "But you can see if there's something else you might like; the menu is great. I don't mind."

I know he's trying to be amicable, but I like that he's showing me something that he enjoys, something outside of what we already know about one another. "I like the idea of you picking."

A look of complete satisfaction crosses his face at my decision as he resumes his perusal of the different things we could order.

When the waitress comes back, Cole confidently rattles off our order. "Could we have a bocconcini, tomato, and basil salad, and one serving of salt and pepper squid to start, please?"

"Any drinks?"

"I'll have whatever beer you have on tap," he answers. Both Cole and the waitress look at me expectantly. Not sure if they card people, or if he's testing me, I go my usual route and don't bother with the alcohol. "A seltzer will be great, thanks."

The waitress gives us a quick nod, and leaves to pass our order on to the kitchen.

"You could've ordered a beer, or wine," he voices. "It wouldn't have bothered me."

"I think I've hit my quota on rule breaking tonight," I joke. His face blanches. "Cole, I'm kidding," I soothe. "I don't actually drink."

"At all?" He sounds perplexed.

I shake my head. "Besides the few shots I had when I kissed Aiden, I think it's safe to say it's not for me."

"So that's how that went down." He visibly swallows. "Is it safe to assume if you go with Aiden it will be your first time at a gay bar?"

"Geez." I place my elbows on the edge of the table and rest my head in my hands. "I sound so fucking lame."

"Elijah," Cole interrupts. He grabs my hands and pulls them down, forcing me to look up at him. "Everyone's been where you are right now."

"Are you sure about that?" I snap. "Because the more I talk, the more evident it is that I don't really measure up."

"Measure up to who?"

"Yo— Everyone." I try to correct my slip up, but the look on his face tells me it's too late.

"Me?" His voice is uncharacteristically low, somewhere between hurt and disbelief. "I don't expect *anything* of you," he spits out.

I catch his anger-filled eyes quickly sweeping around the restaurant before he grabs my hands and places them with his in the middle of the table. He leans over them, his voice harsh and direct. "I don't want anything but your dick in my mouth, so take those unfounded expectations you've put there instead, and leave them in that small as fuck shanty town you came from, where they belong."

13

COLE

J ust as I expected, Elijah rears his head back, seeking some distance and pushes himself into the leather cushioning of the booth behind him. As soon as the words came out of my mouth, there was instant regret. But when he started talking about not being good enough and using underwhelming adjectives to describe himself, I just thought of all the insults his parents had probably been slipping into everyday conversation, and wanted to make sure he knew to never put me in the same fucking group as them.

Without a word or a glance at me, he slides himself across the seat and steps out, giving me his back when he stands, then he walks right out of the restaurant.

"Fuck," I mutter angrily under my breath.

Knowing I need to follow him, I wave down the waitress. She hurries over, her blonde hair swaying with every step, and her best customer service smile painted on. "Is everything okay here, sir?"

"In case our food comes, I just wanted to tell you my

friend and I will be outside. We'll be back in as soon as possible."

"Not a problem, sir," she responds unfazed. "I'll bring you your cold drinks when you return."

As soon as she walks away, I rush through the restaurant and out the door hoping he's getting some air, and not finding his own way back home.

He's standing on the curb, looking down at his phone, the light of the screen illuminating the sadness on his face.

"Elijah," I call out, while walking toward him. "Elijah, please come back inside. I'm sorry."

When I'm right next to him, I repeat myself, and hope he hears the sincerity in my voice. "I didn't mean any of that the way it came out."

Our proximity must weaken his resolve as he turns his whole body to face mine. His eyes are glassy, his long, dark lashes wet and shiny.

God, I'm such a piece of shit.

"I'm so sorry."

Filled with such dejection, he stands still, staring at me, refusing to say a word.

"Please come inside and let me explain myself." Still, he says nothing. "I got defensive," I start. "I didn't want you to think you owed me anything. I didn't want you to think that you had to prove yourself to anyone just because your parents made you feel like that. I didn't want you to lump me in the same category as them.

"I know I have no right to pretend I know you and your parents, or to judge them, but just from the things you've let slip, I don't want to be held in the same regard as them. Ever."

He swipes at his eyes and stares at me, everything about

him in this moment unreadable. Surprising me, he word-lessly walks away, back into the restaurant.

Feeling at a loss, I stare at the back of him, praying that I can somehow salvage whatever is left of this evening.

We settle back into the booth, and the waitress swarms us almost immediately with both our drinks and our appe-tizers. Once we're alone, I watch him stare blankly at the salad that sits in the middle of the table.

I grab one of the small sharing plates and put half of the appetizer onto it. "Here. Have you ever had a Bocconcini salad before?" I ask.

He looks up at me and I immediately notice my mistake. I hold the plate out for him. "Please take it."

He adheres to my request and places it in front of him. "Are you going to talk to me, or just sit in silence while I continue to put my foot in my mouth?"

"I'm not mad at you," he admits.

"But you are mad?"

Looking at me thoughtfully, it takes him a few beats to respond. As expected, he gives me the more adult response to our situation. Taking responsibility and exercising matu-rity. "You were right. I was projecting. And until I can process how not to do that, let's just eat."

I lower my head to avert my gaze, feeling shame at the hands of his poise and control. This is too new and not serious enough for differences to come into play, yet I seem to have brought every single one of his insecurities between us without even trying.

"So, how's your mom?" he asks, catching me off guard.

I give him a tight smile, acknowledging his need to move on from what just happened, but not appreciating it all the same. I'm not afraid of confrontation, but I'm not going to push him if he isn't ready. And maybe this is just real life telling us to quit while we're ahead.

"She's really good," I divulge, not wanting to ruin the rest of our time together. "She was discharged from the hospital just under a week after surgery and her rehab started straight after that. My sister's boyfriend and I decked out the house with some extra hand rails here and there to help her move about." I continue talking as I watch him plate himself some more of the salad. "Thankfully, he and my sister live close by, so I felt less hopeless about leaving to come back here."

"Are you the oldest?"

Wanting him to feel as comfortable as possible, but paranoid my answers will make him uneasy, I keep my answers as light, fun, and superficial as possible. "Yeah. There isn't much of an age gap between Megs and me, so people often confused us for fraternal twins."

"You guys sound close," he observes in between bites.

"As annoying as she is, we are ridiculously close."

"I think I would've liked having a sibling." He flicks his gaze up at me, an apology shining in his deep green eyes.

Even though his childhood sounds like hell, it's still a part of him. It can't be magically erased, or disregarded like it didn't shape him into the man he is today, and I shouldn't expect him to hide his thoughts because I may become unhinged like a madman.

Anybody can see he has the most honest and pure heart to ever exist, and to be reduced to a label by your own parents is anything but fair. And if I focus on the way they mistreated him, I'm going to miss out on the story that's written between the lines.

"You don't have to censor yourself on my account," I tell

him, even though I had planned to do the same thing. "I'll listen to anything you have to say."

His body rises and falls in relief, and I feel the tension sliding off and away from both of us. Our waitress arrives with both servings of steak and the smell of the meat mixed with the portobello sauce sends my stomach into a frenzy.

"This smells amazing," Elijah compliments, echoing my own thoughts.

His focus is on the mouth-watering meal, while I wait, watching, wanting to see his face when he takes the first bite.

His eyes close upon contact and an erection inducing moan sounds from the back of his throat. "God, you really weren't kidding. This is fucking life changing."

Pleased with myself, I dig into my own plate, while he continues to murmur sweet nothings after every mouthful.

"If I lived this close, I would be here every day ordering this," he states. "We absolutely have to come back here."

A rose-colored flush works its way up his neck, passes his ears, and covers his face. I don't acknowledge that it may have been a slip, but rather hope to God it wasn't. "We definitely should. Maybe when you're out exploring the city, we can squeeze it in." My reaction seems to normalize our exchange, slowly shifting the night back to its original mood. "There's some really good places to eat around here, perfect for someone who is too lazy to cook."

"So, you're not a good cook?" he queries.

"I'm not good or bad. I can follow a recipe like it's nobody's business, but I don't actually like doing it. It's depressing cooking for one."

"And eating alone isn't?"

"It seems like that should faze me, but it doesn't. Eating is enjoyable, but putting in all that effort without having someone to show it off to?" I shake my head. "I'm not built for that." Setting my fork down, I take a quick swig of my beer. "What about you? Do you cook?"

"Does pasta and ready bought sauce count?"

"Look on the bright side, at least you can keep yourself alive."

"It definitely helps. There's only so much cafeteria food one can stomach." I make a face at the mention of the university's shitty menu, and Elijah laughs. "It's a small price to pay to almost eat for free."

"The joys of being a student," I muse.

"I just keep reminding myself it's a rite of passage and every other person attending is in the same boat."

"Do you have a job?"

"I haven't been actively looking for one just yet. I've been a bit sidetracked lately, but it has been in the back of my mind." He takes a small sip of his seltzer. "I don't want to get too busy now that I have the research project, but I don't like any free time either. And I want to add cash to my savings for a rainy day."

"Who doesn't like free time?"

"You sound like Aiden," he says flippantly. "It's just a habit I can't seem to grow out of. I work harder and better when I know I have a deadline, or limited hours. There's just something so rewarding about putting yourself under that much pressure, and then succeeding."

"And if you don't? What would you've done if you burnt out and didn't get into King? What was your contingency plan?"

He scoffs, and a cocky smile I've never seen on his face before appears. "I didn't have one."

"What do you mean?"

"Firstly, I did nothing else but study and work in high

school. All day, every day. Secondly, if you give yourself a fall-back option, then you're increasing the chances of failing. You're subconsciously giving yourself a buffer."

I contemplate his theory. "Do you really believe that?"

"It hasn't steered me wrong yet." Placing the fork down on his now empty plate, he reaches for the napkin and swiftly wipes his mouth. "Honestly, without killing the mood, it didn't matter if I didn't get into King. I was getting the fuck out of dodge no matter what."

Curiosity plagues me, knowing that everything about him is tied to his past, and talking about it is the only way I'll know more about him. "So you're never going back?"

"If hell freezes over, sure. People like them are never going to change, and neither am I, so it's a safe bet that I'll leave King and go wherever the wind takes me."

His words are so matter of fact and optimistic, and if he hadn't had that mini meltdown earlier, I would've believed he'd managed to leave that world behind and come out unscathed. But now I know it isn't true. I couldn't imagine any child coping with the rejection of their parents, especially when they refuse to see you for *everything* that you are; knowing it's someone as pure and honest as Elijah is heartbreaking.

Not wanting to risk getting into it again about his family, I change the subject. "How's the research project coming along? Did you guys meet up while I was away?"

"We did," he answers enthusiastically. "We met up once last week, and set up our schedules for the rest of the semester. They really are a great bunch of people."

"I think I picked well," I say with a smirk.

"It's kind of crazy to be a part of it all, to be honest." His eyes sparkle with wonder and excitement. "It's challenging, but it's also something we can definitely accomplish. You were right, you know?"

"I usually am," I joke. "But I don't know what you're talking about."

"It is a once in a lifetime opportunity." He leans over and carefully takes my hand. "Turning it down would've been one of my biggest regrets, so thank you for not giving up on me."

"I had some selfish motives," I admit.

"The end result was still the same."

His thumbs trace circles over the tops of my hands, and the absent-minded gesture is unexpectedly settling.

"You deserve to be there," I reassure him. "And if I have to remind you every now and then, I don't mind."

A deep masculine voice interrupts us. "Gabby has just stepped out on her break," the older looking man informs, referring to our original server. "Would you like some more time to look at the dessert menu?"

Elijah and I continue to watch one another, our hands still entwined, neither of us rushing to let go. If he wanted dessert, I would stay for him, but right now I want him alone and all to myself.

"We won't be getting anything else," Elijah advises, while still holding my gaze. "Is that okay?"

I look up to the waiter who seems uninterested and impatient with us. "Can we have the bill, please?"

Nodding, he begins to clear the table of our plates. "I'll be right back."

Elijah removes his hands from mine and reaches for his back pocket. I reach my hand out to stop him. "Please, let me."

He shakes his head. "Not going to happen."

"I thought you said it was a date," I argue.

"You know very well me calling it that was an embarrassing fuck up, and you and I can't date."

"Humor me," I deadpan.

Just as the waiter returns and hands me the leather check holder, Elijah shifts back in his seat, relenting.

Throwing down a few bills, I close the check holder and hand it back. "Thank you."

I stand up and Elijah follows. Together, we head out of the restaurant, my body close behind his, my hand comfortable on the small of his back.

Outside is a lot busier than when we arrived, the street lights shining on all the couples and families who are now enjoying the bustling streets. Filled with well-lit restaurants, cozy cafés, and an array of specialty stores; it's the perfect invitation for a quaint night out.

"Can we go back to your place?" he asks, turning around and stopping me in my tracks.

"You don't want to walk around, find something for dessert?"

He nervously shakes his head, and selfishly I bask in the fact that he too wants to be alone. His hands land on my biceps. "I think we could use some alone time."

Gripping his hips, I pull him a little closer to me. "You know there's no bed there."

He rolls his eyes at me, but the salacious smirk on his face says otherwise. "We don't need a bed to talk."

I narrow my eyes at him. "You only want to talk?"

"You sound surprised."

"I'm kind of impressed that you can resist all this," I joke, my hand gesturing up and down my body.

He moves his mouth to my ear and whispers. "It's hard. Always hard."

I squeeze his waist tighter, and a light chuckle leaves his

mouth. "Don't doubt that I want you, but I need to apologize for earlier first."

"What?" I rear my head back to get a better look at him. "There's nothing to apologize for. I already did that; I was the one out of line."

"Maybe, but I gave you reason to be."

"I don't—"

"I just want the chance to explain myself."

Acknowledging that this is something he feels compelled to do, I don't argue with his request. "Can we at least stop at the liquor store to get some drinks? The fridge is empty and it sounds like we might need them."

"You mean you might need it," he quips. "I think you're making a big deal out of nothing. It's just talking."

"I'll have you know," my voice turns low and husky, "there's no such thing as 'just talking.'" I sweep his hair back off his face. "Talking is the most underrated form of foreplay."

"Is that so?" His eyes darken with the question. "I think you're going to have to prove it to me."

"Is that a challenge?"

"I'm just saying," he teases. "I'm not going to believe anything until you prove it."

"You don't know what you're asking."

"Try me." He presses his mouth to the corner of my lips, testing my resolve.

Releasing his hips, I take hold of his hand and lead him across the road. We walk in a hurried silence, our destination consuming our thoughts. He chooses to stand outside while I go in and get a bottle of sauvignon blanc and a six pack of beer, because the threat of getting caught and losing my job isn't enough, let's just add trying to coerce a minor into drinking alcohol to my transgressions.

With one hand holding the six pack, and the other clutching the wine to my chest, I step out to find Elijah on his phone.

"Yeah, man, I'm sure," he says to whoever is on the other end of the phone. "You and Callie go. I don't know what time I'll be back." As he's listening, his eyes watch me walk to him, flicking his focus between me and my full hands, he reaches for the wine and takes it off me. "Okay, I'll see you both later."

I don't ask who it is, because it's both none of my business and I don't want him confirming my suspicions.

"It was Aiden," he reveals as we start walking again.

"You don't have to tell me."

"I wanted to."

I tighten my hold on the beer, channeling my irritation somewhere much more appropriate than at Elijah. I'm torn between wanting to know, regardless of my right to it, and never wanting to hear that fucker's name again when we're together.

His shoulders rub against mine as we walk; his touch dissolving the tension.

"Can I ask you something?" I say.

"Of course."

"Why do you tell me?" I take a deep breath. "The kiss? The birthday plans? The phone call?"

"Can I answer when we get inside?"

His need to delay his response keeps us in silence, neither of us knowing how to move on to more trivial conversation.

He keeps himself close to me and the contact makes me feel less on edge about whatever it is he wants to divulge. Every step takes us further down this path of the unknown, where the company becomes more appealing and more seductive. Where the risk is high, but the reward, against all odds, feels great.

When we make it to the front of my place, the anticipation of being alone and vulnerable is palpable. As soon as we pass the threshold, Elijah follows me through the living room and into the kitchen. Standing on either side of the counter, I place the six pack on the top and he sits the wine beside it.

"How do you want this to go?" I blurt out, wanting to avoid any form of silence.

Grabbing a bottle of beer, he twists it open and hands it to me. "Something to keep you company."

Surprised, I take it and lift it to my mouth for a swig. "You buttering me up?"

"More like I'm trying not to scare you away."

14

ELIJAH

I try to keep my composure calm and neutral, despite the way my heart rattles inside my chest. When talking with Cole, I realized how difficult it is to tell him about myself without rehashing the past. Physically I've left it behind; mentally I'm better off away from there. But if I want Cole to know more about me, the ugly stuff is going to have to come out too.

He walks around the counter, his face unreadable. He juts his chin out to the seating area, and together we make our way to the large three-seater. Spreading ourselves comfortably on the couch, we sit on either side, our backs leaning against the arm rests. My body faces his, my arm resting on the back of the couch, and one of my legs bent and resting on the cushion. "The reason I always tell you about Aiden," I start. "Is because he and Callie are not just the first, but the only friends I've had in a little over two years."

Pity flashes in his eyes, passing just as quickly as it came. "I know you know my parents didn't approve of my sexuality. When they found out..."

Swallowing hard, the words involuntarily stop, my voice trailing off as the memory I often keep in its own little box reappears.

I close my eyes and my father's expression of disgust sears itself onto the back of my lids. The way his face morphed;, the different shades of color that matched the change in his mood. It started as a blush, bloomed into crimson, and then his pale skin settled into a chilling blood-red hue. The physical transformation was scary. But it wasn't until my shocked brain registered the words of hate spewing out of his mouth that I realized, my world as I knew it would never be the same again.

"I didn't want to risk anyone looking at me like that ever again," I say before opening up my eyes. "So I stopped putting myself in situations where I would have to interact with people."

Keeping his features stoic, it's easy to believe this is just another run of the mill story he's listening to, but it's the way his eyes soften while staring at me that tells me this is just as hard to hear as it is to tell.

"How did they find out?" he asks.

A humorless chuckle leaves my mouth. "I got caught with my hands down a guy's pants behind church."

His eyes widen in shock.

"His hands may have also been full. With my dick." The visual is enough to have us both laughing and lightening up the mood. "We'd just finished jerking each other off," I explain. "Come was all over our hands. It was fucking messy." The trip down memory lane continues as I remember how it all felt, right before my father caught us. Not just the high from the orgasm, but the complete elation of being able to finally share something so intimate with someone.

"Fuck," Cole interrupts with a chuckle. "I think that would've even scarred my mom, and I've always been out."

Fiddling with the tassels on a nearby pillow cushion, I nervously ask, "What was it like not having to come out?"

Cole shifts, straightening his spine. "It doesn't feel right talking about it."

"Please," I beg. He exhales in defeat, and I give him a stern look. "And don't downplay it."

"I always knew I was gay, I just never realized I was different." He takes a long pull of his beer. "My sister would talk about the crushes she had, and naturally I did too. They were always guys and my parents never flinched."

"Did you grow up around anyone who was gay?"

"No." He shakes his head. "Not anyone close enough to explain how normal it felt, or how comfortable it was."

Sinking back into the chair, I picture a younger, but still confident Cole. "That explains a lot."

He tips his head to the side, narrowing his eyebrows at me. "What do you mean?"

"You're comfortable in your own skin. It's a good look on anyone." He winces like I've insulted him, and immediately I reach for him, placing a hand on his knee. "My upbringing doesn't mean I can't be happy for people who didn't have it like me. What you had is the way it should be."

Standing up, I break the tension and surprise myself. "Can I have a beer?"

Cole jerks up from his seat. "Please, let me get it."

Not wanting to argue, I plop myself back down and wait. In less than a minute he returns, handing me the cold drink.

Lifting the beer to my mouth, I take—what I'm sure is— a pathetic looking sip of the beverage.

I don't swallow it straight away, letting the small amount of liquid sit in my mouth before I find the courage to drain it down my throat. Nothing at all like I expect it to be, the crisp mixture of malt and hops leaves an odd but not unpleasant aftertaste. Quickly, I take another swig and I feel all my senses beginning to accommodate the taste.

Bringing the bottle down, I inspect the ingredients. "I could get used to this."

"That's all I need," Cole jokes. "To turn you into an underage drinker."

"It's college." Raising my bottle, I reach out to him in the universal signal for cheers. The glass of our bottles clinks ceremoniously. "It's inevitable."

Simultaneously, we take another pull before he asks, "So, your family are churchgoers?"

Isn't that the understatement of the year.

"My dad is the well-revered pastor of Kent County Baptist Church."

"Holy shit," he breathes out, understanding written all over his face. "I guess that explains a lot." He leans back, making himself more comfortable. "What was it like growing up? Before the incident, I mean."

"Honestly, it wasn't that bad. Naturally, we were ruled by religion, but it never really felt like a problem; until it was." I hook my arm back over the couch. "I couldn't fault my upbringing up until then. My father was strict, but it came with the territory. And I didn't really have any need to disobey him."

No longer angry at how it all turned out, I can't help but think back on it with overwhelming sadness. I don't miss the family I left behind. There's no connection to the family we became, just a deep sense of nostalgia for the family that we were.

"And after the incident?"

"My dad pretty much disowned me," I say, my voice

thick with emotion. "He did everything but say those exact words to my face." Lowering my gaze, I start picking at the wet beer label, too raw to look at Cole. "I knew his stance on homosexuality when a family from his congregation had come seeking advice about their son, but I was too young to put all the pieces together.

"It wasn't until my friends started talking to me about girls they liked that I started acknowledging the difference. It was a constant stream of boob talk. Who got them over the summer, whose were bigger. And I would sit there wondering how the fuck did I not notice?

"It was then I let myself really focus on what it was I was actually paying attention to." I look up at Cole, who's watching me intently. I feel my cheeks flush, a little embarrassed that I'm telling the man I'm ridiculously attracted to about how I fumbled through high school. "That's when I realized I wasn't noticing Jackie's tits, because I was too busy drooling over Peter's arms."

A smug smile tugs at his lips. "And, how were they?"

Grabbing the cushion between us, I playfully throw it at him. "Shut up, smart-ass."

"You know I'm joking." He clutches the pillow to his chest. "Keep talking about Peter's arms."

I give a long, loud, teasing sigh, feeling a little more comfortable with every detail that slips past my lips. "They were the best thing this fourteen-year-old had ever seen. I would think of him at night and my dick would get hard at the thought. My brain hadn't even caught up to my body back then, just the sight of him was enough. I didn't even need to imagine us doing anything together for me to blow my load."

"I remember those days." He chuckles. "And the guy you got caught with?"

"Alex. His name was Alex," I say wistfully. "He was new to church. His family moved from Oregon, and I remember watching them walk in to the sermon late, nervous but still determined to attend." I rub a hand over my chest, the hurt and loss of Alex as strong as ever. "His mom looked like a Stepford wife and his father was a dead ringer for the dad in the *Brady Bunch*."

"That show is almost a little too old for me," he interrupts. "How do you know about the *Brady Bunch*?"

"Really, Cole? My knowledge of TV shows isn't what's important here."

"Of course," he says sarcastically. "Please, let's get back to reminiscing about your first love, Alex."

I throw a hand over my mouth to stifle the laugh threatening to come out. "Are you really jealous of a seventeen-year-old boy?"

"This is your storytime," he says gruffly. "We can talk about all the weird shit I feel around you another time." He raises the beer to his lips, his eyes boring into mine as he takes a long pull of his drink. I watch the way his mouth purses around the bottle, the way the cords in his neck tense while he swallows, and imagine him on his knees ready for me. Every part of me is enamored with every little move he makes, turning it all into my own secret fantasies. "Are you going to stop staring at me?"

I shake my head, trying to rid myself of my stupor.

"Come on," he cajoles. "I really do want to know the rest of this story."

"Okay," I huff. "But I'm going to turn around and close my eyes."

"So you can think of Alex?" he teases.

I look down at my now visible erection and back up at Cole. "This isn't for Alex."

Licking his lips, he gives me the sexiest wink. "You do you, baby."

I flip him off and angle my body away from his. Sitting upright, I rest both feet on the ground, let my head fall to the back of the couch, and close my eyes.

After a few calculated breaths, I feel myself relax and dive right back into the retelling of the first time I saw Alex.

"His parents were proper in every sense of the word," I continue from where I left off. "But not him. He was dressed from head to toe in black. It was a cross between emo and grunge, but all the churchgoers insisted he worshipped Satan." I chuckle at the memory. "He loved that. He didn't care what anyone thought, and that's what made him irresistible. His confidence was what lured me in. I wanted to be *exactly* like him.

"We started hanging and it was no longer Peter I was imagining at night anymore. Everything changed and I felt my admiration turn into adoration." Opening my eyes, I turn to look at Cole, who's sitting still, hanging on my every word. "I was never going to make a move. Instead, I lied my way through conversations about girls, thinking it's what I was supposed to say. It wasn't until I went to a winter dance with this girl named Jasmine that I realized pretending was no longer an option. She kissed me, and it was horrible. It felt wrong on every level. I wasn't comfortable lying to anyone, but I was even more uncomfortable at the thought of using people to cover up my secret."

Cole's teeth rake over his bottom lip in thought. "And Alex, he just hung around, waiting for you to come out?"

"Well, we were friends first," I explain. "That part always felt natural, but I think he was more perceptive than I realized. Patient too. Maybe because he was a year older than me, or because he knew what it was like.

"Or maybe, just like with you, even when I thought I was doing a great job hiding my feelings, I really was wearing them on my face for all to see."

Cole's face lights up, interest and desire swimming in his gray eyes. He reaches for my hand and I let him take it. The small squeeze is intimate. Comforting and somewhat encouraging, so that I can let all the ugly out, and still sit here, at ease, with him.

"So. after the blunder of the dance, he started brushing up against me more, pushing the boundaries of my personal space, until I knew for sure I wasn't imagining it. Whatever it was between us became unavoidable."

I link my fingers with Cole's and tug him closer. He places the beer he's been gripping tightly onto a nearby table and shifts right beside me.

"I wanted to know," I say, my voice low, my breath shaky. "If I was going to risk my whole world and everything I knew by coming out, I wanted to know for sure that I was gay.

"So, I took the risk. I asked him if he had a girlfriend in Oregon, knowing that Alex would never lie to me. He'd made his stance on honesty so clear." I tilt my head while looking at Cole. "God, I'm stupid." He stares at me in confusion. "Alex used to go on and on about being truthful. He would say you've got nothing if you can't be one hundred percent with your friends. I just realized he was warming me up to tell him the whole time.

"So when he said 'Elijah, I'm into boys,' I could've cried from relief."

With Alex I wasn't an outcast, I wasn't different, and I wasn't hiding. His push for honesty saved my life in ways I didn't realize until after our time together ended. The push and shove he gave me, no matter what the end result was, has been my driving force for as long as I can remember. I didn't want to be someone Alex was disappointed in.

"Then nothing could hold us back. Friendship turned into flirting and then one day I finally got to touch him." Realizing I'm beginning to ramble, I pull away from Cole and bury my head in my hands. "This is awkward, isn't it? I'm sorry if this is awkward. I'm getting carried away. I haven't told anyone any of this. *Ever*. I didn't realize how good it would feel to let it all out."

He plucks my hands off my face and softly presses his palms on both my cheeks.

"I love hearing you talk. Getting to know more about you makes me feel like the luckiest guy in the world. I know you don't open up to many people, and I'm beginning to understand the reasons why." He leans in and kisses the corner of my mouth. "Thank you."

Gripping his wrists, I hold him in place, just staring with amazement that this, right now, is my life. My terms. My story. My version.

"So, that's how you guys ended up behind the church?" he asks, surprising me.

"You really want me to keep talking?"

He slides his hands out of my grip and moves them into his lap. "More than anything."

"Why the distance?" I query, feeling the loss of him immediately.

"Don't look at me like I just kicked your puppy. I'm doing the right thing here."

I look at him expectantly. "I want to give you and your story the respect it deserves. If this is your first time telling it, I don't want my dick to get in the way."

Acknowledging that talking about this has me feeling lighter than I could've ever anticipated, I don't argue. "Fine,"

I huff, scooting back to my side of the couch. "It was supposed to be an extended service with some guest speaker. The day we got caught," I remind him, in case he's forgotten where we left off. "We thought we had all the time in the world. But what I didn't account for was that my dad would notice I wasn't there. And when the other person took the lectern, of course, he came out to see where I was."

As if he's reliving the experience with me, Cole's face morphs into genuine panic.

"What happened after?"

"My father screamed at me till he couldn't physically scream anymore."

"I'm fucking sorry you ever had to deal with that."

I let his empathy soothe me. "You know, that was never the part that hurt the most," I confess. "It was after.

"He stopped looking at me, talking to me; stopped doing things I didn't even realize he'd done in the past, like pat me on the back if he was proud of me or hug me like a father does." Frozen out and left all alone, for the first time I voice out loud just how much that killed me. "He took all the things a child needs to flourish, and he purposefully waited, watching until I wilted."

It's at this point, where the distance he was so determined to keep becomes too much for Cole. He drags me into his lap, wrapping me up, cocooning me in his arms.

"You didn't wilt," he whispers into my ear.

My eyes sting and my throat closes up as I try to hold back the threat of tears. After years of practicing and perfecting how to shut down my emotions, they're on overdrive, filling me up to the brim.

"Elijah." He pulls back, his glossy eyes staring at me with so much conviction. "You were not born to wilt."

The words are like a balm, soothing my freshly opened

wounds. Physically unable to respond, I reach for the collar of his shirt and pull us closer together. I take his mouth in a greedy exchange of gratitude and desire.

"No more talking," I whisper against his lips.

"No more talking," he agrees. "I know what you really need."

Pretty sure his mouth on me is the only thing I need right now, I look at him quizzically. He offers me a knowing smile. "Trust me."

Placing his open hands on my chest, he pushes me back onto the couch. Just as I think he's about to lay himself on top of me, he surprises me by squeezing his big frame into the small gap between my body and the back of the couch.

He maneuvers himself to his side, propping himself up on his elbow. "Come here." He wraps an arm around my torso and shifts me into him, my back curved to his front. Peppering kisses up and down the column of my neck, he guides our heads down to rest on the pillows.

Tucking myself into him, he hugs me. Tight. Firm. It's illogical that this could feel just as good as kissing, but feeling safe and wanted, in Cole's arms, does more for me than I could ever imagine. I can't remember the last time someone just held me.

I needed this. And he knew.

My breath hitches, small gasps of air tearing through the thick waves of emotion. I grip his arms and squeeze him to me, trying to convey how I feel.

I feel his warm breath on my neck and the rise and fall of his body with each inhale and exhale. The moment is serene, peace that I never knew washing over me.

I want to look at him. I want to thank him, but I'm too overwhelmed. Sensing it, he begins grazing his fingertips up and down my forearm, calming down my erratic heartbeat.

"What happened to Alex?" he asks.

"Nothing." I remember how my father tried to embarrass his parents about their son's sexuality, but his parents had his back. They supported their child in all the ways parents are expected to. They told my father if he couldn't be accepting of the people in his congregation, then they wouldn't be a part of it. My dad threw the scriptures at them, and they didn't budge. They told him how they raised their son was none of his business. I envied Alex. "They ended up leaving. Moving away."

"And you never stayed in contact?"

"No," I whisper. "I never even got to say goodbye."

15

COLE

Every word brought a new bout of emotions. Every part of me felt like it'd been dragged through the ringer, trying to fathom how the people who are supposed to love you unconditionally, could be so callous and cruel. It was obvious they'd left scars, their silent and degrading form of punishment infiltrating every decision he'd ever made. It was breaking my heart.

I'd never been more grateful for the love my own parents showered me in than in this moment.

I held on to him, because I needed the comfort. We both did. I needed to erase the look of loneliness off of his face. Try and erase his feelings of inadequacy, and work to process the unforgivable way his parents made him suffer. Especially his father.

Solitude was his only friend, and it pained me. It stoked the protective desire that formed for him from the moment I met him, threatening to engulf me in flames. I couldn't explain the draw or the reasons, but I wanted to keep him safe by my side and hide him away from every little thing that could hurt him.

I move my hand from around his waist and begin to lazily stroke his hair. The thin, soft strands slip through my fingers easier than the styled look should allow.

"I thought my mom would try and stick up for me, you know?" he blurts out, surprising me. Now that he's started talking about his past, it's like he can't stop. "Turns out the loyalty she had to him far outweighed whatever it was she felt for me."

Baffled by how he was repeatedly let down, I let my touch do the talking, hoping he can interpret it for what it is. *I'm here, baby. I'm listening.*

"She was the buffer between us," he finishes. "In her world, she probably thinks she's making the effort, doing the right thing. It's obvious I'll always be the one in the wrong, especially when I'm constantly refusing her poor attempts at communication." He pushes his body further back, allowing himself to be completely comfortable in my hold. "But it felt like such a consolation prize you know? She never once told him he was wrong. Keeping the peace was more important than sticking up for me, and in my eyes she's just as to blame as he is."

"Do you still speak to her now that you've left?"

"She calls," he says with a sigh. "I answer her scripted questions about school and then I rush her into saying goodbye. Rinse and repeat."

I press my mouth to the back of his ear and whisper, "I'm sorry, Elijah."

"Thank you." He grabs my hand and brings it to his lips, kissing it.

We sit in a comfortable, contemplative silence. Something that I've never done with anyone, yet with Elijah it feels so natural and is becoming so easy.

I want every piece of his body, but it's the odd sense of contentment I feel at having him in my arms that surprises me more.

I move my mouth down his neck, leaving soft kisses in my wake. Back up his jaw and settling on his cheek, everything about him is smooth and warm. Turning toward me, he shifts so he's now laying on his back, face up, deep green eyes boring into mine.

His memories from earlier play on a loop, and as natural and necessary as hugging him felt, so does the next thing I'm about to do. I lightly rub at the worry lines in between his eyebrows with my fingers before moving them down the bridge of his nose and then resting them at the tip. I then trace the shape of his pale pink lips; pouty and perfect.

He's watching me with wonder and curiosity, while I take mental notes of every inch of his beautiful face. Reading my mind, he tilts his head up as I lower my mouth to his.

My lips move, slow and tentative, giving this moment the pace it deserves. Despite the desperation that pulses through me, I caress my tongue against his with the utmost reverence. Tasting him. Enjoying him.

"How about we play a little game of catch up?" I ask, my voice hoarse. "Do some things you never got the chance to."

"Like make out?" he jokes, the teasing smirk a contradiction to his eager eyes.

Answering him, I fuse my mouth to his, the distance becoming harder and harder to bear. There isn't the rush, or the usual frenzy that accompanies most of our kisses. Timing and place are not an issue. I kiss him knowing the regret should come but never will. Some crazy part of me wants to try to recreate his youth and give him the experiences he was denied, the touch he was refused. With every stroke of my tongue, I make it my mission to give him all the things he's missed out on. My need to make him feel more than he's allowed himself, more than he's been given, becomes my absolute priority.

He deepens the kiss, one hand settles on my ribs and the other grips my hip, guiding me over him. Putting all my weight on my forearms, I hover, trying to maintain some sort of restraint. "Why are you so far away?" he asks before tauntingly raising his hips, grazing his hard dick against mine.

I take a sharp breath, glaring at him.

"What?" he asks innocently. "Isn't this my teenage fantasy?"

"You want to play it like that do you?" Elijah shrugs, like he's got no idea what I'm talking about. "I'll have you know, before we take it any further, I was trying to keep this some-what G-rated."

I lower myself onto him, giving him all my weight. "You know? Things people usually do before hitting third base."

"But third base was so much fun," he teases, referring to our time in my office. He wiggles underneath me, bringing his eager cock to my attention. "You know, I've never had someone lie down on top of me."

His eyes twinkle with seductive mischief, his face smug as all fuck. I guess two can play this game. "Tell me what else you've never done."

"I'm sure you can guess," he responds, his voice lacking the confidence from earlier.

"Doesn't mean you haven't thought about it, right?" I shamelessly grind my cock into his, trying to keep him from following his insecurities into his own head. "Tell me. When you're alone at night, in your bed, what it is that gets you hard?"

A slight tremor ripples through him, regardless of the trepidation written all over his face. Confused, he ignores the attraction and gives in to the worry, lowering his eyes and shying away from me. I take hold of his chin and steer his focus back to me.

"Don't do that with me." My voice is soft, but there's no mistaking it's an order. With every hesitant breath, his body rises and falls beneath mine. "Don't hide away because you think the things you have to say are embarrassing." I press my lips to his mouth, hoping to relax him. "I know what's going on in that brain of yours," I say, kissing his jawline. "And it has no place here. I want to know *every single thing*."

Peering back up at him, I see the return of desire in his eyes. Right where I want him, I lower my mouth back into the crook of his neck, giving his collarbone a soft bite. "Want me to go first?" I lick up the side of his neck until my mouth sits at his ear. "Want to know how everything about you gets me hard? Want to know how I lay in bed, every night, replaying the image of you on your knees and the sound of you gagging on my cock?"

Shaky hands skim over my sides and settle on my jean-covered ass cheeks. I feel his shaft lengthen underneath mine, and instinctively I press into him.

"That innocence that you're so quick to get rid of," I continue. "Fuck. That's the sexiest thing about you. It drives me fucking crazy how untainted you are." His breath hitches. "You're a fucking prize, Elijah."

My confessions are heavy and unfiltered, but nothing about them is untrue. With my head still buried in his neck, I roll my hips into his, slowly sliding my rock-hard cock against his. Squeezing my cheeks, he guides me into his preferred pace. Up and down, the friction is deliciously maddening. Usually the pace would kill me, slow and steady not being my usual flavor. But with Elijah, the journey is just as fun as the destination.

Wanting to see his face, I raise my head to his. "You feel really good underneath me."

A strained laugh leaves his mouth. "You feel really good on top of me."

"You okay?" I ask, checking in with him. As good as it feels, I refuse to let my body run the whole show. I don't want any regrets with Elijah, or to run the risk of railroading him into anything he isn't ready for.

Smashing his mouth to mine, he gives me the only answer I really wanted to hear. His choice to be in this moment with me has me wading into a pool of relief. Our tongues battle for dominance, while our bodies grind and rut in a flawlessly choreographed dance, moving in a perfect rhythm.

We rock against one another and I'm reminded just how sexy good old-fashioned dry humping can be. Every part of me loving the closeness, the yearning, the opportunity to fascinate him with the simple things.

Clumsy hands find my shirt as Elijah breathlessly tries to work out the buttons. Pulling myself away from his mouth, I rise on my forearms and give him all the access he needs.

Not wanting to rush him, I stay perfectly still, watching his face bunch up in concentration as he undoes each one with determined precision.

When he's done, warm, eager hands splay themselves across my chest, feeling my skin. It's one of the most basic exchanges of human touch, but with Elijah it feels like so much more, like a privilege to be the one to give him things everyone else I know has taken for granted.

"Let me see you," he breathes out, voice rough and needy. I move back on my knees, my shirt open, my dick straining against the zipper of my pants.

Shrugging out of my shirt, I watch Elijah's senses go into overdrive. His eyes roam over my body, leaving lashings of heat everywhere he lingers. "What do you want, baby?" I coax.

Sitting up on his forearms, his hand reaches for my stomach. Fingers lingering around my navel, skimming down my happy trail on the way to my zipper, which he slowly lowers. "I think about you like this," he rasps. "Seeing your skin. Imagining you naked. It's all I see. All the time."

"What else?" I help us both out by dragging my cock out of my boxers. I watch him watching me with his dark eyes and hooded lids, and I thicken in my own hand.

"Fuck," he groans before falling back onto the couch. Gripping his erection, he moans with pained delight. "I'm so fucking hard right now."

"My turn," I order, my gaze flicking between his face and his crotch. His eyes glaze over, and his tongue peeks out, wetting his parted lips. "I know you heard me. Dick. Out."

I watch his chest heave, inhaling deeply, exhaling loudly. Raising his hips, he pushes his clothes over his ass and down to his knees. Freeing his cock, it now rests on his stomach, deliciously hard and long.

Eyes on the prize, I tease him, stroking myself for both our pleasure. "Want this?" I taunt.

"You're loving this aren't you?"

Showing him just how much, I grip the waistband of his

chinos and drag them down the length of his lean legs. Throwing them on the floor, I quickly make short work of my own pants and climb back over him.

Naked, I lean over to kiss him. He presses his palm to my chest. "Wait."

Worried that my birthday suit is a little too much for him to handle, I cautiously pull back. Surprising me, he tugs his white shirt over his head and throws it to the floor.

Wow.

Whether it's the words he gives me, or the clothes he's taking off, every single layer is more beautiful than the one before. Wrapped up in porcelain, his body is lean but delicate. Sturdy, yet graceful. Every line, dip, and curve, showing off his perfectly sculpted exterior. His guard. His protection. His barrier between the world and his unblemished, sinless center.

My eyes continue to rake down his body, stopping at his strained erection. Beads of pre-come decorate his crown, his lechery on beautiful display.

Starting with his lips, I meld myself to him. Mouth to mouth. Skin to skin. Cock to cock.

He's dissolving under my touch, his body languid, his muscles loose. Together we sink into the plush couch, our bodies close, my skin painted over his.

"You feel so fucking perfect underneath me," I whisper against his lips. "I can feel your cock leaking on me."

Elijah Williams ticks all my boxes, feeding my appetite, inserting himself in all my future fantasies. This gorgeous, irresistible, young man is slowly becoming everything I didn't know I wanted, and everything I had no plans of letting go of.

Fingers skim down my spine. They ghost along my

crease and work their way up the same way they came, and back again. Shivering under his touch, I deepen the kiss, trying to channel the wayward currents racing through my body.

I lick the inside of his mouth, tasting his want, filling his need. Firm hands grip my ass, guiding me up and down, setting our new pace.

Hesitation and caution no longer standing between us, I thrust my tongue further into his mouth, wanting unfettered access to him. Placing my hands on his shoulder, I push myself up enough that I'm staring down at him, our hips still connected.

Desperate and thirsty eyes look up at me before focusing back to where my slick shaft glides along his. Needing more friction, I wrap a tentative hand around us, squeezing us together and jerking us off.

His short breaths echo off the walls the faster my hand moves.

"You like watching?" I goad. "See how hard and messy we are."

His dick jerks in my hand, answering me, and I lower my head to take his mouth with mine. Needing more, I breach his lips and suck on his tongue. I make my way across to his jaw and move down his neck, my mouth skating past his collarbone and stopping at his nipples.

Lightly, I graze my teeth over them before slowly licking and biting them. A soft moan escapes Elijah's mouth as I blow hot air on his wet, frigid nipple. He arches as my tongue continues to tease him and my hand continues to stroke him.

"Let me see us again," he pants. "I want to watch us fuck your fist."

The mention of an 'us' makes my dick ache in gratification.

As I lift myself off him, I steal one last kiss before
allowing my eyes to dart to where we're touching. Mesmerized by the action, Elijah adds his hand to mine around our
shafts, our fingers grazing as we watch our dicks buck into
our fists.

Fast and frenzied, we both move at a sloppy and manic
pace. I rut against him, my heavy balls repeatedly pressing
into his.

We're a sight to behold, both of us in a trance. An unfiltered and explicit depiction of desire. I shift my gaze to him,
quick enough to witness the way he's losing control. His face
is a mashup of agony and euphoria, and I revel in it. We're
both standing on the precipice of restraint; needing to let go,
wanting to unload.

"Let go, baby," I coax. "Make a mess for me."

A beautiful whimper leaves his mouth at my instruction,
his body trembling as he spills himself into our hands and
onto his stomach. Chaotic but beautiful, my orgasm follows,
adding an extra layer to the seductive picture.

With one hand still holding us together, he throws an
arm over his head, hiding his face as he tries to regulate his
breathing.

Releasing my grip on us, I move away, sitting back on my
haunches. I wait for Elijah to look at me, wanting to make
sure he sees just how much I enjoyed what we just did. My
fingers swirl around and through the sticky, thick liquid on
his skin.

Slowly, his eyes come into view, just as I raise two coated
fingers and stick them into my mouth. There's no way to
differentiate which taste is whose and I love it. No beginning. No end. Just us.

I reach out and swipe at some more, but just as I'm about to bring them to my mouth, Elijah's hand circles my wrist, halting me.

Sitting up, he moves my hand to his mouth and opens wide for my fingers. Slipping them past his lips, he licks them the exact same way I remember him licking my cock.

"You're trying to kill me, aren't you?"

"I don't know what you're talking about," he says, before going in for another taste. "I just wanted to see what all the fuss was about."

"And did it live up to your expectations?"

"Even better."

Leaning back over his body, I give his mouth a quick, chaste kiss. "I'll be right back." Untangling myself from him, I walk into the kitchen and search for anything that can be used to clean us up.

I open and close drawers until I find one with a few dish towels. This will have to do. I run half of it under some warm water and head back to Elijah.

When I return, he's lying there, content and sated with his eyes closed. I use the wet cloth to wipe up the sticky mess that sits on his stomach. When I'm finished, I throw the towel on the coffee table.

"I'm not ready to put any clothes on just yet." I hold my hand out for him to take. "Want to shower with me?"

Together, we head to the stairs, naked and completely unfazed. As he takes each step up to the bathroom, I'm captivated by the bare sight of him.

He's with me, and he's comfortable in his own skin. It warms up every part of me to be able to witness him like this.

"Switch on the water and I'll search this place for towels, and maybe find some soap," I tell him.

The likelihood of there being anything around to dry us off later is very slim, but even if I have to fucking drip dry, I'm not giving it up. I may have had no intention of doing any of this with Elijah tonight, but I'll be damned if I'm not grabbing all the opportunities with both hands.

I return to the bathroom with my findings, but take a quick look under the sink for something to wash ourselves with.

Bingo. Thank you, universe.

Elijah's already in the shower. Standing under the spray, he hangs his head back and lets the water run over his face. My gaze follows the line of his profile, the tight cords that grace his arched neck, the array of droplets that run and land on every inch of his skin.

My eyes stop on the crucifix that sits still and proud in the middle of his chest. Stepping in the shower, I stand in front of him and hook my finger on the chain.

"Why do you wear this?" I ask, intrigued and confused.

He tips his head down to look at the necklace and then back up at me. "I know my dad's Baptist, but there's something about the symbolism of the cross that I love."

His answer is so matter-of-fact, nonchalant enough that I realize he's misunderstood the question.

"I don't mean like that," I clarify. "I mean, after everything you've been through. Why do *you* wear this?"

His calm and serene expression disappears as understanding settles over his features. I've said something wrong and I have no idea what it is.

"I said my relationship with my dad was bad, I never once said anything about my relationship with God."

"I'm sorry," I sputter. "I just assumed considering how your dad used religion to practically disown you—"

He puts his hand on my mouth, silencing me.

"This isn't up for discussion, Cole." His eyes are hard and his voice is firm. He's almost a stranger. "If you don't understand it," he continues. "That's fine, but I don't need to defend it."

16

ELIJAH

We're standing so close. Close enough that the usual heat between us should be getting ready to engulf us in flames. But it's cold. So cold. And no amount of scalding hot water will be able to warm me up.

Turning, I give him my back and reach to press down the water mixer. A long, strong arm moves around me, stopping me. "Don't. I didn't mean to upset you."

"I'm not upset," I respond defensively.

"Then what is it?" He places his hand over mine, dragging it down to my side, away from ending our time together. He laces his fingers with mine. "I want to understand it."

Squeezing his hand, I lean back into him, exhaustion creeping up on me. "I don't want to talk about it," I say, more deflated than defensive. "I think I've done enough talking tonight."

"Look at me, Elijah."

I feel small and confused, naive and strangely more inadequate in this moment than I have at any other point of our time together. I don't speak about religion and what it means to me. I study it because I'm fascinated with its history, with its transient nature in time, and the way it's been interpreted, translated, and delivered through centuries, but anything beyond that has been one of my best kept secrets.

Cole's reaction would be anyone's. Why give time to something that has no time for you?

I've fought with this myself. Struggled with it, but the deeper I delved, the more I found what I was looking for.

If people could find hate and judgement in God and His words, then I sure as fuck could twist it and choose to only see the beauty and the comfort that I was so desperately seeking.

Religion fueled my soul. My spirit. It became my savior, my refuge, my solace.

Loneliness isn't for the faint hearted; it left me heavy and bereft, and I latched on to anything that could help me rise above it.

I needed strength to survive and that's what it gave me.

Cole's patient breaths sound from behind me, soothing me, bringing me back to him. I didn't want every good thing to be a trigger for something bad. It seemed like it all went hand in hand. A tangled ball of emotions I just can't seem to work through. Every time I think I have one thing sorted, something else pops up.

I didn't want to do this with him again. I didn't want to ruin all the good moments we were having by dredging up shit from the past and giving weight to my insecurities. I didn't want to give him whiplash and have the ghost of my dad ruin this. That man has already taken so much from me and I wouldn't just knowingly hand him anything more.

Finally finding the strength to turn around, I face a wet and worried Cole. Letting my gaze run up and down his body, I take in the man that is my temptation, and possibly my salvation.

"I..." I start, but the words fail me. I don't know what it is I want to say to him. I want to fix it. Go back to that blissed out feeling I was relishing in only minutes ago. Is it always going to be like this? Such immeasurable highs, followed by extremely crushing lows?

Sensing my internal distress, Cole's big hands grip my face. His hold is tight and insistent.

"I'll take your lead when it comes to these things, okay?" He rubs his thumb across my wet lips. "You talk. You don't. I'm not going anywhere."

His words hold so much weight and I wonder if he knows what they do to me, how he's got me all tied up, feeling more than I ever thought I was capable of.

The warning bells still sound in my head, but their incessant ringing seems so far away. There's almost enough distance that every now and then I can forget they exist. I can forget that there is no happy ever after for Cole and me.

Our time together has been short. By all standards and expectations, it should be fleeting and insignificant, but with every passing moment, this is shaping up to be one of the most monumental experiences of my life.

If I'm supposed to walk away from him, consider it impossible. I can't turn away from Cole; the way his steel colored eyes are staring at me, makes me feel like it isn't an option for him either.

Everything has shifted, leaving me with only heart hurting options. Stay and hurt. Leave and hurt. My heart won't survive either choice.

He's not just my professor, he's the man who's changing my world. He's leaving marks on every part of me.

Holding on to his wrists, I get lost in his eyes, imagining

all the possibilities, while my mouth speaks the brutal truth. "I know this is going to end."

His eyes fall closed, like the words are just too much. It's heart-wrenching and twisted that I want the truth to be as hard for him as it is for me. "I don't know how or why or when. I just don't want to waste time with anything else but you and me." I lean into him and plant a surprise, soft kiss on his lips. "The important stuff."

We come together with grace and poise. Savoring. Prolonging. Holding off the frenzy, keeping the delirium we always find ourselves in when we touch, at bay.

He loosens his grip on my face, all the while still moving his mouth against mine. Our tongues tease, every stroke longer, deeper, and more meaningful than the one before. I wrap my arms around his neck. Resting my elbows on his shoulders, I run my fingers through his wet hair, pushing myself closer to him in all the ways I can.

Hands glide down, over my wet body. Settling on my ass, he begins to gently knead my flesh. I press myself into him, two hard cocks resting between us. Content, yet still so eager.

Kisses move down my neck, his mouth sucking at the skin on my shoulder. With his hands no longer touching me, a loud pop catches my attention.

Pulling back, I notice Cole is holding half an empty bottle of body wash, pouring the thick honey milk scented liquid into the palm of his hand.

"You found body wash?" I query.

"I was just as surprised as you are," he smirks. "Now let me get back to business."

Soapy hands start at my shoulders, lightly massaging me. Moving, they find their way to my chest. He takes my nipples between his thumbs and forefingers, rolling and tweaking.

Just like on the couch, I'm at his disposal. His to do whatever he wants to.

Sliding one hand down my stomach, he reaches for my waiting cock. Expertly, he begins pumping my dick, while his other hand continues teasing my nipple. The sensations cause my body to buzz under his touch.

I love the way he makes me feel. The want and need that rises higher with every move he makes.

"You like me touching you, don't you?" It's less of a question and more like a statement dressed in arrogance and seduction. I turn my head, both slightly embarrassed and wholly aroused by his words; he knows what he does to me.

Cupping the back of my neck, he brings his mouth close to my face and whispers in my ear, "You're going to have to do better than that, sweet boy. Tell me, do you like me touching you?"

"So much." My voice is hoarse, but the need is unmistakable. "So, so much."

I didn't know anything could feel this good. I was always too worked up about the rejection from my parents to understand that the rest of the world wasn't them. That I was destined for greater things, and being the object of Cole Huxley's desire was at the very top of that list.

"Give me your mouth," he growls.

Like denying him is even an option, I open up for him. At his mercy, I give him everything I have, wanting nothing more than for him to take it all.

His tongue takes over, punishing me, branding me, ridding my thoughts of anything but us.

He continues to jerk me off, his hand now moving faster, sliding up and down with ease.

I moan into his mouth, my hands pulling at his hair in desperation. The water's sluicing over every inch of us, dripping through his hair, over our lips, down our chests and washing away every single bit of tension and misunderstanding between us. Giving it no room to grow, no reason to breathe.

I cling to him. I cling to this merciless kiss, full of heartache and promises.

I let my mouth do all the talking. With every deep and hungry stroke of my tongue, I tell him all the things I'm too scared to say aloud.

And he listens.

With every tug of my shaft, bite on my lip, sweep of my tongue, he listens.

His mouth starts to follow the drops of water, down my neck, past my nipples, the length of my stomach. Before I know it, his firm hands are gripping the back of my thighs. Separating my legs, he nuzzles his face into my groin, like he just can't get enough.

My body leans back to the tiles behind me, my knees weak, my entire being too consumed by need to even hold itself up.

He licks the underside of my erection before covering my crown with his mouth. Instinctively, my hand pulls at his hair and he hums in pleasure around my cock. His eyes flick up to mine as he begins to work me over, the devious look in his eyes turning me on even more.

"Fuck, Cole."

"What?" he pops off. "I figured I'd get you dirty one more time before we clean up."

"Please don't stop," I pant. "Please. Suck me."

"Turn around," he orders.

Confused, I don't move, my mind taking too long to catch up.

He slaps my ass. "I've got a better idea. Turn around, hands on the wall."

I comply, too wound up to question him, or even care. He has all of me. He can do, touch, taste, tease, every single part of me and there will be no signs of objection ever coming out of my mouth.

His hands squeeze my cheeks, while he takes his time kissing, licking, and biting. "You going to give me this one day?"

"Fuck," I cry out, my brain short circuits, while my dick painfully throbs at the possibility.

He spreads me wide, and I'm sure I'm about to pass out. I look over my shoulder. His steel colored eyes, skilled tongue, and hard cock will be my undoing.

He's all sin, on his knees for *me*, worshiping *me*, like I'm worth it. Like a prized possession. Like there's nowhere else he'd rather fucking be.

I feel a light breath of air on my hole before he circles the tip of his tongue around my rim.

"Cole," I whimper.

"Give me that noise again," he taunts. His tongue presses against me harder, dipping the tip inside.

My breath is erratic, my heartbeat unreliable, my cock aching to be touched.

I bring my hand to my dick and start stroking myself as he devours my ass. His hands snake between my legs and caress my tight balls.

"Cole," I croak.

"Yeah, baby?"

I let my forehead fall to the tiles as a resounding "Ahhh" leaves my mouth and echoes around us.

"That's right, sweet boy. Am I driving you crazy? Imagine when my thick cock's inside you." A slick, lathered finger probes my ass as his words rile me up. "The fucking noises you will make," he mutters.

"I'm going to spread you just like this. Stretch you just enough." A second finger goes in and my body crumbles when he brushes against my prostate.

"Cole, I can't."

He spins my hips around and puts me back in his mouth. Skillfully, he sucks me off, while his fingers continue to graze my sensitive spot, waiting for me to explode.

With one last push, I fall apart. Right on cue, I come. Hard. Hot. Heavy.

He takes his time sucking me dry, milking my come into his mouth. When his mouth slides off me, I shakily drop to my knees, grab his face, and consume him. Desperate to taste myself on him, my tongue dances around in his mouth. Enjoying him. Thanking him. Adoring him.

"How do you taste?" he asks, working out my affinity for after-blowjob kisses.

"Better when it's off your tongue."

"I fucking love when you let go and get filthy," he praises.

"Stand up and I'll be as filthy as you want me to be."

Without hesitation he complies, his thick, veiny cock spilling at the slit, angry and begging for release.

I cover him with my mouth, bobbing my head, working my throat, relishing in his taste. Unexpectedly, he pulls out. I narrow my eyes at him.

"Open your mouth," he commands, while his big hands stroke and squeeze his cock.

Locking my eyes with his, I open my mouth, ready and waiting. With me kneeling in front of him like a supplicant, it takes less than ten seconds for ropes of his come to land on my tongue and drip onto my chin.

"God, you're a fucking sight," he says through labored breaths.

Preening under his compliment, I hold his eyes, unable to look away. Emotions are building between us, too fast to stop them. Everything I feel, I see reflected on his sated face.

Time stops.

My heart does too.

———

DRIED AND DRESSED, I feel overwhelmingly raw and exposed. We're laying down on the couch, Cole protectively holding me, as if he knows I need it, as if he can feel me slowly falling apart. All the talking and the orgasms are hitting me hard, making me feel tender and breakable.

Being as this isn't exactly Cole's live-in house just yet, there is a little bit of uncertainty that follows us around as we trudge through the aftermath of what we just shared.

"I think I'm going to get going," I announce.

"I don't want to push you," he states, "but I can't let you walk out of here if you're not okay."

I squeeze his arms around me tighter. "I am, or at least I know I will be. It all just feels like a little too much right now."

"I don't want you doing things you're not comfortable with."

"No. It's not that," I assure him. "It's the talking. The letting someone in. Bringing it up, giving it air time... it felt real, like it wasn't in my head and I wasn't exaggerating. I just need time to process it."

He stares down at me and I see the hurt in his eyes. Not hurt *from* me, but *for* me.

I place a palm on his cheek. "It's okay. I'm okay."

He swallows hard and presses a soft kiss on my forehead. We sit in a comfortable silence until Cole says, "It feels like we defiled someone else's house."

My body rattles with laughter. "Imagine what can happen when you actually live here."

"Oh, the possibilities," he says with a wistful sigh. "Will you come back?"

"What do you mean?"

He leans up on his elbow and runs his fingers through my hair before taking a deep breath. "Are we going to keep doing this? I just..." Cole doesn't continue, his words for the first time ever sounding unsure and insecure. "At the risk of ruining everything we've shared and reminding you of all the reasons this shouldn't be happening, I need to know what you want. I will walk away if you want me to, but I'm too selfish to let you go without telling you that I want this. I want *you.*"

"I want you too."

They're four simple words. Words we slip into everyday conversations. Words that on their own can have such underwhelming meanings. They're four simple words, but strung together, they hold the weight and power to change everything.

"Are you sure?" he asks.

"About you?"

"About me, about the risk, about it all."

I contemplate what he's saying for the hundredth time, and every time I come up with the same answers. With my vulnerability at an all-time high, I slice myself deeper, open myself up wider. Around him, I don't know how to do anything else but bleed the truth.

"I don't ever want to forget that this was real. Everything you've given me. Keep giving me. Knowingly and unknowingly, in a really short span of time, you've shaken up my world. Made me feel different. Made me feel better. I never want to forget that. I never want to forget you."

"We'll take it slow," he tells me. "We'll work it out."

His confidence returns, every word more certain than the one before. It's what I need, what I want to hear. Knowing I'm not jumping off this cliff and into the beast of the unknown, alone.

"We won't need to hold out or depend on those stolen moments." He kisses me in excitement, and I bask in his affection. "I'll give us so much more."

"I want it all," I say huskily. I pull him back to me, kissing him, showing him just how enticing his offer sounds. "Cole," I breathe out.

"Yeah, baby?"

"Promise me something."

"What?" His voice wavers.

"I said promise me."

"I promise you."

"If it's going to end..." I shake my head. "It's probably going to at some point, and I'm okay with that."

"But," he says tentatively.

"But, if I'm going to get my heart broken, I want you to leave one hell of a fucking scar behind."

17

COLE

I t's been a few days since Elijah left my place. Well, it'll be my place soon enough. He insisted he needed to go home on his own, have some time to unwind. I wanted so badly to crawl inside his mind and make sure he was okay, but unlike the possessed man I felt like on the inside, I was cool, calm, and understanding on the outside.

Elijah also said he didn't want to risk being seen together near campus. As unlikely as it was at this time of the night, his paranoia was warranted. We can't flaunt whatever this is, hoping nobody will notice, or at best become suspicious. It was logical thinking, but it didn't change how much I wanted to drive him home. I wanted to bask in his presence for as long as I could. And as stupid as it sounds, it was the first time I *actually* realized just how dangerous this thing with Elijah was going to be.

I couldn't see past him when I was around him. Everything about him was seeping into my blood and changing my original make up. Before my very own eyes, I was morphing into an unrecognizable man. My priorities were shifting, my interests weren't the same, and that desire to live out my days unattached, seemed like a way of life I almost forgot living.

I was stupid over this boy, and after the other night, I'm finding it really hard to care.

For Elijah, my heart, my mind, and my body seem to be willing to bend any which way. Whatever he needs, whatever he wants, it's a given.

So, right now, against the aching need that sits heavy on my chest, I'm letting him take the lead. I'm letting him call the shots and make the moves. I'm too scared to push him, and I don't want to push too hard and scare him.

In more ways than one, I'm just as new to all of this as Elijah is. What's too much? What's not enough? Am I supposed to feel so invested so soon?

When I'm away from him, the whispers of worry inside my head are incessant. It's a growing insecurity, one that I never had until I met him.

A loud knock on my office door interrupts my midday musings. When the door opens, before I can invite the person in, I'm not too surprised to see Dean Billings at the other end of my office.

The man doesn't wait for anyone. *But why the hell is he here?* Standing up, I run my hand down the front of my shirt straightening my tie, and plaster on an exaggerated smile. I walk from behind my desk to meet him halfway.

"Dean Billings. To what do I owe this pleasure?"

"Cole." In three long strides, he's standing in front of me. Sticking his hand out, I take it with a firm grip. "I just wanted to check in on you. See how your family is doing."

"My mom's doing well," I supply. "Thank you for asking."

"Will you need more time off?"

The question is to be expected, however his snotty tone

has me wondering if he was annoyed I had to fly home in the first place.

"Hopefully not. As of now, I'll be flying home on my own time. On the weekends," I add for clarification. "But if she needed me, without hesitation I would go."

A hint of annoyance crosses his features, and I internally high five myself for ruffling his feathers. I don't know why it never came across when I interviewed for this position, but after meeting him and seeing him with Harper at the orientation dinner, I can't seem to warm up to him.

"Of course," he says. "King is all about family." His patronizing tone doesn't go unnoticed. "And if you need to go, we will gladly cover everything here for you."

The prick is pushing my buttons and it takes everything in me to remind myself he's my superior and that getting on his wrong side any more than this isn't in my best interest.

"Dean Billings. You know I will always endeavor to put the school first. I do not take the opportunity of this prestigious position lightly. Working underneath you is a privilege."

The motherfucker preens, and I want to roll my eyes at how conceited he is.

Pretentious fuck.

"Actually, Cole." He takes a seat on the chair that faces my desk and I follow his lead, taking the seat behind it. "I also wanted to discuss the research project you're heading."

My mind races, immediately focusing on Elijah and the worst possible outcome for this conversation.

"Yes," I say.

"We have some private investors that want to throw more money at it. And to say thank you and welcome them to the King *family,* we're going to put on a black-tie event, show off the oversized, elaborate fake check to our highest performing students and their parents." He flails his hands in the air. "You know? The whole shebang."

What a bore.

"That sounds wonderful," I lie.

"It is imperative you be there, Cole." He narrows his eyes at me, his face no longer relaxed and friendly, his features now severe and stiff. "The board views your attendance with the utmost importance."

No family excuses. Message received loud and clear.

"When will it be held?" I ask, doing my best to not appear unnerved.

"It's still to be confirmed, but definitely in between Thanksgiving and Christmas break. That close to the festive season we will be able to make it worth the school's while. Maybe make it Christmas themed, offer money to a few charities, and allow potential parents to get their feet wet. Really see what King is about. Understand?"

There's no denying King gives as much as it takes, but I'm coming to realize every good deed comes with an abundance of sparkles, glitter, and glamour. Understated is something King will never be.

Just as I'm about to find a way to cut the conversation short, the mention of parents attending the event fills me with dread.

"Just to clarify, the parents who will be attending will be those of the students participating in the research project?"

"Among others, yes."

Motivated by my own personal agenda, I continue with the questioning. "Are the students expected to pass on the invitation?"

"Yes. Handpicked students will be given invitations and expected to pass them on to the family members of their choosing." His explanation puts me at ease. When Elijah receives an invitation, he'll be able to make the call on whether he wants his parents to come or not. But from what he's told me, I don't see him reaching out to them and inviting unnecessary heartache into his life right now. "With such an honor, it's hard to imagine that any student wouldn't want to share their success with their parents."

Not even surprised by his privileged ignorance, I thrust my hand out to him in an attempt to wrap up the conversation. "That all sounds wonderful. It was great seeing you, Dean Billings."

"Please, call me Richard," he says, shaking my hand. "I'm really glad we could have this chat. You're doing a great job. Feedback from the staff and the students has been extremely positive."

Feedback?

I school my face, keeping my smile in place, and my tone light. "That's excellent to hear."

When he leaves, I sink into the chair, confused about his parting statement. Almost certain he said it to throw me off balance, I pull my phone out of my top desk drawer, and furiously type a text message to Harper and Miles.

Me: Is there some kind of professor appraisal I wasn't aware of, or is Billings pulling my fucking chain?

There are a few minutes of silence before Miles is the first one to text back.

Miles: What are you talking about?

Me: Billings just came up to my office. I couldn't work out if he was trying to suck my dick or he wanted me to suck his. The guy's so fucking full of himself.

Harper: You're going to have to elaborate on the dick sucking.

Miles: I'm okay with being kept in the dark about Billings' dick. Thanks.

Me: He came in trying to see if I was going to need any more time off for my mom, and then he did that whole I'm going to pretend to be sympathetic when I really don't give a shit thing. But before he left, he said "You're doing a great job, feedback from the staff and the students has been extremely positive."

Miles: I don't know of any appraisals, but maybe he's just been casually asking around.

Me: Thanks, genius, I got that. But, why?

He sends me a few middle finger emojis. Always the gentleman.

Miles: Trust me. Let it go. Otherwise, you're going to struggle working under him.

Harper: Unfortunately, he's right.

I chuckle to myself, finding their affectionate disdain for one another highly entertaining.

I send through a generic thumbs up and put my phone back in the drawer. I've got class in another twenty minutes and a shitload of work to do.

Dean Billings and his cryptic conversations are going to have to take a back burner.

"Seriously, did you wear the same clothes every day while you lived here? You've barely unpacked." Harper is sitting on my bed, legs crossed, in leggings and an oversized sweatshirt, watching me organize my belongings for the move.

"I told you," I start. "I knew I wouldn't be staying here. And I didn't have Megs here to do it for me."

"Ha. What a slave driver you are. I think I need to teach your sister a thing or two about saying no."

"Well, lucky for me, it's highly unlikely that you two will meet any time soon."

My phone vibrates against the nightstand and Harper's head turns to the noise. I do my best to not seem desperate for it because knowing Harper, she'll see right through me. "Here, let me get it for you."

She picks it up, and I watch her eyes casually sweep across the screen. There's no way she didn't see whose name it is. At this time, there's nobody else it could be. Stretching herself across the bed, she hands it to me.

"Thanks." I try to turn away from Harper's silent scrutiny, but giving her my back would be too obvious. Lowering my gaze to the phone, Elijah's name stares back at me. I unlock the screen to open it.

Elijah: Isn't it ridiculous that I just found the best article on the rise of religious reactive fundamentalisms, and my first thought after finding it was, I have to tell Cole.

I couldn't stop the smile from spreading across my face if I tried. When it comes to Elijah, it's not just the monumental moments. It's the little things. The simple things. The unexpected things. The way he flourishes when he's in his own element, and how privileged I am to bear witness to it.

I quickly type back, trying to ignore the stare Harper is throwing my way.

Cole: You wanted to tell Cole, or Professor Huxley?

The response is quick and perfect.

Elijah: Aren't I lucky I don't have to choose?

I throw the phone back on the bed and wait for Harper's inquisition.

Three.

Two.

One.

"So, you're not going to tell me why you have that ridiculous smile on your face?"

"What, a man can't smile?" I say, busying myself with the piles of clothes in front of me.

"Maybe, if it was the new and improved Miles."

"New and improved," I repeat with a chuckle. "So he's getting some pussy and he's happy. What's wrong with that?"

"Firstly, can we acknowledge that you're deflecting right now, and secondly, you don't need to get defensive about Miles. I give him shit because he takes it so well. He knows he's still part of the three amigos."

"Oh, is that what we are?"

"Well, not if you don't tell me who Elijah is."

I raise my eyes to hers. "I see you got a good look then."

"Pffft," she scoffs. "Like you expected anything else."

I keep folding clothes, a little too worried about what my face will give away.

"You're really going to hold out."

"There's nothing to tell," I lie.

"It's fine. You gave enough away without saying anything, anyway." Resigned, I look up at her. She smiles the second she knows she's got my attention. "The Cole I know is a sex only type of guy. And that, my friend, was not a sex only smile."

"Shut up with your woman logic," I quip.

She raises her shoulders in excitement. "Well, I can't wait till you decide to tell me about him."

An unusual, unfamiliar feeling tightens my chest when Harper mentions sharing details of Elijah. Being tight lipped about our relationship is non-negotiable. I understand why, I just didn't think it through enough to realize that not being able to display our connection would bother me.

"It's new," I concede. "And that's all you're going to get."

"I can deal with that."

Grateful she's unusually agreeable, I change the subject.

"So, when are you going to move out of this place?" I prompt.

"I can't," she snaps, taking me by surprise.

What the hell was that?

Placing my shirt in a box, I stride around to the side of the bed. Sitting on the edge closest to her, I hold her stare.

"What is it?" I ask.

"I don't know what you're talking about."

"You just bit my head off and I'd kinda like to know why."

Hiding her gaze from me, Harper lowers her face. Shifting her shoulders away from me, her body language gets the point across, but it still upsets me to see her clamp up and put walls between us.

"I won't push because I don't like when someone does it to me," I tell her. "But I'm a really good listener. Just ask my sister."

She looks back at me and offers me a sad smile.

She waves me off. "I'm just being dramatic."

"I'm down for drama. Just tell me when and where and I'll be there for all of it."

Scooting over, Harper wraps her arms around my bicep, snuggling into me. "You make me miss my brothers." Tilting my head, I give her a soft kiss on the forehead. "Now that you've unofficially called me your brother, want to actually help me pack instead of watching?"

She laughs, her body shaking against mine. "Sorry, I'm just not that kind of sister."

Snaking a hand behind my back, I grab a pillow and swiftly hit her in the face with it. "Thanks for nothing."

"Cole," she squeals, falling back on the bed in hysterics. Once we both stop laughing, Harper lets out a long sigh. "I should get going."

"What? Why? I need the company."

"Call Miles," she says, letting go of me and climbing off the bed. "I've got some stuff I need to take care of."

Understanding that she probably wants some space, I don't argue. "Let me walk you home then."

"You live all of a minute away. You don't need to do that."

I throw my arm around her neck. "I don't care."

Together, we walk the short distance to her apartment and I reluctantly leave her to her own thoughts.

The whole ordeal has me missing Megs. Dealing with her issues on her own is her typical MO, and Harper doesn't seem to be much different.

Walking back into my mess of a room, I sit on the edge of the bed and pick up my cell. Flicking through my most recent call list, I call Meghann.

"Hey." She picks up on the second ring.

"Hey."

"What are you doing?"

I look around my full room. "Packing without you."

She mock gasps. "What a travesty."

A relaxed chuckle leaves my mouth. "You have no idea."

"Other than that, everything okay?"

"Yeah. I just called to check in on you guys. See how you're all doing."

"I'm good. I'm here at Mom's now, want to talk to her?"

Checking the time, I ask, "Is she okay?"

"Yeah, I've just been mixing and matching up my work

hours these days, so I can come spend a few decent hours here every day."

I hear my mother's voice in the background. I can't work out what she's saying, but her annoyed tone is apparent.

"Here," Meghann huffs. "She wants to talk to you."

There's a rustling sound on the other end of the phone as I wait. "Cole, sweetie, how are you?"

"Mom," I greet, feeling overwhelmingly homesick. "How are you?"

"I'd be better if your sister stopped hovering over me all the time," she complains.

"She's just worried about you."

"Lies. She's avoiding her problems with Trey."

My ears perk up. "They're still having problems?"

"I don't know, I'm just using that sixth sense mothers have. My hip's broken, but my brain's fine, and your sister has not spent this much time away from him in her life." A voice in the background confirms my mom intended for Megs to hear every word. "And if looks could kill, Cole, the one she's giving me right now tells me I'm spot on."

Without giving me a chance to probe any further, she switches her focus to me, and bombards me with the usual twenty questions.

"What's new with you, my darling boy? Sleeping your way through Washington?"

"Besides the fact that it's weird that you ask about my sex life, you're making it sound like I slept my way through all of Chicago."

"Well, the number was very high, Cole. And with your sister and Trey taking years off my life with their drama, I have to pin my hopes of grandchildren on you."

"What would I know about a child?"

"About as much as I knew when I had your ugly ass."

I run a hand down my face, equally exasperated by the direction of this call, and relieved that she's still around to bust my ass every now and then.

"I'm just saying, I look forward to the day you bring home your future."

My future.

The words hit me hard, almost stealing my breath away. It's the second time in just over half an hour I'm reminded of the restrictions, rules, and regulations I have put on me and Elijah. Introducing him to my family would be a big deal. It would mean that I was ready to let him deep into my world. Deep enough that being without him would be impossible. That being without him wouldn't even be an option.

"How's your hip?" I say, too frazzled to even broach the other conversation.

"It's fine, love. A little stiff now that the weather is getting cooler, but I'll be back up and moving faster than you know it."

Her fighting spirit has never ceased to amaze me. There isn't anything in the world my mother can't overcome. "That's what I like to hear."

"You better be coming home for Thanksgiving. I miss you."

"Wouldn't miss it for the world, Mom. I miss you too." She sighs contentedly into the phone. "Can you hand Megs the phone? I want to speak to her before I go."

"Of course, but be easy on her." She lowers her voice. "Whatever it is she's going through, she's still trying to work it out."

"Okay, Mom."

"Hey," Meghann says, annoyed.

"Hey, I just—"

"I don't know, Cole," she interrupts. "I don't know the answer to what's wrong, so please stop asking me."

"Okay," I drag out. "Can you just promise to call me if you need me?"

"I will," she huffs.

"Love you, Megs."

"Love you more."

Hanging up, I'm too wound up to not try to get to the bottom of this. Immediately I pull up Trey's number and text him.

Me: When I come home, we need to talk.

It takes seconds for him to reply.

Trey: Are you okay?

Me: It's not me I'm worried about.

18

ELIJAH

"Expecting a call?" Louis asks me after I check my phone for the hundredth time this afternoon. "Sorry," I mutter. "I'll put it away."

"Dude, I'm not your keeper."

"I know, but you're right, I'm looking at it too much, and I should be concentrating more."

"It happens," he assures me. "We all have off days."

I don't bother arguing or explaining anything to him, because it would be pointless. Truthfully, I am having an off day. I'm getting through the workload, and doing my part, but I'm also trying to balance the hundreds of thoughts filtering around in my brain. I'm trying to compartmentalize and I'm not having any luck with it.

Cole has infiltrated everything. The research project reminds me of him. When I'm doing the homework for his class, I'm thinking of him. When I'm in the shower, I'm thinking of him. And when I'm in bed... He's everywhere.

I'm not necessarily waiting on a message from him, but rather I find myself obsessing over him in general. In this moment it's wondering if he's going to grace us with his presence this afternoon. He's supposed to do some timesheet checks, and I'm on tenterhooks for him to walk through that door.

Since the night at his place, we've spoken on the phone and texted every day, numerous times throughout the day. Considering our schedules are so different, and I'm trying to appear much cooler and more collected than I actually am, it's working for us. But while I find myself completely satisfied by our verbal and intellectual connection, my body aches for him; aches for more.

To try and rid myself of all this pent-up tension, I've found myself running more often and for longer periods of time than I ever have before. I'm trying to channel everything I feel for Cole into one manageable activity.

I feel like I've been twisted inside out, in the best possible way, over this man. He's not just an attractive guy who could keep me around with his skill to wring orgasm after orgasm out of me. He's funny and compassionate. He's smart and interesting. He's the whole fucking package that I can feel myself becoming dangerously addicted to.

"Elijah." Shari's voice interrupts my thoughts. "Elijah," she repeats.

"Sorry." I shake my head and steer my focus to what's important.

"Did you bring the papers?" she asks.

"Of course." Pulling out four plastic sleeves filled with stapled booklets, I hand one to each of the other students.

"This is a detailed report of everything I found out on the change in cultures, the impact of conflict, and the misrepresentation of radicalism within religions." Each of them flick through the information I've provided. I probably could've printed one communal paper for us to share, but I figured this way everybody would be able to dissect the information in their own time, and in their own way. By allowing an array of details, interpretations, and explanations to be collated, I think we're giving ourselves an advantage of an extensive and well-informed submission.

"This is great stuff, Elijah," Jenna praises. "I can't even imagine the amount of time you're putting into research, to be coming across findings of such high quality as these."

"I just can't sleep once I've set my mind on something, so I'll find myself forgetting about the time, completely immersed in the task at hand."

"Elijah, man," Louis says. "You're never allowed to sleep again."

A loud melody of laughter floats between the four of us and I enjoy their understanding and appreciation for my efforts. I'm starting to realize how different it is when you meet people with similar interests and priorities as yourself.

"So, do you guys think we've got enough to submit part one?" The research project is split up into four sections, each one having its own due date to ensure we remain on track and that there's no chance anybody is leaving anything to the last minute. Each section is appraised twice. The first time allows for any feedback given to be addressed and the submission improved. The second time is the final version of the project.

"I think once we add the new information you collected, we should be fine," Jenna answers.

The four of us begin to make more notes and delegations between us, wanting to finish off as much as we can before parting for the night, when a confident and carefree looking Cole strolls on in.

Awareness ripples through me, my body heating up instantly. The mere sight of him enough to tip me on my axis.

"Hey, Professor Huxley," Jenna greets.

Inconspicuously, or at least I hope so, I let my eyes follow his movements and watch him forcefully tear his gaze away from me to focus on Jenna.

"Jenna." He nods at her in acknowledgement. "How are you all today?"

"Good," Shari chimes in, raising a whole bunch of papers up to him. "We just need you to sign off on this weeks' hours and we'll be good to go."

"I can do that." He takes the papers off her and sits at the open space at the end of the table. Directly opposite me.

"Do you guys all have class this evening?" he asks. "Or are you finished for the day?"

"Actually, I was going to say something earlier," Louis looks to me. "I won't be able to stay back tonight. I have another group assignment that's kicking my ass and I don't trust the other students I was paired with to get it done without me."

"No worries, man," I say. "If any of you have plans and can't stay back, don't stress. I can finish off today's stuff, no problem. I'll send it all via email, and you all can double check what I've done, where we're at, and work out what's left."

"Are you sure?" Shari leans over and squeezes my hand. "You don't have to do all that stuff on your own, we can coordinate over email."

"It's fine." I wave her off and catch Cole's stare. "I made plans for after our study session, so I've still got a few hours to kill."

"You're a champ, Eli," Louis adds.

I give them a two-finger salute as they all pack their belongings and file out of the faculty common room.

Pretending we're sharing the space, as opposed to

wanting any alone time we can get, Cole and I wait for them all to disappear out of sight.

Once the coast looks clear, Cole focuses all his attention on me. "Do you really have plans tonight?"

"I do." I groan, letting my head fall onto the table. "I promised Aiden and Callie we'd hang out tonight."

I want to cancel my plans with them. It's on the tip of my tongue to offer, but I don't want to be that guy. The three of us have come too far as friends for me to just ditch them whenever Cole wants me.

"So, I guess it's a bad time to tell you I'm officially moving in today."

My breath gets caught in my throat.

"It's probably an even worse time to tell you I have a beautiful king bed just waiting for us."

I shake my head at him, "You're enjoying this aren't you?"

"Teasing you? Definitely," he says with a smile. "But you not being able to come over, not so much."

I imagine his bed. I imagine us *on* his bed. Fuck it. "I can—"

"No," he says firmly. "You're making friends, new college experiences. I'm not taking that away from you." He stands up, gathers the papers, and walks directly to me. I rise and meet him as he hands me the thick bunch. We both hold on to the stack, as if our hands are actually touching. "Even if I hate every single moment you're with someone else, I will *not* take that away from you."

My face heats up at his sincerity. "You're a good guy, Cole Huxley."

His voice takes on that seductive quality I love so much. "When will I see you?"

Itching to touch him, I try to slide my hand closer to his. "Tomorrow night?"

"I have an afternoon department meeting, and then Miles and Harper are supposed to come over and see the new place. I can cancel."

"If I can't cancel, then you can't either," I protest. "We'll find time." I don't believe the words as I say them, but I don't want us to start finding flaws in our arrangement. Despite the circumstances and the restrictions, I want to continue being hopeful.

"Soon," he says as more of a demand. He skims my fingertips with his own and I revel in his touch. In the knowledge that even if neither of us says it out loud, I'm not the only one stuck in a fog of feelings.

"Have fun sleeping in your bed alone tonight," I tease.

"I'm going to think of you the whole damn time," he rasps.

"You better."

"I'M sure you both said we were studying with pizza," I call out from my room. "I don't see any books."

Callie pokes her head in my room, shaking a bottle of tequila. "There's been a change of plans."

"No way." I shake my head in irritation. Already annoyed and agitated that I'm not spending the night with Cole, Callie's and Aiden's change of plans is of no interest to me.

"Come on," she whines. "You've been MIA for ages and we need to make new memories."

I know it comes from a good place and this was the reason I cancelled with Cole; to have memories with my friends.

"Only two drinks. I have an early class tomorrow," I lie.

"Bullshit," Aiden calls out from his room before coming up behind Callie. "You think I don't know your schedule by heart already?"

I roll my eyes. "You're creepy."

He winks at me. "Most people like it."

"Let me have a quick shower, then I'll come join you." I grab my towels and toiletries off my bed and head to the bathroom. "You think the pizza could be here before I get out?"

"Already ordered." Callie smiles.

In half an hour, I've scrubbed the long day off my skin and I'm stuffing my face with pepperoni pizza.

"So, you seem a little different lately," Callie probes.

"Yeah, man," Aiden agrees with a mouth full of food. "Ever since Callie mentioned it to me, I can definitely see it."

"What do you mean?"

"You're lighter," she exclaims. "Carefree. Dare I even say, happier?"

"I've always been happy," I protest. Maybe not as happy as I am right now, but being around them and attending King, I definitely don't think I've been *unhappy*.

"Did you meet someone?" Aiden interrogates.

"No," I blurt out a little too quickly.

They give one another a conspiratorial look. "You would tell us, wouldn't you?"

"If there was anything to tell, of course." I play cool for the whole exchange, even though inside I'm disappointed that I can't tell them. What's the point in finally having friends if you're still hiding things from them?

"That's enough about me, what's new with you two?" I divert.

"Before we get to that uneventful part of the night," Aiden says. "What are we doing for your birthday?"

"Do we have to do anything?" I groan. "I'd rather we didn't bother."

"It's not an option, Eli," he says nonchalantly. "Pick somewhere you like, or I'm choosing to host it at a gay bar."

"What is your obsession with taking me to a gay bar?"

"Dude, you're recently out and you've never been in a room full of sweaty, hot, and horny guys. It's some top-notch stuff."

"I'm not recently out," I scoff.

"Really? Out of the words hot and horny guys, you're going to focus on the fact that I said you're recently out?"

"Well, I'm not," I pout petulantly. "I just like to keep it to myself."

"Come and troll for dick with me."

I want to wipe that smug, self-assured smirk off his face and tell him I am very content with the dick that I could be getting tonight, if I wasn't sitting here and arguing with him.

"We can go out," I concede. "To dinner and then come back home. Those are my conditions."

Aiden's mouth is just about to open and argue with me when Callie warns him. "Aiden. Let it go. Dinner is perfect."

He glares at her and she rolls her eyes before giving me an unexpected kiss on the cheek. "As long as we get to celebrate with you, that's all that matters."

An odd sense of discomfort and sadness washes over me as I take in the weight of her words. For the first time in a long time, I could see myself getting excited about a birthday, but having to split myself between Cole, and Aiden and Callie sounds exhausting. In a perfect world I'd be able to celebrate my birthday with all of them.

"I'm glad that's all sorted," Callie announces. "How about a shot?"

Just as she finishes pouring the gold liquid into the shooter, Aiden's phone pings. Naturally, both Callie and I turn to look at him.

Before he's even finished reading the text, he's jumping out of the chair and heading to his room.

"Where are you going?" Callie shouts.

"It's an emergency," he supplies, stepping back into the common room and slipping into a black jacket.

"But." She holds up the shot glass as explanation.

"I know, and I wouldn't go if it wasn't an emergency."

In response, Callie tosses down the drink and sinks into the couch, undeniably disappointed. Once again, I feel totally out of the loop with these two.

"What's his deal?" I ask.

She grabs the second shot and drains the glass. "I think he's seeing someone."

"And you're not okay with that," I state. She reaches over for the third glass and I stop her. "Don't. It won't make you feel any better."

"I need to get over him," she says, wiping at her eyes.

I wrap an arm around her and squeeze her close to my side. It breaks my heart to know she loves him and he's too busy to notice. For all intents and purposes, they are the ideal couple. They know everything about each other. They're sexually compatible, and if it wasn't for this huge secret between them, they wouldn't have to hide a single thing from one another.

"Have you considered telling him how you feel?"

"So he can reject me?"

Surprised that the possibility of ruining their friendship

isn't her initial deterrent, I encourage her to find the answers she so desperately needs.

"Don't you think he deserves to know? Or at the very least that *you* deserve to know?"

"Since when are you Mr. Take Life by the Balls, consequences be damned?"

A loud laugh erupts from my mouth. If only she knew. "Some things are worth the risk."

She shifts in my arms and tilts her head up at me. "Elijah Williams, what are you hiding from me?"

God, I wish I could tell her.

"There's nothing to tell. I'm just speaking from experience. It took a lot for me to get here, and get the outcome I wanted... the freedom of finally living the way I want to. I would endure all that, every time, knowing it would lead me here."

She nestles her head in the crook of my neck. "I know you don't talk about your life before King, but for what it's worth, I admire your strength. You are so much more than you give yourself credit for."

A little lump forms in my throat, the gratitude lodged inside my chest. I squeeze her a little tighter and hope she knows just how much those words mean to me.

"Do you care if I go home?" she asks. "I don't want to be here when Aiden gets back."

"I can understand that feeling." I move my arm off her shoulders. "Are you sure you're going to be okay?"

"Unfortunately, I've done this before. I just need a hot shower and a good night's sleep."

"You know I'm here if you need anything, right?"

She rises off the couch and then bends down to kiss my forehead. "Bye, Eli."

"Message me when you get to your dorm," I call out to her retreating form.

"You know it," she shouts as she walks out the door.

As the silence sinks in, I realize I'm here all alone, when I could be with Cole. Pulling my phone out of my pocket, I open my messages and type one out to him. Changing my mind, I delete the text and scroll till I get to the Uber app instead.

I HOPE COLE LIKES SURPRISES.

Walking up his stoop, the nerves begin to creep in and I begin to feel a little self-conscious. *What if he has someone over?*

Ripping off the band-aid, I knock on the door and wait one whole agonizing minute before a bare-chested Cole opens up the door.

He beams, surprise and excitement written all over his handsome face. Knowing that look is all for me, pride fills me up and swallows me whole.

I tip my chin at his naked torso. "I see you're ready for me."

"What are you doing here?" he asks, still smiling.

"My schedule freed up."

"Lucky me." He takes hold of my hand and tugs me inside. The second the door closes, he pulls me to his chest. Hands cup the sides of my face as he brings my lips to his.

Slow and wet, he kisses me like we have all the time in the world. He kisses me with purpose. He kisses me with promise. "I've missed your mouth so much," he murmurs.

Returning the sentiment, I grab his face and kiss him with everything I have. "It missed you too."

A few long seconds pass as we stand there in the middle of his foyer just holding and kissing one another. He pulls back to look at me. "Have you eaten? I've got groceries and could cook something for you."

I rest my hand on his cheek and shake my head. "I'm perfect now, thank you."

Euphoria washes over me as I'm filled with warmth at his attentiveness and consideration. The more time we spend together, the more it shows that this is beyond just physical attraction.

Wordlessly, I walk around him, kick off my shoes, and head straight for his stairs. Two at a time, he's right on my heels as I stop in the middle of his bedroom doorway.

"You don't waste any time, do you?" he teases, wrapping his arms around my waist.

We stand in the doorway and I take in his new, and very large, bed. But surprisingly that is not what catches my attention.

"How the hell does one man have this many clothes?"

He drops his chin to my shoulder. "You're going to have to stand in line with all the other people that give me shit about my wardrobe."

"It's a mini department store."

"It is not."

I whirl around. "You have a shopping addiction, don't you?"

"It's more like a 'I don't like throwing things out' problem," he admits.

"You're a hoarder?"

"Hoarder is such a horrible word. I refuse to label myself as one."

"Cole, you don't need labels." I gesture to the messy bed. "This speaks for itself."

"Well, since you're here, want to help me unpack?" he asks.

I lift up my laptop bag that I brought with me. "I'll help you, if you help me."

He kisses the side of my neck. "What you got?"

"A paper on architecture and paganism."

"I've got a better idea. I'll make room for you on the bed and you study while I make sense of this mess."

"I can help," I argue.

He kisses me hard. "I don't need you to. I just like that you're here."

19

COLE

I move a whole bunch of clothes to the nearby wave shaped chaise lounge that sits in the corner of the room and gesture for Elijah to sit on the bed. "Make yourself at home."

He places his bag down beside the nightstand and then carefully climbs onto the mattress. He places two pillows against the bed head and one in his lap as his eyes sweep across the room. "Tell me once all this is in its right place you're actually a neat, tidy man."

"I have my moments."

"Are you sure you don't want me to help?" he offers again.

I pick up a handful of shirts. "I got this. You need to work on that paper anyway. If we both finish in good time, I promise to make it worth it."

As to be expected, his beautiful face blossoms into an adorable blush. "Stop lagging, Professor Huxley," he teases. "We have things to do."

Reaching into his bag, he pulls out a thick book he would've borrowed from the library. With a cushion nestled in his lap, he opens up to the page he wants and dives into reading.

It catches me off guard how much I enjoy watching him. In his element. In my space. I might not have felt like this about anybody else before, but part of me knows it's not supposed to feel so right when there's so much at stake.

"What are you thinking about so hard over there?" he asks me, looking up from his book.

"Shouldn't you be paying attention to whatever it is you're reading?"

"It's a bit hard when I can practically hear your brain ticking."

I swipe at a bunch of folded t-shirts and head to the dresser. "So, what happened to your study plans?"

"Aiden and Callie had no plans to study; they brought tequila and pizza instead of books."

"Oh." I bite my tongue, always surprised at my reaction to him bringing up his friends. It's pure and unadulterated jealousy. It isn't about a drunken kiss, it isn't because I don't trust him, it's because anyone but me is a better option. And I'm just waiting for him to realize that.

"Aiden got a mysterious phone call and ended up bailing, so I just comforted Callie for a bit before she decided to go home."

"Comforted Callie?" I query.

"Yeah," he answers, his attention half on me and half on the book. "She likes Aiden."

"Isn't Aiden gay?"

"I believe society would put him in the bisexual box, but I really think he just goes where the wind takes him."

"You didn't mention it," I say, giving my back to him as I stuff clothes into the drawers.

"Yeah, it slipped my mind. Along with how they originally tried to lure me in to a threesome."

I whip my head around, not sure whether to make a joke, be shocked, or be jealous. "Jesus, Elijah, that definitely slipped your mind."

He laughs, enjoying my disbelief. "It was a traumatic experience either way. We all try to do our best not to talk about it."

"So, he's not in to Callie?"

An exhausted sigh leaves his mouth, and I can tell he's invested in his friends. "I genuinely don't know. They sleep together, or have slept together, they're both down for threesomes, and they've been best friends forever. On paper it should work."

"Interesting." I continue to hang up clothes, while I mull over the details he's sharing about his friends. It's typical college stuff. The sleeping around, the experimenting. It's usually up to the person to have a little bit of self-control. "Where do you think Aiden went?"

"I have no idea. The sky's the limit for Aiden; I think he'll try anything or do anything rather than face whatever demons he's running from."

"You think there's more to it?"

"Definitely. I know what it's like to need to hide something, but he's even cagier than I am."

Wanting nothing more than to be on that bed with him, I jut my chin out to him. "Keep reading."

"You're the one that keeps distracting me." He lowers his chin to his chest and runs his finger across the pages. "I borrowed this book from the library today; it's better than any of the research I've found online."

"You can find some real treasures in the library, if you look carefully."

"That's how you used to research at college, right?" I look at him in confusion. "I mean, were there even computers back then?"

Understanding dawns on me and I drop my clothes to the ground before lunging at him on the bed. "You fucking little shit, I'm not that old."

He tries to duck away from me. "Just answer the question and I'll determine how old you really are." Tugging the book out of his hands, I rest it beside him and climb up over him.

With my forearms resting on the side of his head, and my groin hovering awfully close to his, I ask, "Do you think about it often?"

"Think about what?"

"How old I am."

He runs his fingers up and down my beard. "Never."

Always saying the right thing, I capture his mouth and sink all my weight onto him. I grind my thickening length into his, loving that it takes him no time at all to get worked up. I'm just about to stick my hands down his pants when he pushes at my shoulder.

"Cole," he says wearily.

"Is everything okay?"

"Yeah. I mean, don't make fun of me for this, but I can't fool around with all this stuff around me."

A few awkward seconds pass by and I wait, expecting him to say he's joking, but it never comes. "Holy shit, you're serious."

He nods vehemently.

"Now I'm just wondering what your dorm room looks like."

"A lot tidier than this."

"Point taken." I kiss him quickly. "You probably need to finish whatever it is you're doing anyway."

A wide, content, and satisfied smile spreads across his face. When we're at King, the annoyance of seeing him and not being able to touch him means I want to do it that much more. Some days I sit in my office and imagine all the ways I could sneak around and accidentally bump into him.

It's embarrassing how much of me it consumes, but having him here in my space? The freedom to touch, the freedom to talk? It keeps me calm, it keeps me sane, it makes me realize that it isn't some twisted infatuation I've glorified in my mind.

But if I have to endure times of discomfort for a night like this, then I'll do it. Without hesitation, I will do it.

Impatiently, I try to get through the shit I own. It's the first time I've ever agreed with anyone who's given me shit for how much stuff I have.

When I finally hang up my last shirt and fill the ensuite with my toiletries, I turn to look at Elijah, finding him diligently writing notes while reading.

"I'm just going to take these empty boxes downstairs and finish up a few things down there before coming back up. I'll be right back."

He raises his hand to me in a wave, unable to take his eyes off the book, and a little part of me swells with pride. I've never met anyone as attentive and focused as Elijah; there isn't a success in the world that he doesn't deserve.

It takes me a little longer than I expected to set up my television. Flicking through the channels one more time, I make sure to check the picture and sound quality. Content enough to leave anything else I have till tomorrow or the weekend, it's finally time to go upstairs and spend some time with Elijah.

Taking the stairs two at a time, I rush through the bedroom door only to find him with his head resting against the bed, his book still open on his lap, and his eyes closed.

He's even beautiful when he's sleeping.

Tentatively, I walk over and take the book off of him. Placing it on the nightstand, I pack up his stationery and put it next to the book.

"Hey," I whisper, running my fingers down his cheek. "Elijah, baby." His long eyelashes flutter at the sound of my voice before opening. "You fell asleep."

It takes a few seconds for his brain to catch up and his eyes widen in shock when they do. "Shit. I'm so sorry." His head moves from left to right, looking for all his belongings. "I'll get going."

"Hey," I soothe, squeezing his shoulder. "You don't need to go. If you can stay, I want you to stay."

His body drops back into the bed in relief. "Are you sure you don't mind?"

A soft chuckle leaves my mouth as I run my fingers through his hair. "No. I definitely do not mind. Do you need something to sleep in?"

He shakes his head, still a little bit disorientated. He swings his legs over the edge of the bed and I step back, giving him space. He stands up and haphazardly pulls down his pants and whips off his shirt.

Clumsily, he climbs back into the bed, under the covers, burying his face in the pillow, while I stand there rocking a semi at the thought of him practically naked beside me.

Walking around to the other side, I switch off the light before shucking off my own shorts. Sliding in next to him, I'm overthinking the sleep etiquette, worried if I plaster myself to him like I want, I'll wake him up.

"Cole," he whispers.

"Yeah."

"Can you hold me?" His voice is soft and faint, the hints of neediness impossible to ignore. Relieved that he's taken the guesswork out of my musings, I turn on my side and reach for him. With my arm snaked around his stomach, I pull his curled body into mine. Unable to resist, I kiss the nape of his neck and squeeze him close to me.

"Thank you."

"I've never had someone sleep in my bed without having sex before," I confess.

His hand skims down my thigh, until he reaches the back of my knee. Hooking it over his legs, I realize I'm now clinging on to him like he's a tree.

Lacing his fingers through mine, he raises our hands to his lips and presses the most delicate, meaningful kiss to the top of it. "I guess it's my turn to give you some firsts."

I don't know how long we lay like that, but having his almost naked body and pert ass pressed up against me is the sweetest torture. It's an underrated experience, the relaxed closeness adding a whole different dimension to our already existing connection.

I hear his breathing even out, just as my own eyes get heavier. My last thought before I let sleep take me is: *I could get used to this.*

FINGERTIPS SKATE up and down my chest, drawing patterns, following my happy trail. My mind has acknowledged someone else's touch, but my eyes are still too tired to open up.

It doesn't feel too early, but considering my daily alarm hasn't gone off yet, it's probably close to six-thirty am.

The movements continue, grazing my nipples and teasing the waistband of my boxers. Elijah's on a little exploration mission, and I have no desire to interrupt him.

Such a contrast to every person I've had in my bed before him, there's no rush to be done. No desire to do anything but lounge around in bed, limbs and blankets intertwined.

Staying in bed overnight with someone was a rarity for me, and the morning after was always a quick dick and dash. I found anything more than the physical gratification irritating. I was selfish when it came to who was in my bed, what we did, and how long it went on for. But as Elijah's hands start to rub up and down my very hard dick, I feel myself wanting to slow him down, wanting to indulge in all the things that didn't matter before.

"What are you doing?" I ask, my eyes still closed, my voice hoarse and gravelly from sleep.

"Enjoying the view," he answers confidently.

"And how is it?"

I hear the rustle of sheets and then feel him move around me. When I feel his weight above me, I open my eyes to find a rumpled and sexy Elijah straddling me.

"Good morning," he greets.

My gaze lingers on the heat that dances around in his eyes and then moves on to the thick erection straining against his underwear.

"Is there something you want?" I tease

He rolls his hips, grinding up and down my cock. Gripping his waist, I wordlessly continue to move him against me, dragging him up and down my shaft, working us both up in the shortest amount of time.

Wanting his mouth, wanting my mouth on him, wanting

everything I can possibly take, I reach out to cup the back of his neck and bring him down to me.

He tastes like a mixture of mint and butterscotch and I find myself smiling against his lips. "How long have you been awake for?" I ask.

"Long enough to use your toothbrush and pop a candy in my mouth."

I lightly slap his ass. "Hop up and I'll be back in a second."

He quickly obliges as I grab my phone to switch off the alarm and head into the ensuite to take care of business. After brushing my teeth and washing my hands, I drop my boxers, leaving nothing to the imagination.

I step out, momentarily stunned that he's as eager and shameless as I am. Running on the same wavelength, he's rid himself of his own boxers and is splayed out in the middle of the bed, running his hand up and down his dick.

Standing at the bottom of the bed, I hold his stare and mirror his actions.

"You're just asking for trouble, aren't you?"

He licks his already shiny lips and smirks.

With his legs now bent at the knee and spread wide open, his hard length and heavy balls are on display, teasing and taunting me.

I crawl onto the bed and nestle in between his legs on my stomach, my head is right up in his crotch. Pushing against his thighs, I open him up as wide as he can go before leaning over and running my length along his taut, warm, skin.

A loud hiss slips through his lips, so I do it again.

"Did you think I was going to catch you stroking this beautiful cock of yours and go easy on you?"

I kiss the inside of his thigh, letting my beard scrape

against his tense legs. I make my way to his dick, but avoid touching it, driving him insane. I move my mouth along the other thigh, enjoying his frustration.

"Please," he whimpers.

I continue taunting him, licking and caressing his balls. Teasing his taint with my tongue, I'm filling up on the musky scent of his skin, driving him as close to crazy as I possibly can.

Hands find the back of my head, wanting me deeper, pushing me closer. I raise my head to smirk at him. "Want something?"

"More," he manages to say.

"More of what?" I roll my tongue over his leaky tip, sliding it through his slit. Back and forth. "More of that?"

"Please," he pants.

I slide myself a little further down the bed, the friction on my own hard cock beautifully painful. I suck one of his balls into my mouth and I feel him shudder.

"More of that?" I continue. "Or what about this?"

I clutch onto his ass, and lift his hips off the bed. Spreading his cheeks, I give a quick, tantalizing swipe of his hole.

"That," he cries out, arching his back. "Fuck, Cole. I want you *there*."

The desperation in his voice is enough to have me come apart. Push me over the edge.

Dropping him on to the bed, I climb over him and slam my mouth to his.

I get lost in all the beautiful things about Elijah. His sweet taste. His unfiltered need. His unrestrained desire. I give him everything I have to offer, one sex filled drop at a time.

Pulling away, I lean over him to reach the nightstand.

Opening the drawer, I quickly grab a condom and the bottle of lube. Throwing them onto the bed, I move back between Elijah's legs and sit on my knees.

"Are you sure?" I ask through labored breaths. "There's no rush."

He grabs the lube from beside me and hands it to me. "There's only one person I trust enough to be my first."

Knowing we were headed in this direction, I hoped to be his first, but now he's voiced it? I'm slowly realizing, I don't want to just be his first... I want to be his only.

I place a hand on his knee and push his legs apart. Leaning down, I kiss behind his ear and whisper. "I promise I'll make it good for you, baby."

He grabs my face before giving me a chance to move away, his green eyes imploring me to listen. "I've waited my whole life to feel this," he starts. "To have a strong, beautiful man pound into me with his thick cock. To have every thrust drown out the years of noise. I want to see the fucking stars with you, Cole."

Not for the first time, Elijah has rendered me speechless. I can feel my blood working overtime, thumping in my veins, trying to quicken the flow and to restart every part of me.

With his heart in his eyes and that desperate plea on his lips, I don't just want to show him the stars. I want to show him the sun, the moon, and all the wonders of the goddamn world.

"Cole," he whispers.

I swallow down the foreign onslaught of emotions wending their way into my heart and give Elijah my full attention. "Yeah, baby."

He runs his hand through my trimmed beard. "Are you okay?"

I press a soft, gentle kiss to his lips. "Better than okay."

"So, you haven't changed your mind?" he asks nervously.

"About having sex with you?" He nods vehemently. "Not a fucking chance."

Returning my lips to his, I lick the seam of his mouth till he opens up for me. Caressing his tongue, I work through the plethora of unknowns, the only way I know how.

"I've wanted to have sex with you since the first time I laid eyes on you," I tell him in between kisses. "And now, you've asked me to show you the stars." I slip my hands between us and grab his heavy cock. "Elijah. Sweet boy, I'm going to show you the whole fucking constellation."

20

ELIJAH

S ealing his declaration with a kiss, Cole's mouth begins to make its way from my mouth down to my chest and past my abdomen. My body breaks out into goose bumps; the lower he gets the harder the waves of anticipation crash underneath my skin.

He sits back on his haunches and squirts a generous amount of lube onto the tips of his fingers.

Louder than I thought, his eyes perk up at my sharp inhale.

"You lead the way okay? You say more or stop, and whichever it is I'll do immediately." He juts his chin out to me. "Now, I want you to wrap your hand around that pretty dick of yours and show me how well you can fuck your fist."

Harder than I've ever been before, it's almost a relief to start stroking myself. It doesn't take long for the pearls of pre-come to reappear and my balls to tighten.

Big, strong hands raise my hips and spread my cheeks. "Don't stop until I tell you to, okay?"

Unable to talk, I continue, my movements slow and

methodical. My muscles begin to tighten as the urge to release creeps up the base of my spine.

"Now close your eyes," he commands. "And relax."

With my sense of sight now cut off, my sense of touch is amplified tenfold. While I dutifully work my length, a slick finger runs up and down my taint.

My body trembles.

"Just concentrate on my voice, okay?" He circles my exposed hole, teasing the rim. "Let go of your dick and put your hands by your sides."

Obeying him is like second nature, an extra layer heightening the sexual tension between us. I clutch at the sheets when the tip of his finger slides through my tight muscle.

"Breathe, baby," he coaxes, as his digit begins to slowly thrust in and out of me. Knuckle deep, he grazes my prostate and it takes all my strength to not come right there and then. Pulling out to use more lube, he returns to my hole, adding a second finger.

"Fuck," he groans. "I can't wait to feel you strangling my cock."

He begins scissoring his fingers, stretching me as wide and for as long as he can. Probing the sensitive bud with every long and hard thrust, every nerve ending in my body begins to stand at attention.

"Open your eyes," he commands, just as he slips in a third finger. My body arches off the bed, the intrusion strangely intoxicating. "You think you're ready for me?" he asks.

Unable to concentrate on anything besides how full I feel, I offer him a feeble attempt at a nod. "I can't hear you," he taunts, pushing his fingers deeper.

Breathlessly, I answer, "I'm ready."

He drags his fingers out, painfully slow, and I whimper

at the emptiness. I refuse to dwell on any bouts of discomfort, but rather focus on the undeniable amount of pleasure that's waiting for me on the other side.

He reaches for the condom and hands it to me. "Want to put it on me?"

"I—" My face heats up in embarrassment.

"Lucky I'm a good teacher, huh?" Placing his hands over mine, he shows me how to cinch the top with one hand and roll the latex down his shaft with the other.

Lowering his head, he presses his lips to mine. Overpowering me into the mattress, his body falls on mine, his sheathed cock digging into mine. His kisses pull me into an overwhelming sense of security and safety. Every taste of his tongue, a delicious reassurance that I couldn't have chosen my first time to be with anyone better.

Using all his strength, he rolls us over so I'm on top of him. He slaps my ass. "Get up on your knees and bring your ass up here." He points to his face. "Don't look so shocked. Don't you trust me? I got you."

Wanting him to know I trust him implicitly, I grab onto the headboard, while I situate myself right above him. On my knees, I look down and see Cole salaciously grinning at the view. Grabbing the lube, he generously pours some into his hands.

One hand grips his cock, stroking up and down, coating the condom with lube. The other helps his digits slide in and stretch out my hole.

One finger.

Fuck.

Two Fingers.

Fuck.

Three Fingers.

Fuck.

I peer down at him, breathless. "You're killing me you know that?"

Holding my hips, he raises his head and plants a kiss on one of my cheeks. "You'll thank me after the orgasm of your life. Now come on and sink yourself on my cock."

I shuffle down his body and hover above his slick, eager erection. With one hand spreading my cheek and the other lining up his dick, he coaches me. "Put your hands on my chest and go slow."

The second his crown touches my rim, I stiffen.

"Breathe, baby. Breathe," he coos.

Closing my eyes, I focus on my breathing as I slowly let his thick cock breach that tight ring of muscle. I hiss at the unfamiliar sting, and Cole begins to stroke my erection. "Inhale the pleasure, exhale the pain. I promise it'll be worth it."

I slide down, lower and lower, until his loud groan confirms he's seated deep inside me. Wanting to watch him unravel, I courageously try and move my body up and down. Working into a bearable rhythm, the original sting is now replaced with a dull ache.

Cole's biting on his bottom lip, his whole face a contortion of concentration.

"Cole."

"Yeah," he says with a strain.

"I want to be on my back," I bite the inside of my cheek nervously. "I want to feel your weight on top of me."

His eyes shimmer with possibility as he takes hold of my hips and pulls me off of him. We clumsily roll over and he wastes no time, wanting to get back inside me.

Spreading me wide, he hooks an arm under one of my knees and pushes my leg to my chest. Lining the tip of his cock with me once more, I feel his purposeful push through every fiber of my being.

The sting returns, but I relish in it; loving how it makes me feel alive. Makes me feel real and, for the first time, keeps me grounded and centered to my reality.

He's deeper than before. Rough. Hurried. Frantic. And I don't want him to stop. I want to feel him till it hurts, till it burns. I want to feel him till I burst.

As soon as he hits my prostate, I fist my aching cock, trying to stave off the inevitable.

"Fuck," he growls, capturing my mouth in a searing kiss. Our teeth clash and our tongues duel as our bodies begin to regulate into an exquisite pace.

I begin to stroke my dick when he stops me. "I want it. I want fucking all of you."

Cupping the back of his neck, I slam his mouth back down on mine, words not enough to convey how much of me I want to give him.

His hand and his cock work together in a punishing rhythm, while our tongues dance along to the same beat.

Releasing my cock, he sits up on his haunches and hooks his arm behind my other knee. With enough leverage, he relentlessly pounds into me. Needing friction, I wrap my own hands around my dick and fuck my fist.

Watching him, while he watches me, is raw and intimate, there isn't any piece of me that isn't on display for him.

Deliciously overworked by his strength and his dominance, I feel my body begin to give in to the temptation. The heat rises through me, wrapping itself around my spine and flourishing inside my chest.

"Fuck, Cole," I pant. "I need the stars."

Just like he said he would, this big, beautiful man, with

his sweaty skin, ravenous eyes, and audacious personality races to the finish line to give me exactly what I need.

Hitting the spot repeatedly, my eyes roll into the back of my head as my balls tighten, ready for release. With every thrust, I see a cluster of white lights twinkling behind my eyelids. As my body soars, they burn brighter, promising the detonation of a lifetime.

When I feel myself dangling off the edge, Cole slams into me with visceral force. I cry out and his mouth catches the sound as he gives me everything he can.

"I need you to let go for me, baby," he says, his voice hoarse. "I want to watch you fly high while my dick wrings out every drop of come from your body."

Gripping my thighs, Cole pulls me close and my body arches at his authority. I feel him shudder inside of me, just as every part of me explodes on his command.

Together, we're a kaleidoscope of color, a chorus of moans, and a collision of bodies.

Cole drapes himself on top of my sticky body without a care in the world. Holding on to him, I keep him close and let the sound of our breathing blanket us. We're not the same two people we were when we woke up this morning, and the way he's wrapped himself around me tells me he feels it too.

Things have changed.

His heart, my body.

Things have changed.

My heart, his body.

"Elijah," he says into my shoulder.

I run my hand down his back. "Yeah?"

"Did you see the constellation?"

"No, baby," I say trying out the endearment out for the first time. "I saw heaven."

"ARE YOU READY?" A fully dressed Aiden pops his head into my room, just as I slip my arms through my jacket.

"I am now."

"Perfect," he responds excitedly. Stepping out of the doorway, he makes space for me to walk through to the common room. "Callie and I want to give you your present before we go out."

"You guys didn't have to get me a present."

"We did," Callie chimes in. "Come and sit down, so you can open it and we're not late for our reservation."

Under Callie's and Aiden's insistence, I finally succumbed to the idea of celebrating my birthday. Seeing as birthdays were never really a big deal growing up, it feels foreign to get dressed up, have people fuss over you, and to give you their undivided attention for a day.

After what happened with Alex, even a simple "Happy Birthday" seemed too much for my parents. Like acknowledging my existence might be the one thing to send them to hell.

I used to be more upset that my mother never made the effort. If there was ever one time I wanted her to act like the caring and maternal woman she should've been, it was my birthday. But as the hours rolled on by, I realized that was just silly kid's stuff. Wishful thinking.

I didn't need to think about her, or let her dampen my spirits when I now had the two best friends anybody could ask for.

And of course, Cole.

The man who spent hours moping because he "wanted to spoil his boyfriend rotten on his birthday."

That's right, he called me his boyfriend. He'd first said it when we were discussing what I was going to do for my birthday. It was casual. Felt like natural progression. I didn't even bother correcting him or asking him for clarification.

I wanted nothing more than to be his boyfriend.

So, after reluctantly agreeing that not spending tonight with Aiden and Callie would set off huge alarm bells, he promised he'd make it up to me this weekend.

I tried to tell him there was nothing that needed to be made up. I didn't need him to fuss. I didn't need anything elaborate, expensive, or over the top.

I told him I only needed him, and he promised that was a given.

In a short amount of time, Cole has become a fixture in my everyday life. I'm addicted. Not just to him, but the man I am evolving into because of him.

I feel comfortable. I feel understood. I feel like me.

Making my way to the couch, I sit patiently waiting, more excited about how happy and content Callie and Aiden are with being in one another's company than my actual present.

While my life had reached great heights after the last time the three of us had tried to hang out, theirs had been a little more awkward and stunted, to say the least.

"Okay, here it is," Callie says, handing me a small rectangular shaped box. "Happy birthday."

I look up at Aiden, and the smile on his face matches Callie's squealing. Putting us all out of our misery, I carefully unwrap the box, peeling off the silver paper one layer at a time.

When I'm finally able to lift the lid off the box, I can't help but laugh at the contents inside. "Are you guys serious?" I ask, looking up at them incredulously. "How did you even get this made?"

I pull out the plastic identification card that now has me listed as twenty-one-year-old Jason Deandra. "Did you guys use my student card photo?"

"It looks awesome, right?" Aiden sits next to me on the couch, plucking the card out of my hands and getting a better look at it for himself. "I can't believe how real it looks."

"I still don't want to do anything but go to dinner," I repeat for what feels like the hundredth time. The compromise for doing just dinner tonight was it was my choice of cuisine and, since they insisted on paying, their choice of restaurant.

It was an argument I was never going to win, so eventually I stopped trying.

"We know," Callie assures me. "But now we can drink saké at Sakéshop."

"Drink what now?" I ask.

"It's a Japanese alcohol. Trust me, you'll love it."

I roll my eyes, because after the last time we all drank together, my trust in Callie and Aiden under the influence of alcohol was pretty much nonexistent.

Aiden pipes in while furiously typing on his phone. "Should we get going? We don't want to be late for our reservation."

"Let me just get my cell and wallet," I say quickly. Before I shove them both in my pockets, I message Cole.

Me: They're taking me to Sakéshop. If you're still up when I get home, I'll call you. I know how you oldies like to go to sleep early.

Cole: Just wait till I see you. I'm going to show you just how 'old' this man is.

I smile, loving our easy-going banter.

Me: Can't wait.

WE'RE SITTING in the Uber when Aiden says to me, "Hey, man, King Koffee just put up another flyer looking for someone to work there. Did you end up going to see if they'd hire you?"

I think back to everything that has taken place since those early weeks at school. Studying. The Research Project. Cole. "No, I didn't end up going in," I say. "I was adjusting to my workload and with the research project, I didn't want to stretch myself thin."

It isn't a lie, but it isn't the whole truth. However, as my bank account continues to dwindle, I tell myself to go in there the next chance I get. It might mean seeing less of Cole, but I know he'll understand that I don't really have any other option.

We pull up to the main street in Georgetown, and the Uber stops in front of a row of fancy restaurants. The sidewalk is bustling with trendy men and women indulging in a night of good food and good company.

I follow Aiden and Callie through a narrow door that leads us to a steep set of stairs.

The light is low and the air around us is tight. "Did you guys bring me here to kill me?" I joke.

"It does make it easy that you came willingly," Aiden supplies.

I back hand him on the shoulder just as we take the last step. In front of me is one of the busiest restaurants I've ever been in. With a low ceiling, decorated in black steel beams and lowly hung black light fixtures that fall directly above each table, it's the perfect combination of formal and intimate.

"Hello, welcome to Sakéshop." A short Japanese lady,

dressed in a traditional black Kimono with cherry blossoms printed all over it, puts her hands together and bows ever so slightly. "Do you have a reservation?"

"It's under Jason Deandra," Callie tells her. I turn to smirk at her, but she's already got a huge megawatt smile plastered on her face, clearly impressed with herself.

As we begin walking through the restaurant, the waitress shouts loudly in Japanese. I stop in a moment of confusion, but as all the patrons look up at us and shout a loud, different response, I realise they just welcomed us to the restaurant.

"That's really cool," I say as the three of us are seated.

"It's my favorite part," Aiden admits. "I love looking up and seeing the reaction of the people walking through. It's endless amounts of entertainment."

Callie reaches for my hand over the table. "Do you like this place? Did we pick a good spot?"

I give her hand a firm squeeze. "This is even better than I expected."

The small dainty woman returns with menus tucked under her arms and a bottle of table water.

She pours each of us a small amount in the already provided glasses and then leaves the menu in the middle of the table.

"Excuse me," Aiden says quickly, immediately stopping her retreating form.

"It's my friend's birthday and we'd like to celebrate with a bottle of saké, please."

She nods and walks away, just as Aiden looks at me knowingly. "You don't eat Japanese and deny yourself saké. It's unheard of."

Feeling relaxed, happy, and content, there's only one person I want to tell.

Picking up my cell off the table, I type a quick message to Cole.

Me: Aiden and Callie really outdid themselves. This place looks great.

The three dots appear and disappear numerous times before his message comes through.

Cole: You deserve it, Elijah. Relax, enjoy your night out. Happy Birthday.

Knowing the words I need to hear has become Cole's forte. After divulging to him my home life, he now reads me like an open book, always offering me comfort and consolation when I need it most.

I begin to type out the words 'wish you were here', but think better of it. Cole doesn't need to feel bad about it and neither do I.

Tonight isn't the night to remind each other of the things we'll probably never have.

Just as I place my cell down on the table, I hear the now recognizable Japanese greeting echo through the restaurant. I raise my head to capture that same moment Aiden loves so much, when I see Cole, flanked by two other people, staring at me.

"Isn't that your professor?" I hear Aiden ask. I can't answer him, all I can do is stare right back at Cole. "What are the chances of him eating out here tonight too?"

Yeah. What are the chances?

21

COLE

When I messaged Harper and Miles this afternoon to join me for dinner, it was probably my most selfish move yet.

I played it by ear with Elijah, and figured I lived close enough to make a last-minute decision about where we would be eating. When he mentioned Sakéshop, it was Kismet. Like the night was mine for the taking, it took me no time to get here.

I was under the impression that if I couldn't spend Elijah's actual birthday with him, then maybe I could be near him... In my head it seemed like the perfect idea; we would share knowing smiles, steal heated glances, maybe sneak off for a secret kiss.

I had romanticized our secret tryst, and as I stand here staring at the horrified look on Elijah's face, I realize me showing up here is anything but romantic.

Three sets of eyes stare at me, a different form of recognition in each. I don't know what made me think I could slip in here and not be recognized. I wanted him to see me, didn't I?

He lowers his head, flicking his hair in his eyes, a habit I haven't seen him do with me in a very long time.

I hate myself for this.

Too busy thinking about how much it was killing *me* to not see him today, and how *I* wanted to be the one that made his birthday better, I didn't consider the position me showing up would put him in.

Unquestionably jealous of his friends, it eats me up inside to not be able to lay claim on him. In the back of my mind, I know that's possessive and brutish, but I can't seem to change it.

There hasn't been a day in the last two weeks where I haven't wanted more. More than him in my bedroom, more than him in my house, more than the quick, stolen moments at work. I didn't expect it to hit me like this.

After we had sex, I thought it would be even easier to stay hidden, because all we'd want to do is fuck each other's brains out. And we do do that. Hard and rough, slow and sensual, we cover it all.

Since that first time, it's almost impossible to not end up inside him whenever we see each other.

He's easily the best sex of my life, and I'm not too much of an idiot to know there's a reason beyond our sexual compatibility for that. We fit together in all the ways I didn't think we would. Our worlds are melding together, tighter and closer than I could've ever imagined, and it's making me crazy.

Certifiable.

Reckless.

Irresponsible.

Irrational.

If I wasn't careful, I was going to end up somewhere neither Elijah or I could afford to be. In the back of my mind, I could hear that little voice telling me where this is heading, and I can't seem to steer it into any other direction.

"Living close to the city suits you, Huxley," Miles teases, oblivious to the tension rolling off me. The waiter leads us out of Elijah's view and further into the restaurant. "It seems like you've settled in and scoped out all the good places."

"Well, we know you don't get out much now that you're all shacked up," Harper teases.

"I'm so far from shacked up right now."

"You're a liar Miles Decker. When you get orgasms on the regular from the same person, you're shacked up."

Harper's voice isn't low, and we get a few weird looks as we pass other tables. I hope they sit us out of earshot of people, because there's no doubt Harper and Miles will be at it all night.

Once we're seated, I look at Miles pointedly, trying to focus on anything else but the shitty feeling inside of me. "Don't try to argue with her ridiculous woman's logic. Just agree with her and she'll drop it a whole lot quicker."

I almost expect her to bring up our conversation from the other week and call me out on my own shit in front of Miles, but she doesn't. And with Elijah in breathing distance, my body relaxes in relief. I don't think I'll be able to handle any form of a Harper inquisition tonight.

The way I'm feeling, I'm likely to tell them everything, and I don't care that they'd be supportive and understanding, I can't risk Elijah's future like that.

I purposefully avoid looking up at him or his friends, as impossible as it is. He needs space, and if I could walk Harper and Miles back out of this place without a fuss, I would've done it already.

"So what do you guys want to order?" Miles asks. "Obviously we're drinking saké?"

I needed something a lot stronger than saké.

"Do you guys eat sashimi? If you do, we could order a few of their platters and share them?" Harper suggests.

Not really in the mood to argue or prolong our time here, I go along, agreeing to everything she and Miles decide.

While they're bickering over the way sashimi is "cooked", I drag out my cell, and against my better judgement, I send Elijah a message.

Me: I'm sorry for showing up like this.

I can't help but look up at his table, which is situated diagonally across from ours, and wait for him to notice the message.

He's subtle when reaching for it, his body language giving nothing away.

Elijah: Don't be sorry.

But I am, I want to shout.

I don't send a follow up text, because best case scenario we'll start text flirting and worst case we'll get into some sort of texting feud which will draw attention to us that neither of us needs.

"Earth to Cole," Harper calls out, waving her hand in my face. "Are you okay? You're being awfully quiet considering you were the one so eager to come and eat here."

"Sorry, I just got distracted for a second there." I put my phone back in my pocket, and pour myself a glass of table water.

"Was one of those kids a student of yours?" Miles asks.

"What?" I almost choke on my water, his observation catching me off guard. "What do you mean?"

"Callie, the girl sitting with those two boys," he says, tipping his head in their direction. "She's in my Juvenile Delinquency class."

"Isn't that your favorite class?" Harper mocks.

"Yeah," I say numbly. "Elijah is in one of my Studies in Religion electives. The other guy is his friend. He's always waiting for him outside of class."

None of what I'm saying is a lie, yet is feels so impersonal it almost could be. He's so much more than just a student. Compassionate and complex, he's everything good that the world needs.

"You get used to seeing students outside of King every now and then," he continues. "If you have a life outside your house, it's inevitable."

A petite waitress with jet black hair walks up to our table, standing directly in front of my view of Elijah, and interrupting Miles. "Are you ready to order?" she asks.

"Yes," Harper answers, taking the lead. "Could we please get the sashimi combo, the sushi set, and the sashimi appetizer?"

"To share?" the lady clarifies.

"Yes, please."

"And some saké for the three of us," Miles adds.

Without another word, the young lady smiles and walks away, just in time for me to catch Elijah standing up from his table and heading toward the restrooms.

Every logical part of me knows I should remain seated. Keep my cool, and have some self-control. But I'm desperate.

I need to see him.

I need to talk to him.

I need *him*.

"I'm just going to the bathroom," I announce.

Throwing the cloth napkin on the table, I push the chair out and stand. With as much restraint as I can muster, I keep my steps even, my gait almost lazy. The complete opposite of how I feel inside.

Once I turn the corner, I'm surprised to see his back against the wall, his head buried in his phone.

"Texting someone?" I ask.

My phone vibrates in my pocket. And Elijah momentarily seems stunned.

"Yeah."

It takes three long strides for me to back him into the wall, my hands on either side of his head. Looking from left to right, I scope out our surroundings, knowing how dangerous this is, but finding very little reason to care.

I need to be near him. I need to explain myself. I need to make his birthday better.

With nothing but earnest curiosity in his eyes, he looks up at me. "Why are you here?"

"I thought," I start, but the words catch in my throat. "I thought I could spend your birthday with you."

He raises an eyebrow, and a humorless laugh leaves my mouth, because I sound ridiculous.

"Not actually with you," I clarify "But by being near you." Embarrassed, I drop my head to his shoulder and groan. "It sounded way better in my head. I'm so sorry for ruining your night."

"You didn't ruin it."

I raise my head and meet his eyes. "You looked mortified."

"I was surprised," he says defensively. He reaches for my jaw. "When you're around I can't focus on anything else. I'll give us away and I'm not ready…"

To say goodbye.

The unspoken words penetrate my skin, sink into my

bones, and turn my blood cold. Stuck between a rock and a hard place, this can't be the only option for us.

"I'm sorry," I say again. "I got carried away. I wasn't thinking clearly."

The sound of a door slamming brings us both back to reality, my body jolting away from his, officially ending my attempt at an apology.

"So, how's your night?" I ask, trying to appear as casual and friendly as possible.

Elijah chuckles at the change, but continues the conversation. "They really went all out for me."

"You sound surprised."

"Nobody's ever done that before." Soft and vulnerable, I watch Elijah struggle to process his feelings. The understanding that for him, life will never be the way it was. From here, it can only get better.

"If I could, I would wrap you up in my arms right now and hug you so tight," I tell him. "Just so you know how important you are. To Aiden. To Callie... To me." I guess he isn't the only one feeling a little bit raw tonight. "This won't be the last time people will want to do things for your birthday. I can promise you as the years go on there will be more than the three of us on that list."

Giving in to temptation, I close the distance between us, possessively resting my large hand against the column of his neck. I let the insinuation hang between us. Let it thicken the air, and the weight of it settle on our shoulders.

I won't correct myself or clarify it. I won't hide under the guise of unknown feelings and guessing games. I've already passed the point where I can justify any of my actions.

Feeling a little bit bold and whole lot reckless, I want Elijah to know that if I can somehow erase our expiration date, I will.

That's where I'm at right now. Feeling it hard. Feeling it deep.

"I really am sorry about tonight." I pinch the bridge of my nose. "When it comes to you, I feel like I'm going a little bit crazy."

"In different circumstances, I would have no problem with crazy."

"I'll make it up to you," I say.

His eyes shimmer with excitement. "You will?"

"Well, not in a place where the restrooms are my backdrop."

Hands dangerously grip my hips. "I'm still coming over this weekend, and now you can give me two presents instead of one."

"Don't be so smug, sweet boy. You know how much trouble it can get you in."

He clicks his tongue. "Only the good kind."

My gaze flickers between his eyes and lips, reading the want, understanding the hunger.

This is why public places are so dangerous, because he's so close, and everything about him is so tempting.

Slowly, I turn my head to the right.

Clear.

Then to the left.

Clear.

Before either of us changes our mind, my mouth is on his like a full force collision. Tightening my grip around his neck, I squeeze as I grind my hips into his. I stake my claim like the crazed animal I am in the only way this forbidden situation allows.

In hidden corners, and dark corridors, I kiss him hard. I kiss him long. I kiss him until I can't kiss him anymore.

"Eli?" Three letters. Short. Sharp. Accusing.

Elijah's head turns first, and I deliberately punish myself by watching his face morph from elation, to all consuming dejection.

This is all my fault. He fucking warned me.

"What the fuck?" Aiden shouts.

My hackles rise at his tone, and I'm about to tell him to fuck right off when Elijah steps in.

"Aiden," he tries calmly. "This isn't the time or the place."

"You think?" he hisses. "You were just sucking face with your fucking professor. In public. Don't try and tell me about time and place."

Shame washes over Elijah, and I'll be damned if I let anyone ever make him feel like that, especially not in my presence.

"You better lower your voice and watch your tone with him," I warn.

"Or what?" he taunts. "You'll hit me? And what will they do when I tell them I caught you kissing a student and you retaliated, huh?"

Aiden momentarily drops his macho act and shifts his focus back to Elijah. "Do you know what you're risking? Everything you've worked for, Eli. Everything," he annunciates. "If anyone finds out, you're going to lose your scholarship."

He voices every single one of our fears, and I hate him for it. I hate him for making them real, and I hate him even more for making the consequences a possibility.

Surprising me, Elijah gets right up in Aiden's face. "Are you going to be the one to tell them?"

Aiden's gaze flicks between me and Elijah. "I can't believe you're with *him*."

It's the recognition of hurt in Aiden's voice that tips me

off. Pieces the puzzle together. "You mean, you can't believe he's with me, and not *you*."

"What the fuck have you told him?" Aiden says accusingly.

Elijah gives me a look that says he isn't fucking pleased, and I shrug. I'm not sorry. I'm not going to let this little fucker run circles around me, and I'm definitely not going to listen to him bully Elijah into feeling regret about anything we've shared.

"I thought you were smarter than this," he says to Elijah. "Smarter than to get caught up in what's probably some sick web of bullshit."

"You know nothing about us," Elijah defends.

"What's there to know? He smelled your innocent ass from a mile away," he sneers.

"How dare you?" I roar. But it's not my anger that makes Aiden flinch.

"Is that what you think of me?" Elijah's voice is eerily calm. "That I wouldn't know the difference between something that's real and something that wasn't?"

"That's not what I said," Aiden argues.

"That I'm just some weak, naive kid?" Elijah continues, his insecurities rising to the surface. "That I would just play nice with anyone who gave me the time of day?"

"I don't know." Aiden shrugs, his face and eyes void of emotion. "Is that what happened?"

I place my hands on Elijah's shoulders and crane my neck so my mouth is right by his ear. "He's baiting you, baby. Don't rise to it." Then I look straight back at Aiden. "Maybe you should stop talking before you say something you can't take back, because he's probably the only guy in the world who will forgive you for some of the shit you spewed tonight."

Livid, Aiden doesn't say a word, but rather he pushes the bathroom door with such force it echoes off the wall behind it. Watching him storm inside, I can sense Elijah's struggle on what to do next.

Unable to meet my gaze, Elijah keeps his head down when he says, "I think I'm going to stay here and wait for Aiden."

"What? After the way he just spoke to you? I don't think so."

"Cole," he says firmly. "I'm going to wait for my friend."

"Is this a joke? He was a fucking asshole to you."

"He was," he concedes. "And that's why I *need* to talk to him."

"What the fuck am I missing here, Elijah? Your friend basically threatened to tell on us, but you want to stay back and comfort him."

He grabs fistfuls of my shirt and kisses me. Hard, needy, and apologetic. "I'm sorry, Cole."

Confused and resigned, I kiss him back. *Me too, baby. Me too.*

Instead of walking straight back to Harper and Miles, I head over to a seated Callie and crouch down beside her. "Callie is it?" She throws her hand on her chest, my voice scaring her. "Sorry, I didn't mean to frighten you."

She looks around the room and then back at me. "Where are Aiden and Elijah?"

"That's what I came to talk to you about." I clear my throat. "Do you think you can go back there and check on them? Make sure they don't kill each other."

Eyeing me suspiciously, she rises from her seat, and wordlessly hurries toward them.

With each step back to my table, the adrenaline that had

been coursing through me lessens. Anger and confusion wasting away until I'm numb.

All of this happened because I thought it would be a good idea to surprise Elijah.

If I had stayed home, this would've never happened. Aiden and Elijah would still be friends, and Elijah and I wouldn't be teetering on the edge of the one thing we both didn't want to do.

I get back to the table, defeated. The expressions on both Harper's and Miles' faces show they're not sure, but also not oblivious to the fact that something just went down.

Grabbing my wallet out of my back pocket, I calmly place two fifty-dollar notes on the table. "I have to get out of here."

"Harper," Miles says taking control. "Go home with him. I'll cover here and see you both there."

22

ELIJAH

S taring at my phone, I will it to ring. To make any noise that alerts me to some form of contact from Cole.

But there's nothing.

Today was supposed to be the start of our weekend together celebrating my birthday, but since the night at Sakéhouse, Callie and I haven't left one another's side. Today we've been vegging out on the couch, my head in her lap, while she mindlessly flicks through the TV pretending like she hasn't spent Thursday night, all of Friday, and most of today waiting for Aiden to finally show up. While I obsess and wonder whether me stupidly telling Cole to leave was me breaking up with him, and not even realizing it.

My only intention was to try and reason with Aiden, salvage our friendship. But he just continued to make his disappointment and disgust in my decisions very loud and clear.

I didn't know what it was with him, whether it was jealousy like Cole had mentioned or he was just worried about my welfare, but when Callie showed up and gave him the dressing down of a lifetime, I realised maybe this, his reactions and his actions, aren't really about me at all.

He'd stormed out of the restaurant without a second glance, leaving Callie and me to both pick up the pieces of our wonky and mangled hearts, as well as the check.

"Are you going to actually do anything with your cell, or just keep holding it like a new hand accessory?" Callie asks, stroking her fingers through my hair.

"I've texted him three times, Callie. Surely he can give me something."

I can't work out if I'm hurt or angry, and the longer this radio silence between us continues, the more confused I become.

He should've never come to the restaurant, and it kills me to even think like that, because I know with every part of my being he came with—albeit slightly selfish—very good intentions. But I know what we're like together. The magnetic force. The combustion. I knew it was making us more reckless. And I knew that that recklessness would eventually get us in trouble.

We've come so far from those two people having dinner at Carne that first night. That had been innocent, or at least just a testing of the waters. But now, we're in deep. Deep enough that I knew we were becoming impossible to hide.

Now it's the weekend, and we had plans. Plans for my birthday. Plans for just me and him.

"Text him again," Callie instructs.

Sitting up, I put my elbows on my knees and rest my head in my hands. "I'm sure that's the opposite of what friends are supposed to say."

"Maybe, but on the off chance he thinks you don't want him, you need to tell him you do."

And I do, don't I?

0
1

1

2

1

I'm confused and frustrated, but I miss him like crazy. I hate this feeling. The unknown, the fear, the anticipation of the worst.

Cole and I aren't supposed to feel like this. Not anymore. Not after how far we've both come. I was so sure we'd left that uncertainty behind.

"I need to head over to King Koffee to try out for this barista job, anyway. Maybe it will take my mind off it all."

"I still don't know why you insist on running yourself into the ground. How do you plan to fit working into your schedule?"

"Callie, hundreds of students work and study. If everyone else can do it, why can't I?"

"Everyone else isn't involved in a research project that has a four-year workload crammed into one."

She's persistent with her argument, and the care factor is cute enough that I don't bother explaining to her—for the millionth time— the ins and outs of the scholarship students at King University.

Holding the back of her head, I steady her as I kiss her forehead. "I appreciate your concern, but it won't be that bad. And if everything turns to shit, I'll have some spare hours on my hands." I rise off the couch. "If I'm going to be miserable, I may as well be making money."

"I think you're overreacting about both of them," she says, stopping me from leaving. "Aiden needs to calm down, but you do not owe him anything, nor should you be feeling guilty about things that were never his business in the first place."

She reaches for my hand and squeezes it. "And Cole. He *will* come around."

"How do you do that?" I ask.

"What?

"Put everything in perspective."

She gives me a sad smile. "I've had a lot of practice. Cole might not be the perfect match for you because of the circumstances, but that's for you and him to navigate. A fight over or with Aiden should not be the reason you end."

I scoff at the mention of Aiden. "He said some really shitty stuff to me."

"I don't doubt it, babe. Just remember, when he comes around, because he will, don't let him get away with it. If someone upsets you, you let them know. And Aiden needs to know. Otherwise, he'll walk all over your kind and forgiving heart, just like he does to mine."

The exhaustion in her voice has me sinking to the couch. "I've been too busy whining about my life, and not spending enough time worrying about you."

"I'm fine," she says, waving me off. "I just think it's time I let this stuff with Aiden go. I'm sorry my realization came at your expense, but if I don't want to keep going around in circles, I have to break my own heart and move on." Unshed tears fill her eyes. "I love him, Elijah. I really do. But I don't like him anymore."

I wrap my arms around her, while she cries into my shoulder. "Here, I've got a little present for you," I say, hoping to comfort her.

She wipes her eyes with the back of her hands. "What is it?"

I pull out an unopened packet of Werther's Originals and she smiles. "I promise they make everything better."

"ELIJAH, YOU'RE A NATURAL," Joe, the owner of King Koffee, tells me. I find it hilarious that's his name, but I don't bring attention to the small things that amuse me. "The job is definitely yours. I'm just going to need a few days to work out the schedule and I'll be in contact."

I put my hand out and he shakes it. "Thank you so much, sir. I appreciate the opportunity."

"None of this sir bullshit, son. The name is Joe."

"Thanks, Joe."

I give him a quick wave goodbye and head out of the shop. Checking my phone, I see a missed call from Cole. Stunned, I stop in the walkway, and a girl walks right into me.

"Shit, I'm so sorry," I say. "Are you okay?"

She doesn't waste any time acknowledging me, turning her scrunched up face and walking away. Finding the nearest bench, I take a seat and hit the call button.

It takes less than two rings for him to answer. "Elijah."

His voice blankets over me, immediately eradicating the tension. God, how I missed him.

"Hey."

"How have you been?" I sigh into the phone, words unable to express the right answer. "Can you come over?"

"Now?"

"Yeah. We need to talk."

I've been miserable these last few days, and prolonging this conversation is only going to add to that. "I'll be there in twenty."

"See you then."

When I arrive at his front door, I have to stop myself from hurling all over the stoop. To say I feel nervous is a gross understatement. My heart is on the other side of that door, and I'm sure I don't want it back.

Anxiously, I knock and then tuck my shaky hands back into my pockets.

The door swings open, and a disheveled Cole waits for me on the other side. I've never seen him so unkempt, so unsure.

It takes everything I have not to run into his arms. To curl into his hard body and beg him to tell me everything will be okay.

His tired gray eyes roam over my body, the low flame of desire for me still there.

He gestures for me to come in, and then leads us through the kitchen. It's awkward and silent, nothing like our usual.

"Do you want a drink?" he offers, standing awkwardly inside his kitchen.

On the other side of the counter, keeping distance between us that I don't like, I ask the only thing I want the answer to. "Cole, what are we doing?"

Abandoning the drink pretense, he bends over, resting his arms on the kitchen counter, scrubbing his hands up and down his face.

"When you told me to leave you with Aiden," he starts. "I was furious. And then I was hurt and shocked, but now I'm just lost." He visibly swallows. "I've never felt like this before, and I don't ever want to feel like this again."

I wait for him to deliver the blow, to tell me that I put the last nail in the coffin when I asked him to go, but it doesn't come.

"I know now how stupid it was for me to show up unannounced. I knew it within ten seconds of seeing your face, and I knew it when I hurtled my bruised ego out of there. It was completely out of character for me, not to mention irresponsible. I could have never predicted just how shitty the night was going to end. And even if I had, it would've been nothing compared to how awful it really was."

He goes silent, as if he's regrouping his thoughts, refusing to look anywhere else but at me.

"I tried to give you space. The unanswered messages… that was me trying to be the adult, and not an asshole. Tried to talk myself out of doing this with y—"

"Wait," I interrupt. "Before you say any more, I need you to know I should've walked out with you that night. I should've left Aiden and my guilt behind in that restaurant and walked out with you."

He stalks around the counter, closing the distance between us, cradling my face in his hands. "If that was the only thing that was our issue, Elijah, I would've been knocking on your door demanding we hurry this shit up and get to the make-up sex everyone's always talking about."

It's a light hearted joke, said at just the right time.

"But I'm stuck here, Elijah. The rules are explicit. In any language, at any school, in every country. Everybody knows this never ends well.

"I know now, more than ever, there's no easy way out of this for us." He runs his thumb across my lips, looking at me wistfully. "I know I should walk away, but when it comes to you, I am a weak, weak man. And so, I'm asking you." Closing his eyes, he takes a loud, deep breath before meeting my gaze again. "I'm telling you. Walk away from me, Elijah."

I shake my head in his hands, "No. No," I repeat. "No, I won't do it."

"We can't have it all, Elijah. And Aiden was right. There's too much at stake here."

He doesn't loosen his hold on me as I continue to shake my head.

"I can't walk away from you any more than you can walk

away from me," I tell him. "Please don't ask me to be the person that ruins this."

"You wouldn't be ruining it, Elijah. What I did the other night, that's ruining it. I set these wheels in motion. All on my own."

I push his hands off me in anger and step away from him. "I spent too many years sacrificing my needs and wants for the greater good, Cole. I won't keep putting myself last."

"Making your education your priority is not putting yourself last."

"I can get an education anywhere."

"No!" he shouts. "No. You are not giving King up."

"Consequences be damned, Cole." My voice is calm, a contradiction to his rage. "I'm not giving you up either."

"Elijah," he warns.

"Nothing you say can change my mind."

"You're going to regret it."

"No, I'll remember it. I'll know that this feeling is real."

I'll know that something very close to love is real.

I don't let my errant thought run free. I keep that card close to my chest, because I don't want to use it like a weapon in battle. When I say those three words for the first time, I want them to hold their worth. I want him to know their worth. His worth.

"Aiden knows, and he threatened to tell, might I just add. Which means Callie does too."

"What, and your friends at the restaurant don't know by now?" I quip.

"That's my point, Elijah, too many people know. It's dangerous."

"Or maybe, just maybe, we could have some people looking out for us, some people rooting for us."

He reaches out for me, and I step back. "Don't come any closer, unless that's where you're going to stay."

The gray in his eyes deepens, swirling like the eye of a storm. Frustrated he can't touch me, the muscles in his jaw work overtime.

"This is how it'll be, Cole. I'll be so close, and you won't be able to touch me. All you'll be able to do is watch, and remember. Remember all the things we had, and all the things we lost."

"You fight dirty, Elijah Williams."

"I fight for what's mine."

He launches himself at me, devouring my mouth like the starved man he is. His kiss is hard and punishing. An aggressive, wordless apology fueled by all the things we want and all the things we can't have.

"I need inside you," he breathes out. "I need to feel what's mine."

Upstairs and undressed in seconds, I'm perched on a bed of pillows, my balls full, and ass up in the air, wanting him to fuck the memory of the last two days without him out of me.

He spreads my cheeks wide, roughly running his lube coated fingers up and down my taint and around my rim. He repeats the motions, touching and teasing everywhere but the place I need him most.

"Cole," I groan. "Please."

I feel his fingers begin to fill me up. In and out, stretching me the way only he knows how. It isn't long before the tip of his sheathed cock is joining in on the action, circling and teasing my hole.

"Ready for me, baby?" I wiggle my ass, and he slaps my cheek. "Smart-ass."

Spreading me apart again, he pushes himself inside me.

The head of his cock slides into me, a slow and delicious burn left in its wake.

He moves his hands to my hips and begins a grueling pace. His grip gets tighter as his thrusts become frantic. My hand reaches for my dick, my strokes matching the rhythm of his hips.

Heavy breathing and the sound of skin slapping skin fills the room. We grunt and moan, the air too thick for anything more. Relentless, he moves in and out, every emotion of the last two days wasting away between us.

"Harder," I call out, wanting to feel it all.

"Any harder, and I'll fucking break you."

"Harder," I say again. "I need it, Cole. Please."

He pounds into me with brutal force, and I let it all consume me. Feeling the hurt, the anger, and the bittersweet gifts the world gives you. The disbelief I would meet this man, and be threatened to lose him every step of the way.

Every stroke becomes our own version of an apology. A sacrifice. A promise.

My body begins to tremble as pre-come drips all over my hands.

In tune with every one of my tells, Cole and his strength push us closer to the edge. "Come on, baby. Come for me. Show me what my sweet boy can do."

His coaxing and endearments are the perfect antidote to his unforgiving thrusts. Hard and soft. The two sides of this beautiful man. *My* man.

Cole's final growl and the possessive thought are all I need.

My orgasm obliterates me. In a fog of exhaustion and satisfaction, I sink into the mattress, Cole's heavy body following.

He lays on top of me, his dick still twitching inside me.

"Let's just stay here," I say, my voice hoarse. "Never leave. Just like this."

Soft lips meet my neck.

"Just." Kiss. "Like." Kiss. "This."

―――――

CLEAN BED. Clean bodies. Cole and I lay naked, twisted up in each other's arms, too wrung out to move.

"I hate to sound entitled--" I say, my head resting on Cole's chest.

"You out of all people, could never sound entitled."

"You haven't even heard what I'm about to ask yet."

"Fine. Shock me."

"Whatever happened to that birthday present you were excited to give me? Do I still get it?"

His whole body stills.

I sit up, turning my body to him. "What's wrong? Did I say something wrong? Shit, there wasn't really a present was there? And now I just sound even worse." I bury my head in my hands, embarrassed.

"Stop," Cole orders. He grabs my wrists and lowers my hands. "There was a present. Or I should say, there is a present. It just feels too soon now."

"Too soon for what?" I ask.

"Maybe those are the wrong words. The present itself isn't too soon. I bought it because I wanted to," he explains. "But after what went down, I don't know if it's a good idea."

"Will you tell me and let me decide?"

He nods. "Give me a second to get it."

I watch his bare ass leave the bed, and admire his back view as he stands in front of his dresser. He pulls out what looks to be a card in an envelope, and makes his way back to bed. With both of us now sitting up, he gives it to me.

"Before you open it, I need you to know, I wanted this for us when I bought it and I still want it now. But I can accept that things have changed, and things may be different between us."

"I promise you, there's no way I won't love whatever this is."

He blows out a long breath. "Just open it. Then decide."

I slip my finger under the sealed flap of the envelope and pry it open. Sliding out what's inside, I see two plane tickets to Chicago.

Chicago.

I look up at him incredulously. "You want me to come home with you?"

"I'm going to surprise my mom for her fiftieth birthday this coming weekend, and I thought you could come with me."

Overwhelmed, I try to organize my thoughts. This isn't some last-minute invite. I'm trying not to focus on how dazed, and a little upset, I am that he spent this money on me. Instead, inside I'm reeling, realizing that this is something he wants. With me.

"Are you sure your family won't mind?"

"I'm going to surprise them," he says with a smile.

"Cole, no." I shake my head. "That sounds like a terrible idea."

He leans over me till I'm lying back down and he's straddling me. "Trust me, you're the best surprise anybody could ask for."

23

COLE

W hen I invited him back home with me, I wholeheartedly wanted him to come; I just had no idea how much it really meant to me until I stuck the key into my mother's front door.

I didn't tell them I was bringing someone because I wanted the shock and excitement of such a monumental occasion as a distraction from the questions that would inevitably come.

He and I just managed to scrape on through what I was sure would be the end of us, and I'm not willing to risk a repeat of that any time soon. If he could win them over, which I had absolutely no doubt he would, the rest of the differences between us would be easier to ignore.

And even if they're not convinced we make sense, I'm too far gone to care.

The week leading up to this weekend was crazy busy. Elijah started a new job, while juggling his usual schedule, and I've been stuck in my office till nine every night working on exam templates and mid-semester grading.

We've had little to no time to see one another, so the

timing of this trip couldn't be better. It didn't hurt that the second we left Georgetown and headed to the airport, our walls slowly started to come down. We didn't have to be those people who secretly worried if anybody saw them staring at one another for too long.

Instead, we got to be the couple that held hands in the Uber, cuddled on the plane, and kissed like nobody was watching in the terminal. And even here, in front of my family, I'm about to proudly introduce him as my boyfriend. Mine. Cole Huxley's boyfriend.

When I unlock the door, I notice Elijah move out of the doorway, hiding out of view. "What are you doing?" I whisper.

"Panicking," he supplies.

I hold in the chuckle, because I don't want to make fun of how nervous he's been. No matter how many times I tell him it's unnecessary, he continues to send himself into a frenzy.

When I texted Megs to tell her I'd arrived, she offered to come and get me from the airport, but seeing as I want to surprise everyone at the same time, I managed to convince her an Uber home wasn't going to kill me.

"Well, you better stop panicking if you want to give my mom the flowers you insisted on buying."

"You can't just go to someone's house empty handed," he says defensively.

"You never come to my house bearing gifts."

"And here I was thinking you liked my dick."

We both swallow our laughter as we pass the threshold. I slip my hand into Elijah's and give him a kiss on the temple. "I promise it's going to be okay."

Knowing we're here, Meghann calls out, "We're in here."

"Who's here?" I hear my mom ask. "You didn't tell me we were expecting anyone. It's eight o'clock on a Friday night."

I laugh to myself because my mom has always had a thing about people coming over past seven thirty. She used to say it was rude.

Leading him through the foyer, we pass the formal dining room that nobody ever uses and steer left into the next alcove that is the family room.

When we come into view, both Mom and Meghann have their eyes on the entryway, squealing in excitement. "Cole!" my mom shouts. "Why didn't I know you were coming?"

Meanwhile, Meghann runs to Elijah and throws her arms around him. "I can't believe my brother's seeing someone and brought him home before even telling me he existed."

Elijah drops his bag and stares at me while awkwardly hugging her back. Giving his hand a quick squeeze, I tip my head in my mom's direction and he nods.

Setting my bag beside the couch, I sit next to my mom and scoop her up in my arms. "I can't believe you're here," she says. "You're really, really here."

Grabbing my face, she kisses my cheeks over and over again. "Mom, stop," I say with a laugh. "There's someone I want to introduce to you."

No longer being attacked by Meghann, Elijah stands there with apprehension and reservation written all over his face.

I hold my palm out for him and he walks toward us until he can take it. When he's right beside us, my mom rests her hand on my shoulder and slowly pushes herself up.

"Mom," I scold, but still help her anyway.

She waves me off. "There's no way I'm not going to stand up and hug the first man my son has ever brought home."

Elijah's eyes widen when he looks at me, and I see the questions starting to pile up. I give him a quick shrug. He was going to work out how much he meant to me soon enough.

His attention shifts back to my mom, as she becomes the second woman in my family to unabashedly invade his personal space.

"Mom," I announce a little more formally. "I'd like to introduce you to Elijah. My boyfriend."

My heart splits into two at the sight of them hugging. Despite the size of the bouquet, they're holding on to one another like they've known each other forever. Elijah desperately needing that maternal touch, and my mother needing the confirmation that I'm doing okay away from home. It's heartbreakingly beautiful to watch my two worlds come together, how Mom and Elijah are inadvertently healing one another.

Pulling away, my mom peers up at Elijah, squeezing his shoulders. "I'm Geena. It's nice to meet you, Elijah."

"Likewise," he responds, handing her the flowers. As if she can't help herself, she takes them out of his hold and wraps him in her arms again. His whole face smiles at the gesture. Like there's nowhere else he'd rather be.

"So, big brother." Meghann grabs my bicep and pulls me back, away from Mom and Elijah. "What's the big secret?"

"I don't know what you're talking about," I lie, while I continue to watch Mom and Elijah enjoy each other's company. "It's been a very busy two months. Moving to a new state. New job—"

"New boyfriend," she cuts in.

"Can we leave lawyer Megs at work tonight?"

Expecting Meghann's smart-ass rebuttal, I'm thankful when the front door opens and a relaxed Trey walks on in.

"Holy fuck!" he shouts. We pull one another into a hug. "It's so good to see you, man."

Elijah must've caught his attention, because he looks between us. "You brought someone home?"

A sarcastic retort sits on the tip of my tongue, but I let it slide. If everyone wants to make a big deal about me bringing Elijah home, then I'll let them. Truth is, for me, he is a big deal.

"Let me introduce you." He gives Megs a quick kiss on the cheek before following me. "Elijah." Both he and Mom turn in my direction. "I'd like you to meet Trey. He's my best friend, and Meghann's boyfriend."

"Hey," they both say at the same time, shaking hands.

"Since I've got a beautiful, full house, do you guys want to eat something? I've got leftovers, or we can just catch up over some coffee."

"Mom. We can do it, you don't have to walk around."

She wraps an arm around my waist. "I've come a long way, honey. I promise I don't overdo it, if I can help it."

Elijah slips his hand into mine, and for the first time in a long time, I feel like I'm exactly where I'm supposed to be.

IT'S MINUTES TO MIDNIGHT, and Meghann and Trey have managed to tell Elijah every single embarrassing story of my childhood. Appreciative the conversation was steered safely away from Elijah and me as a couple, I know tomorrow I won't be so lucky.

"Well, my beautiful family, I have well and truly stayed up past my bedtime. I will see you all in the morning." It's obvious the late night has made her body tired, and it takes a few too many tries to get off her chair. Just as I'm about to get up to walk her to her room, Elijah beats me to it.

As he holds out his arm for my mom to take, I call to her. "Mom."

"Yeah, honey?"

I look down at my watch and then back at Megs. "It's midnight."

Right on cue, the four us begin to bellow out an extremely out of tune version of "Happy Birthday". Like every year we sing it to her, she laughs and then she cries. Elijah goes along with it all, never missing a beat, never feeling out of place. Outside of our time together, it's the most relaxed and carefree I've ever seen him; solidifying that this weekend was exactly what we needed.

Megs takes Mom off of Elijah's hands and helps her get settled into bed.

"I'm going to go to bed," Elijah announces.

"I'll come." I scoot my chair out, but he places a hand on my shoulder, stopping me.

"Stay with Trey, catch up. You haven't seen everyone in months."

Knowing I *need* to talk to Trey, I concede. I tip my head back and he kisses me. Oblivious to why this moment is so significant for us, Trey makes a gagging noise, purposefully trying to ruin it.

He smiles against my lips. "'Night, Cole."

"'Night."

I can't help but watch him till he's out of sight, already itching to be up and in bed with him.

"So, what is it?" Trey asks.

"What's what?"

"The reason you didn't mention him before tonight."

I bury my head in my hands. "Not you too."

"Don't 'not you too' me, I've known you my whole life. You didn't even hide your sexuality for fuck's sake."

"What about you?" I accuse. "You're hiding shit from Megs."

"She thinks that?" The surprise on his face confirms that something's wrong.

"The only thing she told me was that things were weird and she thought you might be breaking up with her."

"What?" He jumps up out of his chair and starts pacing the kitchen. "I would never leave her, Cole. She's my whole fucking world."

"Well, when was the last time you told her that?"

"I'll admit," he says, talking more to himself than me, "I've been moody. Yes, we've both been snapping at one another, but breaking up with her?" He shakes his head. "The only reason I wouldn't be with your sister, is if she didn't want to be with me."

The statement reminds me of Elijah's determination to not let us crumble, to not be swayed by the inevitable and the circumstances, but to fight, and to fight hard.

"Then what is it?"

"I was going to ask her to marry me."

Now it's my turn to be shocked. "What do you mean *was*?"

"About a year ago we decided we wanted to start trying for a family. I bought her a ring the next day, knowing the day she told me she was pregnant I would propose. It felt like the right thing to do. Like we'd come full circle. We fell in love as kids and now we'd be having our own.

"Six months later, nothing had happened. I said we could wait a little longer, but you know Megs... She wanted answers. So, we booked a doctor's appointment to get checked out." He pinches the bridge of his nose, chasing the tears away. "Turns out she was right, there was something wrong, and it's me."

"What am I missing here?" I ask. "There are so many options these days. It won't be impossible to have a kid."

"I'm supposed to get tests performed to see if anything can be done, but I don't want to know, so I've been putting it off."

"So she doesn't know?"

"She had a work deadline she had to meet. I told her I'd go without her. When she asked, I told her the doctor said let's keep trying."

"Trey," I groan. "You've made this so much worse than it needs to be."

"I know, but I didn't want her to marry me without knowing, but I can't seem to find the right time to tell her."

"Nothing will be as bad as whatever scenarios she's made up in her head. You know that, right?"

He nods. "I'll tell her this weekend. At least I know when she's hating on me, you'll be here to calm her down."

"She'll understand," I assure him.

"Yeah... But she'll be angry first."

After a few moments of silence, I slap both my hands on the table. "I think it's about time I called it a night."

"Not so fast. I spilled, now it's your fucking turn."

"There's nothing to tell," I deflect.

He raises an eyebrow.

"I'll tell you one thing, and then you don't get to ask any questions."

"I'm going to regret agreeing to this, but okay, tell me."

"He's my student."

His face falls, but it isn't the shocked expression that surprises me, it's the pity.

"Why are you looking at me like that?"

"You're in love with him."

"I said no more—"

"I wasn't asking a question, Cole," he states. "But maybe you should."

I look at him expectantly.

"When are you going to tell him?"

THE MORNING COMES AROUND QUICKER than I want it to, my body waking up despite my protests. I roll over to hug Elijah, hoping his warm skin will lull me back to sleep, but his side is empty.

When I finally came up to bed last night, I lay there like a creeper, watching Elijah sleep. There was beauty in his moments of peace, where the weight of the world was no longer on his shoulders and he wasn't running himself ragged trying to get all his ducks in a row.

I thought about what Trey had said, and wondered if my deep feelings for Elijah were as obvious to everyone else as they had been to him after only moments of seeing us together. I wasn't intentionally trying to hide them, but there was a huge part of me that was scared to lay them out there.

I don't want rules, regulations, and opinions to tarnish what we have. I don't need the world's approval, but apparently, somewhere in the far recesses of my mind, I needed my mother's.

Curious to where he's gone, I swing my legs off the bed, then rummage around my suitcase for some clothes.

Once I'm all covered up, I make my way to the kitchen, knowing more than likely, he and my mom are keeping each other company.

I couldn't have predicted how easy it would be for them

to fall into a comfortable rhythm. Like they've always known each other. Like it was always meant to be.

Turning the corner, I see Elijah sitting at the breakfast bar sipping on coffee, and Mom serving him French toast. Feeling a little emotional at the sight of them, I struggle to give an appropriate greeting, choosing to sidle up beside him instead.

"Hey," he greets, reaching over and kissing my cheek.

"Good morning, honey. Did you sleep well?" Mom chimes in.

"I would've been able to sleep a little bit longer if someone wanted to stay in bed with me."

Elijah grins at me sheepishly. "Sorry, the smell of coffee and food won me over. You're going to have to try better next time."

"Next time, huh?" I tease, loving that he envisions a next time.

"Elijah, darling. Would you be able to give Cole and me a moment alone?" Like this happens all the time, he doesn't seem to be the slightest bit alarmed by her request.

When I hear his footsteps move further and further away, I look up at my mom. "Is everything okay?"

"I don't know, is it?"

I narrow my eyes at her. "It's too early for code Mom, what do you need to tell me?"

"Don't break that young boy's heart, Cole."

"I..." I stammer. "You think I'm trying to break his heart? What makes you think he won't break mine?"

She glances down at a red envelope on the kitchen counter, then back at me. "I'm just saying the world has not been easy on that pure and innocent young man. Don't be another person who lets him down."

I notice Elijah's handwriting and pick it up. "What's this?"

"Open it and see."

From the outside it looks like a generic birthday card, but when I open it and see Elijah's scrawl all over the card, my heart stops.

"Can I read it?" I ask her

"I'm sure he won't mind."

Geena,

I wanted to start off by saying thank you for allowing me in your home, and making me feel comfortable. I know Cole sprung it on you, but he insisted it would be the best way.

I know this is the first time we've met, and people don't usually lay it all out there, but it's your birthday, and the only gift I have are my words.

Thank you for spending your years raising a beautiful man.

The world needs more mothers like you.

I hope this isn't the last we see of each other, and if it is, your hospitality and hugs will be forever remembered.

Happy Birthday

Elijah

With blurred vision, I look up at my mother. "He's something else, isn't he?"

She doesn't respond, but the small smile on her face says it all.

I run my fingers through my hair, knowing this is the moment of truth. I need to tell her about us. I need to tell her, so she can tell me I'm not crazy. She can attest that he's worth it.

"He's my student, Mom," I blurt out.

Without a word, she turns off the gas to the stove. Putting down the plastic spatula, she shuffles around the breakfast bar and takes a seat beside me. "You think I didn't notice that he looked a decent amount younger than you?"

It's the exact approach she took with me when I finally told my family I was gay.

"What?" she'd said. "You didn't think I'd notice that my son never once looked at his sister's friends when they came over?"

Meghann's friends would shamelessly flirt with me, until I gave her permission to let them down gently. It was embarrassing for all of us.

Grateful for a mother who knows exactly when it is she's needed, I don't waste any more time filling the blanks of my story in.

"I can't walk away from him, Mom." My voice trembles from the thought alone. "I thought I could, and I tried. I swear to you, I tried to do the right thing."

"Honey, there's no right or wrong thing when it comes to who we love."

There's that word again.

"I haven't told him I love him," I tell her. "I don't think I realized I did till this weekend."

"Well, what are you waiting for? A sign from the gods?" she jokes. Slipping her hand into mine, she uncurls my fingers, and raises my open palm to my chest. "Things worth fighting for are never easy, Cole."

"I think I'm going to leave my job at King," I tell her, my body surprisingly feeling lighter the second the words leave my mouth. "There are plenty of other jobs I can apply for."

"You worked hard for that position, Cole. Endless flights back and forth, bending to their will. Are you sure you want to give it up?"

"That's the thing. I don't feel like I'm giving anything up, Mom." Putting my hands on her shoulders, I lean over and kiss her on the cheek. "I went there hoping to gain the experience of a lifetime. Something that no other job, school, or place could give me."

Mom is smiling at me. It's wide and contagious, her teeth on display, the apples of her cheeks a joyful shade of red. I don't realize I'm doing it too, until she finishes my train of thought for me.

"And that's exactly what it gave you."

24

ELIJAH

C ole couldn't keep his hands off me. Not in an 'I want to fuck you right here, right now' type of way, but in a way that let me know that in any given moment he was thinking about me, wanted to be close to me, couldn't get enough of me.

I didn't know if it was because we were at his mom's house, or if it was because we had the freedom to be a couple, or what had come over him exactly. All I knew was I would be devastated when we got back to reality and all this would have to disappear.

It's one thing to touch and feel the person you're with in the privacy of your own homes, but when there were other people around, that tipped my emotions over the edge.

After living with my parents and feeling like I would never get to live and be my normal self, touching with an audience gives me a thrill I can't describe. It's liberating. It's reaffirming. And with Cole and his family, it feels like I'm home.

We spent the day lazing around, feasting on birthday cake. Now, we're all sitting around the coffee table playing poker. Well, they're playing poker, I'm too busy sifting my hands through the strands of hair at the base of Cole's neck; in too deep with all the physical contact.

I have never felt more relaxed, more understood, and more at peace with myself and my choices than I have this weekend.

"Ha. I win!" Megs shouts out excitedly. She and Trey came back over sometime this afternoon, but tonight they're sleeping over, so they can drive us to the airport in the morning. They're a wonderful couple. In fact, they're all some of the best people I've ever met. Especially Geena. With her quick wit and warm heart, she had me like putty in her hands the second she hugged me. I'll miss her the most.

"So, let's up the stakes. I want to know all the juicy details about you two," she points at me and Cole." If I win the next hand that's what I get."

Feeling bold, I speak up. "How about you ask what you want to know and I'll tell you?"

"No," Cole protests. "She has to earn it."

"She's already won two hands, don't let her kick your ass in a third one," I taunt.

He throws the cards on the table in mock defeat. "Fine. Fire away."

Earlier, Cole had mentioned he told his mom and Trey we'd met at King, and that I was his student. He said while their opinions wouldn't have changed anything about us, neither of them is upset or disappointed.

"So how'd you meet?" she starts.

The easy questions first, I guess.

"I ran into him while I was running. Literally toppled both of us onto the ground and sprained my ankle."

Her hands fly to cover her mouth. "Oh my god, how embarrassing."

"God, you don't even know the half of it," I retort.

"So, did he walk you back to your place? What happened after?"

I give the nape of Cole's neck a subtle squeeze, letting him know he can take the reins on this one.

"Actually, he refused to take my help and ran— actually he limped, away as fast as he could."

Cole doesn't even wait for her to ask the follow up question before he dives in. "I didn't see Elijah again until he showed up in one of my Studies in Religion electives."

Meghann's gaze shifts from his to mine and back again. Geena and Trey are watching her just as closely, waiting to see her reaction.

"So you're his professor?"

He gives her a quick nod.

I don't know what I expected, but the silence isn't it.

Trey's the first one to break it by tugging on the end of her ponytail. "What? Cat got your tongue? Just say what you want to say, so we can all move past it."

"What are you both thinking?" she says with much more hostility than I expected. "Cole, you worked so hard for this job. Why would you put it in jeopardy like that?"

He doesn't say a word, and anxiety blooms in the pit of my stomach at her question. I really thought she'd be okay with it. Cole always spoke of Meghann like she understood him, like she always had his back.

I guess, just like Aiden, the backlash comes from the people you least expect.

Moving from behind Cole, I shift off the couch, so I can head to our room. "Where are you going?" Cole asks, grabbing my wrist.

"I think you need to have this conversation without me here."

"No, there's no conversation to be had." He sits me back down, and I want the ground to swallow me whole.

He looks back at Meghann who doesn't look like she's about to back down any time soon.

"Babe," Trey says. "Why don't you and Cole have this conversation another time?"

"Another time isn't going to change the fact that I think he's playing with fire." Her gaze lands on me. "You both are." Straightening her back, she rests her forearms on the wooden table and leans forward. "This isn't personal."

"Like fuck it isn't," Cole bites back. "I've never once attacked your choices. I wasn't that overprotective brother that made it difficult for you and Trey to be together. I saw how happy you were, and that was all that mattered."

"It's hardly the same thing. I didn't have a career I'd spent my life cultivating at stake."

"Look," I cut in. "I get that you're worried for Cole. He and I both have a lot to lose, but being apart isn't an option for us." I tell her things I should've told Aiden. "This isn't something fleeting."

I love him.

"Or something that I can just switch off."

I can't see myself not loving him.

"If there were *any* other way out of this, any other way with fewer potential consequences, I would do it in a heartbeat." Cole squeezes my thigh. "But until that happens, this is the way it's got to be."

"And what if someone finds out, and you both lose?" she counters.

Taking the words right out of my mouth, Cole chimes in. "Then Elijah and I will work it out. *Together.*"

I think he loves me too.

"Fine," she huffs, raising her hands in the air in surrender. "I'll back down. *Just be careful.*"

The conversation officially ends, and somewhat ruins the vibe of the evening. Feeling more angry than hurt, I give Cole a pointed look, and he nods.

With him quick on my heels, we say a hurried and awkward goodnight, and retreat to the privacy of his bedroom.

As soon as he shuts the door, he's hugging me from behind, burying his face in my neck. "I'm so sorry."

"Don't be."

"I didn't expect her to take it like that."

"I get it. I didn't expect Aiden to either." I turn in his arms and take hold of his face. "Maybe she was upset you didn't tell her? Either way, I'm not even that mad about it. It means they care, right? We're stuck in this limbo of what to do and what not to do and there's no way out of that just yet. So until then, we'll deal." My lips gravitate to his, kissing him because I need to feel him, because I want him to feel me. "Regardless of how everyone else feels, we're still together, right?"

"You couldn't get rid of me if you tried."

We stare at each other for the longest time, and I feel those three words down to my bones. I'm irrefutably in love with him.

"Elijah."

"Yeah?"

"I—"

I slam my mouth to his, stopping him. "Don't say it yet."

"What? Why?"

"Because when *we* say those words to each other, I want you to be so deep inside me I can't tell where you start and I end. So close that it feels like our skin's melting into each other." His eyes burn for me and my words, and I wish for the first time this whole weekend that we weren't here. "And we can't do that here. So hold it in for a little bit longer, okay?"

He shakes his head with a smile. "I'll do anything for you."

———

THE REALIZATION that this would be the last time Cole's family would see him till Christmas changed the tune of our goodbye from tense, to somewhat apologetic. I reiterated to Geena I wasn't mad and totally understood Meghann's point of view. But just because I understand her concern for her brother doesn't mean I agree with her. It doesn't mean I'll start forgiving everyone who voices an opinion because they think they know best.

Cole, on the other hand, was mad and remained stoic till the very end. I knew the time between now and Christmas would mend what was broken. They weren't the type of family who would let each other fall to the wayside, and that warmed my heart with a sense of confidence and compassion that I never had in my own.

Now we're back in DC and I'm on pins and needles waiting to get back to Cole's. The sexual tension between us is simmering and almost up to boiling point.

I refused to let Cole touch me at Geena's place. When I feel his skin on mine, all logic and common sense flies out the window; there's no way we would've had quiet, slow sex. The only option was abstinence, and now I'm harder than a fucking post in the back of an Uber.

The worst part is we're not even touching. The temptation on its own is too consuming, let alone an accidental touch that would completely incinerate me.

Even though I know what's coming, it's done nothing, *absolutely nothing*, to diminish the significance of those three words. What they'll mean for us, and how much more secure in our choices I feel. If anything, the anticipation has derailed us. Left us unable to focus. Unable to do anything but wait.

When the Uber arrives in front of his brownstone, the walk up the steps feels ten times longer than it ever has before.

When we step inside, I almost expect him to throw me over his shoulder and run upstairs, but when he chooses to focus his attention on something else, I can't help but wonder if my occasional brute of a man is nervous, and isn't going to say something about it. With that fleeting thought, I decide to take matters into my own hands.

While Cole insists on being an adult and flicking through his mail, I do what any other horny, hot-blooded male would do. I start taking my clothes off in the living room.

Without any hints of seduction or attempts at finesse, I pull my shirt over my head and throw it on the floor. How I take my clothes off matters little to both Cole and me. It's the naked part that's most important.

I hear him clearing his throat behind me, and I smile to myself knowing I've got his attention.

Next are my shoes.

"What are you doing?" he asks.

My socks.

Footsteps sound behind me. "Elijah."

Pretending I'm distracted, I casually turn around and meet his hungry stare. "Sorry, what were you saying?

He gives me my favorite devilish smirk before launching at me. I move just in time, running up the stairs and heading straight to the ensuite bathroom.

He manages to lock his arms around my waist before I even pass the threshold.

Dragging me back to the bed, he drops me in the middle and climbs up over me. "Don't bother running, because I'm always going to catch you."

I raise my hips off the bed, letting him know how hard up I am. "Have I ever told you how much I love when you get unreasonably possessive?"

He lowers his lips to my shoulder, while rolling his hips over mine. "Is that all you love?"

"Oh, is this how we're playing it?"

He moves his mouth up to my face and across my jaw, "I'm not playing anything, I'm just asking."

"What else are you so inclined to ask about?"

Surprising me, he takes the conversation somewhere totally different. "I loved seeing you with my family this weekend. You fit," he says. "Better than I thought anyone ever could. You slipped in like you'd always belonged."

I haven't belonged somewhere in such a long time. Not the right Christian. Not the right son. Not the right friend. But when I was with Cole's family, I felt exactly as he described. It felt like I'd known them my whole life. Like I was part of a group of people who cared what I thought, cared about how I felt. Cared about even the dumb and asinine things I had to say.

"I loved being with your family too," I tell him. He brushes his lips across my collarbone before making his way down to my nipple. "I loved watching you with your family," I add, my fingers running through his hair.

He rests his cheek on my chest and uses the pad of his

thumb to roll my nipple. "I love how comfortable you are in your own skin." He makes a wet trail down my torso with his tongue. "I love how you lose control for me." His fingers unbutton my jeans. "I love that I'm the only one who's seen you like this." My breath hitches and I watch my stomach tremble under his weight. "I love that this never gets old; touching you, wanting you." He drags the jeans down my legs, until all he can see is skin. My thickening cock sits against my stomach, hard and achy.

His lips meet my thighs, pressing wet open mouth kisses back up my body. He takes in the scent of me as he licks his way up my shaft, leaving me hanging for more.

When his body is finally flush with mine, he sits up, straddling me. He looks down at me, his gray eyes vulnerable and needy as his fingertips trace all the different lines and features on my face.

Closing my eyelids, he bends down to give them each a quick kiss. "I love your eyes because they can't lie."

He traces down the length of my nose and over my full lips. "I love your mouth. When I feel it on mine, it's like we have our own secret language."

He rubs his fingers on either side of my temples. "I love your mind, because you're fascinatingly complex."

Then he rests his open palm on my chest and bends to kiss where my heart is. "But this I love most of all. I love it because it's mine. I want you, Elijah," he rasps. "Your heart. Your soul. Your body. Your mind. I want it all."

"It's yours," I say, my voice thick with emotion. "I love you, Cole. It's all yours."

Unable to hold back, we collide in a mess of lips and limbs, my hands fumbling to get Cole out of his clothes.

My eyes roam over his physical beauty, taking in the perfect view of the man who unexpectedly swept me off my feet. Not wanting to rush any part of this, we stare at one another, both of us captivated by the beauty of falling.

Soon enough, we're skin to skin, rolling and rubbing, giving ourselves to each other and this moment. He takes me in his hands. Working me, teasing me, loving me in all the ways he knows how.

My body arches in anticipation as I feel slick fingers breach my hole. Quickly he grabs the lube and the condom and sits up.

I pull the condom out of his hold.

"Make love to me, Cole?"

"Are you sure?"

"I want to feel you, Cole. I want to feel how much you love me, and I want you to know how much I love you." My voice shakes with need. "Please."

I watch him lather himself up with lube, that sight alone enough to tip me over the edge.

"Sit on top of me, baby," he demands. "I want you to see my face when I show you just how much I love you."

Straddling him, I lower myself onto his greedy cock, my hole pulsating for him. Inch by inch, I watch his face morph into complete ecstasy.

Full to the hilt, I whimper at how good it feels.

Fuck," he groans. "This feels better than anything I've ever imagined."

I bounce up and down on his cock, while he wraps his fingers around my length and begins jerking me off.

"Can you feel me loving you?" he asks, our movements getting faster. "Can you feel it, baby?"

"Cole," I warn.

"Tell me," he demands. "Can you feel it?"

"Yes!" I cry out, my body convulsing in pleasure, making a mess between us.

"Today. Tomorrow. Always." he rasps in between deep thrusts before his body follows mine.

I fall on top of him, a malleable ball of skin.

"How long am I going to love you for?" he whispers

"Today. Tomorrow. Always."

25

COLE

S taring at my reflection in the mirror, I fuck around with my bow tie till it looks decent enough to leave the house. Tonight is the King University Annual Christmas Gala at the National Archives. Harper will be thrilled I'm finally getting to see it.

Capitalizing on the already established Annual Christmas Gala, Dean Billings used the National Archives as the perfect backdrop to pay homage to those organizations contributing to our History and Art Department research funds.

The only good thing about tonight is that Elijah will be there. Dressed up to the nines, I'll get to undress him with my eyes, knowing that later I'll get to come home and do it for real.

Since coming back from Chicago, our combined work-load has been borderline unmanageable, but now that the winter break is upon us, Elijah and I plan on making the absolute most of the uninterrupted weeks ahead.

Seeing as Elijah didn't end up inviting his parents, unlike all the other students, he managed to coerce the school board into adding Callie and Aiden's names as his guests for tonight. Things between he and Aiden haven't really changed. Their dorm is being used like a motel, and their interactions have been almost nonexistent.

Elijah has been hoping if Aiden comes tonight, they'll be able to find some middle ground and salvage their friendship. The whole thing has taken a huge toll on Elijah, and I respect his wishes and his loyalty to his friend, but it's going to take a lot more than an apology for me to ever forgive the way he treated Elijah at Sakéhouse.

Just as I'm about to message Miles and ask where he is, he texts me first.

Miles: Just leaving home, see you in twenty.

Me: Thanks.

I pull up Elijah's contact and text him quickly.

Me: How are you getting there?

Elijah: My date got me a limo. Said she's making up for the prom I didn't get to go to. She said she might even let me cop a feel.

I laugh to an empty room, always impressed with how witty he is when he's comfortable.

Me: Did you tell her you like dick? Specifically, mine?

Elijah: After the limo ride. I've never been in one.

In these moments of casual conversation, I'm grateful for Callie, Miles, and Harper. People who are there for you unconditionally. The night at the restaurant may have put a rift between Elijah, Aiden, and Callie, but Callie has really stepped up. And Harper and Miles... Let's just say if there were ever three people who were meant to come into one another's lives at the right time, it's us.

Quickly giving myself a once over, I walk outside to meet Miles. His Explorer sits idling on the street, his empty baby seat in the back, the perfect depiction of Miles' life.

"Hey, man," I greet, climbing into his car. "How are you?"

"I'm doing good, man. Things are really good." The satisfied look on his face makes me happy that after a shitty divorce, he's finally where he's supposed to be.

"Thanks so much for coming tonight. I know you probably had better things to do."

"I'll take any excuse to eat and drink on the King dime. Billings owes me."

As my time at King has progressed, I've come to realize how many people actually dislike Dean Billings. It's a wonder he's actually got a job, considering the rumours circulating about him are never ending.

Ever since the day he came into my office and tried to lay down his law, bringing my family into it, I can't seem to warm up to him.

"So, I wanted to ask you something."

Miles gives me a quick look and then focuses back on the road. "Yeah, what's up?

"Do you think Alexandria University has any openings for a history or arts teacher?"

Alexandria University is where Miles works in the summer. It's still in the same vicinity as King, so I wouldn't need to move or worry about leaving Elijah. It would mean I wouldn't need to worry about a lot of things, namely Elijah and me sneaking around and worrying about getting caught. Add in that there's no Dean Billings, and it's like a dream come true.

Gobsmacked, his mouth opens and closes a few times. "Are you serious? You want to leave King?"

"I want to know I have options," I tell him.

"Can I ask what brought this about?"

"It makes me sound ridiculous."

"Try me."

"It just didn't live up to the expectations."

"So this has nothing to do with Elijah?" he queries.

"While that's definitely a factor, it's surprisingly not the bigger part of it."

Elijah and I have always been up front with what we do and don't want the other sacrificing. While we disagree on the highs and lows of this job, I promised I wouldn't make any rash decisions when it came to leaving King. "Honestly, something feels off. I haven't felt settled."

"I can understand that," Miles says. "I'll be sure to ask around and let you know."

"Thanks, man." Changing the subject, I ask if he knows about Harper's whereabouts.

"She said she was coming, but refused to give me anything else. It's like pulling teeth with her sometimes."

I give him a smirk. "Like you can talk."

"I'm a reformed man," he jokes.

We arrive at the museum and jump out for the valet to take Miles' car. I'm momentarily silenced by the grandeur of the building before me. The columns, the flags, the stone monuments that grace the entryway. It's the perfect place to house history.

Continuing to look around, Miles guides us to the ballroom, while I stare wide eyed at my surroundings like a kid in a candy shop.

"Ok, this looks like where we're supposed to be," Miles says as he walks us through a roped off entryway.

"Are you sure that was the right entrance?"

"Yes. Follow me to the table. They have name tags."

"Are you kidding me?" I whine. "What do we need name badges for?"

"So potential parents can decide if you're good looking enough for them to throw money at your department."

"Fuck that shit."

Miles and I laugh at our own jokes as we dutifully put our name badges in the lapels of our jackets.

"How the hell are we expected to find someone in here?" I ask, the sheer size of the room overwhelming me. Elijah and Callie could be anywhere. Bustling with people, it's almost impossible to recognize anyone with the ridiculously dim lighting. Just as I'm about to text Elijah and try to scope out where he is, I feel a tap on my shoulder.

Turning, I'm surprised to see a distraught looking Callie. My body stiffens. "What is it?"

"Elijah's parents are here."

There's a five second delay between the words that just left her mouth and my brain registering what that actually means. "What do you mean they're here?"

"He's hiding out and I can't seem to get through to him. I've never seen him look so distraught."

"How did they even know about the event?" I signal to Miles I need to go, and then walk beside her as she leads me to Elijah. "Apparently, Dean Billings sent all the parents of students involved in special projects an invitation, as well as telling the students to pass on their own invites."

"You're fucking kidding me," I mutter underneath my breath. "They're the last thing he needs."

"Have they seen him yet?" I ask Callie as we slowly make our way down a narrow hallway.

"Yes. We said hello, and then I made some shitty excuse about how I needed to borrow Eli for a bit and I would bring him back later. He looked like a ghost. There was no way I was going to leave him there."

Stopping myself from hugging her, I give her shoulder a squeeze. "Thank you, Callie."

"Don't thank me yet."

When we turn the corner into a private area and I see a small, scared version of the man I love sitting on a chair and breathing into a paper bag, I want to kill someone.

"Hey, baby." His head whips up at my voice. "Are you okay?"

He continues to hold my stare, while concentrating on his breathing. He takes a few long breaths, releasing them seconds later. I knew his past and his relationship with his parents weighed on him, but I didn't expect to see him like this.

When he seems to have stabilized his breathing, worry and unshed tears fill his eyes. "I'm so, so sorry."

Crouching down beside him, I take his hand. "Why are you apologizing?"

"I don't know what came over me. I've never had a reaction like that to them," he explains.

"You don't need to justify it to anyone," I say sternly. "Are you feeling better?"

"I need to go and talk to them." He rises, and I take his hand and drag him back down to the chair.

"I don't think that's a good idea, Elijah."

"This has been a long time coming, Cole. I need them to know they're not welcome in my life anymore. They have been so absent for so long, especially when I needed them most." His voice cracks and so does my heart. "They don't just get to pick and choose when they want to be parents. It's my life and I won't let them."

"Okay, why don't we try and get them to come in here." I glance up at Callie. "Save ourselves a public debacle."

She gives me a quick nod. "Let me go and find them."

"I have this sick feeling in my stomach, Cole. Like something bad is going to happen now they're here."

"Hey, hey. Stop thinking like that." I tip his chin up to

look at me. "I'm never going to let anything happen to you, do you hear me? I love you."

"I love you too. So much." He cups the back of my neck and kisses me for dear life.

"Oh shit balls," I hear Callie say behind us.

Elijah's body turns to ice, and I whisper against his mouth before turning around. "I got you."

Mr. and Mrs. William are nothing like I expected. Impeccably dressed for the evening, Mrs. Williams wears a long black dress with sequins all over the body. And a man that looks exactly like Elijah stands next to her. Their physical likeness throws me off for a beat. But his handsome outward appearance in a tailored suit can't mask his disgust as he eyes his son.

But then his dad opens his mouth, and the differences between them are like night and day.

"And here I was thinking this beautiful girl that came to get us was your girlfriend," he sneers. "I thought maybe all your book-smarts changed your mind about the gay thing, but here you are as queer as ever."

"Dad," Elijah says, trying to stop him from going any further. "That's enough."

"Who do you think you are telling your father that's enough? How dare you come to this school and bring shame to yourself? Shame to God, in front of all these people."

"Mr. Williams," I interrupt. "I think it would be a good idea if you leave now."

"Leave," he spits. "Over my dead body will a man like you give me orders."

A man like me.

"You still wearing that thing?" He juts his chin out to Elijah, and I notice he's absentmindedly playing with his crucifix. "Such a disgrace you are. God would be ashamed of you."

With strength I've never seen him possess, Elijah goes head-to-head with his dad, standing in his personal space, ready to explode.

"Don't you dare talk about a God you don't know."

His father's head rears back. "A God I don't know?" he roars.

"My God," Elijah points to his chest, "is compassionate. Merciful. And forgiving. My God," he continues, his voice getting a little louder, "has an endless amount of grace. My God doesn't tell his congregation to condemn the sinner. To banish them. My God says time and time again, he who is without sin may cast the first stone. You are not without *sin*. Yet you continue to cast stones at me. And I'm saying it's enough."

He straightens his shoulders, and in a voice so commanding and reverent, he says, "I have suffered enough under you, Dad. I have my God, I have my faith, and I have a man who loves me more than you ever have and anyone else ever will."

Despite the hate radiating off his father, Elijah turns to me with such love and pride. "There's no shame in our love, Dad, and I refuse to be around you if that's what you believe, so, please take your bigotry and stay as far away from me as possible."

Tears streak down his mother's face, and I wonder how many years she's also been suffering at the hands of his father.

Mr. Williams remains as disgusted as ever. Disbelief that the Elijah he knew is not the Elijah that stands before him today.

"I will show you just how far this nonsense of yours will

get you." He looks down at my name tag and back at me, deep disgust etched on every single crease in his face. I hear his thoughts before he voices them, and I know now there is no level too low for this man.

Without another word he storms out of the room, Elijah's mother right behind him, and the three of us are stunned into silence.

Elijah sinks back onto the chair in relief, but I feel it in my bones, it's too soon to celebrate.

"Can you excuse me a second?"

Elijah looks at me perplexed. "Are you okay?"

"Yep. I just need to check something really quick."

Leaving the room, I practically run out to the main floor of the ballroom. Looking through a sea of faces, I try to find anybody that resembles Elijah's parents.

"Professor Huxley," I try to ignore the voice and resume my search, but whoever it is, is persistent.

"Professor Huxley." Turning around, I find Aiden walking toward me.

"What are you doing here?"

"I came to see Elijah."

Unable to focus, I frantically keep searching for them, when a better idea comes to me. Where the fuck is Dean Billings?

"Have you seen Dean Billings?" I ask Aiden.

He looks around. "I don't think so, why?"

"I'm pretty sure Elijah's parents are about to rat him and me out."

"Elijah's parents are here?"

"Focus, Aiden," I chide. "Can you see him?"

I turn my head. Left. Right. Left. Right. Searching the room. Begging that I've got this whole thing wrong.

"Found him," Aiden says.

Following his gaze, I find Mr. and Mrs. Williams staring at me. Their mouths moving at a million miles per hour. Dean Billings looks like he's ready to kill.

Aiden stands in front of me, blocking my view and wraps his arms around my neck.

"What the fuck are you doing?" I ask through gritted teeth.

"Put your hands around my waist," he instructs.

"No."

"Focus, Huxley," he says, throwing my own words at me. "Elijah or the job?"

"What?"

"Who do you pick? Elijah or the job."

"Elijah," I answer.

"I'm so glad I was wrong about you."

He tilts his head, and his next move registers.

"As a mature adult, Aiden, I feel the need to advise you that if you kiss me you will get kicked out of King."

"Good," he says unfazed. "This place turned me into a fucking prick anyway."

"Fuck," I mutter.

"What will it be Huxley? You're wasting time. They're tearing shreds into his scholarship as we speak. Get. Moving. "

I take a deep breath and close my eyes. "For Elijah."

26

ELIJAH

allie's small hand rubs up and down my back as I try to catch my breath. Cole just stormed out of the room after my father, and the adrenaline I felt as I laid my truth at my father's feet is waning faster than I can control.

Initially I was shocked, and somewhat scared, that my parents had shown up tonight, but the young boy in me held out hope that they were finally here to praise me for my achievements at King. That maybe they were righting their wrongs and seeing me for the man I worked so hard to be.

How could I have been so fucking stupid?

Not only did my dad criticize me as well as he always has, but he found my weakness. Desperately, I wanted Cole's comfort, only to dangerously flaunt him right under the nose of the only people who would love to see me fail.

"I have to find Cole," I spit out. "God knows what my parents will say to him. Or what he'll say to them."

"Come on," Callie says. "Let's get this over with and go home."

Leading the way out of the secluded room, I fill my lungs

up with air, trying to steady my breathing and calm my nerves. Nothing could be worse than the showdown with my father–the hard part was done.

But as the large ballroom comes into view, I realize just how bad things could really be. My eyes stumble on Aiden and Cole.

Together.

Kissing.

And *everybody* watching them.

For a single, painful moment, my heart plummets to my stomach. Shock, confusion, and jealousy racing through me; the man I love is kissing someone else.

Why is he kissing someone else?

I feel Callie move closer, slipping her hand into mine. She squeezes my fingers tight. Too tight. I give her a quick, annoyed glance, and she tips her head to the side. Reluctantly, I look behind her, and my gaze lands on my parents staring at Cole and Aiden in disgust. Beside them is a furious Dean Billings, like everybody else, trying to decipher the scene in front of him.

Dragging his eyes off Cole and Aiden, Billings looks back at my father whose mouth is now moving at a million miles per hour.

He points between me and Cole, and that's when it hits me. He wasn't angry and desperate to leave after our confrontation. No. He went to the dean to expose our relationship. To destroy everything I worked so hard for. To destroy *me*.

The magnitude of my father's hate toward me and the lengths he would go to shouldn't be a surprise to me. And it sure as fuck shouldn't hurt like this.

I push away the pain and look back at Aiden and Cole. While their mouths are no longer fused together, the tension between the three of us is still palpable. They're both watching me. Staring. Trying to read my expression.

Cole tries to step to me, but Aiden holds him back. It kills me, but if my suspicions are correct, and the kiss was to take the heat off Cole and me, then distance is for the best.

I see the struggle and the apology written all over his face, and I'm torn between wanting to rush over to him or run away from this whole clusterfuck.

I knew this was always going to happen. Again, my naivety made me believe that somehow Cole and I we're going to come out of this unscathed.

As if my parents were going to easily push aside their years of hate, contempt, and bigotry, and love me because I was part of some huge research project.

Wake the fuck up, Elijah.

Shaking my head, I release my hold on Callie and find the nearest exit. "I *need* to get out of here," I mutter to myself.

"Eli, wait up," Callie calls after me. "I'm sure there's an explanation for it all."

I pull my phone out of the inside of my suit jacket and begin to type in my details.

"What are you doing?" Callie asks, snatching my cell out of my hand. "We have the limo, let's just take it back to your dorm and you can wind down."

"Wind down," I scoff. "I just watched my whole life go up in flames and you want me to wind down?"

"I get it. You're hurt and scared, but let's just get you home and away from it all, and then you can decide on whatever you want the next step to be."

"There's no next step, Callie." My voice cracks. "I've just lost everything that's important to me."

"That's not true," she argues. "It will work itself out. I'm sure of it. We just have to wait till we hear from Cole and Aiden."

Cole and Aiden. Cole's lips on Aiden's

Deep down I know there's a logical explanation to all of this. But as tears threaten to spill, old insecurities and self-doubt begin to follow the well-trodden path back into my brain. In one single moment, I'm no longer the young man taking hold of his new life with both hands. No. In one single moment, I'm now the helpless young man I'm scared I'm always going to be.

Raw and vulnerable, I hold Callie's gaze. "Please, get me out of here."

A SOFT KNOCK on my bedroom door rouses me from my numb-like state. As soon as Callie and I arrived back at the dorms, I went straight to my room, with my suit and shoes still on, and lay on the bed.

The sound starts again, and I realize whoever is on the other side is waiting for me to respond. But I can't. The words don't come.

"Eli."

Aiden?

"Eli, please can I come in?"

Surprised it isn't Cole here wanting to talk, I drag my body off the bed and walk to the door. We haven't spoken in weeks, and now, under the circumstances, everything I wanted us to say to one another pales in comparison.

I try to regulate my breathing and steel my composure. He's my best friend and we need to hear each other out.

Just as he starts his third round of knocking, I swing the door open, unprepared for the worry and anxiety written all

over his face. We both stare at each other, Aiden finally realizing I'm not going to be the one to break the silence.

I watch his throat bob with apprehension before he
finds the courage to speak. "I know I'm probably the last
person you want to talk to, but I'm so fucking sorry, Eli."

After everything that's happened, I'm not sure what it is
exactly he's apologizing for. Should he even be apologizing
if he and Cole just saved my scholarship?

"I don't know what you want me to say," I tell him
honestly. "I don't even know where my head's at right now."

"I want to start at the beginning, but I just wanted to tell
you the kiss—it was all my idea. I think the dean believed
us. Or is at least confused enough to not put too much stock
into whatever your parents told him."

"What were you doing there anyway?" I ask, surprising
us both. "Callie said you weren't coming."

"I was on my way to find you when I found Cole. I
stopped him when he was on his way to the dean and your
parents, and the idea just hit me like a freight train."

"A warning would've been nice," I mutter, even though I
know how unrealistic the request is.

"There was no time," he explains, confirming my
thoughts. "I honestly thought he was going to pick the
school."

I narrow my eyes at him, unsure if this is just specula-
tion, or if something happened between them that made
Aiden think that way. "I guess it would've been the wiser
choice."

He shakes his head. "I was sure he just wanted you for
some innocent, virgin ass." My cheeks flush with embarrassment, Aiden's bluntness not something I'll ever get used to.
"I was coming tonight to tell you that, even if I didn't trust
Cole, I should've trusted you, and been there *for you*. But in

the end, what I thought, what I did or didn't do, and what I should've done, doesn't matter. Cole chose you above his job. He put you first––the way you deserve."

My whole body sags in defeat, my head now hanging low. I should be relieved that Cole's love for me surpasses anything I ever anticipated for myself, but the guilt at what the road ahead of him now looks like because of that makes it difficult to enjoy Aiden's revelation.

"So, what's going to happen now?" I query. "What happened after I left?"

"Billings requested we leave as stealthy as possible after informing us, while it wasn't going to be dealt with tonight, there would be severe consequences."

"Aiden." I rub the back of my neck, trying to find the right words. Trying to push the unexplainable feelings aside and show my best friend the gratitude he deserves.

"Eli, don't," he says firmly. "We're even now. I was horrible to you, and I found a way to make it up to you."

"Aiden, you're going to get kicked out of school," I say, reminding him of how much his actions cost him. "Your parents––"

He cuts me off. "Eli, I hate it here."

In the months I've known Aiden, I can wholeheartedly say this is the most honest thing he's ever said. "What will you do? Where will you go?"

"I don't know yet," he steps closer to me. "I just want you to know, I have never felt more like myself than I do right now. So, whatever guilt you're holding or feeling... it has no place here."

"You're serious, aren't you?" I ask him

"Never been so sure of anything in my life."

"I'm still so sorry," I tell him, my voice thick with emotion. He offers me a soft smile and moves in for a hug. I hold on to him tight, grateful that our friendship survived this. "Thank you, Aiden."

"That's what friends are for."

Stepping back, I rock on my heels, feeling better, but still somewhat unsure. Aiden and I might be okay, but I still need to talk to Cole, apologize for my parents, and clean up the inevitable mess our relationship was always going to cause.

"He's waiting for you downstairs," Aiden supplies, as if he can read my mind.

I snap my head up. "What?"

"Cole," he confirms, in case I was unsure of who he was referring to. "He's in a cab, waiting for you to take you back to his place."

"This whole time?"

"He didn't want to make things worse by being seen coming up here with me. And," Aiden continues with a smirk, "he also said he wanted you at his place, with no interruptions."

Of course he did.

Seconds pass, and my feet still stand firmly on the ground. "Eli, what's wrong?"

"I can't go down there." I bite down on my bottom lip. "I just feel like shit."

He places his hand on my shoulder and squeezes. "Talk it out with him, Eli. He loves you, and you love him. The rest will work out."

"I should go change." Quick hands drop to the lapels of my suit jacket and hold on.

"No, you look good like this."

I tilt my head to the door and he nods. Unsure and uncertain, I make my way down what feels like a hundred flights of stairs. Instead of taking the door that leads to the campus coffee shop, I take the door that leads out to the main road, not even a little bit surprised to see Cole leaning against a Yellow Taxi Cab, his arms folded and ankles crossed.

He looks every bit the confident, authoritative and driven man I fell in love with, but it's the storm in his gray eyes that gives away just how precarious and fragile everything is in this very moment.

Pushing off the car, he urgently walks toward me, clasping my face in between his hands.

"Fuck, I'm so glad you're here right now. I didn't think you were coming down."

My eyes dart around, checking our surroundings, not used to Cole touching me so close to campus.

"We don't need to worry about that anymore," he says, reading my mind. "But I'll explain more when we get to my place?"

It's more of a question than a statement. Him asking if we're okay enough to be at his place; together, and alone.

Knowing we need to hash everything out regardless of my fears of the outcome, I wrap my fingers around his wrists and offer a nod. His hands slide away from my face and into mine, and he turns and leads us both inside the back seat of the cab.

We sit close, our thighs brushing up against one another. The silence is permeating, but the back of a cab with another person listening in on our heartbreak isn't an ideal situation.

I keep my hands clasped together, knowing one single touch will destroy me.

Late and dark, it takes us half the time to arrive to Cole's apartment. Against my better judgement, I follow him inside but stop myself from walking in any farther than the foyer.

"What are you doing standing there?" Cole asks "Come inside. Sit down and talk to me."

My gaze meets his, and my heart pounds against my rib cage. The moment has come, and the way he's looking at me, he knows it too. I hope he knows how sorry I am that I have to do this, and how much I love him. How much I'll always love him.

I clear my throat and blurt out the words I never wanted to say. "I think we should break up."

27

COLE

I want to tell myself I heard him incorrectly, but that little piece of shit voice inside my head reminds me this was inevitable. From the very beginning there was too much stacked against us. I knew that, but I was sure we could overcome it. Hell, after tonight, we should be able to overcome *all* of it.

"No," I respond bluntly. The words leave my mouth quicker than I can tell myself to pull them back, but it's the truth. Being without him isn't an option for me, and he's going to have to give me a fucking good reason as to why it is for him.

"I apologize for it all," I say quickly. He narrows his eyes at me in confusion. "Talk to me. Talk to me so I can make it right."

He shakes his head at me. "You think I want an apology?"

"Don't you?"

"You don't have anything to apologize for."

"I kissed someone who wasn't you," I supply bluntly.

"That you did," he says, matter of factly. He tips his head

back and looks up to the ceiling before returning his eyes to mine. "And while the visual hasn't quite left my mind, that isn't what this is about."

I cringe at the harshness in his tone. It's well deserved, but I hate knowing I'm the one who's making him feel so off balance. "Then what is it?"

We stare at each other in silence, both of us–for the first time ever–not on the same wavelength. I really thought we would be arguing about the kiss, but now it's clear this is about something else entirely. Something so much more significant.

"I can't be responsible for you losing your job."

"That's what––"

He raises his hand in the air to cut me off. "Please hear me out Cole, I don't want you to make those sacrifices for me."

"That isn't your call, Elijah." I step to him, and he bristles. The small movement alone makes me want to crawl out of my own skin. I try to school my breathing as I coax myself to give him space. "Elijah, baby," I say softly. "That isn't your call."

"Yes, it is," he shouts. "When it's at the hands of my parents, it fucking is."

"They were going to rip that scholarship straight out of your hands," I scream back. His face is red with rage, and my heart aches for him and the world he's forced to carry on his shoulders.

"And you should've let them."

"No fucking way."

"You're going to lose your job. Not to mention Aiden will be expelled." The anger between us rises, both of us unable to remain calm and collected, the threat of loss and heartache too real to contain.

"We both knew what we were getting ourselves into. It was our choice."

"I can't have it on my conscience, Cole," he says, nothing but pain and anguish on his face. "Knowing my parents did this to you. I just..." Like a gavel, he hits his coiled fist into the wooden door behind him. The loud thump enough to say all the things words can't. "They wanted to hurt me, and you should've let them."

Unable to take the distance, I meet him toe-to-toe, purposefully invading his personal space. He raises his eyes to meet mine, and the devastation brings my blood to a boil.

"I will never let anyone hurt you like that. Over my dead fucking body," I seethe. "I will not stand by and let them do that to you. We didn't know each other back then for me to stop it, but now they'll have to go through me. I don't want anything they say or do to touch you."

Exhaling a large breath, he lets his body slump against the door. I feel his defeat before I hear it. "I thought they might've changed." His eyes close and I watch the corners of his mouth turn down. "They couldn't even wait and let themselves see everything I've achieved in the last six months."

"Stop," I interrupt.

He ignores me.

"It's like he came to point the finger," he continues. "Just to say 'I told you so; you're still the same piece of shit son that you've always been.'"

"Baby, stop," I beg, letting my forehead fall to his. "They don't know you. They've never known the real, beautiful you."

"Why don't they want to know me?" His tear-filled eyes open and lock on mine. "Why?"

Refusing to bear witness to him beating himself up, I

slip one hand behind his back and the other under his knees, scooping him up in my arms and heading straight for my room.

When I place him on the edge of the bed, his head hangs low between his shoulders; he doesn't argue or question me.

Even beaten down and broken, Elijah looks beautiful in his suit. Shopping with Callie to find the perfect one, I wasn't allowed to see him in it till tonight.

Lowering myself to my knees, I slowly push his legs apart and settle in between them. Taking hold of his chin, I tip his head up until his tired eyes look at me.

"I didn't get to tell you how gorgeous you look in your suit."

The saddest smile graces his lips, and it takes everything I have not to kiss it all away.

Wordlessly, I untie his leather shoes and place them beside his feet. I quickly take off his socks and place my palms on his thighs, then straighten my body till we're face-to-face.

"Not that long ago, you told me you fight for what's yours." My hands skim up the soft material, eventually pushing his suit jacket off his shoulders. "I know they hurt you, but you're mine now." My fingers work the buttons on each of his cuffs, and then slowly undo the ones down the length of his shirt. I keep my focus on his face, not letting myself be tempted by the inches of bare skin coming into view. "And I too fight for what's mine."

Reluctantly, I release my grip on his shirt and leave it hanging open, denying myself of a single touch.

Cradling his face in my hands, I bring us closer together, our eyes instinctively closing. Our noses are touching, our mouths only a breath apart. "This is not how we end." I feel his pulse quicken at my words. "Nobody gets to take you away from me. Nobody gets to destroy what we have."

One hand clutches the back of his neck while the other slides down his neck, past his collarbone, and stopping right on top of his heart. "Please," I whisper, my voice hoarse and thick with emotion. "Tell me you know that."

Firm hands slide around my waist, and soft, wet lips glide against mine. "I love you," he says before pressing his mouth against mine.

It's only been a few hours since we last kissed, but after everything that's happened, this feels like coming home. Like we made that risky, grueling trek through all the lies and secrecy one last time, and we're finally where we're both supposed to be.

Together.

Slow and tentative, the tension between us and anger from earlier is far off in the distance as we finally allow ourselves to enjoy the taste of freedom and possibilities. His tongue dances across the seam of my mouth before plunging between my lips and searching for its mate.

The kiss changes from soft to deep to hungry; desperation clawing at the surface, both of us needing to be sated.

My hands glide over his naked torso, pushing against him till our mouths separate and he falls back onto the mattress. "Let me finish undressing you," I tell him, eyeing his erection and rising up off my knees.

"No," he says, surprising me.

"What?"

"Take your clothes off for me." It's not always easy for Elijah to be so forthcoming, but when he does, there's no question that I'll always give him what he wants. "I just want to stare at the reason why I'm the luckiest man in the world."

My heart swells inside my chest at the compliment, making it harder to do anything else but smile at him. He sits back up and grips on to my belt buckle. Pulling me back between his legs, he stares up at me with the most honest and content look in his eyes I have ever seen.

"You take care of me like nobody ever has. You make me feel things I never thought I would have the luxury of feeling, and your love..." I run my knuckles down his cheek, words failing us both. "Your love leaves me wanting for nothing."

"Tonight you sacrificed a lot for me." He shakes his head at me before I can argue. "I'd be lying if I said I don't harbor guilt over it, or that it won't come up again for us, past tonight. But above all else, there's one thing I *need* you to know."

"You don't need to say it, baby."

"I *want* to. I want you to know I would give up the world if that was the only way I could have you. Because King, and everything else there is, all means nothing if you're not by my side."

"So, it's okay for you to make that choice and not me?" I challenge.

He lets his head drop, taking a deep breath, before meeting my gaze again. "I don't feel worth––"

"Please don't let those words come out of your mouth." I know the run-in with his parents is the catalyst for all his insecurities, but I won't let him talk shit about himself. "Not here. Not now, and *never* between us."

He offers me a soft nod, and I cover his hands with mine and push them away. "Let me strip for you." His mouth lifts in a shy smile, my plan to lighten the mood hopefully working. "Isn't that what you asked for?" I tip my chin up at him. "Lie back down."

Instead of lying flat on his back, Elijah sits up on his elbows, his gaze on me like a second skin.

Finally, I shuck off my suit jacket, like I've wanted to all night. Returning to the buttons on my shirt, I take my time undoing them, teasing him.

My dick twitches in my slacks as the mood between us shifts. Haphazardly, I discard my shirt to the ground and watch him palm his own hardening length.

I unbuckle my belt and let the sound of the opening zipper echo around us. I pull myself out of my boxers and leisurely begin to stroke.

Elijah's tongue peeks out of his mouth, licking his bottom lip seductively. "You want a taste, Sweet Boy?"

"I'll take whatever you give me."

"You always know just what to say, don't you?"

Sitting up, he reaches for me, and I let him; both of us pushing my pants and boxers to the floor. Kicking off my shoes, I quickly step out of the bunched-up material, and Elijah's warm hands wrap around my shaft.

His hot, wet mouth follows, taking me all the way to the back of his throat. My loud groan bounces off the walls as his tongue explores every inch of my cock. Reaching the crown, he laps up my pre-come, spearing the salty slit. "Fuck, baby. I need inside you. I need to come *inside* you."

Like teenagers, Elijah and I planned that tonight would be the night I went bare. After getting tested and being given the all clear, experiencing this with him––a first for both of us––on a night where we celebrated his successes seemed like the perfect backdrop to what would top off our amazing night.

Now, the significance is more poignant. Because after tonight, what has happened both in and out of this bed will change us forever.

Elijah's mouth pops off my dick, and I waste no time getting him naked. He shifts himself to the middle of the bed, and I crawl on the large king bed to follow.

He's fucking beautiful. Each time more so than the last. I slam my lips to his, tasting him, feeding off him, working my mouth over the expanse of skin at my mercy.

I move down his neck, lick his nipples, and stop at his leaking cock. My eyes flick up to his, taunting him as I suck him off.

My tongue and hands work in tandem, jerking him off, massaging his balls, and spreading his pre-come all the way down to his hole.

The second I slip a finger in, Elijah loses all coherency, breathy moans the only noises he's able to make.

"More." I add another finger, and his request turns into a beg. "Please, Cole. I need more. I need *you*."

"Let me just get myself lub--"

"No," Elijah huffs. "Just you. The way we are right now."

Slipping my fingers out, I spread Elijah open and begin to pepper kisses on to his ass cheeks. Working my way closer and closer, my tongue begins circling its way to the promised land. Elijah shudders with every swipe as I move my hand to continue stroking his cock.

From hole to tip, I make sure he's as wet and slick as he can possibly be. There's no doubt I want to be inside him, but I don't want to hurt him.

I settle between his legs and give a tug at my aching dick before lining myself up. I try to regulate my breathing, telling myself not to go too hard or too fast. I push the tip in first and still, the skin to skin contact almost too much to handle. "Fuck," I groan. "I'm gonna go all the way in," I warn. "Okay?"

"Please, Cole. Please. Plea--"

The word is cut off by a delicious whimper as I swiftly thrust myself deep inside him.

"Shit. Cole," Elijah gasps. "You feel incredible."

I frantically piston into him, mesmerized by this new and unparalleled sensation. "You feel so good, baby," I croon. "So fucking good."

Elijah's hands circle his cock as he demands I go harder.

"Any more and I'll split you apart," I tease.

"You know that's what I want," he says. "After tonight...I..."

His voice trails off and heat-filled eyes collide with mine. Words are useless as I push into him. Deeper. Faster. Grazing his favorite spot with every unrestrained stroke.

I give him what he wants. I give him what we *both* need.

Raw.

Exposed.

Vulnerable.

Hurt.

Real.

And so fucking in love.

"Oh fuck. Cole," Elijah calls out as I watch his come beautifully decorate his chest. Spurred on by the sight, I pick up the pace and find my own release, my body handing over the remaining pieces of my heart.

Looking up at me with an intoxicating mix of reverence and desire, I know he just gave me the same gift in return. As my dick pulses to the same beat as my heart, I know we are one in all the ways that matter.

Mind, body, and soul, he's mine and I am his.

This life, with him, is it for me. No matter what we face, or where we go, it will always be the two of us.

Elijah and Cole.

Cole and Elijah.

Gorgeous and sated, Elijah glows with satisfaction and happiness. A look and a feeling that *I* so proudly put and want to keep there. "I love you so fucking much, Sweet Boy," I tell him.

Wrapping his hands around my neck, he pulls me down onto his body and whispers in my ear, "Today. Tomorrow. Always."

EPILOGUE
ELIJAH

NEW YEAR'S EVE

I t's New Year's Eve and Cole's house is a cross between a hotel and a disaster zone. With Geena, Meghann, and Trey staying here, what usually feels like a spacious home, now feels like a matchbox.

After Cole asked me to move in with him, I told him having Christmas Day at *our* house would be the only thing to sway my vote. When in reality, I had no willpower when it came to denying Cole. Saying no to him wasn't in my vocabulary and that handsome fucker knew it.

The truth is, I didn't want to stay in the King dorms any more than he wanted me to. After the whole kissing debacle at the University gala, being the talk of the town was something I didn't want to have to get used to.

Photos of Cole and Aiden kissing spread like wildfire. But as the story itself unfolded of how my parents had dropped my name to Dean Billings first, gossip mongers were desperate to try and get the whole story.

Initially, I had felt so guilty that these two men had

purposefully jeopardized their futures to save mine. But the more I saw them, and how happy and carefree they were right now, the more I realized that this was the perfect outcome for all of us.

Cole and I wanted to be together without any restrictions. We didn't want to have to look over our shoulders, or worry about rumors. So, when Dean Billings told Cole he could return to work after a two-week suspension, Cole politely handed him his two-weeks' notice, and said goodbye. He was careful not to burn his bridges, despite really wanting to give the dean a piece of his mind. But he's been happier in the last few weeks than in all his time teaching at King, despite how much he loved the students and the class material. Seeing as there was no proof an actual relationship took place, Miles, Cole's friend, is certain he'll be able to get another job at any school, and we'll be able to have our uncomplicated happy ever after.

As far as Aiden goes, he's the happiest I've ever seen him. One day he'll tell his story, and we'll all be better for knowing it, but until then, he's coming and going as he pleases, doing exactly what it is he wants. No longer the young moody man I had become accustomed to, Aiden is taking care of himself, and it's such a beautiful sight to see.

I've tried a few times to apologize, or to at least thank him for what he did, but he's told me over and over that he has no regrets. If anything, he's finally, for once in a really long time, excited about the possibilities for his future.

I check the time, and there's another hour and a half till everyone comes over for an impromptu New Year's Eve party. After our Christmas dinner went so well, everyone wanted to ring in the New Year just the same way.

Cole is off buying last minute knick-knacks with his

mom, and I'm almost certain Trey and Megs are having sex in the main bathroom.

When Megs had arrived in DC over a week ago, the first time we'd seen each other since the argument at Geena's house, she spent a whole day obsessively apologizing. I told her a million times she didn't need to, but the sentiment won't be forgotten all the same. And she and I have gotten to spend some quality time together this week and have come to realize that we actually have a lot in common, besides us both having Cole's happiness as one of our top priorities.

"Oh hey, man. I didn't know you were here." Disheveled and a little bit flushed, Trey walks into the room, and I would say my assumption on the couple's extracurricular activities was spot on.

"So, do you usually have sex in the bathroom when nobody's home? Is that some kind of new fetish people are into these days?"

"You know what, Eli?" Trey says, trying to stifle his smile, "I'd say you're hanging around Cole too much, because you sure as shit weren't this smart-ass-y the first time I met you."

"Really Trey? Smart-ass-y?"

He flips me the bird than calls out to Megs. "You can come out, babe. He knows."

When she comes into view, I throw a dish towel at her and she quickly catches it. "Wash your hands and then help me make this pasta salad."

Forty-five minutes later, Cole and Geena are here, and we're about fifteen minutes from our guests arriving.

"This stuff looks great," Cole says, his finger heading straight for the homemade French onion dip.

"What are you doing?" I slap away his hand. "I didn't watch your mom cook all day so you can just ruin it all."

Geena laughs from behind me. "This is why you're my

favourite, Eli." She looks at Cole. "At least he doesn't try to take all the credit."

The doorbell rings just as I've finished setting the table with the variety of food Geena made. She specifically requested everyone tell her their favorite dish, so she could make it for tonight. She really is selfless, and in the short time I've known her she's been more of a mother to me than mine ever has.

Once I stood my ground with my dad, my mother didn't even bother with her weekly fake calls. We were done and, surprisingly, I'm nowhere near as upset as I thought I would be about the loss.

Everyone piles in the house at the same time, punctuality clearly everyone's speciality.

"Hey." Callie walks in first, heading straight to me and kissing me on the cheek. I catch Aiden walking in behind her, smiling at his phone like a loon

"What's he so happy about?" I ask.

"That's the new him," she informs me. "Smiles all the time."

"It's actually kind of creepy."

"Tell me about it. I've known him my whole life and I've never seen him smile this much."

"Hey, man," he says when he and Cole finally stop talking. "Thanks for inviting us over."

I raise an eyebrow at Callie. "He's even got manners."

"Ha. Ha. Very funny," he quips.

"And jokes too," Callie adds.

Everyone starts taking their normal seats around the house, like we've done this a million times before. It isn't long before Harper walks in, and then Sophie and Miles with little Joey in tow.

I stand back, watching everyone, admiring how this

beautiful band of mismatched people managed to find their way into one another's lives.

With her mobility getting stronger every day, Geena is in her element, fussing and fighting over all of us. The food and drinks keep on coming as we all flitter from one to another talking about everything and nothing all at once.

"Can I have everyone's attention?" Callie clanks her fork to her wine glass. "So, most of you don't know, but I love lists and New Year's resolutions. If you don't, now you do."

A small chorus of laughter fills the room.

"Anyway, back to my point. I would like to propose that we all announce one New Year's resolution we'd like to achieve. Doesn't have to be personal, doesn't have to be big. And then next year, we come back and see if we achieved it."

"Ok, and if we don't achieve it?" Harper asks. She's spent quite a bit of time at our place lately. Man, do I love calling it that. *Our place.* And I know she has something going on. Although she hasn't shared, Cole and I just do our best to be there for her until she's ready.

"Then we don't achieve it, I guess."

"I just know, people in this room have become my life-long friends. Certain people," she looks at me, and everybody's eyes follow, "have inspired true and honest change, and I want to keep up that momentum. If I know at the end of every year I have my best friends by my side, then maybe I'll do more. I'll be more. I'll be the woman I really want to be."

Aiden swoops in next to her. "And I think that's enough wine for tonight."

Callie's face heats up in embarrassment and I don't want that here. Especially not for her. "Well, personally, I love this idea of Callie's. You all know that the past few months have had a lot of ups and downs for me, and I wouldn't have been able to get through it all without each and every one of you. So I'm up for some continued positive change and honesty. So, I'll take a turn." I stand up and hold up my glass. "My New Year's resolution is to not fall in love with my new arts and history professor."

"Hey," Cole shouts from beside me. I feel his hand slip into the back of my pants and give my ass a quick squeeze. "You're going to pay for that," he murmurs into my ear.

"I can't wait."

"So, was that the resolution? Or are you two gonna fuck in the living room?" Trey teases.

"Trey," Geena scolds, pointing at Joey. "Do you want your mouth washed out with soap?"

Meghann and Cole drown out the idea, while Harper begs Geena to do it in front of everyone.

"So what's your real New Year's resolution?" Cole asks me, while everyone else is either bickering or laughing.

"I just want to be happy," I admit. "I want to be this happy, all the time."

"I think I can make that happen."

"Yeah?"

As Cole opens his mouth to answer me, the doorbell rings. I look around, everyone accounted for. "Are we expecting someone else?"

"Actually, I am," Cole says, an excited grin spreading across his face.

He slips his fingers between mine. "Come with me."

"What is it?" I ask

"Just follow me."

"It's for me?"

He gives me a quick nod and then opens the door.

"Hello," the guy's eyes flick from the brownstone number on the bricks and back to Cole. Kind of hidden, he can't see me, but I can see him. "Is this Cole and Elijah's place?"

"Yeah, man," Cole says. "Are you?"

His hair is a different color, clothes less grunge, more surfer, but his eyes and smile are exactly the same. "Alex?" I come into view.

"Holy shit. Elijah. It's so good to see you."

He goes in for the bear hug. Personal space and boundaries have never been concepts he's understood.

"How are you even here?" I ask, looking between both of them.

"Well, Cole found me on the internet. Kinda stalkerish," he adds. "But I'm glad I answered his email.

"I thought of you a lot over the years, man. And seeing you, out of your home town, in college and with a boyfriend, I'm fucking impressed."

A little bit tongue-tied, I lean into Cole, and just like that he does what I need him to.

"Come in, man. Come meet everyone and get some food."

I hang back and watch everyone take him in. They greet him as if they've always known him, and it's a beautiful reminder of how far my life has really come.

Pulling Cole aside, I hold his face and bring my lips to his.

"What was that for?"

"You're my boyfriend, I don't need a reason to kiss you."

⸻

THE NIGHT GOES ON, the food getting replenished and the drinks getting topped up, there's nothing but smiles and laughter all around. Alex and I decide, since he lives locally, we should catch up in the new year and share what our lives have been and have become since the last time we spoke.

Seeing as we were about to ring in the New Year, and we have no plans for this to be a one-time catch up, Alex is enjoying himself, floating from person to person. More often than not, I catch him and Aiden huddling together, laughing with the familiarity and comfort of something more than friends. It makes me happy and nervous all at the same time.

Crammed together the lounge room, we sit on every piece of furniture we can, watching and waiting for the ball to drop.

As the countdown begins, I look at Cole. "Why did you contact Alex?"

"What was your New Year's resolution, again?"

"To be happy," I answer obliviously.

"Exactly." I can hear the numbers fall away in the background. "My one job is to keep you happy, Elijah. I saw an opportunity, and I ran with it."

"Thank you." I kiss him again, just as I hear everybody shout a loud "*ten nine eight seven six five four three two one.*" A quick glance around the room and I see Geena, Harper, and Callie hugging. Trey and Megs whispering, Sophie and Miles making out like teenagers on the couch, with a sleeping Joey laid out on their laps. And of course, Aiden and Alex. Lips locked and ready for either heartache or happiness; no one knows at this point. But I'll support them both whatever comes.

I wouldn't want this bunch any other way.

"I love you, Cole."

Time stops.

"I love you too."

My heart does too.

Did you enjoy Devilry?

If you'd like more of Cole and Elijah, please head over to
my website and check out their bonus epilogue.

http://www.marleyvbooks.com/bonus-epilogues/

Want more MM Romance from Marley Valentine?

Check out her best friend's brother romance, Without
You.

Available on AMAZON in e-book and paperback.

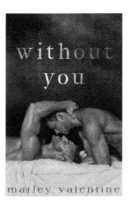

"Tragedy brought us together, but something stronger made me want to stay."

Julian was the boy next door. My brother's best friend, he fit with my family in ways I never could. While he and Rhett went on to play house, I left the only life I knew, desperate for a fresh start.

Until everything changed.

Heartache came along, and the aftermath of my brother's death was here to stay. I was now face to face with Julian more than I ever wanted to be.

Being around him brought up all my insecurities, forced me to deal with hard truths, and conjured up feelings I had no business entertaining. He wasn't the man I thought I knew. He was complex and layered, and inherently beautiful in all the ways I'd never noticed.

Not on another person.

Not on another man.

Not until him.

ACKNOWLEDGMENTS

Andrew and Jaxon, these books are nothing without you two by my side. I love you.

Mum, Steph, and Chris, I love you.

Jacob, when you came to me with this idea, I didn't think our schedules would ever clear up enough for it to happen. *(Sybil, we finally did it, and we got to share your beautiful covers with the world. The wait was worth it, yeah?)*

I couldn't be happier with how it all turned out. This series pushed us in more ways than one, and I'm so glad I got to share the whole experience with you.
Thank you for reading Devilry. I know it isn't your usual cup of tea, but as always, you came through LOL.

Sybil the work you did on our promo material, is out of this world. Your talent has no limits, and we are so grateful you're on our team. Even if we drive you crazy, we know you love us just as much as we love you.

Laura, thank you for always being there to talk through a story line, to read a scene, or to talk me off the ledge I so often find myself on when writing. Your excitement about my books, always helps me push past the finish line.

My beta team: Jodi, Michelle, Shauna and Lupita. I couldn't have done it without you guys. You don't complain about the deadlines I put myself and you guys under, and you're always there when I need you to read something last minute. Thank you, Elijah and Cole would not be here without you.

Jodi, everyone thanks you for the GIFS. Please, don't ever stop. #MMMondays need you

Shauna, your extra eyes on Devilry, saved my life, and made a world of difference. Thank you

ellie, as usual, you put up with me. I don't know why, but I've learned not to ask questions.

Michelle and Annette from Book Nerd Services. Your work with my ARC team exceeded any of my already high expectations. The organisation, the support, the general boost you have given my books and my brand will never be forgotten. I'm so grateful we crossed paths and hope I never have to do a release without you.

My street team. You ladies kick ass, each and every day. Thank you for your faith and support, always.

The ladies at Enticing Journey, thank you for your work. Always above and beyond professional.

To all the people who listen to me bitch and moan on the regular. Sybil, Kacey, Celia, Bianca, Ella, Donna, Diane and Brenda, you get me through life. Thank you.

And last, but definitely not least, to everyone who took a chance on my first MM book, whether it was your first Marley book or your first MM Romace book, I wouldn't be here without you.

If I forgot someone, I'm sorry. I still love you, and you guys know the drill by now. Eat McDonalds on the regular and stalk Charlie Hunnam.

Much Peace and Love.

ABOUT THE AUTHOR

Marley Valentine comes from the future. Living in Sydney, Australia with her family, when she's not busy writing her own stories, she spends most of her time immersed in the words of her favourite authors.

Marley Valentine is also half of Remy Blake; a male and female author duo, paired up to have some fun writing steamy, short reads with insta love/lust and a HEA. You can expect twice the debauchery in every novel they write.

Other Books by Marley Valentine:

Devastate | Deviate | Reclaim | Revive | Rectify

Smuttily Ever After (A Bloggers Anthology) | Without You

King University Series

Depravity | Devilry | Debauchery

Find Marley

www.marleyvbooks.com

Manufactured by Amazon.ca
Bolton, ON